Praise for *Kiss the Joy As It Flies*

"Sheree Fitch has created in the character of Mercy Beth Fanjoy a great heroine—wise and sexy, extremely funny, full of determination, desire and grit, unflinching in the face of sadness. Here are all the firecracker hurts and fears of being an independent woman and ultimately, the rare and undiluted joys of same. This book is a joy ride."
—Lisa Moore, author of *Alligator* and *Open*

"An engaging character, Mercy is compellingly drawn and charmingly flawed."
—*Globe and Mail*

"*Kiss the Joy As It Flies* is a wonderful read: warm and wise, funny and sad, with a rich cast of characters. A fable of the everyday that embraces life even as it faces dying."
—Will Ferguson, author of *Spanish Fly* and *Happiness*™

"*Kiss the Joy As It Flies* is a marvelously funny, dark, irreverent novel with fully realized characters who take us by the hand to lead us through Fitch's complex and memorable woods."
—Meg Wolitzer, author of *The Ten Year Nap* and *The Position*

"*Kiss the Joy As It Flies* is funny and heartbreaking and thought-provoking and sometimes all three—and more—at once. Fitch made us wait a long time for her first novel, but it was worth it. It's a rare and lovely book."
—*January Magazine*

"Highly readable, emotional and humorous…Mercy is the type of woman you enjoy getting to know. She's spirited, strong yet vulnerable, ambitious yet normally flawed…[*Kiss the Joy As It Flies*] is lighthearted, at times laugh-out-loud funny but it has grit, real substance."
—*Fredericton Daily Gleaner*

Kiss the Joy As It Flies

SHEREE FITCH

Vagrant Press is an imprint of
Nimbus Publishing Limited
PO Box 9166, Halifax, NS B3K 5M8
(902) 455-4286   www.nimbus.ca

Printed and bound in Canada

Cover design: Heather Bryan
Interior design: Kathy Kaulbach, Touchstone Design House
Author photo: Lucinda LaRee

*This novel is a work of fiction. Names, characters, places, and incidents are either
the product of the author's imagination or are used fictitiously. Any resemblance to
actual persons, living or dead, events or locales is entirely coincidental.*

Library and Archives Canada Cataloguing in Publication
  Fitch, Sheree
  Kiss the joy as it flies / Sheree Fitch.
  ISBN 978-1-55109-781-7
  I. Title.

PS8561.I86K57 2010   C813'.54   C2010-903055-9

The Canada Council | Le Conseil des Arts
for the Arts | du Canada

NOVA SCOTIA
Tourism, Culture and Heritage

We acknowledge the financial support of the Government of Canada
through the Book Publishing Industry Development Program
(BPIDP) and the Canada Council, and of the Province of Nova
Scotia through the Department of Tourism, Culture and Heritage
for our publishing activities.

Mixed Sources
Product group from well-managed
forests, controlled sources and
recycled wood or fiber
FSC www.fsc.org Cert no. SW-COC-000952
© 1996 Forest Stewardship Council

For my mother:
her laughter,
her wisdom,
her love,
her prayers.

He who binds himself to a joy
Does the winged life destroy
He who kisses the joy as it flies
Lives in eternity's sunrise.

William Blake

Moreover, the need to become a choice-maker heroine is a jolt to many women who mistakenly assumed that they already were.

Jean Shinoda Bolen

PROLOGUE

From the sky, looking down, were you a dove or a raven or a yellow-bellied sapsucker, were you a passenger in a plane or a helicopter or a hot-air balloon floating over the small North American city of Odell, it might appear that the city itself and all who lived there were tucked inside a nest of emerald green feathers. The fortunate trees not yet stricken with Dutch elm disease or devoured by longhorn beetles grow so close together their leaf-heavy branches sway and touch, creating a natural arc, a verdant canopy that appears to hush and protect the entire downtown core. You might glimpse the river through the foliage—a sudden flash of ribbon winding through the town and around it like the loopety-loops of a G clef sign.

Were you from a country where the landscape is pockmarked by land mines, where souls endure poverty, starvation, and war, and where homelands are ravaged by sickness and genocide, Odellians might appear not only privileged, but safe and somehow exempt from disaster. Nothing could be further from the truth.

Were you to get up close, really close, to a four-storey teal brick building and take a look in the window, you might see a solitary, hardworking, serious-minded woman in the midst of a crisis. If you watched for a while, you would conclude that disaster had, in one sense, permeated her entire life. You might ask how it was that along these streets of stately elms so many secrets could be hidden in the full light of day, marvel at how so many lives intersect and collide, and consider how fragile each heart. Like this woman, you might find yourself laughing and weeping at the sheer mad joy of all of it.

In times of distress, the sound of one's own voice can offer solace and alleviate apprehension. Never underestimate the power of your own <u>vox humana</u>.

—from Oral Speakman's *Anxiety Busters: Voicing Our Fears Aloud,* as recorded in Mercy's quotebook notebook

In a green room on the fourth floor of the Odell Medical Clinic, Mercy Beth Fanjoy studied her toenails. They were pink. Geranium pink.

She was naked. It was Tuesday.

As she gazed at the bare bum of the boy in the Norman Rockwell calendar, her universe tilted sideways and quaked. It was as if a fault line formed and cracked through all four chambers of her heart. She inhaled deeply. Vapours of rubbing alcohol, iodine, and antiseptic soap stung her nostrils. She clutched her stomach. The pompom balls of cotton in the glass jar on the cabinet bloomed into small clouds—momentarily floating before her like the ones in the sky that very morning. Mercy blinked in an effort to regain equilibrium, as if rapid eye movement and facial twitching might stop the alarm bells ringing in her head or whisk away the unpleasant news: exploratory surgery within the fortnight.

It was a much too beautiful day and Mercy Beth Fanjoy, at forty-eight, was much too young and robust to seriously entertain the idea of death. But there she sat: naked, shivering, thinking of Lord and Lady Baden Powell and the Girl Guide motto. *Be prepared.* It flashed in neon, a rusted hotel vacancy sign creaking inside her head. *Be prepared.* The words triggered the smell of wood smoke and canvas, of pine needles and outdoor latrines. The soundtrack of an old summer camp song filtered into the room. Voices of diabolical ten-year-olds echoed in her inner ear:

The worms crawl in and the worms crawl out.
They go in your ears and out your snout.
Dodo dodo dodo dodo dodo do- do- do- do- do.

"Well, I'll be cremated," she wailed, silencing the creepy chorus. She clapped three times and clasped her hands as if in prayer. Swinging her legs back and forth, she watched her pink toes pendulum-sweeping the floor.

Perceptions shift when the world rolls over on its belly. Illusions about oneself shatter. "Some Girl Guide I turned out to be. Be prepared? For this? Well, I certainly never bargained for terminal disease and premature death, not even after my mother's cancer scare. No, not even then, not really. I would not entertain such morbid thoughts, I told myself and then I banished Death from my mind, yes I did. Suffering? Banished. Death? Banished." Mercy's voice rattled around the empty room. "I quit smoking. I've exercised moderately. I've avoided trans fat. And yet, here I am, very possibly a malignant woman." This was the moment the outwardly competent, ordinarily composed, solidly built Mercy Beth Fanjoy disappeared. Her replacement was a quivering human jellyfish blob of angst.

"So we'll see what's there when we get in there. How's that? No need to worry until we have to," Dr. Wiggins wheezed in his phlegmy voice, wiping his hands on a paper towel as he re-entered the room. Mercy hurriedly covered herself, tying a paper Johnny shirt around her midriff as

Wiggins turned away. With his left foot, he pressed the pedal of a chrome waste can in the corner. The lid slapped open, briefly exposing the contents within: rubber gloves, razors, syringes, cotton swabs, Q-tips, tongue depressors, bloodied strips of gauze, and crumpled wrappers from bars of chocolate.

The lid clamped shut with a nasty twang. Wiggins flashed Mercy a slight, reassuring smile and tried to straighten his stooped shoulders. Then he shuffled towards her, stopped, and reached for her hand. Calmly, step-by-step, he explained The Procedure.

"You're just kidding around!" Mercy wanted to say. "You've made a mistake, haven't you? Dr. Wiggins? Well, haven't you? Ever? Once?" Ordinarily, Mercy was an impossibly hopeful type. But today, even she was cognizant of her own denial. Today, even her hopes were dashed.

Wiggins droned on while Mercy stared blankly at his face.

"Worry? Who, me?" she interrupted. "Waste of time."

"You haven't heard a word I've said, have you?" he asked kindly.

Mercy blinked. "Pardon me?"

Wiggins grunted and reached for a leather-bound medical book. "It's called laparoscopic surgery. Mercy, are you listening?"

Mercy nodded like a bad actor playing an eager student in a medical television show. "Excuse me. But. What. Exactly is. A. Laparoscope. Dr. Wiggins?" she asked, her eyes widening then narrowing, her brow pleating. Wiggins pursed his lips, twisted his mouth from side to side, then thoughtfully reached for his pencil and prescription pad. He began to draw.

Walter Wiggins, beloved but overextended physician, loving father and faithful husband (on the second go-round), fly fisherman and amateur magician, had cared for Mercy since childhood. He detected the razor edge of panic in the way she'd suddenly lowered her voice and chewed off her words. As he sketched, he bit down on the side of his tongue. He turned the pencil sideways and shaded parts in. His paunch, like a pregnant woman's in the last trimester, heaved up and down. The high-pitched train-whistling congestion in his chest alarmed his patient.

For a few seconds, Mercy forgot about herself and scrutinized Walter Wiggins; the wiry hair growing out of his ear lobes, his nose a map of broken blood vessels, huge hands that belonged more to a carpenter than a healer, but hands ever competent and sure. Other than the raspiness, Mercy concluded Wiggins appeared normal: Old. Tired. Overweight. Busy. Kind. Possibly a recovering alcoholic. She waited as he put a few finishing flourishes on what, after all the effort, she expected to be a masterpiece of anatomical genius. Wiggins turned the pad around and displayed a crude diagram of a laparoscope and, beside it, an etching of her pelvic region. The drawing looked to Mercy like a distorted game of hangman, but she was flattered he'd made her so slim.

"The problem area is behind and to the left here," said Wiggins, tapping the paper. He circled her navel with red marker as he continued his explanation, creating a perfect bull's eye. His language turned technical; his words were few, his voice robotic.

"I see," said Mercy from time to time. "I see. Sharp instruments, lasers, and lights are involved." Dr. Wiggins didn't laugh at her feeble attempt at humour. Usually, he was a jovial sort. This sudden stoniness unsettled her.

"You can get dressed now, Mercy," said Wiggins. He patted her shoulder then left politely.

"Sweet Jeezuz," she whispered. This one utterance seemed to pop a cork of inhibition. A volley of oaths followed in a sentence that contained every profanity Mercy Beth Fanjoy knew. The swearing was uncharacteristic but the talking to herself was habitual. Ever since she'd read Oral Speakman's *Anxiety Busters: Voicing Our Fears Aloud*, Mercy's nattering to herself had actually increased because she was no longer ashamed of the tendency. After all, self-help author Oral Speakman reassured her and his millions of readers that "audible self-talk is not abnormal. In fact, solo singing and dancing with mops and other household implements is beneficial for many who live alone and even for some who live with others." Mercy had purchased the book on a recommendation from Dr. Goldbloom, the family therapist she'd visited just twice. The therapy had encouraged a horrific eruption of hives, but the book was an excellent find. She only wished now she hadn't skipped the chapter "Old Age, Decay, Suffering, and Death."

Mercy crossed her arms and hugged herself, and began rocking back and forth. "There, there," she whispered, as if trying to soothe a lost child. "It will be okay." Her voice broke as she told herself this necessary lie.

Mercy hopped off the examining table and scanned the room, as if searching for a way out. She squinted at the eye chart, reading it line by line, then inspected several framed crayon drawings and a poster entitled "Your Inner Ear." She marvelled at the sensuality of the language used in the naming of parts.

"Utricle, cochlea, vestibule, superior canal," she whispered. "The bony labyrinth," she said slowly, with an accent. For a second she envisioned a sacred holiday destination, a miniature Stonehenge in the chambers of the *auris interna*. Her mind, it seemed, had a mind of its own. She paced heel to toe in a semicircle and halted directly in front of a floor-to-ceiling shelving unit. Dragging her finger through the greasy film of dust, she wrinkled her nose and clucked in disapproval. Years back, she'd been the one scouring this office with scalding water and baby shampoo. At home, in her middle bottom dresser drawer, she still had a stash of old business cards.

Mercy Maid
Fast 'n' Fastidious. Reasonable Rates.

From the highest shelf, a papier mâché dragon scowled down at her menacingly. Below it, a bobble-headed ceramic doctor grinned from his perch next to a needlepoint pillow that warned: Do No Harm. Weak-kneed, Mercy swivelled around, rushed to the sink, and splashed cold water on her cheeks, drying off with a scratchy paper towel.

Hundreds of children stared out at her from years of school photos haphazardly thumb-tacked onto a corkboard above the doctor's desk. In the upper-right-hand corner, beside a flapper baby—a bald five-month-old wearing a rosebud hair band—Mercy spotted her one and only child. Belle, twenty years ago, aged eight. Mercy kissed her own index finger and reached out to touch Belle's face. The picture fell. Mercy snatched it up, and cupped her daughter in the palm of her hand.

In the photo, Belle was missing a front tooth. Her hair was plaited in the long black braids Mercy had tied with perfect red satin bows. Belle's wide smile didn't match the shyness in her eyes. Had she been able, Mercy knew her daughter would have hidden underneath the uneven fringe of bangs across her forehead. With great care, Mercy pinned Belle's picture back on the wall. A nail popped and the board swivelled sideways, threatening to fall. Mercy tried to save it and crashed backwards, catching the glass jar full of cotton swabs and rescuing the corkboard, but the pictures cascaded in a slow-motion avalanche to the floor.

Stooping to her knees, she gathered up the thumbtacks first, then sorted the mess of pictures according to size. Some were no bigger than postage stamps. Her hands were shovels; the picking was slow and awkward. Were she a person of faith, a believer, a person who prayed, it would have been an opportune moment to do so. Something like a sob hiccupped in Mercy's throat and chest. She issued a long sigh and began chewing at her lips, determined not to cry. This was no time for weakness.

Mercy normally considered any activity that was not useful a kind of indulgence. She reconsidered, just then. Just what *was* the appropriate reaction when exploratory surgery might be the most exciting up-and-coming event in your life? A sudden urge to scream overwhelmed her. She pinched her nostrils and coughed. The impulse passed.

"Bust this anxiety, Oral," she griped, and finished gathering up the pictures. She stood up—too fast. A wave of wooziness slammed her. Her legs buckled. She plunked herself back down and thrust her head between her knees. The dizziness lifted, blood rushed to her head.

Fumbling blindly for the blood pressure kit and the small rubber-nosed reflex hammer on the table above her, Mercy hauled the paraphernalia into her lap. Two months of training as a nurse's aid had given her some rudimentary first aid skills that came in handy from time to time. With the confidence of Florence Nightingale, she wrapped the sleeve over her bicep, velcroed it in place, slipped in the small black football-shaped pump, plugged in the stethoscope, and squeezed. As she suspected, her blood pressure was low. She didn't bother testing her reflexes. Her legs jounced around like two crazed jackhammers. Worried she might be going into shock, Mercy scrubbed her hands together fast and hard and slapped herself on first the right cheek, then the left. This only resulted in making her cheeks sting. Then Mercy remembered a fear-busting strategy from Oral Speakman. "Pretend to be two other very talented people rolled into one instead of yourself, and feel the infusion of energy and greater confidence! Dream you are Ella Fitzgerald and Frankie Sinatra combined! Sing!"

"Well, what the hell," muttered Mercy. She began belting out a jazzy version of "O When the Saints." She snapped her fingers. Starting to feel exhilarated, singing with gusto and zest, she stood. Solo dancing, graceful and half-naked, she thumb-tacked the pictures back onto the corkboard in a stunning sun-shaped collage.

The people in the overcrowded waiting area down the hall lifted their heads from their reading. What was that ungodly sound? they each silently wondered, not looking at one another, but shifting to attention, like a pack of beagles on alert. A man wearing blue jeans and a white T-shirt beneath a herringbone tweed blazer paused while composing a text message on his BlackBerry. The receptionist stopped filing.

"What's that sound?" a three-year-old finally asked his mother. He wore striped overalls over a red T-shirt and miniature sneakers. "Is someone getting a vathhhinATION?" he asked, his voice rising in alarm.

"No honey, I think it's somebody…" His mother's voice trailed off. The others watched her, hoping for an answer, waiting for enlightenment. What on earth was that sound? In the earnest pause that followed it was clear she was a mother wondering whether to lie or tell the truth. She listened again, her platinum head tilted to the left, fidgeting with her earring as if it were a listening device. At last, with a ladylike guffaw, she blurted out, "…somebody…singing! At least, trying to."

The waiting room erupted in laughter. Then someone's cellphone rang—to the tune of "Yellow Submarine"—and they quickly turned from one another and returned to themselves.

Mercy, oblivious of the laughter and goodwill she'd help

spread in that wallpapered waiting room, continued her improvised scat. Oral Speakman's anxiety-busting strategy actually worked. Her spirits *were* lifted. With Speakman-like verve she bellowed, vocalizing and visualizing all her worries tied in a balloon that floated up and away, bobbed in an endless blue sky and disappeared, her negative thoughts vanishing into the ether. Creative visualization was something she'd always considered somewhat ridiculous, although she recently conceded (for Belle's sake) that, indeed, happy thoughts might have a placebo effect for some. In any event, there was nothing to lose now.

She glimpsed herself in the mirror and tossed her hair over her shoulder, tucking the few strands of grey behind her ears. She stifled a laugh. Her cheeks were flushed, her eyes sparkled, and Mercy saw herself as if for the first time. She was *alive*. Her giddy frame of mind dissolved.

On the projector screen inside her head, Mercy envisioned herself melting like the Wicked Witch of the West into a thick waxy puddle that swirled into the eye of a hurricane. Snowflakes burst forth from that Cyclopean eye, flying like doves whose feathers morphed into trembling ashes on the tip of a burning cigarette. The ashes spiralled and she whirled off into...Nothingdom. Utter blackness. That was it, she thought. Ashes. Ashes. We all fall down.

She paced the room, her heart thumping in her ears. For the first time in her life Mercy felt not just doomed but damned. Stretching back on the examination table, she studied the polka dot holes on the ceiling tiles. What if she'd been wrong all this time? What if hell was not just here on earth but a real place, like some believed? An underground Grand Canyon filled with fire? Mercy began to sweat. There was a stabbing in her heart, as if a miniature pitchfork had hold of it and was sending electromagnetic shocks through her entire body. Hell. Hades. Inferno. Since adolescence, she had never given the notion a second thought. Theologically and politically, Mercy had long ago declared herself an underdogmatist. This was an original Mercy Beth Fanjoy word, one she coined herself in her weekly column:

Underdogmatist: *Anyone who lives on this planet is an underdog. Anyone who doesn't belong to any other ism, subscribe to dogma of any other ideological stance, or know what they believe from day-to-day. There is consistency in inconsistency. Self comes first. After that, one's greatest gifts must go to serve the greatest needs. No church. No party. No comfortable certainty.* (O Me of Little Faith. "Mercy's Musings," *OO*, June 90.)

Mercy had supporters. "It would make the world a better place if we were all underdogmatists. I agree with you!" That one was signed by "your secret admirer and most loyal fan." But Mercy also received hate mail for the column: "When you don't know where you stand, you don't stand for a thing! That's when Satan slips in sideways. He preys on wishy-washies like you. Pathetic. Selfish! Underdog. Woof. Woof." That letter was signed by "a conservative of great conviction."

Now, with heart-cracking clarity, Mercy acknowledged that underdogmatism had its downsides. No dogma, no manifesto; no manifesto, no organization. She had no helpline to call at a time like this. Her best friend, Lulu, would fret and hover. Her mother would only tell her, as always, to pray, and praying was out of the question. As for turning to her daughter in a time of crisis, Mercy decided there was no need to worry Belle—yet. She was such a busy young woman these days. Besides, like so many mothers, Mercy preferred to think Belle still needed *her*. This trick of mind infused Mercy's days with meaning and her nights with insomnia.

Mercy bolted upright and the room spun around. She focused once again on her sad, chipped toenails, wiggling her toes. The pedicure-massage, her first ever, had been a birthday present, compliments of her mother and daughter.

Mercy's feet had once been much appreciated. "And did

Feet First

A relaxing, revitalizing spa experience for weary soles.

Claim before December.

those feet in ancient time/walk upon England's mountains green?" she'd been asked once by the lover who rattled off the poetry of William Blake as he nibbled her toes. Mercy blushed, remembering. It was so long ago now it seemed like a dream.

A big-boned woman, Mercy's generous bosom extended

like a tea tray over narrow hips and wishbone legs. In profile, she appeared slightly off balance, ready to tip forward over child-sized feet. Sometimes, at day's end, and even though she always wore sensible shoes, the bones in her wee feet screamed with pain. Now her foot ailment seemed laughable, the least of her worries. Hadn't she read somewhere once that after death, hair, fingernails, and toenails kept growing? *The worms crawl in and the worms...*She covered her ears in an effort to drown out the sound. Where to run? Where to hide? What to do?

Time and Death. A formidable duo. Time ticked. A monstrous whirr and buzz in Mercy's belly. Death pawed. A hungry beast.

Ribbons of sunlight streamed in through the slats of the venetian blinds. Dust particles danced like fireflies. For a moment the examining room seemed luminous, almost speckled with glitter. Mercy sliced her hand through the bars of light and shadow. The fine hair on her arm caught the dazzle. It warmed her momentarily until she saw that the ribs of light across the floor looked exactly like the rungs in a jail cell or the spindles of a cage. The room itself was one big death trap. The automatic sweat sprinkling system buried somewhere in her scalp switched on at high frequency. A ginger-haired, amber-eyed woman on fire, she tugged a paper cup from its dispenser and turned on the taps.

Then, as if from the next room over, Mercy distinctly heard a tapping on the wall. This was followed by the voice of her Aunt Gladys. "What you need to do, Mercy, is remember Faustina. And me, too, of course." Mercy started at the voice. Faustina, the beatified Polish nun, and Gladys, her beloved Aunt Gladdie, were both dead. "Perhaps hearing voices is a beginning symptom of whatever disease I have," she mumbled, both sarcastic and mournful.

Mercy squeezed her eyes shut, trying to swallow. Fear curled and puckered her tongue, as if she'd been licking a penny, something she'd done once as a child—before swallowing the penny, choking, being rushed to emergency, and almost dying.

"When in trouble, write!" Rifling through her purse, she found her coiled notebook and pen. "Scrub the floor!" was another of Gladdie's beliefs. Gladdie spent her life with a mop in one hand and a pen—for writing to pen pals all over the world—in the other. Mercy clicked her pen five times. But her hand shook, and her fingers cramped up.

The next horrifying thought she had was how exposed she'd be, dead like that. Everyone would discover how disorganized she really was. No one would believe the chaos she was hiding. The things! The clutter! Overstuffed closets. Trinkets in drawers. Tupperware containers of junk.

Admittedly, nothing she owned was valuable enough to warrant an estate sale, but this didn't stop her from picturing her mother and Belle making cardboard signs and tacking them to telephone poles all over Odell.

Garage Sale

This Saturday.

435 Charlotte Street.

Home of Mercy Beth Fanjoy.

Everything must go.

Visions of strangers and, worse, her friends milling around in her bedroom, rummaging through her dresser drawers, holding up the one pair of thong underwear she owned, made her wince. She saw the scene clearly:

"Well, look at this. Who would have ever thought Mercy Beth Fanjoy, of all people, would be into lingerie from Lacy Lola's? She was always such a practical woman." It was Miss Flouncy-Bouncy Suzy Homemaker Vonda Kitchen, from high school. Even in Mercy's reverie, Vonda sounded like a squeaky toy mouse and her nose, dusted with freckles she'd once claimed were fairy's footprints, crinkled in disapproval.

"Stanfield's cotton briefs, I would've thought. Boxer shorts. Yep. Here they are."

Ricardo, Mercy's hairstylist, appeared. He shook his head, looking just like he did when inspecting Mercy's split ends. He loved to spin her around, go nose to nose with her, and say: "When will you ever learn? Between appointments, con-di-tion!" Ricardo sniffled a little and gnawed at his thumb, his hand in a balled fist of genuine grief.

"Whoopee and would you lookie here?" twanged a tooth-less man in a black baseball cap. It was Gordie Duggan, Sporty Gordie, from her ninth-grade prom.

"Is that a—? It's purple? A purple *vibrator*?"

"What is that thing that looks like a thumb on the side with those two horns for?"

"Does it work?"

"Batteries are dead."

Mercy pictured some instant camaraderie, a wave of amusement clutching them all as Ricardo pranced about in her bra.

One giggle turned into more and then—hysterics! Mercy scowled. She had been to many an estate sale and auction and witnessed, more than once, the nonchalance and banter among people looking for a bargain. Was there no respect for the dead whatsoever?

Dead meant she wouldn't be there to defend herself. She wouldn't be there to tell them the sex toys and lingerie were a joke from Lulu for her forty-fifth birthday. She wouldn't be able to tell them that she'd never used the Horny Little Devil vibrator and other pleasure majiggies. No one would know the truth.

"What's in the next drawer—whips and chains?"

"Socks. Just socks is all. Bee-you-tee-ful, though. Yep. These socks in the bottom drawer look hand-knit. She must've been quite the knitter. Look!"

"Leg warmers? Did the woman ever throw *anything* away?"

"I wonder what paint colour this is on the walls."

"I'd say it's Hydrangea Blue. I saw a can in the basement. Maybe you can get the number off of that."

In her mind, Mercy saw them moving on, like a gaggle of Canada geese, leaving her dresser drawers open, revealing the tangled mess that was, she now feared, symbolic of her truest self. Ropes of costume jewellery, hair accessories, toenail clippers, tweezers, nail polishes, dental floss, panty liners, Q-tips, silk scarves, leotards, Mother's Day cards, diet diaries, personal journals, foreign coins, rocks, shells, sea glass, lipstick, the lingerie—all of it, everything—was mixed in together and overflowing, spilling out the contents of an entire life and spelling out clearly how little control she had over it.

Mercy cracked her knuckles and flapped her hands like she was shaking out a thermometer. She'd done the research and watched the report aired by the BBC, CBC, and CNN three times: A recent British study actually linked the tidiness of dresser drawers to personality traits. "Apparently, it's been discovered that men who keep their sock drawers in order make 'good' husbands." (What's in His Drawers? "Mercy's Musings," *OO*, Mar. 03.) In that column Mercy pondered what "good" meant. Loyal? She'd never had her own husband, good or otherwise.

She would die as she had lived—single. Alone.

This thought writhed inside her; a venomous snake of desire bit her ankles and all her dormant Kundalini energy surfaced. Perhaps it was death's sudden squirm. All the things she should have done, might have done, could have done, would have done, came rushing forth. When this tsunami wave of dismay washed over her and subsided, Mercy saw, with clarity, all those things she'd left undone. She turned the page of her spiral notebook, clicked her pen five times, and began to write.

After a lifetime of playing with words, Mercy made a disheartening discovery. Words offered little comfort in the face of a major hyperventilation moment. Nonetheless, she pressed the nib sharply into the unsuspecting page. At first, she wrote furiously, as if to keep up with the frenzied beating of her heart, as if she could scare death away with the loops and swirls that joined together so magically to make words, words to make sentences, sentences to make sense out of it all. Usually, the pen was a wand, casting a spell, transforming the energy, busting anxiety. Not today. She spread sheaves of paper over Wiggins' desk. Slowly, painstakingly, she wrote and re-wrote.

Sweet Jeezuz, Sweet Jeezuz! I knew it. I'm dying. I knew it. I told the cat this morning. I did. I said BB, I think the news will be bad news. I feel it in my belly. Here, feel it. Lump, not just fat. A lump. I should never have voiced it out loud! Exploratory surgery, the doctor said. I need a plan of action if I want to get these few things done. Mercy, focus. Be succinct!

Mercy wrote and scratched out. She wrote but the words only sputtered from her pen. She crinkled up pages and tossed them like baseballs across the room. She tore pages in two. Then she did it. She asked herself the question: Were she to die in this upcoming surgery by some accidental slip of the knife or heart failure, what would she most regret not doing? The brain babble stopped. Each word was a sword. Some jabbed, others sliced, but the confusion was gone. She wrote firmly. She made a list.

Things To Do I've Left Undone
1. Call my mother and make her hand over the note.
2. Reunite Belle with her father.
3. Finish and publish my book.
4. Destroy incriminating evidence (RP letters).
5. Determine the identity of my number one most loyal fan/stalker/secret admirer.
6. Solicit Lulu's help and figure out how to dispose of the Horny Little Devil and other pleasure chest toys.
7. Take belly dancing lessons.
8. Have sex at long last with The Animal Man.
9. Forgive and make contact with Teeny Gaudet.
10. Travel. Anywhere. Get the hell out of Odell—for at least a day.

Mercy gulped for air as she reread the list. She crossed out *belly dancing* and scribbled instead, *Lose five pounds.* She then wrote "Note to Self: This is one week you must follow through!"

The sharp "click" sound of a door, like a shot from a starter pistol, ricocheted from down the hallway. Mercy could hear Dr. Wiggins heading towards the room, whistling. *No time to worry*, she wrote. *This is No Big Deal.*

Dr. Wiggins knocked on the door, but still Mercy didn't

move. She had days, maybe hours, to confess her sins, right her wrongs, and clean her dresser drawers.

No Big Deal, she wrote again in the notebook. *Breathe and Get Dressed,* she scratched. Worry sucked away positive energy and—like crying—was useless. The fear made her stomach curdle like lemon juice in cream. But she would go home and tackle the list. Oral Speakman, that multi-millionaire advice guru author, encouraged plans. Maybe Mercy could write a self-help book. She'd call it *Death Strategies*—except to have a bestseller she'd probably have to do the dying part first.

Wiggins knocked louder.

"Yes?" Mercy called out.

Dr. Wiggins stepped into the room.

"Mercy? Mercy Beth! Why aren't you dressed yet? What's all this paper?"

Mercy crossed her legs and backed away, flung one arm over her breasts and tried to cover the rest of her body with the small, coiled notebook. Then she passed out.

"Mercy! Mercy! *Mercy!*" Dr. Wiggins' voice roused Mercy. She came to fully then, only to find herself sprawled on the floor, a coat thrown over her. The berber carpet beneath her buttocks scraped worse than sandpaper.

"Take it easy." Wiggins was wiping her forehead with a warm cloth.

"What happened?" Mercy blinked and sat up.

"You tell me."

Mercy shrugged, her eyes springing leaks. She lowered her head. One tear dripped off the tip of her nose.

"Try not to worry until you have to. You've just worked yourself into a full-blown panic attack. Breathe." Wiggins leaned over her, checking her pulse.

"Easy for you to say. And that's exactly what I was doing!"

"Hyperventilating is not breathing. Talk to me slowly. And I repeat: this could be nothing. Cysts. Fibroids. I wouldn't lie to you, would I? I've known you since you were a kid."

"Read!" she said, but her voice broke and warbled. She sounded like a sick bird chirping. *Ree-eeead.*

"Say again?"

Mercy handed him the notebook and blew her nose with the Johnny shirt.

The doctor adjusted his glasses and turned his back. Mercy realized this was a signal for her to get dressed.

Dr. Wiggins let out a long sigh. "Sweet Jeezuz," he said.

"Sweet Jeezuz" was a phrase used by many Odellians in-stead of "well whataya know" or "damn it" to indicate amaze-ment or disapproval. It was considered no less offensive than "holy mackerel." It was also the name of Mercy's first dog. Before he was trained, every time he had an accident, her mother yelled, "Sweet Jeezuz! Bad dog! Bad! Sweet Jeezuz, pee on the newspaper! Or Sweet Jeezuz, Sweet Jeezuz, are you stupid?" Soon they noticed the poor thing came running every time she said it. And finally he refused to respond to his proper name, Bubbles. So, "Here, Sweet Jeezuz!" they called for him. "Roll over, Sweet Jeezuz!" And, when he ran away, "Have you seen Sweet Jeezuz?"

These days, her mother used the phrase as a simple term of endearment. It was an ecstatic uttering for Jesus Christ Lamb of God, light of light that taketh away the sins of the world. Cassandra Fanjoy-Rutherford spent a lot of her life doing devotions in a religious community called the People of the Church of Faith and Light and Celestial Vibrations.

"Sweet Jeezuz, that's quite the to-do list!" Dr. Wiggins was making clucking sounds. "Number four? Incriminating evidence? What did you do? Commit murder?"

"No. Adultery. Years ago. I told you about it. But I kept let-ters. They have to go," Mercy said in a matter-of-fact tone.

"Right, right, I remember. That was when you lost a lot of weight." He continued reading. "A book, eh? I've got an idea for a novel myself. Wouldn't mind running it by you sometime. Stalker?"

"Well, more like an anonymous fan. You can turn around. I'm dressed."

"And is The Animal Man who I think he is?"

Mercy looked up at the ceiling and began to hum.

"Sex is the best idea on the list. Very good idea. Travel, too."

He handed back the notebook and let out a long whistle.

"Those first two have me worried. You sure you really want to open up all these cans of worms? Let sleeping dogs lie and all that. And besides, like I said, we don't know anything yet."

"That 'yet' sort of sticks in my throat. I'm just going to tidy up some things. Feng shui my life." She began gathering up her clutter of papers.

"Say what?"

"Forget it, Doc. And forget you read this, okay?"

"Well this'll keep you busy anyhow. Not that you're ever at a loss for things to do. So if you have more questions, if you're having trouble sleeping or anything, just call, okay?" She nodded. "And," he chuckled like a jolly department store Santa, "be a good girl and say your prayers."

Mercy winced at this display of paternalism. "I don't go to church and I don't know how to pray, or even if I believe in God, let alone reincarnation," she said, her voice prickly.

Dr. Wiggins looked as if he had just been given too much information.

"Reincarnation? I didn't say anything about reincarnation. Don't go asking me for answers—I'm an Anglican!"

It was a vestry joke. He began lifting folders from his desk as if he'd misplaced something. Mercy didn't laugh. She began to cry. Wiggins stopped shuffling. He placed the tissue box where she could reach it.

"Look, Mercy, it's best to under-react in times like these. You might want to take time for a little rumination, eh?

Get it? Do a 'Mercy's Musing' on rumination?" he laughed, then wheezed, then coughed, then snorted in through his nose, making a sound like a shovel hitting a sudden patch of concrete in the winter.

"Pull yourself together now." He patted her shoulder, twice. "Atta girl," he added.

Mercy was a horse being readied for a race by a jockey. Under-react? Compared to who? Or was it *whom?* she pondered. And just how did one do that? She'd always been prone to what she considered a slight excessiveness, even if, technically, that was an oxymoron. Her mother had a theory about what she considered her daughter's over-the-top reactions to life's usual bumps and bangs. "Mercy, you were born sunny side up, you know—head first but face up not face down, wide open with no protection from the very start. Most babies are face down and curled. I was in labour forty-eight hours. I'm no doctor, but I think this trauma and open-armed entry have everything to do with your extreme sensitivity to smell, light, and loud noises. I would like to rebirth you by baptism as a Vibrationist. If you consent, of course." Of course Mercy did not. Would not. Would never. Let her mother and her congregation shake and rattle and quiver before some Almighty God and Great Conductor. As far as Mercy could tell, though they were nice enough and peaceful, the Vibrationists were all infected with some kind of virus she had no intention of catching.

Mercy finished buttoning up her coat, grabbed her purse, and headed towards the door.

"Mercy?" Wiggins' voice was muffled.

"What?" She was still trying to process the word "under-react."

There was no reply.

"What?" She looked back.

The doctor was staring at her with a stunned expression, like he had to pass gas and couldn't. His face turned as red as the maple leaf on the flag behind him. "Are you okay?" Mercy clutched her throat and rushed towards him. Wiggins shook his head no. He appeared to be holding his breath.

Then she saw. He was wiggling his ears, one at a time, just like he used to when she was little. Dr. Wiggly, she used to call him.

Mercy leaned down—he was such a pot-bellied elf of a man—and gave him a hug that almost cracked his rib cage. She inhaled his leathery smell, remembered her manners, and mumbled something. It was a sound as close to gratitude as she or anyone else might muster, under the circumstances.

Walter Wiggins closed the door of his office and broke wind. It was the exertion—all that ear wiggling. He plunked himself down in his swivel chair so hard it lurched and he almost toppled over.

"These wheels will be the death of me," he grumbled. He regained his balance and hen-scratched a few additional notes in Mercy's file.

Linda, his nurse and receptionist of twenty years, poked her head in the door, and wrinkled her nose.

"There's a man here who says he has an appointment about a lighting system for your house—lord! Beans again last night, Walt?" She fanned her hand in front of her face.

"Sorry. I'm just an old fart. Come in for a sec would ya?"

"Do I have to?" she grimaced. He gave her the boss look.

"Sorry, Walt." She closed the door. "This is serious, isn't it? Mercy, I mean."

He nodded. "Oh dear." Linda was fond of Mercy personally, and a fan of "Mercy's Musings."

"Yep. It is. I've a phone call to make, so tell the others I'll be running a bit over." He cleared his throat and gazed down into his open, empty palms, looking from one hand to another, as if reading a newspaper.

"Walt, are you crying?" Linda had never seen such a stricken expression on his face. She pressed her hand against her lips in concern. Her voice got lost somewhere in her throat.

"Mercy's going be fine, isn't she?" The question hung there—a squeaky sound of hope, a door hinge that needed a squirt of oil.

"That all depends on what you mean by 'fine.' I'm concerned for a lot of reasons." Wiggins sniffled and cleared his throat. "I'm okay. Don't be staring at me like that. Maybe it's time to retire again. This time for real."

Linda nodded and wrapped him in a bear hug. Wiggins blushed like an adolescent boy and shrugged her away gently, then blew his nose.

"Second hug in five minutes. I'm a lucky man."

"Need me to get a number for the phone call?" He shook his head no. This was a number he knew by heart.

For the second time in his life, Walt Wiggins was going to betray his Hippocratic Oath. He silently prayed this would do no harm. He was certainly violating doctor-patient confidentiality. As chair of the ethics committee with the College of Physicians and Surgeons, he knew he was walking a thin line. By the time he finished dialing, he figured he could justify the decision, if he ever had to.

"Hello."

"Cassie, Walter Wiggins."

"Walt! Am I due for my physical?" There was a slight tease in her voice. Cassandra was seventy years old and still a flirt.

"I've got to talk to you. About Mercy."

"Is she okay?" Cassandra's heart spun around her rib cage, as if attached to a small propeller.

"How about I say it like this—you'd better ask her about

that yourself. And…"

"What? What?"

"I'm calling to warn you. You'd better be prepared. She's going to ask again. About the note."

"Why do you think that?" Her voice had lost all its warmth.

"She told me. Cassie, if she's going to start up again about the note, we've got to—"

There were whispery mewling sounds on the other end.

"Cassie, are you okay? Are you still listening?"

"I am."

"Now. To be on the safe side, we'll need to get all our ducks in order. If you want, I can refer you to—"

"I have my church so I won't need any shrink or lawyer or anyone to get me through this thank you very much. You are a fine man. If you hadn't been so happily married—SWEET JEEZUZ, stop!" Cassandra's dog, Sweet Jeezuz the Fourth, was on the back of the sofa, barking. "But I'm very happily married now as you know. And you are too. Maybe another life." The Vibrationists, though Christian-based, believed in reincarnation.

Walt chuckled. "Don't be teasing an old man like that. My heart!"

"Well. In any event, there's no problem. About Mercy, I mean. There was no note, remember? I'll do like always. You know, handle this crazy idea of hers like I always have."

"Cassie, I think…I think you might want to reconsider. I mean, could be it's time to let her know what all really happe—"

"Don't go there, as they say these days! Don't even think it."

"Well. Then. Okay. I'm here if you need me."

"That gives me great comfort, old friend. God bless you."

Cassie hung up. Her heart thrashed around at full throttle, a propeller out of control. When she glanced at herself in the mirror above the telephone table, her image shattered into a million pieces. Shards of glass pierced her, puncturing her lungs and heart and vital organs. As if blinded and suffocated, she grabbed the table and blinked, opening her eyes as the feeling passed. She re-established her bearings, grateful, as always, she was still intact. Then, she applied her lipstick and smacked her lips.

"B! P! Baden-Powell. Be prepared," she rallied herself. "And thank you, Jesus, for guiding Walter Wiggins to make the phone call. I can be well prepared now I've received this gift of kindness. It is a sign of your mercy. A warning sign." Still, Cassandra shivered with trepidation, her head buzzing with questions. What was wrong with Mercy? Something serious? The doctor had been deliberately evasive. It had to be something dire; why else would Mercy start up about the note again? "Enough spinning these old tires of worry," she chastised herself. "Straighten up and get down to business."

Cassandra Fanjoy-Rutherford, though like her daughter in many ways, had faith and prayer and extra special armour in her personal survival kit. She was a great believer in rituals. She had a wonderful tactic—developed long before the days of creative visualization. It was simply her little Game of Signs. As she tied a blue scarf fashionably around her neck, she imagined it as a banner that read, "Proceed with Caution." Then she sorted through her jewellery box until she found the sacred talisman. She bowed ceremoniously, her chin to her chest, as she draped a gold necklace over her head. A gift from her first husband, the chain held a fourteen-carat gold charm of Nefertiti's head. To Cassandra, it was her personal hotel doorknob sign, a finger held up to lips. "SHHH! Do not disturb!" on one side. "Housekeeping," on the reverse.

"Keep this house. O lord. I pray...Please. Keep it safe by night and day. Mmmmmm..." Cassandra Fanjoy-Rutherford had long ago mastered the strange art of anxious humming. The resulting sound was hauntingly beautiful.

Each day of her adult life, at precisely three o'clock in the afternoon, Gladys Marie Fanjoy, along with millions of other Roman Catholics, kneaded the beads of her rosary, prayed the chaplet of Divine Mercy, and recited the Divine Mercy prayer. Imagine, if you will, Gladys beseeching young Mercy, "to stop, pause, pray for the world and everyone in it. Glory be to Faustina." Gladys transformed the facts of Faustina's life into a kind of Grimm's fairy tale, a ritual bedtime story for Mercy.

"Once upon a time, long, long ago, in the country of Poland, there was born a blessed child, a girl child, the third of ten children. Her name was Helena Kowalski. Helena. Helena. Helena. She worked hard for her family and joined the Sisters of Our Lady of Mercy—the order after which you were named. Helena gave her life over to Jesus when she was only sixteen, yes, just as she was budding into womanhood. It was then she was given the blessed name of Mary Faustina. She worked in lowly jobs, cooking and cleaning, carrying and scrubbing. Yes, dear, a little like Cinderella. Then one night Jesus came to her. 'I do not want to punish aching mankind,' he told Faustina. 'But I desire to heal it, pressing it to my merciful heart.'"

Then Gladys, smelling like lilac talcum powder and moth-balls, leaned close to Mercy and showed her the diary and picture of beautiful Faustina and another of Jesus with rays of light, one red, one white, emanating from his chest. "Every day of your life, Mercy Beth, I want you to know there are people who care. It just makes you realize how much goodness there is. And that healing can happen. Remember that, whenever you are hurting."

Mercy still had one of the small statues of Faustina that Gladys had left her in her will. She still kept Gladys' framed picture of Jesus' emanating heart tucked in her children's bible, on top of the illustration of Jesus in blue robes, arms outstretched, beseeching: *Little children, love one another.* Now here she was, a grown woman feeling just like a little child, fondly remembering her late Aunt Gladys and wondering if a prayer to Faustina, the angelic-faced first saint of the twenty-first century, might stand her in good stead. Have mercy upon Mercy? No, she shuddered. It was simply too ridiculous.

It was not quite noon as Mercy shuffled through Dr. Wiggins' waiting room softly singing, "O When the Saints." She brushed by a kind-eyed man in a tweed jacket, close enough to catch his scent. He wore cologne, something she did not normally like in a man, but this fragrance was subtle. Gingery. Lemon. Caught off guard by a sudden surge of lust, Mercy shivered, slightly embarrassed. It was a long-forgotten sensation. Downright miraculous, the human body! she couldn't help thinking. Cervix, ovaries, clitoris, uterus, vagina, Saskatchewan. She giggled, remembering the silliness from childhood. Still, the heat inside her roared like a furnace clicked on for the first time in years.

"This is your sacral centre. Kundalini energy and desire stir from your solar plexus, Mum," Belle informed her during the last yoga session they'd shared.

"Is that the same thing as horny?" Mercy had asked. Belle, who was in a headstand at the time, had not been amused.

The gingery lemon-smelling man grinned at her like a game show contestant. Even in passing, Mercy couldn't help but notice his dimples, how deep they were, like two, small, bottomless whirlpools. How she longed to plunge her fingers in, test those waters, swirl in a barrel made for two to the edge of their very own Niagara.

"Did you get a vathhination?" shouted a little boy just then, breaking into her fantasy. He was dressed in overalls and did not have dimples. A bubble of thick green mucous ballooned from his left nostril with every exhalation. Mercy felt doused with cold water. And why was everyone in the waiting room staring at her, as if trying not to laugh?

"No honey. Not today. No needle for me. Dr. Wiggins is saving it just for you!" she replied, immediately slapping her hand over her mouth. Was it her imagination or was there a collective intake of breath? The boy shrieked in terror, then began to cry—a croupy sound like the barking of a sad seal. In shock, the mother cradled the boy in her arms, rocking him furiously, looking over the top of his head at Mercy. The door slammed behind Mercy with an offensive belching sound as she made a clumsy exit.

"Wasn't that Mercy Beth Fanjoy?" someone whispered.

The man in the glassed-in booth in the parking lot of the Odell Medical Clinic took the parking fees, grunted "g'd day," and surveyed all the comings and goings in his square cement corner of the world, while he watched the sports channel on a miniature television. He loved his job. His name was Pete. Although most people would not be able to recollect his face were they to see him elsewhere, Pete would recognize them, no matter who was playing or what team was winning.

Every day he saw folks in various stages of sickness and health leaving the parking lot, looking relieved or sad, impatient or distracted, in pain, distressed, stressed. Pete was ever grateful he was not one of them, happy to be the gatekeeper with no immediate need of medical attention. The invisible man. An arm extended. An upturned palm. Today, he was keeping his eye on the Raptors game and a young mother as she struggled to secure a screaming toddler in a car seat, a greying couple passing arm-in-arm discussing the pros and cons of angioplasty, a teetery geriatric woman baby-stepping along. As well, there was that tall woman who'd sprinted past him. She'd raced into the vintage car in row M and for the last five minutes appeared to be having some sort of a breakdown. Pete silently wished her well (he often did this to the panic-stricken) then cheered as right on the buzzer Toronto scored a three-pointer from half court.

Finally, after fifty-two furious strokes with the hairbrush, calm settled over Mercy. As she reapplied her makeup in the rearview mirror, an elderly woman in blue hobbled by. Wisps of cloud-white hair sprouted from under a woolen tam. Her wizened face with its pointy chin was a perfect triangle. Her coat swallowed her. Wing-shaped lapels flapped; she was a woman poised for takeoff. She passed by close enough for Mercy to notice the dragon's head carved on her cane. The woman was wearing lime-green gloves. The colour plunged Mercy into the past.

"LIME! Lime-en-essence," her childhood friend Teeny Gaudet, in a voice filled with wonder and mirth, was whispering in her ear. "Over there, Mercy! In front of the window! I saw first. One of mine."

In the world according to Teeny Gaudet, whenever a person spotted lime green or smelled the smell of oranges, this meant guardian angels were close by. If the lime green was actually worn by a person, and the person had blue eyes, whoever noticed first could claim the angel as their own. Mercy had surmised, even as a child, that this was just superstition. And as an adult, Mercy most certainly did not believe in angels.

"Still. Better safe than sorry," Mercy heard herself saying now as she cranked down her window. "LOVE those gloves," she shouted out. The woman ignored her. Mercy rolled up the window and shifted from thoughts of angels to caskets and worms. Going back to her makeup, she concentrated on outlining her lips.

A car alarm went off nearby. Mercy sighed and started the ignition in her HubbleyCraft. The car was so old mushrooms once sprouted from carpets covering the floorboard. It was a gas-guzzling 1969 black Cadillac Deville, the convertible she'd inherited from her good friend Harold Hubbley a few years back. Recently cleaned and Scotch-guarded in an effort to cover the mildew smells, the car had "character, real character," as Hubbley used to boast. Mercy loved the Deville and drove the vehicle with the same confidence she wrote her name. Despite whatever greenhouse gases her daughter regularly accused her of emitting, even now, with the surgery on her mind, as she heard the motor purr and eased into traffic, the car made her smile.

Then, on an eye-squintingly brilliant day, on a day people went about their ordinary business and their ordinary lives and smiled their ordinary smiles, Mercy drove through the city of elegant elms, trying to forget her bloated watermelon belly.

A huddle of teenagers in the park, uniformly dressed in dark, sack-like outfits, lit cigarettes and postured themselves in a way to suggest sinister and cool. Behind them, a band of eager, athletic types played basketball. Mercy longed to stop and join them. The backdrop of trees was a glorious mix of crimson and orange and the sky above so punchy blue it seemed to crackle. Mercy smiled, admiring a squirrel skittering along on its tightrope run high above on a telephone wire.

Just look, she thought, how a person could be broken-hearted or terrified or in the midst of turmoil and pain, and how the rest of the world kept rolling right along. How often people brushed by each other. They greeted each other normally and replied *fine fine just fine just fine yes just fine thanks and you* when really they might be in a crisis or mired in grief or despair. Life was such a death-defying act. An egg juggle. It was marvellous really, though. Wasn't it?

Past the uptown malls and drive-through takeouts, past the high school, past rows of brick apartment buildings, down the hill towards the centre of town, Mercy rolled on. She travelled zigzag and drove slowly, purposefully detouring, past the streets of bungalows and split entries built in the sixties, houses now weary and faded or newly re-sided with vinyl, inhabited by aging arthritic parents of friends now grown and moved away. Here she was, right in front of Teeny Gaudet's house. The lawn was trimmed and mint green. A new walkway set in fieldstone led to the front door. Hanging pots of petunias still bloomed. Or were they plastic? Mercy thought she saw a figure move in a chair by the window. The television was on. "Can I have a cup of tea, Mrs. Gaudet? Yes, it has been a while! Tell me, how *is* Teeny?" She could just imagine the look on Mrs. Gaudet's face. "Mercy! I knew you'd come by sooner or later. I've missed you."

Further on were the wartime homes that clustered around that den of iniquity, Odell University, including the house she'd lost her virginity in. Right there on Reed Street, in that basement, in a rec room with black walls and a red shag carpet, on a round bed beneath a furry blanket. The setting was neither romantic nor original but, unlike so many girls, Mercy's first encounter had been pleasing. She'd had a thumpingly good time: copulation in perfect time to a heavy-metal drum solo.

Mercy scrounged frantically in her purse for The List. She uncapped a pen with her mouth and spit the top into the passenger seat. She placed the notebook on the steering wheel and circled the number 8 on her list three times. *Have sex at long last with The Animal Man.* "Noah," she whispered.

"Shit!" Mercy stopped just in time at a red light. "Shit!" she said again, walloping her head on the steering wheel. The horn squawked in protest. A red Mustang overstuffed with teenagers honked back and then idled beside her. "Nice car, lady! Are you like Batwoman? I'm BUTT-Woman," a brunette with braces yelled out. The car swerved dangerously close and roared ahead of her. One of the girls stuck her rear-end out the side window in a full moon salute.

Mercy rubbed her forehead. Then she leaned on the horn and gave them a third-finger bird sign right back. Her pedal foot trembling violently, she pulled over to the curb as soon as she had turned the corner. Sucking in air like a gulp of water, she breathed.

She smelled rain coming. Although she had a keen sense of upcoming weather conditions, Mercy wasn't always accurate. Storms blew in, sometimes, without warning. People died. Reaper storms, they were called.

Mercy signalled and manoeuvred out onto the street once more and rolled on, trying to forget. A few moments later, she coasted by Phoenix Place, the building that housed an insurance company as well as the entire operation of the *Odell Observer*. The red brick facade and ornate arches were newly restored. At one time (despite her lack of solid journalistic credentials), Mercy proudly claimed a cubicle of her very own, complete with a nameplate on her desk. That privilege had been taken away when Stirling Cogswell died. He had been her first editor, mentor, and dear friend. Mercy missed his sanity and wisdom terribly. "He was a true permissionary," she'd said in his eulogy. "A permissionary is one who gives another permission to have faith in their unique authentic selves and yet challenges them—always—to go the next step. 'Onward ho!' he used to say. 'Onward ho!'"

Right now, going forward was all she could do.

A few moments later, she signalled left by the old hospital—now a hospice and addictions clinic. On the other side of the street was the Glooscap Animal Shelter. She eased into the parking lot and considered going in to talk to Noah Perley. The Animal Man. But she was totally flummoxed. How, she wondered, did one proposition someone, exactly? She was forty-eight years old and she had forgotten how to approach a man, if she had ever known at all. Too bad Teeny wasn't still a friend, Mercy thought, snickering to herself. She'd have a line or three up her sleeve.

She turned off the ignition and sat. Beside the animal shelter was a gingerbread-style Victorian home. It looked like a large family residence until you looked closer and noticed the bars on the windows. It was Odell's shelter for women: Ferguson House. This reminded Mercy she had another deadline. She'd agreed, pressured by Belle, to produce an educational brochure on domestic violence for the R.A.N.T.S.—the Radical Angry Necessary Tirading Sisters of Odell, an organization that had always intimidated

Mercy. Sensing a lot of anger in their membership and true to her underdogmatic principles, she'd never joined up. Belle, the current treasurer, doggedly claimed the "energy" was shifting.

"The Rage Age has given way to The Sage Age," she argued. "A new wave of interfaith, interracial, wise, spiritual women rising to change the world is happening, Mum."

"Really?" asked Mercy, trying hard to catch a fraction of her daughter's enthusiasm.

"Really!" Belle nodded.

"For instance?"

"Women like Oprah." Belle continued, "Women like Aung San Suu Kyi in Burma, like Maya Angelou, like Mrs. Johnson in Liberia."

"Mrs. Who in where?" Mercy knew she was not in the know. "Like Hillary Clinton?"

The brochure was due for International Women's Day. Mercy was well pleased with the title, "From Survival to Thrival," but so far it was all she had. Now she counted the months on her fingers. March 8 was less than five months away. Would she still be around? Who would finish the brochure if she could not?

She started the car again. "Under-react," Wiggins had had the nerve to say. She hadn't known it was a word until he'd uttered it. Her face grew hot. Her stomach knotted. Deep, slow breathing did not help. Pausing at another stop sign, Mercy watched as a man in a motorized wheelchair whizzed across the street. An antenna on the back of the chair wobbled in the wind and a red flag flapped above his head; a water wheel turned in Mercy's stomach. She pictured spiralling, mutating cells and wanted to vomit.

"Stop feeling sorry for yourself, Mercy Beth," Aunt Gladys' voice sifted in again from the ether. "Remember Faustina." But Gladys, believer in angels and the visions of saints, admirer of popes and the beatified Polish nun Faustina, was still dead. Dead dead dead. Belief or no belief, you still die, thought Mercy.

"To hell with Faustina," Mercy muttered. "Sorry Gladdie, but I'm so not ready!" she wailed. "Not anywhere goddamn ready." A car behind her leaned on the horn.

"Sweet Jeezuz!" Mercy yelled. Her voice was hoarse. And because she'd refused Dr. Wiggins' kind offer of medication, she changed direction and drove to the liquor store. Mercy wasn't much of a drinker, mostly because it didn't much like her, but she thought she might want a sip later, after class tonight. (She wasn't prepared for that either.) After buying white wine, a chardonnay, and a pack of menthol cigarettes, which she vowed not to smoke, she decided to head downtown for coffee.

A few minutes later, driving into the heart of the Odell historic business district, she turned on the radio. "In the headlines for October 17, 2006, the population of the United States reaches the three hundred million mark; two trains collide in Rome, killing one and injuring countless others; and a woman from Odell, Mercy Beth Fanjoy, a wannabe everyone and a washed-up nobody, might have ovarian or stomach or some kind of cancer. Those are the headlines, now here's the news." Mercy switched channels until she found classical music.

"Verdi's *Ernani*," the host announced in a hushed tone. Mercy turned up the volume. Perhaps, she thought, if she were to wage a battle with death, surely this music would keep her inspired and give her resolve. Just then, a plane roared by in the sky, a giant dart, a potential missile, piercing the blue beyond. The rumble drowned out every last rhapsodic note. The music was lost.

"More coffee?"

Before Mercy answered, Bee reached into her apron pocket and put two creamers by her cup.

The Coffee Mill Restaurant, downtown Odell's major gathering place, was located on the lobby level of the Odell Hotel on Electric Street. "The hotel is no Château Frontenac," tourists said, "but the food's great."

The hotel was impressive in a pretentious, ornate, wrought-iron way. It was *Odell's oldest and most conveniently located hotel*, the website declared. But the restaurant was something of a contradiction. There was still a great greasy spoon menu in an atmosphere of faded elegance. To the gentrified or those from away, it was reminiscent of another era, when women studied etiquette and knew to remove their gloves when serving tea. To the locals, it was a diner.

The dining area was spacious, the scalloped tin ceiling high, the colour of thick cream. Small light fixtures bloomed like inverted toadstools around a gold-leafed chandelier in the centre of the room. The Coffee Mill easily accommodated its loyal, daily clientele as well as the transient hotel guests. The row of booths claimed by regulars hugged one wall. The rest of the seating area was more formal: oak tables for two or four sparkled with good silver and fine china set

on white linen tablecloths. Green linen serviettes, folded skil-
fully, sprouted from cut-crystal goblets. Carpets swirled with
Loyalist blues and Acadian reds. The seat cushions matched
brocade curtains tied back with thick, gold-cord tassels.

Whenever she entered the Coffee Mill Restaurant from
the foyer of the Odell Hotel, Mercy felt she was vanishing into a tapestry. She normally liked this feeling. The last
booth overlooking the river had been her writing booth since
her student days, when she discovered that the white noise
of a busy place helped her write. The easy clang and clat-
ter gave her focus. The office at the *Odell Observer* was too
frenetic, and at home she was tempted to sleep.

"Honey, you okay? You're looking kinda peaked today,"
Bee said.

"I'm just a little tired, Bee."

"Know the feeling, don't I just? You're working too hard,
hon."

Bee moseyed over to the next table.

B-e-e.

"That's me, busy as a bee," she'd said, when Mercy asked
that first time if it was a typo on her name tag. That was over
twenty years ago. Mercy watched Bee with admiration. How
did she do that? She always seemed so relaxed and able to fill
everyone's coffee cup at the same time. And smile. Mercy knew
Bee had not had an easy life. What Mercy did not know—or
want to know—were the details. At present, Bee had one son in
jail, a grandchild she'd never seen, a mother in a nursing home,
and a bi-polar ex-husband who turned on her whenever he was
off his meds.

Today, Bee was wearing white sneakers and pink ankle
socks with frills on the cuff. A Cape Bretoner, she called ev-

eryone honey or hon and wore her hair in a high ponytail. It swished past her tailbone when she walked and was pulled so tight off her face it smoothed out her wrinkles. Once, she undid the ponytail and shook out her hair, and her face crumpled. "I don't need no Botox, hon. Detox, maybe, but none of that botulism stuff. Got that back there in the kitchen, ha!"

"Seeyalatergators," she shouted out as some police officers left. "My worst tippers," she muttered to Mercy as she flew by.

Mercy was mesmerized as Bee performed her acrobatic balancing act. Platters of dishes were perched along her left arm up to the elbow joint. Stacked plates in the other hand were tucked under her chin. She twirled and opened the door to the kitchen with a bump of her behind, swivelled sideways, absorbed the momentum with her hip, thrust again, and disappeared. Mercy was suddenly overcome with love for Bee. She stifled the urge to cry like a child whose dog had run away.

Hormones and death, she thought. Would it be safe to go out in public? She hid her face behind a menu, hoping to regain some control.

Even in the happiest of times, Mercy had a propensity to be maudlin. Maude Lynne she'd been dubbed by one of her readers. And sentimentality especially was one thing her readers (except for her number one most loyal fan and secret admirer) had warned her she should be wary of. But the death clock was ticking. Tick, tock. Now it was on rewind and she was talking to Cogswell in his office many years ago. You can't please everyone, Cogswell was reminding her. Again. Most of her life Mercy and most women she knew kept on trying to do just that. Please others. Seek approval.

"Critics—positive or negative, right or wrong—are a waste of time. Also, beware the lobster-pot mentality! Don't let the buggers at the bottom claw you down into the pot!" Cogswell had warned. "I say be diligent. Ignore the critics! Get over yourself. Do what you must! But also ponder the words of William Blake: Opposition is true friendship."

Now, in the Coffee Mill Restaurant in the Odell Hotel, Mercy made a vow. She turned to a fresh page in her notebook and wrote:

For the next ten days, I do not care what anyone thinks.

She then added an affirmation:

Yes. I am determined to embrace this as an opportunity. Two weeks is enough time to resolve a few things. I shall hug this fleeting thought of death to my bosom as a gift, a friend. Except I would have been such a good grandmother. Grand mother. Was I?

Mercy stopped writing. She had a flash of Belle, sitting in a chair, nursing a baby, with other children at her ankles, gazing up at her. A fire roared as she talked lovingly to her angelic offspring.

"Lord save us, Mercy! You look so serious. Writing an obituary or something?" Bee was peering over her shoulder. "More coffee?"

Mercy covered the page. She who hated dramatic scenes in public places was ready to blurt out, "I love you, Bee."

"Deadline pressure?" Bee asked, perching on the edge of the seat opposite her. Leaning forward, she studied Mercy's face.

"You could say that," Mercy nodded.

"Well, you look like the wrath of God. Go home."

"I'm going soon enough. A few more notes for class to-night."

"One of these days, I'm going to take one of your classes. My book'd be a bestseller! My life story would curl your toes, rot your socks, stab your heart, and make you wet your panties." She hopped up and waved to a man in the corner.

"I'd love that, Bee. I really would. And I always say everyone has a story to tell. But I'll bet you wouldn't learn a thing from me. Gotta run."

"Aren't you forgetting something?"

"What?"

"Your fortune, honey." Bee reached into her never-ending apron pocket and handed Mercy a fortune cookie.

"Thanks, Bee."

On the way to the car, Mercy cracked open the cookie and two small banners of paper fluttered out—butterflies dancing out of a cocoon. Two! Mercy chased after them. Two! It hap-pened sometimes. She trapped them with the heel of her shoe, bent down to pick them up. She straightened up, pleased with herself, and shouted out, "Got ya!"

"*Pardonnez-moi?*" A man wearing a yellow windbreaker over a tweed blazer blocked her path. "*Je ne comprends pas.*" He smiled at her but Mercy thought it was an indulgent kind of smile, one reserved for children or crazy people or those with visible disabilities. He looked vaguely familiar. It was the dimpled man from the doctor's office! A deeply dimpled French man. His eyes were delphinium blue.

"Litter! Litter!" she sang out, smiling. "Can't have that!" Mercy waited. He stared, and then shrugged. A knapsack slung on his back, he rolled his suitcase up the wheelchair ramp away from her. In his other hand was an old-fashioned doctor's bag.

Mercy waited until he entered the hotel.

She turned back to the fortune cookies. Carefully, hopefully, she looked down at the two small pieces of paper in her hand. One was completely illegible, like a Rorschach ink blot test. It reminded her of an amoeba. The other one was blank.

Back in the car, Mercy screamed. She screamed and screamed, all the way up and down the hill, at the top of her lungs. Fear of death strategy number one: primal screaming. She was hoarse but almost orgasmically released.

When she looked through her windshield next, the world was on fire. Every leaf on every tree had transformed into candle flames, as if each tree was haloed in golden light. Mercy blinked. Leaves were leaves once more. No haloes. This trick of light had not happened to her in years but she needn't have been surprised. It was fall in Odell, and there was a gilded, bronzed feel to everything. Maybe, were there a heaven, it would be like a crisp fall day in Odell...pleasant enough if you had a sweater on.

Just before she turned from Smythe onto Charlotte Street, Mercy spotted Lulu coming out of Goodfood's Grocery. Not telling her best friend in the world what was going on with her ovaries would be dicey. She considered just driving by. Even if she did have her fair share of flaws, she was no liar.

"Omission *is* lying," she'd always told Belle, crossing her fingers behind her back. "Lying is wrong, a sin even, to those who use that sort of language."

That rather absolute and deeply held opinion came from a lifetime of experience and from her mother's refusal to acknowledge the existence of the note Mercy's father had left behind after committing suicide when Mercy was a child. Now it was the number one item on her list of things to do. Her mother and her huge omission. "Big lie. Sin-sin-suh-in," hissed Mercy.

She tooted the horn and waved at Lulu, turning into the parking lot.

"Hey!" Lulu reached through the car window and hugged Mercy's neck. Her breath smelled of mint and coffee.

"How'd it go at the doctor's? What did he say?" Pumpkin earrings dangled from Lulu's earlobes.

I'm maybe dying, Mercy wanted to blurt out. "Everything is fine! Menopausal stuff. So, a-okay. I'm busy. Class tonight. On my way home to do some research."

"On what?"

Success stories of ovarian cancer victims?

"The expression, 'keep a stiff upper lip.'"

"Haven't you done that one before?"

Lulu—Mercy's friend since first grade—was a mother of three and happily married to Hap Kunkle. She had been an elementary teacher for twenty-six years and had a filing system for a brain. A genius of organization with a heart bigger than the Milky Way, Lulu was one of the living saints of the universe, in Mercy's eyes. "Only saints or lunatics would put in long days with children not their own," she often teased.

Lulu said she chose elementary school because she preferred children to adults and wanted to work in a profession where she could believe most people were hopeful types. "And I get to wear colourful clothes in seasonal themes every day—and my Converse Hi-Top sneakers. I can accessorize with outlandish jewellery and pretend it's all for the sake of the children, especially the ones with ADHD. Bright colours and shiny things help keep their attention."

"Mercy?" Lulu snapped her fingers in front of Mercy's face.

Mercy was having her own attention deficit challenge at the moment. She stared at Lulu, who was wearing a black feather boa-like scarf over an orange turtleneck, black denim jeans, and orange sneakers.

"Mercy!"

"What?"

"I said I think you already ruminated on stiff upper lip."

"No. I don't think so."

"You have so! I gave that column to Whiny Wanda. It's one of my faves. You called that column 'Soul-Seekers, Soul-Suckers, Stoics, and Other Annoying People.' Remember?"

Remember? Mercy nodded, rolling her eyes skyward. Some Odellians had gotten up in arms about the term "soul-suckers." Mercy was told by a certain C. Beres that the soul-sucker column was "undignified" and she should "stick to motherhood, domestic affairs, and recipes. Why encourage vulgarity?" Mercy was shaken at first. Like always, Stirling Cogswell, editor and gentleman, gave her some much-needed and sage advice.

"There will always be those who try hard to maintain a sense of decorum, those watchdogs who fiercely guard the fine veneer of gentility glazed over this city," Cogswell said with considerable cynicism. "This is essential, or else all would indeed be lost!"

"Lord, Mercy. Are you okay?" Mercy was staring into

space, smiling, fondly remembering Cogswell. She could use a little of his no-nonsense approach today.

"Yes! Right. Sorry. Time to switch jobs, I guess. Seems my mind is like a tippy canoe these days. One more piece goes in my brain-pan and it's information overboard! Gee, not bad." She pulled out her coiled notebook. "Brain, tippy canoe."

"That's more like it!" Lulu was accustomed to Mercy's odd asides and note scribbling. "Want to do late lunch tomorrow? I've got a spare hour."

"How about a sweat in the steam room?" Mercy replied.

"No, I'd be no good for the rest of the day. You trying to lose weight again?"

Mercy nodded. "Aren't I always?"

"How about supper Saturday night then? Hap's barbecuing."

"Call and we'll see." A horn honked behind them. Lulu flashed a perky grin and dashed off.

As Mercy headed home, she consoled herself with thoughts that her loved ones, when the time came, would rally together. They would make broccoli and cheese casseroles and rolled asparagus tip sandwiches, and drink gin and tonics. All in her honour. After a great party, they would hire that company that specialized in memorial boat cruises. What was it called? *The Orinico*. They would play Eva Cassidy's version of "Somewhere Over the Rainbow." Recite poems. Linking arms, they would scatter her ashes in the waters of River St. John.

Upon her arrival home, Mercy waded through a puddle of mail at her front door. Shuffling through bills and flyers, she found a self-addressed, stamped 8 × 10 manila envelope. Anger crested over her with such force she kicked the wall. BB yowled in bewilderment and skittered away. Mercy knew the envelope held only more bad news. Clutching it, she opened the doors to the garden and scrutinized the neglected, tangled mess she now realized was a better metaphor for her life than her overstuffed dresser drawers. She needed to prune.

"If you want to do a good job at anything, the proper tools are required!" The admonishing voice belonged to Fiona Featherstone of *How Does Your Garden Grow?* It bleeped at Mercy like some intercom system installed in the yard. For years, Fiona had been an integral part of Mercy's Sunday morning ritual. After a one-hour walk, then time with the "Book Review and Lifestyle" section of the *Globe and Mail*, a pot of coffee, and a chocolate croissant, she tuned in to Fiona on the Home and Garden television network.

Folks: Do you have the proper tools? What's more, do you know how and when to use them?

The truth was, Mercy was afraid to prune. There were blades involved; she was klutzy. And left-handed. She could not imagine cutting into a loaf of bread decently, let alone something living, like a plant. And there was the whole matter of where to snip—above the node or below.

Nodes. "Once you begin to notice," Mercy said to no one but the floppy-faced sunflowers gone to seed, "once you are in danger, the language of death is ubiquitous. Every-fucking-where, as Hap loves to say. Death metaphors, like disease itself, can run rampant." She clutched her stomach. The lump felt bigger than it had before the doctor's appointment.

The manicured garden—once a tiny Eden—had grown wild under Mercy's somewhat jaded green thumb. Still, Mercy preferred this riot of colour to a tidy landscaped look. To her, this gnarled garden was a magical sanctuary year-round, a place she could imagine elves beneath toadstools, Shakespeare's fairies cavorting in a ring, and the long-dead poet William Blake and his wife in naked ecstasy, talking to angels.

She had been much too neglectful lately, however. Today, she saw only how the garden sprawled. Monstrous weeds thrived, chaotic as Medusa's serpentine curls. At the moment it seemed to mock her in a cruel reminder and manifestation of her internal system of roots—capillaries, veins, and arteries. She remembered the dreaded black knot she'd found on her chokecherry trees last year. A blight that spread like cancer.

"What you need to do is cut off any branch that has been affected at the node that is right below and, hopefully, a comfortable distance from the black knot." Mercy pictured a scalpel.

Was it the same for black-knotted ovaries? she wondered. Black-knotted pancreas? Black-knotted intestines?

Taking a deep breath, she turned the manila envelope over many times before opening it, as if she could change the wording of the letter with some ritual or spell. She unfolded the paper. At least it wasn't a form letter.

Dear Ms. Fanjoy:

Thank you for your query. Although I am intrigued by your biography ideas, and I admire your empathy in the sample writing, I regret to say we have no place for "Healer, Hooker, Homeless: Three Women of Old" on our list. I like it but I don't love it. Frankly, the work I say yes to has to speak to me in some extraordinary way. Also, I'm not sure you can execute. These ideas seem extremely ambitious for a writer with no real publishing track record. Why not consolidate some of those columns you've done over the years and add some new ones? A combination of serious and humorous. You might want to get an agent and try a regional press. Alternatively, you can always self-publish. Many people do and there is no longer the same stigma surrounding vanity publishers as there once was. Or perhaps publish an e-book. Good luck!

All best,

Henrietta Hawkes

Every word from the pen of Ms. Hawkes was a pin, stabbing, and by the end of the letter, Mercy's abdomen, which was a lumpy inflatable mattress to begin with, was punctured. So much for her dreams of the Great Fictional Biography. It was as if her very lifeblood was gone, vacuumed out through her navel.

The hummingbird feeder was as empty as she was. Mercy filled it and checked the other, which she'd made herself with a kit from Canadian Tire. She brewed a cup of lemon ginger tea, sat in a wicker rocker on the small flagstone patio, and began preparing for her evening class.

No sooner had she sat down than the next-door neighbour's cat pounced into the yard, a squawking blue jay in its mouth. Mercy had no special fondness for blue jays. She considered them selfish and common. Nor did she find any joy or beauty in their *weedle-weedle* song. But this possessed, demented cat was diabolic. And the bird in this instance was certainly the underdog.

As usual, BB performed outdoor surveillance from the window. Mercy vaulted from her chair and spun into mother-bear action, yelling and waving her hands.

"HSSSS," she spouted out, as catlike as she could.

Momentarily distracted, the cat let the bird escape. Its warbled throat song became one of strangulation. The blue jay tumbled along the ground, a chipped piece of sky. The cat waited and watched, blinked up at Mercy once, then nodded in BB's direction, as if to say, *Watch this, okay?* He pounced on the bird again, batted it between his paws, and seized it with his mouth again. But still he didn't kill it. The bird thrashed and squawked.

The cat stopped. Watched. Circled. The crippled bird tried valiantly to fly. The cat pounced again, toyed with it between his paws. Like a pitcher, Mercy thought, nonchalantly tossing a baseball from one hand to the other, before he wheeled and nailed the player on third trying to steal home. Then suddenly, as if bored, the cat let go.

"Fly!" Mercy screamed. "Fly!" But the bird staggered drunkenly a few inches and flopped. The cat did a three hundred and sixty degree turn, leaping high, and struck again. Mercy waved her arms then stomped the ground and rushed the cat.

"Fuck off just fuck off fuckfuckfuckfuck off fuckoff!" she clucked. "Get out of my yard you goddamn murderer." The cat looked at her evenly. Mercy lunged. She was paw-swiped, the cat's claws sinking into her flesh. Mercy screamed and snatched her arm away.

"Mercy?" It was Mrs. Cattalini. A humpbacked, lavender-scented devout Roman Catholic, Mrs. Cattalini was also an old friend of Auntie Gladys' and an actual survivor of the Halifax Explosion. She was also the owner of Trixie, the sadistic, murdering cat. Mrs. Cattalini was going out, as she did every day at this time, to walk her midget-sized husband around the block. He had just suffered his third stroke in three months. "Mercy?"

"Mrs. Cattalini! Your f-fucking cat is killing a bird in my yard. Come get it." Mercy was near hysterical.

"Well, well. Cats do that, dear! It's not a disaster. No need for that kind of language. Your Aunt Gladys would be ashamed. Calm down! Here puss puss. Here pussy." Trixie padded proudly back to Mrs. Cattalini, tail feathers in its mouth.

"Is it dead? The bird?" asked Mrs. Cattalini. Mercy saw a set of eyes peeking through the cedar hedge.

"No! Not yet. But almost."

"Call Noah," said Mrs. Cattalini. "Maybe he can save it."

"Fuckfuckfuckjustfuckrightoff. Pussy pussy." It was Mr. Cattalini, laughing and drooling.

"Joe, stop it! Now see what you've started with that profanity, Mercy."

Mercy ran into the house, grabbed a dishtowel and found a shoebox. The blue jay was under a bush by the time she returned. Clots of blood, like dollops of blackberry jam, dribbled out of its breast and belly. She wrapped the bird in the cloth and felt it tremor faintly. A tiny beating heart in her hand. Feathers still floated in the air. But the creature was alive.

Noah, The Animal Man, the man of Mercy's dreams, he-who-she-wanted-to-have-sex-with, was not at Glooscap Animal Shelter when she burst in. "Can you save this bird?"

The pimply teenager's eyes widened. "I don't know. I'll call Noah right away."

"I have to go get ready for work. Will you call and keep me posted? I don't have a cell but you can leave a message."

The girl nodded with compassion. "Yes, but at the Glooscap Animal Shelter, Mother Nature and the Great Creator have an understanding. If it's time for an animal spirit to pass—"

"It isn't time! I know it! I'll pay," said Mercy. "Anything! This bird *has* to live."

The girl's eyes widened. She tried to hug her, but Mercy squirmed away. The girl hugged the box instead and handed Mercy a business pamphlet on which was printed the prayer of St. Francis, the sayings of BIG EAGLE, and Noah's twenty-four-hour hotline number.

Mercy drove home, grief-stricken. It was raining. Even if she knew how to pray, in this instance, she did not know whether to pray for life or for death. How much suffering before death was the cure? Who decides? Time death time death time death, repeated the windshield wipers.

A few hours later, Mercy pulled into the parking lot of Darcy D'Avery Hall and pulled out her list again.

Things To Do I've Left Undone
1. Call my mother and make her hand over the note.
2. Reunite Belle with her father.
3. Finish and publish my book.
4. Destroy incriminating evidence (RP letters).
5. Determine the identity of my number one most loyal fan/stalker/secret admirer.
6. Solicit Lulu's help and figure out how to dispose of the Horny Little Devil and other pleasure chest toys.
7. ~~Take belly dancing lessons~~. Lose five pounds.
8. Have sex at long last with The Animal Man.
9. Forgive and make contact with Teeny Gaudet.
10. Travel. Anywhere. Get the hell out of Odell—for at least a day.

With the viciousness of an attacking cougar, Mercy scratched out number three, tearing the paper. There'd be no book. Sooner or later, she realized, it catches up with you—all the lies and omissions, procrastinations. At the bottom of her list she wrote:

Who was Darcy D'Avery that this building bears his name?

He might have been a good guy but he's dead just the same.

Mercy laughed. She laughed the way insane people laugh when they realize they are sane but just ended up crash-landing on the wrong planet.

What will be my legacy? Who will even care?
Will anyone remember Mercy Beth was here?

She scribbled another question, this one not in verse:

Why is it that times of crisis seem to heighten one's sensibilities, so that everything resonates?

Still in hysterics, she clutched her stomach and bit her lip. "I laughed so hard I thought I'd die." What an expression, she thought now. The next question put an end to both her laughing and her note-taking:

Why haven't I felt this alive always?

Mercy clambered out of the car, strolled leisurely into the cafeteria, ordered a double cappuccino, and made her way to class. For at least a few hours, she would forget, be safe, and let others not so fortunate worry about death and dying. And only much later would she drink that glass of wine by the fire, admit the terror, and cry herself to sleep.

"Life is...just one big challenge. Write without editing for five minutes."

Mercy trumpeted this brilliant opener to her class the evening of the first day she seriously contemplated the eventual and perhaps imminent possibility of her own death. So much for leaving her worries behind. She winced and then attempted to mask her emotions with a grin so wide her jaw almost locked in place.

Her unsuspecting students greeted her as usual with small half-smiles of expectation. Then they bowed their heads and approached the page and opened themselves and their words spilled forth.

The class of eight participants consisted of fledging writers and one who had published a poem in an anthology by a vanity publisher. Mercy anticipated the group would unite, eventually, but they were only just starting to trust her and feel safe with one another.

They knew by now that Mercy Beth Fanjoy, popular *Odell Observer* columnist, was a non-linear thinker who relied on themes for coherence. This loose structure was not an excuse for what seemed to be a lack of organization, but, she assured them, a conscious choice, a willingness to be open to the energy and creative flow of every class. "Themes like resilience, loss and recovery, or appearance versus reality, or—well—the list is endless. Themes make for a kind of blueprint for each class, in a connect-the-dot, make-your-own-meaning type fashion. You can and will form your own picture."

Mercy positioned herself from the beginning in the role of Holy Fool and Socratic questioner. She permitted herself to be vague and to answer questions with questions. With the efficiency and courage of a midwife, she birthed the hidden gifts and stories she was thrilled to see in everyone. Her approach to teaching writing was based on a book written in 1904 called *The Write Truth*. Most of the time, publication was not the goal of her students, so she encouraged all participants to strive for authenticity in the weekly writing exercises.

"So explore the themes and, more importantly, find the recurring symbols in your own lives. Where are the parallel lines? The lines of intersection? And ultimately you will find clarity and insight due to the thematic patterns you uncover, discover, and recover. And there will be more questions spurring you on to even greater illuminations." She'd seen it happen time and time again. The class was therapy for many. For others, it was merely a distraction or hobby—some dedicated the time to preparing a memoir, a scrapbook of words that would one day be left behind for the grandchildren. "But what could be more important than that?" she asked them to consider. "Neither fame nor fortune."

"You have a bad habit of answering your own rhetorical questions," one student wrote on last term's teaching evaluation form.

For Mercy, teaching these many years was her own lifeline, another freelance job she'd stumbled into, work that paid decently and helped her stay afloat. Treading water, drifting, staying afloat, waterlogged, bloating, drowning—these were recurring motifs in her life.

At times, even she wondered how she did it, especially when Belle was little. "Single parenting must be so challenging. How do you juggle so much?" Cogswell asked her once. "Why not write about that, Mercy?" he'd encouraged. And so she did.

"I'm a plate spinner. But every plate is overloaded and I feel like things are going to crash around me every second of every day." (The Planet of Plate Spinners, "Mercy's Musings," *OO*, Sept. 89.) Plate-spinning Odellians empathized and responded enthusiastically.

"Well, if you hadn't confessed, we'd never have known," wrote her most loyal fan and secret admirer. Yet they loved that she did confess; in fact, it was that ruthless honesty in exposing her own faults and foibles that made her column so popular. Folks even started using the plate-spinning metaphor on their own—in coffee shops, in conversation, in emails to their friends, on posters for International Women's Day. Mercy was ecstatic. This cross-pollination of ideas was gratifying to her. She was not a territorial woman when it came to ideas that, after all, were rarely ever original, and really, a dime a dozen. It was a different matter when it came to her invented words and phrases. Or when it came to her daughter. Mercy admitted she had overly possessive tendencies around Belle. Killer mother-bear instincts, in fact. She preferred not to think about this side of her nature too often.

Those who knew Mercy best were neither surprised by her personal admissions nor overly impressed by her pearls of homespun wisdom. They were sometimes irked upon re-

alizing they had been the source of one of Mercy's rumina-
tions, but they got over it. Those who loved her worried
about how frantic she seemed, how hard she worked. Some
thought she might have an undiagnosed anxiety problem.
Lulu, for example, encouraged her to drink decaf and not
take on so much extra, especially the teaching.

"But I need the money. It's a non-credit course and I
don't have to mark, just read, and I'm not teaching really,
Lulu, not like you. It's more like 'facilitating' or 'guiding.'
Besides, I like it."

"You can still burn out doing what you love. Would you
just please slow down some?"

"You should talk," laughed Mercy and gave her friend a
hug. Lou-ease. She was a more focused person than Mercy,
certainly. Calmer, at least on the outside. Louise was the real
teacher. She transmitted her entire being into each of the
children in her care.

"Lulu actually loves every one of the crusty-nosed, whiny,
little knee huggers like they were her own!" Teeny Gaudet
once remarked. Teeny, the author of *Maybe My Baby* as
well as the *Burt the Burping Bear* series, insisted you didn't
have to have children or even like kids in order to write for
them—let alone love them. Lulu, on the other hand, Lulu
loved. But while Mercy was less jaded than Teeny, she was
no Lulu. At the very most, she was a listener, an instructor.
The Lifeline class at Odell College for the Department of
Continuing Education did not require a teaching certificate
or love. Tolerance, maybe, but not love.

Dr. Demmings had hired Mercy because he felt her life
experience and newspaper work made her more than quali-
fied. "From a TV guide writer to a columnist in ten years!

This is a most impressive curriculum vitae." In Odell, that kind of progress elicited respect from some, envy from others, and indifference from most.

During that first interview, Dr. Demmings talked mostly to her breasts. "Yes, very impressive." Mercy smiled and took a deep breath, which she hoped made it look like she had *a heaving bosom.* Dr. Demmings needed to add another course as desperately as she wanted the job.

"Thank you. You won't regret hiring me." She smiled at Demmings when he told her she was hired. It all worked out just fine and Dr. Demmings never did more than ogle. He never did get very good at not getting caught looking.

Lately, Mercy was looking for a change. The Lifelines course had started to bore her. This was both surprising and discouraging—her very own syllabus for the course argued that "each voice was unique and important and that everyone needed to tell their story." If this were true, it should never grow redundant. Hoping to rekindle her former passion for teaching, she reframed old notes and recently proposed a course called Every Body Has a Story.

"Writing is, after all, a healing art," she smiled, ending her presentation with what she considered a clincher.

"Says who?" asked Dr. Demmings. He had the kind of stray eyebrow hairs that quivered like antennae. Boing. Boing. He was waiting.

Mercy stammered. "Well, well—"

"I'll think about it," he said, and dropped the file folder on his desk along with a stack of other folders that made him appear to be a busy, busy man.

As the class continued to scribble, Mercy doodled at the edges of her margin: *OH my ovaries. OO! Oh.*

She hadn't thought of it before but maybe the course title Every BODY Has a Story would attract survivors of childhood abuse and domestic violence, people with chronic pain and terminal disease. A dying crowd. She wasn't ready for that. Mostly seniors attended Lifelines class. They were a healthy lot for the most part, and almost too agreeable.

"Stop," Mercy barked out now. The class seemed to freeze in place. This obedience embarrassed Mercy.

They shook their heads wisely as Mercy continued babbling on about life's many metaphors, rubbed at their liver spots, and wheezed yes yes yes my dear oh lord yes don't we know life is a challenge made up of smaller obstacles all along the way.

"A journey, such a journey," sighed Lincoln Grover.

"A voyage," agreed Ernestine Perkins.

"An odyssey!" Brent was a small-boned, waxy-skinned man with a face twitch. When he talked, he held his hands on either side of his head, as if putting his head in parentheses. Mercy wondered if this was how he somehow kept the twitch under control. Sometimes she wondered if Brent had epilepsy or Tourette's syndrome, and might at any moment launch into a string of expletives that would give half the class a coronary. At thirty-five, he was the youngest and, besides Lincoln, the only other man in the class. He had a degree in English literature and was able to sprinkle in literary references from time to time.

"A quest of mythic—" he began.

"Or maybe—maybe just some humdrum boring road trip," Mercy interrupted. Even to her own ears, her voice was harsh. "If it's a road trip, you're lucky if you get a pit stop to pee let alone a rest stop, spread out a blanket, a gingham one, red, and have a real picnic with fried chicken or maybe cucumber sandwiches and devilled eggs and nice cold root beer. And then it's back out on the highway to more traffic, congestion, potholes, mudslides, and yes, even fatal accidents caused by deer. So do we whine? No. Not us. We are not Odysseus exactly, not Sisyphus either, thank god, but Hercules, yes! For if we write we can use these tests slash labours for purposes of our narrative arc, creating our own mythologies, transforming negative into positive, shit into compost." Her voice had raised an octave.

Ernestine pressed two fingers against her lower lip. Lincoln scratched his temple. The rest looked at each other to gauge how they should react to this uncharacteristic interruption. Mercy lowered her head. "No offense. On the other hand, maybe, maybe it's just like—I forgot who said it once—life is just a dash between two dates on a tombstone." There was a shocked silence. She really had gone too far. Mercy cleared her throat and walked back behind the desk. "Next exercise. Write this down. 'I'm having trouble with…' Fill in the blank. Begin and write for ten minutes."

They bowed their heads and obeyed at once and it seemed to Mercy that the sound of their pens and pencils scratching the paper made soft, whispering sounds of forgiveness.

In the lavatory stall, beside two verses of obscene doggerel, some phone numbers, and a crooked valentine that said "Ruby and Heather forever," Mercy noticed a message in tiny letters: local astrologer and psychic, call 454-6732. She memorized the number by remembering Canada's centennial was the year 1967 plus her daughter's bra size. She flushed and washed her hands.

Perhaps she shouldn't have had that last coffee. Her heart thrashed. She brushed her teeth—a technique she used when she quit smoking. It helped calm her down. "Up and down in and out over under. There you go. Something you can do, Mercy. Brush your teeth." That was death strategy number three, she registered mentally, as she returned to class. Now number four. She counted how many steps it took to get the length of the corridor. "Counting is also a good and healthy preoccupation," she imagined herself saying in her own self-help book. She stopped outside the classroom, afraid the class had mutinied in her absence and left after her rant. Should she confess to them it had been quite a day and even she had her limits?

No, of course not, keep up a brave front. Forward ho! "When you're in a peck of trouble and the world seems to deride/ Don't you let yourself forget it, there's a sunny side!" Mercy hummed. It was a Gladys song. She smiled ruefully and re-entered the room.

"Five more minutes and then we will share." She flashed them what she hoped was a genuine look of encouragement. Gladys of the Glad Heart encouraged her to smile no matter what. *Accentuate the positive. Eliminate the negative. Don't mess with Mr. In Between.* Who knows, she thought as she studied the members of her group, maybe some even welcomed her exuberant outburst of pessimism tonight. Mercy was told once that her joy and positive attitude were suspect as well as irritating: "It grates on those of us who cannot summon it up easily," wrote a student on her last evaluation. "Not all of us have such confidence or lead such privileged lives."

Mercy suspected the comment had come from a burlap-faced, urine-smelling woman named Sadie. "But what makes you think I do? Why, when you do something reasonably well, do people believe, or rather assume, you do it easily?" Mercy wanted to write back. Instead she wrote, "Assumptions are Lethal," for the Double-O. ("Mercy's Musings," *OO*, May 94.)

Just then, a hand shot up.

"Was it okay if I wrote it in verse?" It was Ernestine.

"Oh. Dear. Well. I'd rather you write closer to the way you'd talk for this exercise." Mercy tilted her head, "Do you understand what I mean by that?"

"Conversationally?" asked Ernestine.

"Is that an adverb?" Brent said out loud.

"As if you were writing a column of your own," said Mercy, sending Brent what she hoped was a piercing, intimidating look, quieting his grammar police.

"Let's call it Ernestine's Everyday Ordeals." Mercy suggested.

Ernestine's eyes glowed. "I can do that!" she said, and began writing anew.

Mercy knew, from her own essays in the *Odell Observer*, that writing about the mundane allowed one to process and work out a whole tangled mess of thoughts. It was all she could do, in any event, not having bona fide journalistic credentials. It was amazing to her that she had readers, ones who were, for most part, appreciative folks. At first she'd been so timid.

"Trust your audience," Stirling Cogswell advised. A quiet, patient teacher, Cogswell gave Mercy the break she needed. At the same time, he handed her *Bartlett's Quotations* and William Strunk and E. B. White's *Elements of Style*. "Each, a writer's bible," he'd advised her, patting Strunk. "Always. You must go back to fundamentals. One must know the rules before one can break them." He was right. Mercy still consulted those rules. In gems like, "Place yourself in the background" and "Prefer the standard to the offbeat," she found not only a way to teach Lifelines but also a coded philosophy for daily living, a philosophy she wished she followed more consistently than she did.

With some modifications, Mercy found Strunk's instructions on writing style helped her with personal style and guided her in social etiquette and moral conduct.

MERCY RULES
Do not overeat, over-drink, or over-talk when in a crowded room.
Be discrete when giving out personal information.
Remember: No one wants or needs your whole life story.

Do not say: "I'm hungry as a horse" when on a dinner date.
Over dinner, listen and say, "Well, what do you think?" first and
lower your eyes and say, "I don't really have an opinion, just a
few thoughts."
Even in the column, suggest, don't preach.
Ask politely for the meanings of words you are unfamiliar with.
Dress in neutral, muted shades. Blue, black, beige.
Never pretend to be more educated than you are.
Try to catch your first thought before it flies out of your mouth.

But like the Ten Commandments, Mercy seemed doomed
to break these rules too, over and over again. Mercy Fanjoy,
a slow lifelong learner.

As for Bartlett, the range of topics the quotations inspired
over the years—well, there was no end. Just last week she'd
begun her rumination with, "Charity begins at home, but
what if you do not have a home?" She'd been told by the current editor to discuss the problem of homelessness springing up in their town centre. How she'd wrestled with that
column, wondering why she'd agreed, pretending she could
handle the tough social issues. She had a social conscience,
but she was not the flag-waving, placard-carrying type.
Sometimes, she felt like such a fraud. But there was the day
Belle had burst in and slapped the paper on the countertop,
kissing Mercy on the cheek. She was wearing a shirt that
said, "Stop bitching, start a revolution."

"You rock, Mama! Awesome." That praise, coming from
her daughter (who'd always been so difficult to please),
pleased Mercy to no end.

"I just wrote the truth," she said modestly, as if the truth
were the easiest thing in the world to find.

"This is your best writing ever," said Belle, opening the fridge. There was a peace symbol on the back of her shirt. "Got anything good to eat?"

In that column on the homeless problem, Mercy pointed out how Odell was changing, how they shouldn't look the other way. "As you pass them, look into their eyes not just their outstretched hands, and imagine it is your son or daughter, father or mother. Take them for coffee. Ask them their names. Donate to the soup kitchen. Let's not ignore REALITY," she warned. (Fearlessly Facing the Faceless. "Mercy's Musings," *OO*, Oct. 06.)

She got yelled at the next day by three teens with multiple piercings and arms bruised with tattoos. Even though they shaved their heads and wore clunky black lace-up army boots that made her think of Nazis and torture and Anne Frank and heroin, a sudden genuine sadness for all their angry young hearts and the broken hearts of their parents had overwhelmed her. She wanted to do everything she had publicly asked others to do and sincerely tell them she loved them. Instead of putting her head down and walking on when they asked, "D'ya got any spare change today?" she asked if they would like to go with her to The Coffee Mill. "We don't want your frickin coffee," one of them hissed. "Shit, what is it with folks today asking us for coffee!" Mercy was thrilled; *she had readers.* For her, this translated into r-e-s-p-e-c-t.

"Mercy?" The entire class was looking at her, expectantly.

"Sorry. Yes. Ten minutes are up."

"Can I read what I have?"

"Sure, yes, go ahead Lincoln."

"I've been having trouble with girls," he began. He was

eighty-two if he was a day. "I'm still having trouble with them, ya know."

Mercy watched all of them, shaking and hooting with laughter, then Lincoln, laughing harder than anyone, looked at her and nodded.

"Well it's true. It is. Flora Atkinson, not one month widowed, is calling me five times a day."

"Tell her you are already taken," piped in Ernestine, who batted her eyelids in exaggeration. This set them all off again.

As Mercy joined in, it seemed for several seconds as if their belly laughter had been rehearsed. The uncontrolled merriment danced in undulating waves of sound, in an ebb and flow of mirth that filled the room, spilled down the corridors, and roared back in on them, a kind of symphony cresting in crescendo. Their hearts quivered and bloomed wings. It was as if they were all flying, zipping around the classroom in a rhapsody of joy, a painting by Chagall.

I do love them, Mercy realized then. I do, I do. I've loved everyone who has crossed my path and shared pieces of his or her life with me. Oh hell. I see. I see I love everyone. People are all so beautiful. All of them. They really are. Even my mother. Even Teeny Gaudet. No one will know how I feel now, not ever, because I will die and I will have told no one. Listen! Can you hear me? I love you bunch of laughing folks, you tired-out lonelys, you empty nesters, you, you geek-faced epileptics, you misfits. ALL of you. All of us. I am you. You are me. One body. It really is like that, isn't it?

Mercy turned towards the blackboard. Someone from a class that afternoon had written, "Consider the lilies of the field." Mercy shivered as a wave of whole body goosebumps washed over her.

The laughter subsided and Mercy felt their eyes on her back. She turned and gave the next exercise. "I am going to give you a smell. When I say begin, without thinking or editing, write for five minutes. The smell is: oranges. Oh, one more thing: When I say stop, write in at once, wherever you are, the word 'Amen.' Okay? Okay. Begin."

The result was an astounding, frenetic flurry of images and impressions that, had they been penned by James Joyce himself, would have elicited pages of critical analysis.

Everyone had a spark of genius in them, Mercy had come to see over the years. All they needed was to believe it themselves. That was her only job when it came down to it. To validate the creative genius she saw in everyone. *Almost* everyone, Mercy thought now.

"Any personal metaphors to end this evening?" she asked.

Jean—Mercy thought that was her name—put up her hand. "I know this is probably going to sound strange, but..."

"Jean, this class is about finding your voice. Do you realize you apologize every time you open your mouth?" Mercy intended kindness but the woman's whining and insecurity in the midst of this experience of oceanic love and faith for the universe was a pinprick in the balloon of her euphoria. Her tone was scolding—a scrub board rubbing sound.

"I'm sorry," she replied. Brent snickered behind his hand. "And it's *Jan*."

"Right. Jan. I'm sorry."

"It's okay—no one ever remembers my name."

Oh dear, winced Mercy. Jan the faceless. Jan the nameless. Capital V for victim emblazoned on her forehead. "And what is it you intended to say?"

"Today's personal metaphor?"

"Right. Go ahead."

"I am just a footprint in sand on a beach the tide keeps washing away." Mercy blinked rapidly and coughed into her hand in an effort to block the surge of hysterical laughter she felt. But she was far too kind to say what she was feeling, and as an underdogmatist she related to the idea despite herself. Besides, she was having a genuine eureka moment. "Janet— Jean-Jan! You just gave me an idea! If we feel we are forgettable when we are alive, how will it be when we are dead?"

Jan nodded her head. "Exactly. I've often wondered that," she said, her lips closing in a pitiful pout and head tilt. Mercy ignored her and addressed everyone else.

"For next week, let's write our obituaries!" she yelled. "Serious or funny. As if it were going in the *Odell Observer* tomorrow. No. Let's aim high and modify if and when we have to: the *Globe and Mail* "Lives Lived" column. Yes. Let's. Let's write what we want them to remember. Okay?"

One by one, they nodded. Jan Muir was radiant. When she smiled, with her small, sharp teeth and mop of curls, Jan reminded Mercy for all the world of a miniature grey poodle, not unlike Sweet Jeezuz the first.

When she got home, Jan Muir watered her plants and laid out her clothes for the next day: a beige pleated skirt and a beige sweater. She took out her home and dream journal. The class was stranger than usual tonight, she thought, and, yes, perhaps it had disintegrated into morbidity. She wrote the following:

Mercy Fanjoy rarely gives assignments. There must be a rhyme to her reason, and besides, we trust her with our lives. At least, the parts we select, the lifelines we dare to throw out to one another and choose to share. Every week, it's like giving your palm over to a fortune teller, or one who claims to see who you are by reading it, as if somehow all those heart lines and love lines and life lines are who you really are, and all your worst traits too, your darkest secrets are laid out and shine in the light like silvery stretch marks. For a second, you feel vulnerable and exposed, then wholly seen and even understood. And miraculously, you are not judged, but told, instead, you are infinitely worthy of love. If you were a person prone to using figures of speech you might say this is a possibility that makes your heart do a triple somersault of joy.

At the same moment as Jan Muir closed her journal in an exclamation mark of happiness, Mercy, half asleep in her living room, took another sip of wine. She was employing the singing drinking death strategy.

"Ayy men Ayymen Ayymen," she slurred, imagining an old friend, Isaiah Livingstone, in her living room, clapping his hands. Aymen. He was singing. Ayymen! Isaiah Livingstone had been a classmate at Odell University, one of a small number of foreign students and an ordained Anglican minister. Brother Izzy, he liked to be called; a missionary to white folks like her.

"Comin' to service this Sunday?" he used to ask every week.

"I'm too big a sinner, Izzy!" Mercy normally laughed off his invitations.

Izzy would laugh too. But then one day, very quietly, he replied, "Seventy times seven, Mercy! Jesus forgives seventy times seven."

To which she said, "Izzy, I have more than four hundred and ninety things to confess to."

"That means infinity, Mercy Beth. That's how much forgiveness Jesus has for you. It's never too late to be born again. The Divine Calendar's got dates available for being born again and again and again."

"The Divine Calendar?"

"Yes. God's timetable. You think you're busy? Just imagine." There was a twinkle in his eyes. "You, Mercy Fanjoy, need to go to Africa some day. Go to my home. Then you'll understand. It's all about surrendering to God's plan, not yours."

"Izzy, give it up. I think you'd get along well with my

mother," Mercy had teased, but squirmed beneath the intensity of his gaze. "Africa. Honestly, I'd rather see Paris first." Mercy giggled and punched his arm gently. "And knock off the God stuff, okay?"

Izzy, she now penned at the bottom of her list in the coiled notebook spread out on her lap. *Find coordinates.*

Bleary eyed, she looked back up the list, reading number one out loud. "Call my mother and make her hand over the note."

"I might have had to live not knowing what my father's last message was, but I'm not going to die not knowing," she said to the cat. "Even if the tests are negative, even if my own death is only a faint and distant probability, I'm getting those words." She pointed her finger at the cat. "Right?"

The cat blinked and nodded. "A good strategy will be necessary, Mercy. Skilful means required. I think it best if you bring up the subject of the note in a public place. The Coffee Mill, maybe. Or church. Even better."

"You are so wise, old cat. Good advice. Belle was right. You Buddhists are experts in skills training. Yes, somewhere public. There's still too much potential for violence."

"Your mother is older now. She's mellowed," Buddha-Belly reminded her with great equanimity.

"Not *her* violence, BB. Mine."

Dear Cassandra and Sweet Pea Mercy:

Today I discovered I am dying of a rare

neurological disease. I have three months left to

live. I want to spare you the agony of watching me

suffer. Forgive me if this is an act of cowardice or

selfishness. For me, this is my final act of undying

love. I will watch over my girls from heaven,

Gabe

—FAREWELL NOTES, MARTYR VERSION #3
BY TEENY GAUDET AND THE SCRIBE TRIBE

"Shout out! Do nooooot hold back!"

On Wednesday morning, Mercy overslept. One arm in the sleeve of her coat, she'd plunked a bowl in front of BB, dashed out the door in record time, and squealed out of the driveway. Cursing every red light, primping in the rear-view mirror whenever she could, Mercy sped to the People of the Church of Faith and Light and Celestial Vibrations in the HubbleyCraft. Now, as she thundered into the tiny, claustrophobic room in the basement of Gleaner's Dry Cleaners, she regretted her haste. Her sweater was inside out. Her socks didn't match. She wanted to charge right back out, not just hold back, as Brother Hubert was suggesting.

Brother Hubert's warm-up was delivered in jubilant tones. "Lift up your voice like a trumpet! Glory be to God in the highest Alleluia. Lord when I listen it's not my ears no nay and it is not the keys of a piano I'm tuning. I am simply translating the vibrations from heaven to the earth. They come through they come through they come right through my entire body out my fingers and then the celestial tap tap tap ting ting clang! One pianooooo's not the same as another of course, but it very much depends upon the one playing the instrument of God just how tuned into that divine frequency they are. Have to admit I have my favourites...Take Doctor Berkshire—may he rest in peace with the Lord—I tuned his piano for twenty-five years and like to think the music he made, the composer he was, the sweetness of the glory of God Almighty came out somehow because I may have done my proper work and...listened with a pure and humble heart to serve the Lord my God Almighty and yeah yeah Alleluia Sweet Jesus may he have found the note! The NOTE! The NOTE! That one perfect note he needed to create his last symphony because I lovingly stroked the keys of that piano and blessed it and prayed over it and gave to it vibrations that whisper of the Holy Spirit, what is it that we most need to hear, needs us all to hear...at any given moment and so..."

Hubert "Hugh" Rutherford, piano-tuner, Cassandra's long-time companion and husband of one year, would keep going for as long as he felt moved by the spirit. He spotted Mercy, and waved her in, not missing a beat. Mercy slipped into the chair beside her mother, moving it closer. The scraping sound made folks look at her in agitation.

"Mum?"

"Well, would you look at what the cat dragged in?" her mother whispered. Cassandra smelled like she'd just bathed in a pool of gardenia petals. Even this early in the morning she was her usual well-turned-out self. Today, she sported a sapphire suede pantsuit and black patent heels. She glowed. Mercy was overwhelmed with a sudden desire to touch her mother. She wanted to sniff her deeply, lay her head on her lap, and ask her to sing a lullaby. But to do so would be to confess her fear of death, a lack of faith, the confusion of her heart. This would only be painfully embarrassing and entirely inappropriate. Instead, Mercy smiled bravely, as if enchanted by her mother's familiar greeting.

"Good to see you—ach!" she sneezed. Her nose dripped. She groped in her pockets as if a tissue might miraculously appear there, until her mother, ever prepared, waved one in front of her face.

"Still allergic to me, I see. Did you get a haircut?" Mercy's hand flew to her hair. She fluffed it up and patted it down as she nodded her head. Her mother reached out, tucked a loose strand behind her ear, then cupped her daughter's chin, trying to make eye contact. Mercy focused her gaze, as if in rapt attention, towards the makeshift altar where Hubert now played the vibraphone.

"It's a good look on you," Cassandra continued, still examining her daughter's face, as if looking for blackheads to squeeze or traces of aging or, worse, as if in Mercy's face she could get answers to some unasked questions. But then, unexpectedly, Cassandra leaned forward and kissed her daughter tenderly on the forehead. Every time Cassandra moved, waves of gardenia perfume sprinkled the air.

"Welcome Sister Mercy! Glory be to the GOD of joyful vibrations! You are welcome to pray with us." Hubert launched into a new round of praise.

Mercy slumped in her seat, praying only to render herself invisible. This talk of vibrations rekindled memories of that Beach Boys song. More shocking yet, she pictured the purple plastic Horny Little Devil vibrator at home in her drawer, the one she had yet to dispose of.

"Vibrations vibrations vibrations," the congregation repeated.

"Hi Mercy! Quackkkkkquackkk!" Dodie Potts shouted over.

"Hi, Dodie! Quackkk," Mercy said back.

Dodie was Odell's adopted special person. Her gnarled body was unnaturally small and ever shrinking. In profile she was bent forty-five degrees at the waist. Her physical appearance was most disconcerting when someone, especially a child, encountered her for the first time. Dodie's face was a Halloween mask—a twisted sideways map of miniature potholes and crevices, of errant moles and whiskers—and her eyes were small, startled lower case o's. Dodie worked as a school crossing guard, and every day she could be seen trundling along, covering a three-block radius as she delivered the *Odell Observer* in her little red wagon. Since she was a child, Dodie Potts had quacked.

"Where BELLEMUHCEE? Quackkk," she shouted out.

"Home, Dodie. Quaccck." Mercy, like everyone, knew quacking back was the only way to silence Dodie.

The members of the congregation smiled at Mercy with reverential benevolence, teeth not showing, heads cocked sideways to the left, their eyebrows lifted in what looked like a ritual church salute. Then, they began to vibrate. The People of the Church of Faith and Light and Celestial Vibrations didn't shake exactly, or roll or quiver or quake. They *vibrated* when filled with the Holy Spirit.

The Vibrationists' particular way of vibrating was something they were taught at first but that eventually became an involuntary reflex. It looked to those on the outside as if maybe these were people with near to bursting bladders, their jiggling so much like the dance of children in snowsuits with no restroom in sight. At best, they were joggers bouncing up and down on the corner waiting for the walk light to change.

Right now, they were all wiggling towards Mercy.

"Can you come outside for a second, Mum?" Mercy's voice was shrill.

"Is there something wrong? Is it Belle?" Cassandra clutched her throat.

"Not Belle. But yes, it's urgent." Mercy stood up as the congregation, undulating in a wave comprised of forty or so people, moved closer. They stopped when she stood. Mercy clasped her hands in prayer at heart centre as Belle had shown her in yoga and bowed her head many times. She kept nodding while she backed out of the doorway. They were all watching her, their heads cocked to the right now, their foreheads so wrinkled Mercy thought of the poster of the Shar Pei dogs she'd seen at the Glooscap Animal Shelter. Worried souls, all.

The rare, almost miraculous appearance of Mercy in church unnerved Cassandra. Shaking in fear, not in resonance with the Holy Spirit, she lit a cigarette as soon as they were outside. She'd been practising a look of surprise since Wiggins phoned. Although she knew a query about the suicide note was forthcoming, she could never have anticipated this ambush. Her disbelief was genuine. She concentrated on blowing smoke rings.

"Mum, when are you going to quit?" Mercy asked in her most irritating, sanctimonious, recovered-smoker's tone of voice.

"Soon. What's so important that you came to church at eight in the morning?" Cassandra scraped a flake of tobacco off her lip.

"Please listen carefully and don't say anything when I am done. Think about it first," Mercy pleaded, trying not to sound desperate.

"Fine." Cassandra blew more smoke rings and tapped her shiny toes in two-four time.

"I want the note. It is very important to me. I need to know what he wrote. Why he left us. Okay? That's it. I want the note."

"The note? The note? You mean the divine note Hubert was just going on about? I knew one day you'd see that the Vibrationists—"

"Mother!" Mercy began to gnaw her lower lip. "Please!"

"What?" Cassandra widened her eyes in feigned innocence.

"You know the note I mean." Mercy gently touched her mother's arm.

"You mean the note you imagined. Well…you can stop with the drama over this false memory you have. I've told you, you must have dreamt it—there was no note. Do you hear me?" Cassandra pulled her arm away, stomped on her cigarette, and walked towards Temple Hall. "Call me later?"

"No. You call me when you are ready to give me the note."

"There was no note."

"Mum! I'm asking and for once I want the truth."

Cassandra Fanjoy-Rutherford slid her hand in her pocket, clutching her pocket watch compact. It was real sterling silver, a Yours Truly Beauty bonus for being top national sales rep, spring of 1962. Engraved on the back were her initials—a dignified 'C' and an elegant 'F'—and the phrase *Beauty is timeless*. The watch stopped working long ago, but she was never without her mirror. Mercy watched as Cassandra drew on a new set of lips, smacked, and closed the compact. She shot her daughter a piercing look.

"Mercy, trust me. There was no note."

Cassandra turned and soldiered on, marching up the walkway and re-entering Gleaner's Dry Cleaners. The door swooshed shut behind her. Mercy's eyes burned. Cassandra hadn't missed a beat.

"Note? What note?" Mercy jumped and spun around.

Old Stinky waved, sprawled on a bench a few feet away. He straightened up and patted the seat beside him. Mercy obeyed, hoping she was upwind of him. She couldn't recall seeing him on the way in. Old Stinky began to whiten his face, as he did every day, using some sort of grease paint, layering it on until he looked like Marcel Marceau miming a homeless man. Where his supply came from Mercy had never thought to ask. Now she recognized the bottles— Yours Truly Beauty cosmetics from the All Occasion Fun for Beauties product line.

"So—what's new, Old Stink?"

The junior vibraphonist played the closing hymn and the doors of the temple—Gleaner's Dry Cleaners—were flung open wide. As the members of the congregation of the People of the Church of Faith and Light and Celestial Vibrations filed past Mercy, they whispered: "Rest your troubled mind, Mercy. Healing beams." Mercy bristled, knowing that during the prayer session, Cassandra must have asked they say prayers for the misguided soul of her daughter, Mercy. A few Vibrationists approached and touched her forehead at her third eye chakra. "Holy Spirit heal this child," they whispered before Mercy managed to squirm away.

"You're still here? Hi, Stink." Her mother skirted by. Mercy jumped up. Dodie took Mercy's place on the bench. "Where Bellemuhcy? Allwetallwetallwet. *Quack.*"

"Home, Dodie. Not wet. Home." Home was always a good answer if you wanted Dodie to stop quacking. Mercy chased after her mother. For a second she wondered if emotional blackmail was the way to get what she wanted. *Mother, I have a dying wish!* No, she decided, that would be her very last resort.

"I'd like to speak with Hugh."

"You already did."

"Not 'you.' Hugh. Hubert." For the first time that morning, Mercy got a reaction.

"This is OLD family stuff!" Her mother's thin-lipped hiss was clearly audible.

"Well Cassandra, if I'm not family by now, what am I? If I can help tune up someone's life, bring God's harmony to them, you know I will." Hubert caught up to them both.

Hubert Rutherford was ten years Cassandra's junior but to Mercy he seemed older, like maybe he was born ancient, one of those babies folks called an old soul. Mercy thought of him as a gallant man, perhaps reincarnated from the days of chivalry. Hubert held Mercy by the arm, under the elbow, and cradled her hand in his gentle bear paw. His palm was warm and soothing. He led her a few paces off so they could speak in private.

Nodding all the while, Hubert listened to Mercy with his eyes cast downward, turning the brim of his hat around in his hands like it was a steering wheel. It was a brown fedora, with a small green feather in the band. He was never without it.

Cassandra looked a little like someone had just shoved her face into a pie. She lifted her eyes to the clouds. Old Stinky farted and laughed, Dodie quacked, the music faded, and Cassandra took out her compact. Her hands were shaking. After she touched up her face, Cassandra smoked, sending nervous, sidelong glances in the direction of her daughter and husband in their conspiratorial huddle. She winced as the last of the Brothers and Sisters filed by. Their repetitions of "Peace be with you, Sister," lingered, almost cruelly, long after they were out of sight.

"Peace be with you," echoed Cassandra. But there was no light in her eyes, and not even a trace of her ordinarily stunning celestially vibrational smile.

Hubert Rutherford thought his wife, Cassandra, moved like the capital letter L. A swirl of grace. A sauntering cat. They were still in the parking lot, and she was walking Sweet Jeezuz. He watched Cassandra tend to the business of scooping the poodle's waste into a plastic bag, tying it in a knot, and portering it dutifully over to a garbage can. Hubert chuckled; Cassandra was offering effusive congratulations to Sweet Jeezuz for a job well done. Then she rubbed noses with Sweet Jeezuz and tucked him safely under her arm. Cassandra possessed a tenderness towards the dog that she found difficult to extend to two-legged creatures. But she wasn't alone in this. The world was filled with people who preferred to be in the company of those who did not speak. Hubert supposed that was one of the reasons she'd chosen him. He was a man of few words and harmony was his middle name. He was a man who heard God in the silence and therefore believed silence really was the best reply.

"I love this woman and want to help so help me do thy will. Amen," he prayed now as his wife sashayed back towards him. Cassandra climbed back into the cab of the truck, still praising Sweet Jeezuz. Hugh made a decision then and there.

"Cassie, I have been given an assignment."

"What is it now?" She knew each of his vibrational tones.

This tone meant business.

"Not what. Who. Mercy."

"Mercy is just being silly."

"She says she saw a note the night her father died."

Cassandra poked her tongue under her upper lip, sucking it through a gap in her teeth. Hubert cringed at the sound, knowing it signalled his wife's distress. If she knew how unattractive this habit made her look, she'd cut her tongue right off, he thought. But Hubert was not the sort of man to criticize.

She fiddled with the radio, turned up the volume. Hugh reached for her hand.

"Cassie, *please*. Turn it off." She did, but then swivelled her head sideways to look out the window, and began to hum.

"Sometimes you are worse than a child!" he teased. She stuck out her tongue.

"So, tell me, was there a note?"

Cassandra hummed louder. It was "Row, Row, Row Your Boat." She looked at him sidelong when they stopped at the corner. He was a dashing, grey-haired, kind-eyed man. "The first time I laid eyes on him, at a national conference of PCFLCV followers, I thought of Maurice Chevalier, the French actor!" she told her bridge club.

They'd courted long distance for many years, and finally Hubert moved all the way from the warm west coast to what he called this "strangely beautiful, half-frozen little city," to be with her. "The only things I really miss," he said, "are the ocean at my doorstep and the redwood trees and the Nanaimo bars." Cassandra didn't bake or eat sweets for fear of gaining weight. She was, however, a fine seamstress. Now, she pulled out the pillowcase she was embroidering.

"Was there?" he asked again.

"He is not your enemy," said a little voice in her head. "Tell him the truth." Cassandra inhaled and scrounged in her purse for her thimble.

"Yes, there was." Her voice jabbed as the needle pricked the cotton.

"I see." Hubert coughed, and pretended to adjust the heat.

They drove on in silence for a few minutes. Hugh did not hear God. He heard a series of sirens screaming. He heard twenty-one cannons firing.

Cassie looked in the glove compartment as if she was going to find the appropriate words there. Like most times, she broke the silence first.

"I have my reasons, Hugh."

"I'm a very good listener."

Cassandra, ever the stoic one, started crying then. It was the kind of weeping that came from tired, heart-broken children, crying that went on and on and on, rising and falling, rising and falling, cresting and fading until a new round began. Sweet Jeezuz whimpered with her, nosing under her chin. Cassandra's head was buried in her hands as the dog, so small and pathetic, tried to lick through his beloved master's fingers to kiss her face. It was a futile effort.

Hugh eased into the parking lot, turned off the engine, and took his wife in his arms to stop her shuddering. He'd never probed for details of the suicide before, believing personal information was something a person offered freely. He was a private man, not given to sharing much of his own past, not because it was sordid or anything he was ashamed of, but because it had never occurred to him that his life was of much interest to anyone other than himself.

Now he would need to know more. He had been chosen

to help both these women. When Mercy pleaded with him after church, those topaz eyes of hers so filled with sparks, he recognized she was a woman on fire with spirit of some sort. Maybe even the Holy Spirit. "Please Hugh, you will be the ONE who persuades her. I know it." Mercy had left a bracelet of white finger marks on his wrist from squeezing so hard. "I'll try," is all he'd promised. He turned now to Cassandra. "Okay, honey. Let's go in to breakfast now."

"I'm a sorry sight," she said, looking in her pocket mirror, reapplying lipstick.

"You're not. You're beautiful as always."

"I can't, Hubert." She smacked her lips. "I can't give it to her." She clicked and unclicked the compact, then slipped Sweet Jeezuz into her purse.

"What did the note say?"

They walked towards the Coffee Mill entrance. "I can't tell you."

"Why not?"

He opened the door. Cassandra stopped. "Oh my God. You don't understand, do you? At all. It is…it is…beyond… what any mother…it's too horrible."

"I'm a grown man, Cassandra. I can handle it. Mercy's now a grown woman. She would rather know than not know."

"She wouldn't though. She really wouldn't. You wouldn't either."

"Cassie, is there the remotest possibility—hear me out here—and I mean this in the kindest way—that the way you are looking at things and the conclusion you've reached could be…wrong? Just plain wrong?"

"Wrong? Did you say wrong? I am not wrong. I know what's best for my daughter. Wrong. Wrong?" She stomped through the open door.

"Problems in paradise?" It was Bee. "The usual?" They nodded and slipped into their booth by the window, over-looking River St. John.

Cassandra gave Hugh a look of such righteous indignation that had it been another topic he might have laughed. Had the woman really, ever, not once considered there might be another point of view as valid as her own? he wondered. Was she ever wrong? About anything? He decided to take another approach.

"What if you hadn't read the note, Cassie?"

"I wish!" There was a trace of bitterness. "Don't think I haven't thought about that."

Hubert watched his wife closely. Cassandra cradled the cup between her hands as if its warmth soothed her arthritic knuckles. She blew into the cup. "I think I would be a different person," she said finally.

"How so?" He folded his arms, as if to brace himself.

"Well, less tired for one thing. I wouldn't have had to live with the same recurring nightmare all these years. It's not as bad as it used to be. Since we've married," she added softly. "I'm hungry, let's eat." She smiled.

He reached across the booth, cupped his hand over her ears and kissed her forehead.

"That's more like it; my lovebirds are back!" chirped Bee on her way by. Sweet Jeezuz yapped.

"I so did not hear that!" yelled Bee over her shoulder.

Hubert, man of God, disciple of Christ, piano tuner, con-duit of vibrations, lover of Cassandra, chewed slowly. He felt a steady rumble in his belly, like bowling balls beginning to roll in some underground alley. To Vibrationists, this distant thunder spelled danger. And then he heard, he was sure, another sound, like the panting of a hungry animal, something evil approaching, getting closer, sniffing at the very edges of their harmonious life.

In the days ahead, Hubert sensed tuning into the Divine Frequency would be difficult, if not impossible. He thought of David and Goliath and "Onward Christian Soldiers." He envisioned Daniel in the lion's den. Then, he silently repeated the Vibrationists' simple three-word Hymn of Hims. Shadrach, Meshach, and Abednego. Shadrach, Meshach, Abednego. Not only had they withstood the fiery furnace, never once faltering in their beliefs, but they were wise men. In his former life, Hubert believed they had been his next-door neighbours, ones he'd shunned. The very repetition of their names set all his spiritual tuning forks humming. This Hymn of Hims, for him, spread vibrations of fearlessness and faith, vibrations needed when darkness approached or, worse, settled in, and truth would be put to the test.

Fear not!

The Grand Conductor's voice was like a tap of a baton.

Fear not!

On a frigid night in November in the early nineteen sixties, Gabe Fanjoy, husband of Cassandra, father of Mercy, brother of Gladys, waded into River St. John and never walked back out. The tragedy was recorded in the *Odell Observer* as an accidental death. Mercy was five years old on that calamitous night, an unfortunate age, as she was too young to remember her father clearly and too old to forget him entirely.

For most of her life, the word "father" caused a dull toothache sensation inside her head. Sometimes, Mercy sensed a presence—a murkiness hovering beside her that was so palpable she was tempted to reach out and touch it. These experiences were disquieting. Mercy, therefore, preferred not to think of Father at all. Instead, she thought of Daddy, the dashing man grinning out from photographs. Her favourite picture of him was a faded clipping from the *Odell Observer*. The month before his death, he'd been featured in the "People in Your Neighbourhood" section. "Gabe Fanjoy, Man of Letters. He carries the weight of our words on his shoulders," the caption read. Gabe Fanjoy had been a postman. That postman who went fishing. The man who got swept away in the undercurrent of River St. John.

This morning, the river was the colour of barbed wire. The air was crisp, the sun a flirt. From time to time, light winked through the weave of cloud as if breaking through layers of tissue, illuminating the green and bedazzling the river.

Mercy marched heels first, head up, chin forward, fists clenched. She took great pleasure punching the air, and pedalled her legs from the hip flexors, like a marathon walker in training for the Olympics. After her mother's stonewalling, she'd gone home and tried to contact Belle again. There was still no answer and she'd left five messages since yesterday.

"Hi honey, it's late but can you call?"

"You must be sleeping or out, call even if it's late, okay?"

"Belle, something to discuss with you and I know you are busy but...call?"

"Belle? Me? Call."

"Well, me again. It's morning now. I know I'm being a pest and violating your boundaries but please—this is urgent."

On the last call she breathed into the receiver as if in distress, then hung up. The message button flashed red. Eagerly, Mercy grabbed the receiver. But it wasn't Belle.

"Mercy, Noah. The blue jay's pretty bad, eh? Wanted to let you know that it's alive. Made it through the night. Call, okay?"

Rather than call and before she could lose her nerve, Mercy had laced up her sneakers, and was now clipping right along. If she took the long way, it was about an hour to the Glooscap Animal Shelter.

Mercy passed others on the trail—joggers in spandex and headbands, a rollerblader with kneepads and helmet, a man in a suit talking on an ear-wired cellphone, a coffee mug in hand.

"Dow Jones," she heard as she passed. She made a mental note to see about her will.

Mercy picked up her pace. Her arms were like pistons now and she saw only the trail ahead until she almost plowed down a man crossing her path. He smelled of sardines and wobbled back and forth, his cup held out. Mercy stopped.

"Are you new in town?" she asked. The man was squinting at the sky as if the sunlight hurt his eyes. He teetered. Mercy dropped a loonie in his cup and heard it plop.

"What the hell are you doing? Jeezuz, that's my coffee, lady." Then he burped. Gravel crunched as Mercy sped away.

Mothers with toddlers in monster-truck strollers rolled toward her. Mercy stopped to let them by, beaming at the children. One of them began to scream.

"Wasn't that Mercy Beth Fanjoy?" said the first mother.

"Who's she?" said the second, who was new in town.

"Mercy of 'Mercy's Musings,'" the first replied. "Aren't you reading our local paper yet? And she works at Occasionally Yours Stationery and Office Supply store too. Manager, I think."

"Assistant manager," corrected the third. "And who does she think she is—the mayor or something? The way she struts about. Look at her go. Like she owns the trail. Mercy's Snoozings, if you want my opinion. She was right nasty to Dylan yesterday in Dr. Wiggins' office."

Five minutes later, Mercy settled on a bench to catch her breath and gather herself together, rehearsing what she might say to Noah Perley. "Oh how long have I longed for you?" She laughed out loud. Maybe it would be wiser to invite him for a kayak trip first.

Today there were a few kayaks out on the water. A team of rowers worked in perfect unison, making it look effortless as they criss-crossed the river. Under the overcast sky, at this bend of the trail, River St. John was a deep navy blue. There was no breeze and the surface was a perfect mirror, bevelled at the edges. The trees on the riverbank opposite were in duplicate. This made it difficult to tell where the water ended and the earth and sky began. This mirage was beautiful. Mercy Beth felt like a woman in an impressionist painting. All she needed was a parasol. And a lace, mono-grammed handkerchief. And a title. Woman on the Verge. Of Death, maybe.

Aunt Gladys shook Mercy awake the night the suicide hap-pened. She had smelled of Minard's Liniment, and her breath was a fleecy tickle in Mercy's ear. As if she were confiding a secret, she spoke slowly:

"Now you will have to be very brave. Just like Goldilocks when the bears came home. Can you do that? You mother will need you. Angels have come and taken your father. He's gone in a chariot of fire to be with God and his heav-enly family, Amen. Come on now, dear. You have to get up, Mercy."

Mercy jumped up from the wooden bench and began to speed walk again, pummelling the air. She needed that note. The Note. The one her mother insisted did not exist.

"I know what I saw!" she'd screamed at her mother, how many times?

"There was no note."

"There was!"

"You were seeing things."

"I was not!"

Even now, that moment still ran like an old home movie when Mercy wanted it to.

Her mother, curled up in a corner of the sofa, was sipping tea and munching on a crust of toast. Mercy wanted to poke her to see if she was real, afraid she was just a stuffed doll of a mother someone had placed there. Cassandra's small, pinched face with no makeup combined with such uncharacteristic stillness terrified Mercy. Gladys was rambling on about Jesus when the doorbell rang.

Sergeant Hector Ross came jangling in the door, in banana-striped trousers and brown serge coat, all keys and buttons and brass. At the sight of him, Cassandra sprang to life. She wailed, stood up, then collapsed in his arms. Mercy was confused. Gladys tried to usher her niece into the kitchen to have hot chocolate, but Mercy held her ground. After a momentary tug of war, Gladys finally picked her up to take her away, but not before Mercy saw Hector Ross hand over the note.

It was white and crumpled up in a ball, an almost-perfect paper snowball. Flopping over Gladys' shoulder, Mercy watched her mother smooth it out and read it. Her lips moved but she made no sound. Then she turned it around and around in her hands, examining it with the same expression on her face as when she held a puzzle piece and couldn't figure out where it belonged. She began pounding Hector Ross' chest. She threw down the note. He picked it up. He handed it back to her. That's what Mercy saw before she had hot chocolate and watched the sun come up. A screaming sun in a blood-red sky.

"I did not imagine that sky," she muttered now. "I did not dream the note." The urgent croak of a bicycle bell scraped behind her.

"To the left, the left, the left!"

Mercy jumped out of the way just in time. The cyclist swerved and almost toppled over, but planted a foot down, balanced, and remounted. He scowled at her. "Geez, are you deaf?" he shouted over his shoulder. "I gave you plenty of warning. What more do you need?" He cycled off and Mercy, hugging the left side of the trail, kicked at the gravel. The man was still haranguing her. "You'd better watch it, lady. A lot of the other bikers only ask once." Mercy looked around as if he might be talking to someone else and then she wandered off-trail, dreamily strolling towards the river-bank. It was more peaceful walking closer to the water. The ducks, like feathered numeral twos, bobbed on the surface of the waves. The water lapped against the shore repeating, like a gentle mantra, *the note, the note, the note.*

The first time Mercy asked about the note, the note that never was according to Cassandra and the police and newspaper records, she was ten. She'd figured out by that time that it was not an accident and the river didn't reach out and grab people at all. Her father, the mailman, had not gone willingly after hearing God's SOS distress signal from heaven, as Aunt Gladys had tried to persuade her.

Like most nights, Gladys was upstairs quilting. Mercy and her mother were in the rumpus room. Cassandra was trying to memorize the names of her latest Yours Truly Beauty items and concentrate without puckering her face or moving her lips too much as she practised her sales pitch. Her face, which most people considered beautiful, was slathered in a mud mask the exact green of fresh duck doo. Mercy was eating Halloween candy while watching *Tarzan* on television.

The day had been emotional. As it was the anniversary of his death, they'd been to the graveside that afternoon. While chewing a candy kiss, savouring the thick molasses juices sloshing around inside her mouth, Mercy blurted out the burning question: "What did Daddy say in the note, Mom?"

The Yours Truly Beauty products came in three times a year: spring, fall, and Christmas. Those items were wrapped in candy apple cellophane and nestled in bright green plastic trays. Voluptuous bottles with metallic gold caps filled with powders and lotions shone like stars, dazzling Mercy every bit as much as Cassandra did.

At one time, Cassandra had one hundred and twenty sample bottles lined up on her dresser in perfect formation. Mercy spent hours counting the bottles and mixing the contents together, pretending they were magic potions with which she would save the world. Other times, she took them out and played movie star with Aunt Gladys.

"Look at us, all gussied up!" Gladys would say, and spin around, gin in one hand, a straw in the other. They pretended they were in Paris, smoked the straws like cigarettes, called each other Fifi and Brigitte, and said: "*Mais oui! Mais oui! Ah quel dommage!*" Mercy's mother rarely played with them. To her, beauty was serious business.

Mercy's timing could not have been worse. With a whole new product line she had the responsibility to sell and promote, Cassandra was distracted and under considerable pressure.

"Ey?" Cassandra responded lazily. In the language of their home, "ey" meant, "What, dear? I didn't catch that; you'll have to repeat your question."

"The note. What was in the note?"

Her mother never asked what note. Instead, she walked across the room and yanked Mercy up by the elbow off the floor. The candy kiss juice went down the wrong way. Mercy choked. It sputtered out her nose.

"Who told you about a note? Gladys?"

Mercy shook her head.

"Answer me, Mercy Beth. Who said there was a note?" Cassandra stood screaming, her face cracking open. Mercy was first stunned and then somewhat fascinated, watching the cucumber facial mask split apart, her mother's pores like the magnified freckles of some monster. Mercy's fascination soon turned to alarm. She could barely breathe let alone answer her mother.

"Answer me, I said!"

"Daddy did." It came out in a gargle of molasses juice.

"What? Don't you ever, ever—"

Cassandra grabbed Mercy by the shoulders, lifting her off the floor, shaking her daughter like a dirty carpet.

"Well, he did! He visits me all the time! And I saw it." Attacked, Mercy struck back, a belligerent, trumpeting child.

"There. Was. No. Note. Hear me?" Cassandra slapped the air as though Mercy were a fly she was hoping to swat away from her face, then her head, then her cheek. She slapped harder and the thorn on her silver rose bracelet nicked the top of Mercy's ear. Mercy screamed when she felt the blood, but Cassandra's yelps were louder as she clenched her fists while pounding her child's small back. Mercy scrambled out of her clutches; her mother's nails, sharpened to a point and polished white, were suddenly witch's claws.

Mercy made it to the top of the stairs and forever remembered the soft rescuing arms of Aunt Gladys and the smell of Minard's Liniment against the wailing sounds of her mother, a sound Mercy thought better belonged to a tortured animal caught in the teeth of a steel trap.

The Glooscap Animal Shelter was in sight. Mercy balked. She wished now she'd phoned ahead, as Noah had requested. The idea of propositioning him made her chest ache; rejection was so humiliating. She still had no idea how she might approach the topic. *Hi, Noah. I just thought I'd drop by and check on the bird. Incidentally, I'm not sure how much time I have left to live, myself, so I'd like you to make wild passionate and deeply spiritual love to me. Can we get a room at the Sweet Grass Sweat Lodge, maybe?* And what if the bird had died?

Her back throbbed. Pain speared her stomach. Mercy Fanjoy, the human shish kebab. Every ache now seemed suspicious. She hadn't slept much last night, thinking of her lump, her list, and Hades. Maybe she could call Doctor Wiggins and get that prescription for sleeping pills. How she wished he still made emergency house calls—like he did back then.

"Lollipop?" Dr. Wiggins kept green suckers in his black bag. He held a tiny flashlight in Mercy's eyes. He stitched up her ear and promised when she was good as new he would show her the secret of how to wiggle her ears, one at a time. After tucking Mercy in bed, he bent down and kissed the tip of her nose and shuffled away. Mercy lay motionless in bed, straining to hear his words. His voice was firm and patient. He'd soon soothed her mother's sobs to sniffles. Wiggins agreed not to report the incident on the condition Cassandra seek immediate rest and relaxation.

Cassandra went on a two-week vacation. She returned wearing a white pleated mini-dress with navy blue polka dots. Tanned the colour of creamy taffy, her skin glowed. Her hair was silver blonde from the Miami sun. She wrapped Mercy in a cloud of coconut oil when she hugged her hello.

Cassandra never said she was sorry. Not really. She cried for a long time beside Mercy that night after her daughter was asleep, all the while whispering, "My baby oh my baby." There was never violence again. There was no need. The note, solid and silent as a rock, became a permanent wedge between them.

Now, taped on the inside of the screen door of the Glooscap Animal Shelter, was another note:

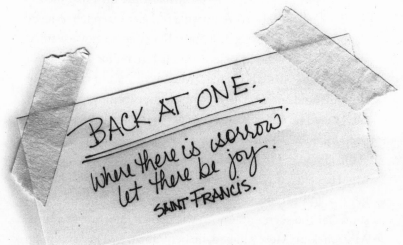

Relieved, Mercy did a sharp about turn and headed back the way she came. Even with Saint Francis' healing prayer, she felt grim as oatmeal. Remembering could do that. It could suck you into quicksand grief and guilt. Quagmire you in the past.

"Suicide. *Your* father committed *suicide?*" Teeny had her hands over her mouth.

"Yes, suicide."

"I'm so sorry, Mercy." Lulu's eyes brimmed with compassion.

"But that's a sin," said Teeny. "A biggie."

. They were in junior high. The asphyxiation death of Mrs. McPherson, the grade-eight geography teacher who'd crawled into the trunk of the family station wagon to die shortly after a diagnosis of pancreatic cancer, was an uncommon tragedy in Odell. There were no school grief counsellors in those days. During a memorial assembly the students were told only that she had suffered a sudden illness.

Mrs. McPherson was one of Cassandra's customers and the family, horrified by the funeral parlour's attempt at beautifying the corpse, appealed to Cassandra for help. Gladys warned Mercy that the suicide was stirring up a lot for her mother. It seemed that Gladys considered Mercy old enough for an honest conversation.

"As you figured by now, Mercy, your father killed himself and your mother will most likely never get over it."

Yet it seemed to Mercy that her mother was her usual stirred-up self. All she said when she returned from McArthur's Funeral Home was, "those damned morticians need a good seminar on skin tone colours." Mercy watched as Cassandra lit a cigarette and exhaled in exasperation and continued. "Molly McPherson was a fall if there was ever a fall and they tried to make her a spring. They used a yellow base when they should have been using blue and you'd think they would know that a teal blue silk scarf at the neck could do wonders to accentuate the rosy highlights. Poor Molly. How unselfish. Imagine sparing your family like that."

For Mercy, Teeny, and Lulu, the incident was an inspiration.

"Your father, Gabe Fanjoy," proclaimed Teeny, "was just like Mrs. McPherson. And Jesus Christ."

Calling themselves the Scribe Tribe, the girls became ghost writers of sorts. They lit candles. They used a fountain pen. Teeny was the leader and scribe, Lulu and Mercy her apprentices in the forbidden art of writing a dead man's words.

Dear Cassandra:
I do not want to prolong your suffering. Such is the depth of my love. Cherish forever our Mercy.
Gabe

The martyr version of the note kept them busy for a month and might have satisfied Mercy. Not so for the melodramatic Teeny Gaudet, who got so carried away she even started typing the notes.

Dear Cassandra:
Others will think me dead. The truth is I want to leave you with the dignity that accompanies widowhood instead of the pity and guilt of an abandoned woman and child. I loved you once and it pains me to think of never seeing darling Digger again, or hear my Sweet Pea calling out my name when I come home

each evening. But I have found my true love and cannot live without her.

Amelia and I met in a restaurant while I was on a coffee break. We are moving far away where fantasy is better than reality.

I wish you well.

Gabe

At first, this version was troublesome. Gabe's body had, after all, been recovered.

p.s. I have floated a decomposed body out to shore and fitted it with my dentures. I hope you get some insurance money.

"So maybe your father is not dead!" suggested Teeny.

"Oh, dear," said Lulu.

Hopeful, Mercy searched the phone book for names and found one G. Fanjoy in a nearby town. Mercy Fanjoy, teen detective, had scored. She dialed and waited.

-Hello.

-I'm looking for Gabe Fanjoy.

-I'm Greg.

-Is this...Daddy? It's Digger.

-Digger? What kinda name is that?

-The name you gave me. Remember? Because of the worms I used to dig up for you before you went fishing.

-What the hell? Worms? You crazy or something?

-Daddy?

-Honey, I ain't nobody's daddy.

Pounding the pillows on the bed, Mercy had worked herself into a state of hysteria when Gladys appeared by her side.

"For the love of God, girl, what's the matter? Where does it hurt?"

"The note. What was in the note, Gladdie? What did he say?"

Mercy watched as Gladys seemed to blush in reverse, growing pale beneath her sunburn. Just back from Florida, her aunt's skin was peeling like paint off an old house.

"If you stop your blubbering, I'll tell you what I know."

Mercy blew her nose, nodding.

"*If* there was a note—and I'm saying 'if' here, okay—no one but your mother and Hector Ross read it and they refused to talk about it. Your mother..." She paused and touched Mercy's ear tenderly before she continued. "Well we know about that day, don't we? I've asked before, Mercy, and all she ever says is, 'Some things are better left unspoken.' She must have her reasons. Let it go, dear heart."

That's when the betrayed husband version of the note was born.

"Why haven't we seen it before?" shrieked Teeny. "Your mother would not let anyone know because it would reveal her 'transgressions.'" This was a word Teeny Gaudet had been using since second grade.

"Your mother is the wayward woman, an ex-Catholic, a transgressor if there ever was one." Teeny shook her head. Even Lulu agreed this could well be so.

"So my mother drove my father to his death?"

"That is correct," said Teeny. "She is an s-l-u-t."

"Teeny!" Lulu thought she'd gone too far, but Mercy nodded. Her mother was an adulteress. It was the worst of words, all three agreed, then clicked their pens.

Dear Cassandra:

I have discovered that you have been having an affair with Hector Ross, and in fact, that you have never stopped seeing him. I guess I have always known that Sweet Pea was not my daughter. Her hair should have been curly, like mine. Genetics. I hope you three can be happy now that I am out of your way. I simply cannot live with this pain in my heart. It is stabbing me like lightning, piercing me like poison darts, jabbing me like the jagged edge of a Campbell's tomato soup can and the soup is my blood which spilleth forth.

Yet my love for you remains with you forever amen,
Gabe

These purple prose versions were written at the same time the girls were studying metaphor and simile in English class. Hector Ross was cast in the role of the other man because Mercy knew her mother had dated him briefly in high school and a year after her father's death he started to appear on Friday nights. He wore a slimy, pumpkin-coloured leisure suit and offered Mercy a bag of Oreo cookies before whisking Cassandra out for supper at the Chinese restaurant. The romance only lasted about a month and then, according to Gladys, the good sergeant was transferred to Regina to teach physical education at the RCMP training division. But the way Teeny figured it made sense. "They waited a decent interval of time so no one would be suspicious. After discovering you cannot create happiness on the back of someone else's misery let alone death, they broke it off."

The note game did not help the increasingly strained relationship between Cassandra and her adolescent daughter.

"Why are you so hateful?" Cassandra asked one Saturday night after Mercy locked herself in her bedroom. "I've told you before, no parties unless there is parental supervision."

"A lot of fun a party with parents is!"

"Mercy..."

"Leave me alone!"

"I'm your mother, not your enemy. Unlock this door! There are rules here."

"Murderer! Murderer! You killed him!" Mercy slipped the binder of mock suicide notes through a crack in the door. She turned up the stereo louder. She knew her mother hated Jethro Tull. But even Jethro didn't muffle the distressed sounds of Cassandra thumping the furniture around. Victorious in her revenge, Mercy plugged in her earphones and danced.

In the eleventh grade, Mercy ran away.

Dear Cassandra: I just can't take it anymore. Sorry, Glad-die. I'm so glad we had this time together. So long. Love Mercy.

Mercy knew with the last line, Gladys would think of sitting together eating popcorn on Thursday night watching *The Carol Burnett Show*.

Mercy ran all the way to a classmate's house—empty of parents for the weekend. There was Golden Nut wine. Mercy spent most of the night telling Timothy Webber he could not touch her breasts and barfing vomit the colour and consistency of melted chocolate ice cream into a pink plastic garbage can.

When Mercy went home—in the back of a cruiser at five o'clock in the morning—she was still drunk. Cassandra was a dirty, grey, terry cloth mess, her puffy eyes betraying her stone-cold face. She shook her head in disappointment and went to bed.

"Oh honey, thank god you're all right," said Gladys.

Mercy wasn't exactly all right. She had alcohol poisoning and slept most of the next day. She woke when Gladys brought in a tray of food: Campbell's tomato soup, with unbuttered toast and coffee ice cream for dessert. Mercy sat up, reaching out in reflex, to hug her in gratitude. Gladys caught Mercy's wrists.

"I could beat you within an inch of your life, young lady. But you are too strong and I am too old and that never gets anybody anywhere now, does it? But I would like to take my crochet hook and stitch those lips of yours together. Your mother is only human and I've watched you treat her like some kind of criminal this past year. If this is still about your father's suicide and why he left you two then I'm going to give you the best piece of advice you will ever get: Sometimes in life, Mercy, there are questions to which there are no answers. Accept that. Trust me, you can't, you don't want to know everything. Only God—" then she'd lost Mercy, who continued to watch her aunt's lips move, pretending there was no sound coming out.

"God, Gladdie? God? Oh. The Great God. The one who's so great he hurts innocent kids by taking their fathers away to help him get his job done? Taking care of the world. Well, from what I see, they must all be on vacation." Gladys got up like Mercy had poked her in the stomach, and left, slamming the door. Mercy kept going. "God, Goofy, Daddy, Mickey Mouse, Jesus, the whole shitload of them messing up, Aunt Gladdie. All messed up." She threw her tray against the wall. The bowl shattered, soup splashed, then dripped slowly, like blood oozing out of the floral wallpaper. The ice cream was a soft mocha puddle on the rug. Mercy raged on. "There is no God—only fucking fuck-up-ed-ness! Hear me?" she screamed, a scream so loud she was immediately hoarse.

Mercy cried herself to sleep that night. She would never accompany Gladys to mass again, not even at Christmas.

The note game stopped. A kind of truce followed. Cassandra befriended Teeny and Lulu, seducing them with Saturday night makeup parties. The topic of the note was strictly forbidden, but Cassandra eagerly provided stories of her courtship and love affair with Gabe Fanjoy.

"We saw *The Glass Menagerie* the night the new theatre opened and afterwards I had rum and raisin ice cream and Gabe told me if I ate enough of it I'd get drunk. Such a tease. I wore a pleated Black Watch skirt and hunter green sweater set—that was one of his favourite outfits. Said I had legs better than Betty Grable's. They're still pretty great, whatya think?" The three girls nodded.

Cassandra was Regional Sales Representative for Yours Truly Beauty by then, having been top sales rep for five years running. Even in her late thirties, she was a walking advertisement for her products. "I feel a little guilty leading people to believe I use the Yours Truly Beauty line," she confided to the girls. "I'm allergic to most of the products. Cameo soap for washing, witch hazel for astringent, and Pond's for moisturizer. And once a week, put your face over a mixing bowl of boiling water, and a towel over your head to clean your pores and that is all a woman needs." Those were her fundamental beauty tips to Mercy and her two friends, although she was never short of other helpful suggestions.

"Never wear pants with an elastic waistband. Lipstick is all a teenager needs. Anything more and you'll look cheap and the boys will get the wrong message. And Mercy, honey, you really shouldn't hunch your shoulders like that; you have a beautiful bosom. It's supposed to stick out. Look how Teeny walks—so straight."

But Mercy already felt like she stuck out enough. "I'm too tall, too gangly, too bull moose in the china shop, too eager, too shy, too much of all the wrong things, not enough of what seems to be needed to just fit in," she complained to Teeny, who nodded in sympathy. Mercy was certainly not anything like her mother, who, had her life been different, could have been a movie star. "People often tell me I look just like that actress—oh, what is her name?" Cassandra Fanjoy inhaled and smiled, then snapped her fingers. "Ellen Burstyn! Yes, Ellen Burstyn. She does look a lot like me."

Lulu and Teeny nodded in agreement and admiration. Mercy entertained the idea of her father and mother as glamorous movie stars, madly in love, torn apart by Gabe's suicide—prompted by the diagnosis of a deadly disease. It was the only acceptable version.

Mercy even tried to convince herself she'd imagined the note on that terrible night long ago. But truth has a way of surfacing. Circumstances shift, and the hidden, unanswered questions re-emerge with a vengeance.

Once, she dreamt of a miniature paper sailboat floating on the waves of River St. John, folded just so—a pop-up, origami, bird-like boat. There were words: large block letters in bright pencil crayon. The note. Mercy plunged in after it, thrashing through the icy river, grasping the paper triumphantly, treading water as she tried to read it. The words were blurred, the message lost. She watched as it floated away. Then she remembered she could not swim.

When she'd opened her eyes that night, she was sitting up in bed, her left arm outstretched in the dark.

The United Empire Loyalist Cemetery was an Odell tourist attraction. Mercy entered and strolled around, still lost in thought. The headstones were works of art. Sir Frederick Odell himself was interred in the first row by the river. Mercy wondered if her ashes could be buried beside her father and Aunt Gladys in Spring Garden Acres on the other side of town. Gladys was a vibrant, healthy ninety-year-old when she "passed over." She'd fallen downstairs on her way to her quilting and never recovered. The quilt, based on Faustina's image of Christ, was called "Divine Mercy."

"Gladys," Mercy whispered. "Gladdie, I'm scared. And Gladdie, who will be here for Belle?" She heard Gladys' commanding voice: "Give Belle my statue of Faustina and she'll be just fine. Get the quilt finished. It is hers. Faustina will have mercy on Belle, our precious Belle."

"You hold within you precious life," was exactly what Gladys had said when Mercy first confided in her that she was pregnant. Gladys was tenderhearted and non-judgmental but firm about what Mercy should do. "You must have the child then place the baby up for adoption—to parents who can take care of the child. There is a very good home in Halifax. I can make arrangements." Initially, Mercy had agreed, but after the first flutter kick in her belly, she changed her mind. Her mother did not take the news well, and went into shock. Finally, she confided in her two best friends: She would have her child. She would raise it alone.

"Mercy, are you nuts?" Teeny had shrieked and grabbed her by the shoulders.

"I *said* I can raise the baby myself. My mother did." Mercy pulled away and held her head high.

"But your mother had Gladys," Teeny pointed out. "And you'll have to leave your nurse's aid course."

"Not to mention we'll have to know if what your father had runs in the family," Lulu chimed in. Mercy pictured a little demon with winged feet flitting through the branches of her family tree. Lulu rambled on, as if reading the pages of her psychology textbook: "Yes, we have to know if it was some serious mental disorder like schizophrenia or manic depression or multiple personality or something. Genetics are out of your control."

"And just who is the father? I thought you were only ever with Sporty Gordie? What other secrets have you been hiding?" demanded Teeny.

Today, as Mercy walked over the lumps of earth where caskets were buried and bodies were only heaps of bones or dust, she recalled that night in shimmering detail. Her revelation happened at the very same spot, on "The Green," in this graveyard. Getting drunk in the Loyalist Cemetery was almost a rite of passage in Odell. Teeny and Lulu drank while Mercy remained as sober as the tombstones they sat on. The river had just receded after a messy spring thaw. The earth was spongy and Teeny was wearing heels, so she'd climbed on the hood of the car, where she danced on the roof and howled at the moon. "United Empire Loyalists.

You-nightly-hump-the-Royalists. Mercy's gonna have a babeeee. Imm-a-cu-late Con-cep-tion," Teeny bellowed, a broken record, until finally she'd fallen, one leg through the sunroof and the other splayed across the car roof. Teeny in the moonlight—it would be a snapshot in Mercy's mental album forever.

Where Teeny performed, Lulu had counselled. Even now, Mercy could almost smell the gin on Lulu's breath, feel Lulu grabbing her arm, pinching her flesh. "You need to know more. You need to get hold of the note. You need to know your baby's DNA!"

"Well you go ahead and ask my mother, Lulu, okay? I'm not going back there. She shunned me, remember? And I do not want to know if she tells you what was in the note." This was a lie as fat as Mercy's beluga belly and they all knew it.

Lulu took Cassandra out for Chinese food, straggling in late a little tipsy.

"God, she's a character. What stories she's got. She sure loves her work." Lulu laughed as she kicked off her shoes. Cassandra was a volunteer beautician at the Odell Rehabilitation Centre at the time, the beginning of her career in palliative-care beauty for breast cancer patients.

Lulu made herself at home on Mercy's sofa. "First, she gave me the lowdown on her work. If you feel you look good, you do feel better. It's a mental thing, she said. Even if we are dying, we women still like and deserve to look good. Mercy, did you know she even offers workshops where they get folks to visualize their own after-death experience? After one workshop, a woman told your mother she couldn't visualize dying until she'd first tied a purple ribbon in her hair. Imagine! Women and hair! It matters. Outward beauty *matters*,

your mother said. I agree." Lulu imitated Cassandra's man-
nerisms uncannily as she related the evening's events.

"Hey, I've got a new shade of lipstick she said was good
for your skin tone." Lulu produced the tube from her satchel. "She told me about being in the middle of buffing up the
fingernails of one of the burn victims and the woman starts
telling her how she got there. Seems her husband dumped
a bucket of gasoline on her and lit a match. Christ almighty.
Your mother said Christ almighty! Like it's a prayer, almost,
but you're never sure with her, eh? And your mother says
the woman's hands were just limp, like there was no bone in
them, like wet cardboard when you pick it up. But she had
beautiful, long, hard nails. She said: 'And I tell you, by the
time I was finished with her, there was a smile on that poor
woman's face.' And I don't doubt that for a second, Mercy,
knowing your mom."

"So…"

"Oh yeah. Not to worry, Mercy. Your mother says if it was
a mental disorder, it was one of those temporary insanity
things. As far as she knew, he was fine. Talked to himself a
lot, she said, but then again who doesn't do that from time
to time, eh? How's babycakes tonight?" She patted Mercy's
tummy.

"Lulu! THE NOTE? What about THE NOTE?"

"Right, THE NOTE. Want some tea?" Lulu turned her
back on Mercy and plugged in the kettle. "Well, she got
quiet when I asked her. This real sad look came over her
face—like for a minute maybe she even considered telling
me. 'What note?' she said finally and then she wouldn't say
anything else. Sorry."

"SEE?" Mercy screamed.

Lulu brought the tea to the table. She took Mercy's hand. Hesitating, she asked ever so gently, "Mercy, do you think maybe you might have been...you know, seeing things, like maybe you *did* dream it?"

The rage Mercy flew into that night convinced Lulu there was indeed a note.

Now the sun was in hiding and the river was the grey of lead pencil. Though it was muggy, Mercy shivered and exited the graveyard. When the time came, Mercy thought, she could ask her mother more about how to wear a turban to make it look less obvious she was undergoing chemotherapy. She walked faster.

Soon she was at the bend in the river equidistant to home. She could go forward or back but decided instead to take a detour and walk the pedestrian bridge to the other side of the river.

Odell Downtown Development and City Hall had done a wonderful job with the Millennium Riverbank Revitalization. Even at night, River St. John was filled with light.

"The old Train Bridge now links South Side to North Side and it looks like something European, not that I'd know, not ever having been to Europe. But I think it's Odell's very own Arc de Triomphe, hugging River St. John, a graceful braceleted arm, linking one side of town to the other." (Bridging the Gap. "Mercy's Musings," *OO*, May 04.)

There were a few others like Mercy, who strolled along, mostly couples holding hands, talking to each other. They were all taking advantage of the warm spell, more proof, as if anyone needed it, of global warming. Winter was only weeks away, and Mercy wondered if there would be snow. There had not been enough for cross-country skiing in recent years. At least, come spring, there'd be less chance of flooding.

Mercy stopped in the middle of the bridge, went over to the railing, crossed her arms, and rested her chin on top of her wrists. She looked down into the cognac-coloured river. Light filtered and slid through the current as it eddied around the support piers beneath her.

As her eyes swept the length of the Odell Green and Electric Street, she saw how far she'd come and how so much had changed. Odell was more beautiful than it had ever been. How she'd miss this place. How she loved this place. How she'd loved biking here with Belle when she was little. And how nice it was still, to come down with Lulu on her lunch break sometimes for those speedy walk'n'talks, and she had even learned, on days like this, how soothing it could be to enjoy strolling in leisure. She had finally come to appreciate this kind of solitude.

"Alone is not the same thing as being lonely," she whispered. Like you must have been, I guess, Daddy? And it was muddy back then, just a worn path, I suppose. And littered, no doubt, with beer bottles and wrappers. All garbage and mud. A thick pudding kind of mud. And it would have been cold, wouldn't it? Cold and dark and clammy. Mouth-of-killer-whale dark as you walked along. And not a chance in hell anyone would have spotted you, taking off those wing-tips, placing them toe to toe on a flat rock, tucking the note under your wristwatch, wading slowly, oh so slowly, into the current as if you were trying to ease yourself in for a moonlight dip.

Well, that is how I picture it. But it wasn't because you were lonely, was it, Daddy? Because, you know, don't you, that I've missed you every single day of my life since the night you left.

Daddy?

Daddy, what was in that note?

Daddy?

Oddie, affectionately known as the Nude Dude, was the cupid-like statue that adorned the fountain outside City Hall. Work crews removed Oddie every winter and placed him somewhere indoors. Today, a horseshoe of spectators had gathered to watch. Mercy joined them.

The statue was lifted from the fountain, wrapped in rolls of bubblewrap, placed in what looked like a coffin, and carted off. Mercy laughed, remembering Teeny's insistence that it was a gender issue: "It's because all of the mayors have been male and they live in fear that Oddie's pecker might freeze and fall right off."

The crowd dispersed. At the corner of Electric and Regent streets, Mercy headed towards home.

It wasn't as if she had seriously contemplated jumping off the bridge today, though she had gone overboard with what Oral Speakman would call "catastrophizing." The surgery could go fine and the lump could be nothing, she kept repeating to herself. Besides, there was her father's legacy. Even if she were terminal, suicide—even a *mercy* killing— was out of the question. She would not do to Belle what was done to her. The only time Mercy felt true despair was when Belle pulled one of her little disappearing acts, as it seemed she was doing at present.

Mercy trundled up her front porch steps, then flopped down on the swing. The tree house Hubbley had built for Belle was still cradled in the branches of the giant elm above her. Mercy could almost hear her daughter's laughter, see her grinning down, feel her nestled on her lap.

"Mummy, where do the leaves go when they blow away?" Belle was four at the time, a serious child. Mercy, even in reverie, could almost feel the small brown face against hers. "Mummy?" Sometimes, if they were lying down together, to get her full attention, Belle would take Mercy's head between her small hands and say sharply, "Mummy!" as if Mercy were being a bad little girl and Belle was the mummy.

"I'm thinking, Missy Belle."

"Sink hardah, Mummy!"

"Okay, I've got it. They all blow to a tree in the middle of the forest in the middle of the world. They fly onto this big tree and they all glow and they glow so bright that the moon sees The Glowing Tree, even at night, and the moon reaches right down and plucks up the lucky ones for stars!"

"Nonono. The moon has no arms, silly Mummy!"

"Yes she does. We just can't see them. And she hugs us all the time. Like this! ERRghnumnumnumnumie." Mercy squeezed and kissed her daughter until both their hearts were full.

Mercy bolted upright and barged into her house. The swing swivelled on its chain and rocked back and forth wildly, as furious as Mercy felt when those memories found their way in and she realized she no longer had any baby to rock. Belle was grown and gone. One of her more poignant musings, From Motherhood to (M)Otherhood ("Mercy's Musings," *OO*, June 99.) had struck a chord with many empty nesters. That was then, this is now, she'd reminded herself and her readers. Now, she continued to roar through her house, upstairs and down. She'd suddenly remembered she'd forgotten to love and be loved, something she thought she might get around to—sooner or later. Mercy realized with sharp certainty she would never know what it was like to sit there on that swing, sipping tea, with someone who might call her darling or sweetie or hon. She'd often wished there had even been someone she could chastise gently, the way Lulu did with Hap. With some envy, Mercy marvelled at people who loved each other well, overcoming inevitable grievances with a wellspring of devotion. "At least I have Belle," she reminded herself. "Some people only have themselves. They are the brave ones."

A car overturns, trapping a child.

The mother, wounded, desperate, and alone, rolls the car off the child, as easily as if turning back a quilt. Incredulous witnesses relate the incident on the six o'clock television news. Years later, they will mesmerize their grandchildren and the telling will become family legend. Grandmother herself will be the heroine of the tale, the tiny fearless woman who lifted the car single-handedly despite a broken collarbone.

The story will be repeated to inspire hope, to let the little ones know that ordinary people perform extraordinary feats. Some people, just as miraculously, do survive life-threatening disease. Imminent surgery to examine an unusual *abdominal protrusion*—a pair of words Mercy typed into her computer's search engine—was nowhere near as dramatic as a car crash. Car accidents and other disasters were things Mercy thought of whenever Belle did not return her calls. This was irrational—Belle had no car. Still, the mere thought of her daughter in danger created a burst of energy that overtook Mercy. She bustled into the kitchen, where she prepared a toasted tomato sandwich and brewed a pot of Earl Grey tea. As she ate, she perused her list, with renewed determination.

Things To Do I've Left Undone

1. Call my mother and make her hand over the note.
2. Reunite Belle with her father.
3.
4. Destroy incriminating evidence (RP letters).
5. Determine the identity of my number one most loyal fan/stalker/secret admirer.
6. Solicit Lulu's help and figure out how to dispose of the Horny Little Devil and other pleasure chest toys.
7. ~~Take belly dancing lessons~~. Lose five pounds.
8. Have sex at long last with The Animal Man.
9. Forgive and make contact with Teeny Gaudet.
10. Travel. Anywhere. Get the hell out of Odell—for at least a day.

Circling number one, Mercy phoned her mother and left a message. "Mother, Mercy. Wonder if you have reconsidered and will give me the note. I would appreciate this act of kindness. You know my number." She ticked three check marks beside number two.

Knowing she shouldn't, she copied numbers down from her old green address book and phoned around to several of Belle's friends: "Hi! This is Mercy Fanjoy. I'm wondering if you've seen Belle lately. I just seem to keep missing her. Well, anyhow if you do, tell her it's not urgent-urgent, but that I did call…to tell her…tell her there's a FedEx package here for her."

She looked at the empty number three on her list, and pencilled back in *Finish and publish my book*. She dialed Eunice McTavish. "Eunice. Been a while. It's Mercy. Can I come over sometime to brainstorm and talk over some ideas with you?"

Eunice was ten years Mercy's senior. They'd met when their children were toddlers in the Swim 'n' Gym program at the YMCA. Eunice, the oldest mom in the playgroup when older mothers were few, had adopted a child from Rankin Inlet in the Canadian North.

"What a sweet little Eskimo boy!" Vonda Kitchen said that first day.

"He's Inuit, not Eskimo," Eunice smiled, with not a whit of hostility. Vonda took offense and ignored Eunice from that day forward.

It was hardly surprising that Mercy and Eunice gravitated towards each other: Mercy, the youngest in the group, with an illegitimate child—a bi-racial child, no less—shared little common ground with the married, middle-class mommies. In the third week of class, Mercy casually mentioned to Eunice she was thinking of getting a full-time job.

"I really don't want to leave Belle. I don't want someone else playing with her when I should be the one. And I don't want to wear pantyhose every day. So, if I could do something at home...My mother suggested selling Yours Truly Beauty but as you can tell, I'm not into makeup. I don't bake, so Saturday morning selling bread at the market won't work either. That was my friend Lulu's suggestion. She came up with a logo, 'Loaves of Mercy.'"

"What would you like to do?" Eunice asked as they floated their children on their backs in the pool.

Mercy was startled at the question. A handsome woman, Eunice had short-cropped auburn hair and thick brown eyebrows. Her skin glowed and she moved in an athletic, confident, woman-golfer sort of way. In front of this educated, professional woman, Mercy was suddenly shy. "I don't really know."

"Do you have any ideas?" Eunice looked at her directly, as if she cared. This sudden attention combined with the chlorine smell made Mercy almost sick to her stomach. "I'm cleaning a few houses. It's not bad money."

"Money's important. But what do you dream about?"

"Dream? Oh. Well, you know. Writing romance novels and making a bundle," Mercy giggled, remembering Teeny calling them panty-wetters. "I like writing, and it's something you can do from home," she continued.

Eunice arched her eyebrows in surprise. "A writer. Aha! Would you like to come for coffee at my place tomorrow?"

Mercy and Eunice and Belle and Nathan became the best of friends. Eunice knew the managing editor of the *Odell Observer* personally. Eunice eagerly set up a meeting with Stirling Cogswell, and another at the employment office, after coaching Mercy on interview etiquette.

At the moment, after making three phone calls, Mercy was feeling connected enough. Her eyes scanned the rest of the page and settled on a note to herself about Isaiah Livingstone. She hauled herself upstairs and flicked on the computer, sending a query to the alumni office at Odell College.

An hour later, Mercy was still at the computer, having Googled so many sites on ovarian cancer she was bleary-eyed. Under "funeral services for agnostics" she'd found three hundred and ninety thousand sites. After downloading a pattern for sewing one's own cremains bag, cleaning another dresser drawer, and leaving a mess in the middle of the room, she wandered back downstairs, played a while with BB, and went out into the garden to find peace among the weeds.

"How's your bird?" It was Mr. Cattalini, peeking over the

hedge, bringing her back to the moment.

"Alive. Still alive. I just called and checked."

"That's good, Doris."

"Mr. Cattalini, Doris isn't here anymore. It's Mercy."

"Mercy? You mean that girl you took in who got herself knocked up? What about her? She still around?"

"Joseph!" Mrs. Cattalini reprimanded her husband, the merriment obvious in her voice. "You know Mercy, for heaven's sake. You're just up to no good!" she chuckled.

In her rocking chair, Mercy smiled indulgently and closed her eyes. Both hands cupped, she placed them over her belly, thumbs inward, and touched either side of her navel. Now that she was most likely carrying death, she was grateful she had once carried life.

The morning Mercy discovered she was knocked up, as Mr. Cattalini had so candidly reminded her, she'd studied her young body in the mirror in awe. Instead of crying, she'd giggled, reached out her hand, and touched her reflection in the mirror. Inside her was a baby, curled and shaped like a lima bean, no bigger than a pea. Mercy remembered a storybook page—all scarlet red and royal blue tapestry hiding a mile-high bed. *The Princess and the Pea* was one of her favourites. If you were truly a princess, you could feel a teeny little pea through all those layers of mattress. Could a baby be felt through all the layers of her skin, muscle, tissue, and bone?

She'd been enchanted, giving little thought to the long journey ahead or what she would do, let alone where she would live. After her initial awe turned into distress and her mother disowned her, she'd resided temporarily with Lulu and her family. Gossip spread like wildfire in Odell, and it wasn't long before Mercy found herself applying to rent a basement apartment. The landlords, Doris and Harold Hubbley, had settled into the upstairs of the small clapboard house at 435 Charlotte Street upon their return from living ten years in the United States.

It so happened that Harold had just suffered a minor car accident; his left leg was broken in five places.

"They're getting on anyhow," Lulu's mother informed Mercy, her eyes dancing. "They need someone to help out on grocery days, maybe do a little light housework, take them to some doctor's appointments. They have a small bachelor apartment with its own entrance." Mercy could have it for a reasonable rent.

The apartment was clean and cozy—a bit musty smelling and the pea green shag carpet was atrocious—"Preggers can't be choosers," Teeny had joked. Lulu agreed. Mercy signed a lease.

The day Mercy moved in might have been the loneliest day of her life, had it not been for her girlfriends. After Lulu and Teeny helped Mercy unpack the green garbage bag that held all her worldly possessions, the girls lingered.

"I'll be fine," Mercy said.

"I know," Lulu replied, her bottom lip aquiver. Teeny kept hugging her. Within minutes of their departure, Doris knocked timidly on Mercy's door. She was a fleshy woman who wobbled slightly, a smiling apple-cheeked garden gnome.

"I've got some old dishes and cutlery and wondered if you could use any of this before I send this box on to the Anti-Poverty Association?" Doris grinned, exposing a jumble of large tea-stained teeth, all jousting for position in her small, puckered mouth. She held out a fine china gravy boat—an odd choice for a welcome gift perhaps, but Mercy thought it was beautiful.

Harold knocked, just as timidly, later that night. "Figured you might not have many groceries yet. I made some beef stew s'afternoon. Want a bowl?" He held it out.

When Mercy nodded no, he looked her right in the eye and said, "Honey, if you don't eat my beef stew, I'm gonna shovel it down your throat."

Taken aback, Mercy had burst into laughter. That's when she learned a person could laugh and cry at the same time— a sun shower, one of life's secret survival strategies. Harold hobbled in the door on crutches, took Mercy gently by the wrist, sat her down at the table, and gave her a spoon.

"I'll go get some milk. You'll need to be drinking lots of that."

Odd, mused Mercy now as she rocked back and forth, how the past serves the present. The topic of the week's column was teenage pregnancy. Perhaps it was too close to the bone. She was also too close to deadline and was feeling the pressure. Mr. Cattalini was long gone but Trixie the cat was slinking over. Without thinking, Mercy picked up a rock and threw it, aiming for the cat's head. She missed by a mile. The cat hissed and Mercy hissed back, then bolted inside.

She found her rug-hooking basket and rummaged until she found the sunflower she'd been working on for over four years. She stayed at it about three minutes and gave up, yet again. Being left-handed was a curse in a world designed the other way round.

Mercy rattled around the place she called home, like a single marble rolling around in an empty shoebox. She loved her home: the cramped well-cooked-in kitchen; the cozy yellow sunroom, with its tangled jungle of plants; the blue-and-white bedroom that lacked action and passion; the paper-strewn office; the spare room with Belle's few things, a mess of magazine clippings and collages half done, glitter paint spilled on piles of old newspapers, yarns in bundles for all the rugs she'd never hooked. She cherished every rumpled, cozy, cinnamon-smelling inch and corner of the house. Mercy was grateful. She had a home. The house needed a new roof and the foundation was cracking and Mercy had been worrying where the money to fix it would come from. She'd pictured herself growing old in this house. But then, so had Doris. Wandering into the dining room, Mercy touched the gravy boat Doris had given her that first day. The small piece of fine china had been a constant, always full of change. Running her fingers over the pattern never failed to remind Mercy of Doris. And kindness.

She picked up the photo of the four of them—Doris, Harold, Belle, and herself. It was Christmas Day and she'd put the new camera on a tripod and set it to auto. With ten seconds to rush back to the group, she'd only managed to wrap them all in her arms and sit on the edge of the chair beside Harold before the shutter winked three times and snapped.

They'd known it was Harold's last Christmas even then. Doris had shiny puddles of grey under her eyes. Belle had just smoked a joint. Harold's face was the yellow of dried mustard, and his eyes were bulging out of their sockets like the eyes of a seal, glazed over with morphine. Her own face was hidden in that half shadow, like something Picasso might paint.

Mercy kept vigil with Doris as Harold was dying. It wasn't a peaceful saint's death. He fought until the last second, clutching her hand before going under the last time, crying out something that sounded like snow. "No. No snow." He was peaceful and for a few minutes Mercy kept his hand in hers. It was warm, and got warmer, it seemed, before it began to stiffen.

She'd moved upstairs with Doris after Harold died and bought the house a year before Doris was taken to Sunny Acres Seniors Complex.

Every Friday morning, Mercy visited Sunny Acres. She held her nose for fear of being sick. It was the smell—sour milk mixed with boiled cabbage and Mr. Clean. Mercy, however, could still sniff the smell of death and rotting flesh underneath. The air was humid, thick as Vaseline.

She usually read Doris a story from *True Confessions* magazine. Every time Doris asked how Harold was, Mercy lied and said, "Fine, just fine." Then she would chit-chat about the weather, jabber away as she shaved the stiff bristles of hair off Doris' chin and upper lip, gently applied Aloe vera gel over the area, brushed her hair over her baby pink scalp, and put her in a fresh flannel nightie. Later, she would feed her friend and former landlady cubes of green Jell-O one by one with a baby spoon and read some more, until Doris fell asleep and dreamt of only God knew what, or maybe, and this is what Mercy most feared, she no longer dreamt at all.

The tidying up of things did not come easily. Undertaking fearless personal inventory was not for the faint of heart, as Mercy was discovering. She found the effort to focus and compartmentalize more challenging by the moment.

Intense pain burrowed a hole inside Mercy's abdomen as suppertime approached. She pretzel-twisted and writhed on her yoga mat. Applying pressure to her abdomen, she pressed in, prodding with her own fingers the way Wiggins had. From what she could tell, the growth was shaped like Italy. How appropriate—a boot-kick in the belly. The jarring sound of the telephone ripped through her. She jumped up and lunged for it.

"Belle?"

The woman, whose name was Mrs. Appleby, spoke as if she'd rehearsed the words. "Unfortunately, Isaiah Livingstone passed away in August. If you check last month's issue of the *Alumni News*, there's a lovely obituary. The death was due to complications from pneumonia."

"Dead? Izzy died? He was younger than I am!"

Mrs. Appleby, who was used to people asking her to repeat news they did not like to receive, said only, "I'm sorry. Yes. Mr. Livingstone has expired."

"Expired?" Mercy gaped at the phone as if she could peer through it and see the woman. "Sweet Jeezuz, who uses that word?" she wanted to yell into the receiver. "Expired? Expired?" she yipped again, her voice rising in accusation, as if the office manager of the *Alumni News* was somehow personally responsible for Izzy's *expiration*.

"I'm sorry Ms. Fanjoy. I called as a courtesy instead of emailing. I have someone on the other line." With that, the line went dead. Completely dead. Dead not expired.

Mercy was fuming. "Isaiah Livingstone was *not* a bottle of pills, a magazine subscription, a loaf of bread, a container of yogurt. How can any halfway-sensitive human being use that word!" she wailed to Buddha-Belly. The cat blinked in solidarity, empathizing completely with his master's righteous indignation, at the same time bored with her redundancy and inability to accept impermanence. Mercy just wasn't there yet, was all. He sighed and licked his paws.

Mercy charged into the television room and rifled through the magazine rack on the wall beside the sofa. With violent impatience, she yanked it down. Back issues of the *Odell Observer* (containing her personal favourite "Mercy's Musing's" columns) spilled onto the floor. She thumbed high speed through the pages of the *Alumni News* and there he was, grinning up at her. Ebony skin, white teeth, those all-forgiving eyes.

Over the years, as was the way with so many relationships, Mercy had often wondered where Izzy was and what he was doing, and sometimes Mercy would find herself lost in a fond memory of Isaiah Livingstone. There was that one particular evening, however, she would sooner forget than remember.

Soft but steady rain had been falling all that day. By evening it streamed down streets, swirling into the sewers, gurgling in a steady comforting rhythm along the eaves of the library. Their original seven-member study group had dwindled to two and theirs was a comfortable, Tuesday night routine of a few years, predictable and safe. That night, when Isaiah and Mercy left the glare of the building and walked into the darkness, the air wrapped around them in layers soft as thick, black velour. Despite the rain, the evening was surprisingly warm.

Isaiah offered his umbrella to her, and she, being the taller of the two, had accepted. It was a handshake of sorts, as if they had agreed upon something. Mercy opened the umbrella, cocooning both of them under the network of steel ribs and black dome. Linking arms felt natural, although it was not something they had ever done before. The touch, perhaps because it was rare, electrified them both.

They manoeuvred past puddles, towards the downtown. The trees, mostly elms and maples, a few oaks, were studded with tear-droplets of rain silvering the branches and leaves. The asphalt pavement beneath the street lamps seemed newly tarred and greased. They veered down streets so glazed with light it was difficult to see. As they continued winding their way through what seemed like a low-ceilinged tunnel embedded with stars, Mercy was overcome with an emotion she was not familiar with. She realized she was happy.

Then there it was. The thought. The dangerous thought that lurked like a sinkhole about to cave in, spoiling the moment of bliss, and if Mercy were not careful, if she let the thought get any traction, she might plummet into despair. Still, she couldn't help wonder what a person's life might be

like with someone trusted always by your side. With someone specific, say, someone like Isaiah Livingstone. To be
huddled like this, two birds in a cage, safe against the wind
and rain. Just then a gust blew the umbrella inside out and
Mercy, chastened, wrestled with the ribbing. Soon they were
back under the dome and protected once more.

They spoke little. The silence was soothing and familiar.
Izzy didn't speak much, in fact. When he did, his face lit up
and he smiled, speaking through his gap-toothed grin. His
English was still limited, and oftentimes he spoke only to ask
Mercy a question—always one he knew would get her going.
Then he'd allow her to babble on.

"A brave man," Mercy teased once, "you giving me an
open invitation to muse out loud. Or maybe crazy. Izzy, you
must like the sound of my voice almost as much as I do."
Mercy was never afraid to admit to her many peccadilloes.
She figured almost everyone was on a never-ending self-
improvement journey. Strange thing was, Izzy seemed to
enjoy her just as she was.

"Keats' Theory of Negative Capability, Mercy. Explain fully," Izzy would say. Or, "de Chardin said the ills of this present
world are but growing pains. Do you agree? Why or why not?"

But this particular night, Izzy had no questions and so
they walked in silent harmony—a tall white woman and a
small black man under an umbrella through the streets of
Odell. Their footsteps scraped and clicked on the cement,
and echoed, the tease of a tap dance. Odell was suddenly a
hollow place, a nether world they were leaving behind in a
space outside of time. They roamed as if expecting to see
new terrain around the next bend. Mercy felt certain she
was not alone in feeling this way.

At the corner, where it was their habit to say their farewells politely, a car sped by, slicing through a puddle, splashing up a wave of water that crested over them both. Despite the umbrella, they were drenched.

"Ass—" she stopped herself from finishing. Around Izzy, perhaps because of his collar, Mercy often self-censored, willing her higher self to emerge.

"HOLE!" Izzy finished for her, throwing his head back, hearty laughter booming into the street and up to the heavens, and like a boomerang ringing back down to earth. The two of them, inebriated with joy and dripping, laughed like two sodden fools, gasping for air.

Laughter of the kind that makes a person clutch their side can, at times, be the heat that melts the iciest armour, releasing the deepest of inhibitions. Rules of decorum are all but forgotten. Leastways, that would be Mercy's excuse.

"You are soaking, sopping wet, Izzy. Come home with me. I'll give you dry clothes," she said, her angular face dripping with rain.

"I'm fine Mercy. It's not far." He cocked his head and turned, walking backwards.

"Izzy, it's across the bridge, and—well, here, take your umbrella—but really it's a good thirty minutes after that. You'll catch your death of cold. Please come to my place."

His hands in his pockets, he shrugged in surrender.

"All right mother. I accept your kindness." He walked back towards her, and huddling under the umbrella, they skip-hopped all the way to Mercy's apartment in the Hubbley basement.

Mercy paid Robbie the babysitter, who eyed Izzy rather suspiciously then bustled about. Embarrassed at the chaos in her small apartment, Mercy apologized as she picked up cereal dishes from that morning, a freshly laundered stack of Belle's clothes, piles of books and papers from the table. She tripped slightly as she rushed to put on the kettle.

"Mercy, slow down, woman. Stop apologizing. Do you forget where I come from?" Did Izzy mean Africa or his own little hovel on the north side of River St. John? It didn't really matter. Mercy was suddenly ashamed at her North American house pride. "I'm sorry," she said.

"I said stop apologizing!" Izzy was laughing, shaking his hair like a wet poodle, spraying the kitchen.

"Here's an old pair of sweats and a towel. Have a shower. Hand me out your wet things and I'll pop them in the dryer. I'll have tea made when you're done." Mercy tried to sound matter of fact though she was suddenly awkward, realizing she was instructing the man to undress.

"You are wet too," he replied, unbuttoning his shirt.

"Don't worry about me," she smiled, trying to avoid sneaking a look at his chest.

Isaiah retreated to the bathroom and Mercy sauntered into her bedroom. She began undressing, aware at the same time of the very attractive man (a man of God no less) standing naked in the steaming shower, just down the hall. It brought tears to her eyes. Not tears of lust so much as tears of another kind of longing. All she wished for, really, was that the two of them might lie down together, underneath the covers on her bed, and for once she would know what it was like to fall asleep in the arms of someone she truly loved. For she loved Izzy, of course she did—as one loves a friend. Mercy's loneliness that night pushed her to a kind of boldness. She did not, as she had once seen in a film, strip naked and enter the steaming shower. How she longed for the boldness of Teeny Gaudet. Instead, she wrapped her terry cloth housecoat snugly around herself, and prepared cinnamon toast and tea. When Izzy, his face scrubbed and shining, sat down at the table, she placed the food before him.

"Thank you. In the room the women come and go, talking of Michelangelo," he said. "Discuss, Mercy. Explain fully, please." But Mercy was not in the mood for the lamentations of T. S. Eliot, or any academic discussion whatsoever.

"Do you want to see something so beautiful you cannot even begin to imagine it?" she asked with what she hoped was a tantalizing but not overly seductive gaze. Izzy stopped chewing and swallowed, his Adam's apple bulging out and disappearing again.

"But that is how I see everything," he said slowly, his eyes shyly scanning her face. It was not the answer she expected.

"You do, don't you?"

"I do," he smiled, and wiped his mouth with the napkin.

"Well, still," Mercy reached out and took his hand, "you have not seen this, come on." She led him down the hallway and opened the door to the room.

"Belle," she whispered. "Asleep."

The room smelled of little girls' dreams, the plastic of skipping rope handles and rubber dolls and animal crackers and strawberry shampoo. A night light glowed amber. Belle's black hair fanned out on her pillow, swirling like the rays of a sun in a primitive painting, and her face was open to the room and the sky beyond the room and the heavens beyond any sky.

"See," whispered Mercy. "A miracle."

"Indeed," he replied, his buttery breath on her neck like

a tickle.

For a fleeting moment suspended in time, Mercy pretended she and Izzy were like Lulu and Hap, or any other couple lucky enough to gaze in upon their sleeping child, to share that moment of wonder and awe and heart-wrenching beauty and feel the magnification of joy because oh how much better it was when that joy could be shared. Belle shifted slightly and Izzy placed a hand on Mercy's arm. Then they tiptoed, like proud parents, back out of the room.

"I'd better be going," he said then. Crestfallen, Mercy nodded and watched as he retrieved his coat where she had draped it carefully over the radiator. "You can bring my clothes to school."

"You don't have to go," she said, realizing at once she'd erred in the worst of ways.

Izzy met her gaze evenly. "But I do," he said, the certainty in his voice like cement.

"I meant. I am so….You must think…." Mercy knew it was no use and felt the humiliation all the way from the soles of her feet to the sockets behind her eyes.

"Hush," he brushed his fingertips to her lips. Mercy watched him turn, and as if in slow motion, Izzy floated towards the door. He let himself out into the night and the rain. Out of her dream.

Even now, these many years later, Mercy burned with shame. She threw down the *Alumni News*. She'd lost contact with others who knew him, so there was no one to call who might share her grief and weep with her, knowing that the world was a lesser place without Isaiah Livingstone praying for its salvation. "Just because I can't pray has never meant I've disregarded the prayers of others," she sobbed into BB's fur.

The sky outside was twilight indigo. The windowpanes blackened and wind whistled through the chimney vents. Right then and there, Mercy decided on her travel destination. *Zanzibar* she scribbled beside number ten on her list. Then she sat. Mercy kept sitting in the dark and let the house grow cold as she mourned and longed for the grace of her long-forgotten, all-forgiving friend. Was the death of Isaiah an omen? *See the baby! Aymen. Wrapped in a manger. Aymen. Aymen. Aymen Aymen.*

Buddha-Belly snuggled up to her, resting on her stomach, tamping the flesh where underneath a war was being waged. There was nothing quite as comforting as the touch of fur, as an old cat's purring, except maybe human touch of any kind or the sound of a heart—even if you can hardly hear it—just beating on.

When I was a mother of babies
I rocked them made things
    better
When I was a mother
    of toddlers
I helped them with whatever
When I was a mother of teens
I prayed when they went
    wild.
Now I am a mother
    of adults
Helpless as a child.

— Foxy Moxy Roxy Galpal
    Greeting Cards

When in a regular pickle
remember, where there's
a Dill there's a way.

If at first you don't
    succeed, cry and
        cry again.

—Mercy's quotebook notebook

On Thursday morning, Mercy sat in her favourite booth in the Coffee Mill Restaurant in the Odell Hotel, writing her last will and testament. She wore a powder-blue sweater, her favourite. The wool was pulled and gave the effect of a giant cotton swab—it was that soft to the touch. Mercy stroked the sleeve thinking of the bloody feathered breast of the blue jay, shivered, and hugged herself. For over fifteen years, she'd worn this sweater for comfort whenever she'd been troubled.

Perhaps I should be buried in this sweater, Mercy wrote, then remembered she wanted to be cremated, her ashes scattered in the waters of River St. John.

She tapped her pencil on the page.

Today, she'd stopped trying to avoid or control the morbid thoughts. This in turn released her from her initial fear and sadness. She was now an amazingly efficient can-do sort of woman, a transformation in only a day after a lifetime of believing herself to be a hopeless procrastinator. Now she was smiling and thinking blissfully: Will wonders never cease? People can change. It's as if an angel, the angel Candonow-done, has visited me! Mercy had decided it was in this very restaurant her memorial service would be held and she had even selected what songs she wanted played.

Mercy stopped writing and wondered if for the service

Belle would favour the standard to the offbeat, as Strunk advised. A hat to hide the purple hair, a turtleneck for the tattoo, and a few less tongue rings perhaps? Mercy easily pictured herself on her deathbed leaning close, whispering to her daughter. She would clasp her hand and then, with the sawdust-smelling rotting breath of the dying, utter her last words: "Shave your armpits if you wear something sleeveless, okay honey? Just a thought. Looks do matter."

At the moment, although Mercy was unaware of this, she herself looked soft and feminine and pretty in an offbeat way. She wasn't, in fact, a pretty woman, if you took her features one at a time. Her best feature was her pore-less skin, which her mother said was just plain genetics.

The man who'd positioned himself in the booth directly in front of her nodded and grinned, then stared unabashedly. He had thick, naturally curly hair—something Mercy was fond of in a man. She caught his eye for the third time and he smiled again and saluted her. It was the French man with the deep dimples! She frowned back, giving him what she hoped was a glacial stare, dismissing him with a glance at her watch.

If Belle did show up, Mercy knew she would have to listen to her long-winded excuses and pretend this perpetual lateness was somehow justified. When at last they'd finally talked, it hadn't exactly been a pleasant conversation.

"Mum, you called a bazillion times and then, like, everyone I know? And said you have a package for me?"

"Belle. Hi. I've been worried!"

"Why? Never mind answering that. You're always worried. Once an anorexic, always an anorexic, eh? I'm great, Ma.

More than great. Sheesh. What's in the package? Can you tell? I'll come over and—"

"Can you meet me for tea. Today?" Mercy tried to be nonchalant.

"Not really."

"Well it's something I want to give you in person."

"I thought you said it was a FedEx package."

"Oh, no, I think I said I'd FedEx it if I had to."

There was a whoosh of breath, exaggerated exasperation. "All right. How about ten?"

"At the Coffee Mill?"

"Fine."

"Love you."

"Ditto."

Mercy folded the will and reached into her satchel for her lined yellow notepad. If Belle did not show as promised, she had Plan B. Contingency plans were always a good thing, especially since Belle could not always be relied upon to keep her promises. Besides, as Belle often said by way of excuse: things change.

Dear Belle:

Here I sit waiting. I've been cleaning out my drawers and the attic. Amazing how the past gets lost unless you open up old drawers. There is much I have not told you about your conception and birth. I feel this is as good a time as any. I wanted to do this in person. ~~*But you are not here, not that I'm overly surprised. I know you have better things to do these days.*~~

Your Birth

I think I told you that after I was asked to leave my nurse's aid training program, the only job I could get was clerking at Laura Secord Chocolates.

There I was, trying to eat as healthy as I could, for your sake. At home, mostly, thanks to Doris and Harold, I managed. But in there every day? The French mint chocolate bars, chocolate-covered almonds, hazelnut clusters, and my favourite—dark chocolate, rum-filled truffles—were too much to resist.

Think of your superhero Xena the Warrior Woman on steroids. Imagine a whale pregnant.

My face broke out. I gained thirty-two pounds and got varicose veins. I was forced to scoop out ice cream sideways when my belly got in the way, got freezer burns on my wrists, and permanently warped my spine. (Yes, Belle, feel guilty—children can cause you pain from the very start.)

The day after Valentine's Day, as I was dismantling the "chocolate & lovers" display, removing a life-sized cardboard cupid from the front window, my water broke. Ana, the store manager, grabbed a mop before she went for the phone. When Howie Bell from mall security saw a crowd gathering outside of the store, he rushed in. (See Angels Rush in Where Fools Dare to Tread—Thank Heavens! "Mercy's Musings," OO, May 78.)

A father of three and therefore well-acquainted with the look on a labouring woman's face, especially when she's down on her hands and knees, rocking back and forth, Howie wasted no time. "We're going NOW!" he yelled and barged through the crowd.

He wrapped his coat around me. We slipped and slid through the mall parking lot to his emerald green Jeep. Howie is five-foot-five. I was Hulk Hogan to his Thumbelina. How he ever managed to hoist me up into that seat without a forklift is noth-

ing short of a miracle.

It was one of the longest and bumpiest rides of my life. And that day we were hit with a sudden blizzard. Cars were off the road. We zigzagged all the way down Smythe to Woodstock Road, where the old Victoria Hospital used to be.

"Find your focal point, focal point," he was saying. I hadn't attended Lamaze classes, and I was moaning. The whole time I thought he was cussing at the cars or God or me. Something about the fucking point. (Excuse my French.)

By the time we reached the Emergency, I'd crawled as far underneath the glove box as I could. The pain! Howie left the Jeep idling, grabbed a wheelchair and squealed me in to the admissions clerk. He was panting almost as hard as I was. Then, he blurted out—for all to hear, "This is Mercy. She's going to have a baby. I'm not the father!"

The clerk frowned and lowered her voice. "Sir, we can do tests later if you wish, but really, is now the appropriate time?"

"He's not the father!" I shrieked. "He's just security!"

The poor woman dropped her pen.

Howie Bell and I bonded for life and you, babycakes, became Belle, which, as everyone knows, is French for beautiful.

When I returned home, Lulu and the Hubbleys had everything ready. The wicker bassinet was by my bed, the change table right outside the bathroom door. A pile of flannel nighties and cloth diapers were folded and ready to go. There was a month's worth of groceries in the fridge. I still have the sign they planted in the snow beside a snow-woman and snow-baby on the front lawn that day. "Welcome home Mercy and Belle."

On Tuesday, before entering Dr. Wiggins' office, Mercy

had taken a peek at a three-week-old baby swaddled in blankets.

"It's so nice to see that some people still use receiving blankets and keep their babies warm and womb-like in sleepers instead of dressing them like miniature football players before they are a month old," she gushed. The mother had shifted away. Mercy was dismissed. This depressed her. "I probably sound like one of those overly talkative lonely women who get on a roll and never shut up, one of those well-meaning but somewhat spineless women in the Anne Tyler novels I love so much," she smiled in apology. Pretending she had to go to the bathroom, the unfriendly mother stood up and left.

"Okay, so I'm a woman with a lump in my belly who lives alone and I'm happy for the chance to talk to someone who might talk back. Is that so wrong or pathetic?" She'd mouthed these words silently as she leafed through *Newsweek*.

O Belle, time flies. I've become a middle-aged woman with strongly held child-rearing opinions.

Your Father
Your looks come from your father. Lucky you. Your father, whom I have to confess I didn't know all that well before your conception, was Chinese, maybe Japanese, or so I thought at first. I was too afraid that if I asked him he might be offended. Right off, and as I've often told you, he was a nice man. A quiet, gentle man, and he wanted to be a doctor. I think he was very smart. You've obviously inherited his intelligence and passion for the healing profession.

When I told him I was pregnant with his child, he left uni-

versity in two days. I was not surprised. As you know, the only other man in my life, my father, disappeared suddenly when I was five years old by committing suicide. But I'll not dwell on that now. This is about your father, not mine. I should be fair. It was the end of summer and he had graduated and was going back to his country that fall.

We met (not at a campsite as I think I suggested once) while I was working as a file clerk in the Faculty of Science before I entered my training. Whenever he came into the office, the secretaries (or so it seemed to me) were suddenly so busy they didn't have time to answer his questions. He was extremely hard to understand. So, maybe because I was patient and tried to listen until he almost finished a sentence, he liked me. Still, when he asked me out, I was taken totally by surprise. I mean, he was so little, and I'm so big.

Your father and I would have made a very odd couple. Making love with him was, as they say up on the Miramichi, a pretty uneven teeter. Too much info? Sorry. After he left, I tried to get a phone number for him. Then I just thought, leave the poor man alone. He obviously was not ready for parenthood. It's not like we were madly in love. Two misfits looking for comfort. But here's what I want you to know, Belle: You might have been an unplanned baby but you were never unwanted.

Grambo
Hang on. It's quite the story. Your Grambo did not speak to me until three weeks after you were born! Imagine! Then she almost fainted when I told her the reason you had such distinctive almond-shaped eyes was not because you might be Down syndrome (Yes, that's the first thing she said when she looked at you!), but because your father was Bhutanese. Yes, for a long

second there, I thought she was going to disown me again. That was something she'd been threatening to do since her conversion to the PCFLCV, shortly after my father's "sudden" death.

Did I ever tell you how my mother's conversion happened? Two Witnesses came to the door and I let them in. ("You opened the gate to them, why not your heart?" she carped for years.) My fault.

That glorious day, they left a copy of Awake! with my weeping mother. I can still see her standing at the window in her pink velour housecoat, her hair a rat's nest, mascara smudged, a tissue crumbled like a carnation in the ball of her hand as she waved to them until they were out of sight.

Somewhere in the literature, she found words that spoke to her loss. She was baptized not as a Witness but in the People of the Church of Faith & Light & Celestial Vibrations, within three months. Total immersion. They do have one thing in common with the Witnesses. They shun.

"I shun you. Shun you!" she screamed the night I told her about you, Belle. Shun? Shine? Shone? The fact that I had never embraced the Vibrationists had been a sore point for a while but one she lived with. I honestly think she finally had the excuse she wanted. She could wash her hands of me and look the members of her congregation in the eye. But I guess this first shunning didn't really count. That day she discovered you were biracial, like I said, I thought I'd get shunned again.

"Bi-what? Bhu-where?" she said on her inhale. She bit her tongue and said very slowly, on the exhale: "Was he a Christian man?"

(She's certainly come a long way. Hasn't she?) Although your father and I never got around to discussing religion, I bobbed my head up and down as if my neck was made of coil, like one

of those dashboard Snoopy dogs. She got fifty nods in response to one question.

"Well. Then." Her voice was crustier than a five-foot layer of ice. "We believe all races and colours are one under God," she said as if it were a page memorized from the Bible. (It was.) "Acts 10, verses thirty-four to thirty-five," she continued. "And Peter opened his mouth and said, 'Truly I perceive that God shows no partiality, but in every nation one who fears him and does what is right is acceptable to him.'"

At exactly that moment, you burped and spit up on her sweater. Honey, your sense of timing!

After she got cleaned up, she mauled you, inspecting your fingers and toes and all. You were wearing a blue nightie smocked with pink thread. Store embroidery but still, it looked good with your skin tone. I still have it. Your beauty got to her.

"Mercy," she began, while blowing her nose, "I've prayed over this. And I forgive you." My absolution was delivered as she inspected the contents of a phlegm-filled Kleenex.

Was I supposed to say thank you? I wondered as I watched her. Amazing. Just who did she think she was? And what had I done to her exactly? Belle, my darling child, I vowed that day that there would never be this kind of tension between us. (Well, I had no clue back then.)

"Do you need anything?" she asked me as she was putting on her coat to leave. She was finally taking in her surroundings. "Besides a kettle?"

"Like, everything?" I was trying to keep it light, Belle, I was.

"You don't have any end tables," she said. I started to laugh, but then I realized she was dead serious.

"And a little bit of lipstick is not going to hurt you."

I had a good cry after she left. Maybe because I realized she

*must have once loved me as much as I love you. She said she
was very touched that I named you Belle. She thought it was
a derivative of Belliveau, her maiden name. I can see how she
made the connection, and I let her think what she wanted. What
harm is there in that? But I digress.*

Mercy's pen ran out of ink. She reread the letter. Bee was
chirping away to a group of regulars—two police officers
on their afternoon breaks. "So I says to him, I says look
mister, we got coffee, we got tea. You want that GD fancy
stuff, give me starter money and I'll open up my own coffee
shop. Then you can have your soy chai latte triple cappuccino frappuccino skim mocha macchiatto café au lait with
bullshit for whipped cream for all I care, but you're still
gonna have to sit your sorry arse right down here to drink
it. It'll be a cold day in hell when I serve coffee to go so you
can walk around like every other idiot with a Styrofoam cup
velcroed to your hand and your cellphone glued to your
ear. I'm a waitress, I told him, so tell me how can I wait on
anyone in that much of a hurry? HA!"

The officers, who laughed and shook their heads, offered
up their cups for refills. Every day Bee Godwin, raconteur,
seemed to pour salvation as well as coffee into mugs. Mercy
inhaled, found another pen, and resumed writing, hoping
these brief anecdotal sketches of her own would help her
daughter in the ways her restless, hungry soul most needed.
Perhaps, before the surgery, Mercy would be forgiven for
her own errors of omission.

So to the real reason I have written this. Hope you don't fall off your chair. As you say, things change.

After a lifetime of telling you otherwise, I really think I'd be okay now if you were to contact your father. It is your choice. But I had Vincent Fitzgerald do some detective work a while back and I know where your father is and how to reach him. I called him today. Call if you want his coordinates. His name is Jigme Tenzing. He lives in Nova Scotia. He would love for you to call, he told me. I said I could not guarantee that, of course. It's your choice, dear. And call me after you read this, okay?

Love, Mama

The tea was cold. It was 11:45 and Mercy had scheduled lunch with Eunice McTavish at noon. Realizing Belle was going to be a no-show, she swept pens and notebooks into her purse, second-guessing herself and the idea of some movie-of-the-week father-daughter reunion. It would get ugly, she suspected. If Belle chose to contact her father, this meant she'd discover that the good man had expressed the wish to have visitation rights since Belle was ten—a wish denied by Mercy and her lawyers. Also, Belle would learn there was a bank account with fifty-four thousand dollars in it—the three thousand a year for eighteen years of child support that Jigme had paid. Mercy had saved the money in a trust fund for Belle and used it as collateral for her small mortgage. Of course, Mercy intended the money to go to Belle when the time was right.

Mercy rubbed her forehead furiously, scrunched her eyes, and opened and closed her mouth several times to unlock her jaw. She'd been muttering to herself as she read. Mr. Pardonnez-Moi gawked at her as if she was a crazy woman. She signalled to Bee for the bill.

"Yes?" he said. The man thought she was waving at him.

"My bill. I was asking for my bill."

"Yes," he grinned.

I'm hopeless, thought Mercy. His smile. Those eyes. She scolded herself: Think of all those normal-looking murdering psychopaths and perverts. Looks meant nothing these days.

Then, the same way it had washed over her in the car on Tuesday before class, Mercy was overcome with a fit of laughter. The man began to smile uncertainly. Mercy laughed harder when she saw the alarmed expression on his face. She laughed and began to snort, she laughed and gasped, she laughed with no sound, just a kind of air-sucking desperation. She laughed high then low, in circles of sound, she laughed and began to choke, tears streaming down her cheeks. She clutched her stomach. She grabbed a notebook to hide her face and a new sound came out, a kind of *who-who-who-who whooting* sound, her shoulders and torso shaking. She would die right here, right now, in the Coffee Mill, death by laughter seizure. The dimpled man was now looking from side to side, almost terror-stricken. The *who-who-who* changed to *kerckerckekrch*—Dodie-like quacks.

Bee rushed over with water.

"Are you okay?"

"Kerckkerchhummhmmuhmmm. Humm. Kerckwhoo!" Mercy convulsed and nodded. She stood up, crossed her legs, as though on the verge of wetting her pants.

"Mercy?"

"Hehuhhuhuhkerck." She simmered down some and took a sip of water, giggled and sprayed the water out her nose and mouth all over the table, and began a new bout of laughter. By this time, Bee, the man, and all the other customers in earshot were laughing, too.

"Mercy! Mercy!" said Bee.

It took Mercy almost three minutes to come to a stop. Her jaw ached. Her breathe was ragged. Her entire body was unravelling like a fraying rag. She sat there, undone, unable to find edges with which to tuck herself back in.

Bee slid into the booth and hugged her. "Oh, honey. You are not yourself. Thought that yesterday. Belle? That little earth muffin stood ya up again?"

"She's so busy these days. She only said she'd try to make it." Despite her valiant efforts, tears slipped down her cheeks.

"Well, never mind. This might cheer you up. I brung it."

"Brung, brought, what?"

Bee handed her a recipe card. Bee's Beet Soup.

"Fantastic!" Mercy looked it over. What had once started as an exercise to help Bee improve her literacy skills had now become Bee's hobby. Each recipe card was a small work of art. The recipe was in calligraphy, and in the margins were exquisite, miniature watercolours of vegetables. Mercy gave her a hug. "I'll make a pot this weekend."

"Call me if you have any questions. See ya tomorrow."

"*À la prochaine*," said the dimpled gentleman as Mercy passed.

"*Au revoir*," she gave him half a smile, afraid if she smiled fully she might lose it again.

On the way to Eunice's house, Mercy dropped Belle's letter into the mailbox of the bat cave she was living in. Mercy had gone in once, but it just depressed her terribly. Belle was clean enough but she had nothing besides cushions, candles, paints, music, and yoga mats. Her bed was her portable massage table. On the walls were posters of the Dalai Lama and Buddha, the Vietnamese monk Thich Nhat Hanh, the Virgin Mary, Jesus, Whoopi Goldberg, and

Sanjay Gupta, health reporter for CNN. There was also a life-sized cardboard cutout of Xena the Warrior Woman and a small statue of Faustina, one of Gladdie's. The apartment had reeked of patchouli.

Simple was admirable, though, and Mercy was grateful that Belle was getting better. A vegan and three years drug free. A yoga teacher and a raindrop therapist.

"Just what is a raindrop therapist?" Mercy had mistakenly laughed out loud when Belle first informed her what she was studying.

Belle answered in a huff: "An energy balancing mind-body medicine that combines aromatherapy and massage and works through the electromagnetic field of the body, curing disease and mental instability and restoring harmony."

"Drip drop, Belle." Mercy hoped teasing might soften her negativity. Belle's crestfallen face revealed otherwise. "Honey, I did some research. It sounds like quackery to me. One website I found says some oils might even be toxic. You could poison someone. I've gathered some notes together…"

"Mercy, are you crazy? Drip drop, yourself. That girl is getting herself better! Do you want her to waste away to nothing again? I'll give her the money for the course if you help her with the rent." Humbled by her mother's insight and tenderness toward her daughter, Mercy had agreed. These days she could handle most of it; the vegan part Mercy still felt too extreme. A decade ago, Belle had been diagnosed with borderline anorexia. Plunged into guilt and fear, Mercy's instinct was to fatten her up and keep her safe. She wanted to protect her daughter from her worst self. Belle *was* better. She was a good soul when she was stable. And she was in love. She was seeing a very nice young woman. What more could any mother want?

The very incredible Eunice McTavish lived in a buttery yellow clapboard house with black shutters in the historic downtown district of Odell with her husband, Gerald, a petrologist. Eunice met Gerald in the Northwest Territories in the seventies when she was doing a paper on *inuksuit*. "Signs Sacred and Directional" had launched her career. The couple stayed north after they married, living in various communities before returning south.

Earlier that morning, after her run, Eunice had been clattering about her kitchen, a skunk stripe of perspiration down her back, her face shining, her hamstrings burning, when she heard Gerald in the shower. She ran her tongue over her upper lip, tasted salt, and began to peel off the sweat-soaked clothes moulded to her body. By the time she got to the bedroom she was naked and shivering. She opened the door and joined her husband, who was surprised to see her—but grateful. He handed her the bar of soap, and turned. Eunice washed his back. She slid the bar of soap up and down, making a wide soapy trail, teasing him until he could stand it no longer and turned around.

"My rock man," she said. "My rocket man," she was soon panting.

An hour later Gerald was saying, "Whoever said twenty-five is better than sixty did not have you for a wife."

Eunice shivered with pleasure remembering, but now she was running late. She found herself resenting Mercy Beth and her midday interruption when the doorbell rang. She heard Nathan greeting Mercy and went down.

"I've got a favour to ask," Mercy said five minutes later, as they settled in at the table.

"Ask away."

"Do you know anyone I can turn to for editorial advice? I am moving ahead with my book project."

Eunice sat up. "Oh, The Book." Mercy had been talking about The Book for years but never seemed to get around to writing it. Today, Eunice heard a new tone in her friend's voice. And she saw, in the set of Mercy's jaw and the straightness of her shoulders, that she might actually mean it this time. She leaned forward in her seat, studying Mercy's face.

Mercy talked in spirals, reminding Eunice of the way wind blew outside her bedroom, sometimes soft and gentle, then a gust, and then a whirlwind. Eunice only half listened to the words, knowing by cadence when important information was coming and knowing when it was just air bubble blowing time. She noted Mercy's body language instead. She was twirling her napkin as she spoke. Besides, she knew Mercy would end with the same question. And she would have the same response.

"So what do you think I should do?" Mercy finally blurted.

"What do you want to do?" Eunice shot back, on cue.

"I want to write a good book," Mercy exclaimed.

"Why?" This was not Eunice's usual follow-up question. She usually said, "What do you need in order to do that?"

and let Mercy stutter out her response. Eunice helped herself to more salad.

"Why?" Mercy was not prepared for this. She'd never asked herself the question, let alone answered it.

"Why." Eunice nodded and speared a cucumber with her fork.

Mercy looked down at her plate, silenced.

The phone rang and Eunice excused herself. "I've got to take this," she said, as if relieved she had an excuse to leave.

Mercy dreamt of The Book often. A hard-covered book with a sapphire-blue, matte-finished jacket, the cover copy read:

An amazing chronicle of the lives of three brave women!
She saw her own hands as they opened the book.

For Lulu Lutes, who always said I would/believed I could; and R. P., who told me I was "a unique"; and Stirling Cogswell and Eunice McTavish, the permissionaries who gave me my start; and all the teachers I ever had since grade one; and Belle and Doris and Harold and, and and and...

Mercy realized she had a tendency to be overly grateful, but in fact she felt like that—grateful—most of the time, like she was indebted to everyone who ever gave her the time of day.

After the academy-award-winning-speech-list dedication came the advance praise blurbs and starred reviews.

I have rules. I don't blurb. I don't make exceptions unless the work is exceptional. Point taken? —Tamara Grete O'Dow

This book has historical authenticity and lively, plot-driven prose. —Jacinthe Irvine, *The Globe and Mail*

"A damn good read! MERCY RULES." —*People Magazine*

"Like one of those page-turning mysteries; the classic ones, with a cast of characters you won't forget after the plane has landed." —*Montreal Gazette*

"Mercy Beth Fanjoy has gotten too big for her bootstraps. Now she thinks she's going to be a writer. Her magnificent obsession with three dead women is perverse. Who does she think she is, Christina Gaudet?" —*Odell Observer*

The daydream usually ended there, with a scratched-record sound, the book catching on fire and burning to ash. Ashes, ashes. Goddamn Teeny Gaudet showing up even in her daydreams. Teeny Gaudet, her former friend. A published writer of some thirty books including *Burt the Burping Bear*. She now had her own talk show on a cable radio station.

"Do you ever see Teeny anymore?" her mother asked from time to time.

"Ms. La-di-da blows in from New York, does book signings and fundraisers, and blows right back out. No time for any of her old friends. Well, she always has time for Lulu, who seems content with getting crumbs and never fed up with the offer to do a quick lunch or, worse, get up at some godawful hour and meet for breakfast."

"What on earth ever happened between you two?" Cassandra had asked then.

"It's private." Mercy had always managed to deflect the question. For the longest time, Lulu tried unsuccessfully to reconcile Mercy and Teeny.

One day, on one of their walk'n'talks by the Odell Green along the river, Lulu gently brought the subject up. "Teeny is hurt by your withdrawal. She says she totally understands why, though, Mercy. She won't tell me what happened, but she takes all the blame."

"And so she should," sniffed Mercy.

Lulu, whose valentine face could never quite look stern, raised her voice. "She said she was sorry, Mercy. Heavens! What happened, anyway?" Lulu stopped and faced her.

"Never mind. You don't need to know. It was bad enough to ruin our life-long friendship, okay? I am not a very forgiving person, I suppose." Mercy stooped and tied up a sneaker lace.

"Is it possible that you are now just a little bit jealous of Teeny's success, Mercy? I love her but even I'm envious. Her and my three sisters! I'd give anything to travel like that. Just a dash of glamour now and then, you know?" Lulu walked faster.

"Glamour and Teeny do not go together in my books," Mercy said with a touch of bitterness, and jogged to catch up.

Teeny, who hailed from the roughest side of Odell, was a bright student and was offered scholarships to university right out of high school. Mercy made higher marks their final year in English class. As far as Mercy was concerned, all Teeny had really accomplished was to breed more rudeness into the world.

"Why would I envy anyone who wrote a book called *Burt the Burping Bear*?" she asked Lulu. "Maybe I should write

Pee Pee the Pissing Cat. Now there are all these belching, ignoramus adults encouraging their children to see who can burp loudest, or burp five in a row, or have a contest to see who can burp 'Silent Night' the best. Honestly. Some people."

"You are so envious and so…competitive."

"I am not!"

"You are so. And judgmental."

"I am not. I'm opinionated, maybe. Call it an occupational hazard."

"And while some schools have actually banned the books, Mercy, the *Burt the Burping Bear* series has done a lot of good to encourage some of the more reluctant readers in my class." Lulu's voice was rising again. Her face purpled the colour of plums.

"Right, and Teeny makes a bundle," snapped Mercy.

"And buys her parents a new house. And donates to good causes. Bitterness does not become you. Making money is not evil. I'm happy for Teeny—look what she's had to overcome." Lulu's voice wavered.

Lulu was referring to the herpes that left Teeny sterile not to mention the over-the-top scary abusive boyfriend from college.

"I suppose," said Mercy, sensitive to Lulu's increasing agitation with every sentence. "And it's not easy, I'm sure. I mean, you know what they say about the kids' book industry."

"No, what?" Lulu's fists were clenched.

"It's a bunny eat bunny world."

It was the only argument they'd really ever almost had. It ended in hysterical laughter. Lulu and Eunice. Where would

she be, Mercy often wondered, without those loyal steadfast
friends?

"Mercy?" Eunice, back from her phone call, snapped her fingers in front of Mercy's face and began clearing the lunch dishes. "Sorry about taking so long. Your three minutes are up. If you don't know why you want to write the book, then you aren't halfway ready."

"I am so!" Mercy rose and helped clear the table.

"Then answer the question. Convince me."

"Okay. Granny Ross was an amazing healer. She saved a whole community from smallpox. Canada's first nurse. Gregoria…she was this wild Spanish sexual woman, a vivandière, a camp follower, a hooker, really. She may even have been the mistress of the Duke of Wellington. Imagine. She ended up in Annapolis Royal, had six poodles, married an old curmudgeon she called 'my *bruta besta*.' And then there's Shaw T'laa—Kate Cormack—the real discoverer of gold in the Yukon gold rush, according to Stirling Cogswell. But she lost everything. Including her daughter! Tragic. Really tragic. Amazing women and they've just sort of vanished. None of them have gotten their just deserts."

"Desserts! Speaking of which, want some ice cream?" Mercy nodded yes. Eunice continued talking over her shoulder. "So you want to rescue them from oblivion? A kind of feminist revisionist history."

"Your learnin' is showin', as my mother would say. That's your world, not mine. One little book. A fictional biography type of book is what I want. I don't want to rescue. I just want to remember, to celebrate lost lives of great women. To inspire young modern women who think they have a hard go of things."

"I see," Eunice said crisply. "That would be what feminist revisionists seek to do. And you did go to university. Don't go all anti-academic on me."

"Sorry. I wasn't really. But I want mainstream readers. I just want an editor who will understand and have faith in me. I have a great idea—and they wouldn't even let me try. Look what Ms. Hawkes wrote—"

Mercy handed over the letter. Eunice read it slowly, arching her eyebrows now and again. She exhaled, and spoke as if picking words with great care. Her tone was tender.

"Well, what if this is a realistic assessment? Maybe you should start by doing what she says. And maybe you should ask what these women mean to you personally." Eunice's words were colder than the ice cream on Mercy's tongue.

"I just told you."

"No you didn't. You said what you wanted the book to 'do'—the message you wanted to send. You never said why you picked these three. How do they speak to you? Not a bad thing to ponder." Eunice sounded bored, as if the conversation was wrapping up.

Then, it was as if Mercy's stomach swelled into a balloon, inflated and then released—whipping around like a ballistic missile in the McTavish kitchen. She clutched her abdomen, kneading the area around her lump. She could feel it through all the layers of her clothes. Her stomach rolled, shrivelling inward. Then something snapped inside.

"What? I—I—suppose you think *I* need healing, *I* need sex, *I'm* invisible, abandoned by my daughter, and will die alone? And not make any difference whatsoever? Right. Well, not all of us are as competent as you, Eunice! Or intelligent or, you know, as clear-headed or useful or—"

"Mercy!"

But Mercy was gathering her purse and her query letter. "I was even going to ask you to read it. Suggest how to sharpen it. Forget it." Mercy stampeded away, upsetting her bowl, rivulets of ice cream on the floor streaming in a perfect wake behind her.

"Please—don't hurry out. Wait now!" But Mercy kept going, dropping one of her envelopes, slamming the door behind her.

Eunice, the amazing Eunice, whistled.

"Sweet Jeezuz! I guess I must have hit a few buttons too many. Well, good. Get angry and get going, Mercy Beth." Eunice watched as her friend hightailed it down the street, her coat flapping behind her, her head held high, looking like she might trip at any moment.

On that October day, Mercy Fanjoy was a woman striding the streets of Odell with renewed purpose. Energy and breath. When you realize fully there's only so much left, you make wiser choices.

The attic smelled of pine and soggy compost. In the dimness, the eaves glowed amber. "Like viewing the world through a jar of honey held up to the light," Mercy whispered in BB's ears, twirling the two of them slowly around in a circle. She was wide-eyed open, childlike, mesmerized by the glow.

Behind stacks of boxes and piles of old magazines, Mercy eyed the birdcage in the corner. Swiping away a gauzy nest of cobwebs, she clutched the neck of the stand and unhooked the bowl of the cage, tucking it safely in the crook of her arm, its wired ribs against hers. As though the cage were made of glass, Mercy, in strange, slow gyrations, waltzed the cage downstairs. In the kitchen she scoured the rust away with scalding, sudsy water. Whistling as she worked, her spirits lifted.

"Maybe the bird will recover better in a nest of its own," she suggested to Noah when she'd last called Glooscap. "I have just the thing. I'll bring it by tomorrow."

For a while, the cage had been home to a startled-looking spider plant, which had unfortunately suffered and died from Mercy's zealous overwatering. She'd painted the cage purple and whenever the urge to rearrange furniture jolted her awake, as it often did in the middle of the night, she shunted the cage from corner to corner, room to room.

"This damn thing," she'd say to BB, "is nothing but an eyesore! And it's all because of you I don't have a bird!" BB would only look at her smugly. Eventually she'd stashed the piece of faux Victoriana away in her attic. Now here she was, lovingly ironing an indigo piece of flannel. This she planned to fold in threes and use as a liner for the bottom of the cage. The blue jay would have a fine bed to recover on.

Keeping busy helped Mercy forget what she now visualized as an ever-mutating tumour. Regrettably, she was incapable of erasing the memory of her insane outburst at Eunice. The tips of her ears flamed. She cringed, remembering, ice-cold shame like a hand clamping down on the nape of her neck. Whatever had possessed her? Eunice, who was only ever kind and helpful, did not, in any way, deserve that sour spew of vitriol. Perhaps, Mercy admitted to herself, it was time to confide in someone about the surgery. Maybe she needed to stop doing everything and just concentrate on her list. Or her deadline. This week's "Mercy's Musing's" column was going nowhere.

Stella? Hey there, where are you? Mercy. Would you tell Ted I'm not going to make deadline this week? I think if you check you'll find it will be the first time ever. In fact, I'm taking a few days off. No big deal, I've got a flu bug, I think. I always had one column in reserve in case this happened. I looked it over this a.m. Making a few changes, and then I'll send it in an attachment. Just email if you need me. I'll be checking. Ciao.

She resumed cleaning the cage. The reserve column was a rumination on "Home Remedies and Household Hints."

This was not something she had to research much. She had years of experiential wisdom. Mercy sprayed stain remover on her rag and filled the sink to let it soak. She glanced out the window. The Cattalinis, going out for their stroll, waved at her. Drying her hands on her apron, she retrieved the book she'd purchased on her way home from Eunice's. Mrs. Cattalini was an avid reader. She dashed off a quick note.

Dear Theresa: I am so sorry about my rather offensive language and the turmoil yesterday. I hope you enjoy this book. It is set during the time of the Halifax Explosion. I loved it! I thought you might like to read it out loud to Joseph. I'll have you over for tea sometime and we can discuss it. See you soon. Incidentally, the bird is holding its own. Mercy

She slipped the note inside the book, hastened next door, and slid the gift through the mail slot. Across the street there was a lively ruckus, the Ferris children and their mother. They were putting up Halloween decorations, hanging stuffed sheets from the branches of an elm tree, stretching cotton batting to make cobwebs over railings. "Hey Mercy! Want to come over and help us?" Mercy waved and quickly retreated from their gaiety.

"Not today, I'm late on a deadline."

Love one neighbour, lie to another, she chastized herself. Had Cogswell been alive he would have said, "Work with it Mercy. Don't you know, every contradiction is an invitation to explore?" *Exploratory surgery*. She swallowed, typing it into the computer's search engine. She closed her eyes, pressing the search button, not at all convinced information-gathering was as healthy an anxiety-busting strategy as Mr. Oral Speakman positively—almost smugly—guaranteed. Mercy's experience was different. As Cogswell often said and Strunk advised: less is often more.

Three months after Mercy started doing the weekly television guide for the Leisure section of the *Odell Observer*, Stirling Cogswell had called and requested a meeting. Mercy was anxious, having only met him the once, briefly and safely with Eunice by her side. The fact that Mercy would have to squeeze the meeting in between two of her housecleaning clients only increased the pressure she felt. She changed clothes, perched outside his office door, fidgeting and occasionally smiling at the receptionist who'd promised it would only be a few moments.

"I don't know what's keeping him," the receptionist said after about twenty minutes. Her voice was a relief as it droned though the tedious silence. Her hair was the colour of egg yolk and piled on her head in layers, like a hat made of rose petals.

"It smells like Ajax in here. Can you smell it? No. Lysol? Pine-Sol?"

"No, Javex," Mercy corrected her, reddening. "Bleach."

"Did you take a bath in it?" the receptionist sniffed in exaggeration and waved her hands, fan-like, in front of her face.

Mercy couldn't tell whether she was being hostile or not.

"I just came from my other job," Mercy sniffed back. "I'm a cleaning lady by day, TV guide writer by night."

Mercy was hoping she sounded sardonic. This was a new word she'd discovered doing the TV guide. It was amazing what she was learning by reading capsules of television sit-coms and old movies.

"Here." The nose-sniffer opened up her drawer.

"What?"

"Come here," she whispered fiercely, eyeing the closed door. "Quick."

Mercy approached her desk as if she was in a conspiracy. "My name's Stella."

"Nice to meet—" Mercy began.

But Stella sprang up then, squirted the air in front of Mercy and pushed her through a mist of perfume.

"Divine Musk. He loves it. And relax. I just started here, myself. He's a nice man. Not like my old boss. Close your eyes." She sprayed a little cloud around Mercy's head.

The door opened.

"Mercy Fanjoy?" said Mr. Cogswell, and sneezed.

"Really, Stella, you've overdone it with that air freshener this morning." Cogswell was taller than Mercy, and rail thin—the same width from the front as sideways. He was probably a redhead at one time, Mercy surmised, judging from the freckled skin, but he was as bald as Mr. Clean.

"Well," he'd started in that day, after his sneezing attack. "I see you're having a good time with the movie synopses these days." He blew his nose loudly. Mercy politely looked away.

He'd actually read her movie summaries? So he was about to haul her across the carpet. What could she say to defend herself? I am grateful; do not get me wrong. This job is so damned tedious, and though I'm tempted to plagiarize word for word, my high school English teacher taught me better.

"I was just jazzing them up a bit," Mercy smiled. "I'm still trying to figure out colon and semicolon use."

The Wizard of Oz had been her latest write-up:

Saturday at seven. Channel 4 CHSJ. Don't miss this all-time favourite for young and old alike. Get the popcorn, gather round, and click your heels three times. You're never too old to dream of somewhere over the rainbow.

"I know I got carried away." She took his silence as agreement. What she expected was something like, "Mercy, we can't have this sort of self-indulgence. This is the real world, not a creative-writing class." Instead, he smiled.

"You're doing fine. Ready to move up a notch?" He leaned back in his chair.

"Yes!" she squealed, her entire torso nodding in agreement. Just in time, she remembered Eunice's advice to not appear too eager. "Well," she drawled coyly, leaning back herself. "I still have my clients…"

"Clients?"

"My housekeeping clients. It depends on how much time you're asking for," she continued, somewhat too expansively. "I didn't realize it would take so much time from my business to just write a few paragraphs."

"There's an old joke among writers, Mercy—goes something like 'this letter would have been shorter if I'd had more time.' See, writing is rewriting and revising and pruning. How to say so much with so little. But you're doing it."

This was all the encouragement Mercy needed to surge forward once more.

"Actually, Mr. Cogswell, I have what I think is a fantastic idea." She rummaged in her purse.

"You do?" he sat up in his chair, cupping his chin in his hands, covering his mouth.

Mercy bashed on. "Well, the *Odell Observer* has this women's page every Friday. It's okay. I mean, pretty standard stuff. Recipes, household tips, fashion, and well—this is almost the eighties, Mr. Cogswell. Where are the articles on daycare, affordable housing for single parents? I mean, how about a weekly section—not just a page—just for women called something catchy like 'Movers and Shakers.' You could profile successful, outstanding women in the community. Like Eunice McTavish! You could tackle a few issues more relevant to our everyday lives. You could review books there, too. It would be so inspirational to younger women and older women, too—women trying to do something with their lives." She finally took a breath.

Stirling Cogswell scratched his whiskerless cheek.

"By 'you,' you mean you?" His eyes twinkled.

Mercy bobbed her head and shrugged. "I see things sometimes," she admitted sheepishly. "I can see this. Eunice said I should run it by you. Here are my notes." Her hands were shaking. He took the notes, placing them to the side.

"Well, that's a great idea, but I had something a little less ambitious in mind for now. I've been in touch with a local animal protection agency and shelter. There's a need to have a weekly roundup of animal news." He was writing something down.

"Pardon me?"

"People love their pets. Stray dogs, cats, reported abuse, fines against those who have mistreated animals. That would be a popular column." He took off his glasses, rubbing the bridge of his nose, his flesh indented so deeply he might have been wearing nose plugs.

"Would it be by Mercy Beth Fanjoy?" she asked hopefully.

"You mean would you have a byline?"

She nodded.

"Well, it's really just information gathering. You'd be compiling, not really writing." He watched her closely.

"A compiler," she repeated. It reminded her of something to do with hemorrhoids. "I do love animals," she heard herself saying. "I had a dog when I was little but he ran away. I still dream about him. But now I don't have any pets, or know much about them. Not really."

"You don't have to be a cop to report on crime." He laughed gently.

Mercy imagined herself spending a day with a dog catcher, giving a riveting account of the capture and imprisonment of a dog: *Ain't nothing but a pound dog.*

"So you're throwing me to the dogs," she said.

He chuckled. When Stirling Cogswell laughed, his upper lip stuck on his overbite.

"Are you interested?" he repeated.

Mercy nodded.

He handed her the piece of paper he'd written on. "Call this number. Ask for Noah Perley. Tell him Cogswell sent you."

"Okay. Thanks." Mercy started to leave.

"Mercy?"

"Yes?"

"Didn't you forget something?"

She looked around her chair. "I don't think so. I only had my purse."

"Money?" He was putting her notes in a file folder.

"Pardon?"

"You didn't ask about money." He stood, towering over her.

Mercy was mortified. "Remember, negotiate," Eunice had warned her. "Say it, Mercy—*knee-gooo-she-ate*. And ask for more than he offers."

"Right. Money. Well—"

He named an hourly figure, up a notch, just barely, from the TV guide.

She asked for fifty more cents.

"Sure. And see how it goes with your other work—if it's too time-consuming, we'll talk. Get back to me in a few weeks, anyhow."

"Okay," she said. "Thanks, sir."

"Call me Cogswell. 'Movers and Shakers,' eh? It's a good idea."

Mercy walked away, the praise making her want to burst into song.

Stella looked at her as she left. "Are you okay?"

"Never better!" Mercy gushed.

As planned, she met Cogswell after one or two "Animal Watch" items. Mercy was surprised when the swollen bone where his eyebrow must once have been began jumping slightly, and he said, "Would you like some more work?"

She took a deep breath. "Pardon?"

At this, Cogswell reached under a pile on his desk and produced a bundle of books. "We get these freebies from publishers and we've got no one to review them. You've got a little one, yes?"

"Yes, Belle. That's her name," Mercy said proudly, digging in her wallet for a photo.

Cogswell took the photo and nodded. "She doesn't look like you."

Mercy nodded. "Her father's daughter. Except he's not around."

Cogswell ignored this personal revelation. "And you read to her?"

"Night and day. She loves books."

"Well, review the ones you want and you can keep the books too."

"A reviewer? Me? Mr. Cogswell, I don't have more than my high school education. Shouldn't a reviewer—"

"Have an opinion and know why they think what they do, but never forget that it is only their opinion and point of view and not *the* truth. Someone who keeps asking, What is excellence?" He'd stood and turned his back to her, searching his bookshelf, still talking. "Eventually, Mercy, you should check out university, but at this point, here's all you need to begin." He placed another book in her lap. It was his own dog-eared copy of Strunk's *Elements of Style*. "Never stop referring to it, no matter how many degrees you put behind your name. That is, if you want to stay in the biz."

"The biz! I am breaking into the biz!" she announced an hour later to Eunice, hugging her in gratitude. She phoned Yvette Leblanc, her employment counsellor. Yvette also had a line on a job as assistant sales manager at Occasionally Yours, the stationery and office supply store. Yvette wondered if she could handle it all. "Ab-so-fucking-lutely!" Mercy shouted to the ceiling after she hung up the phone.

At present, with a more quiet kind of confidence, the kind she'd long admired in Eunice McTavish, Mercy finished composing two emails. One went to her secret fan and loyal admirer, and another one to another publisher about "Healer, Hooker, Homeless: Three Women of Old." She'd reinserted number three back onto her list. She'd show Ms. Hawkes. Eunice too, for that matter. True, her so-called career ladder was more like a shaky rope ladder, but she'd learned a little about persistence.

"Onward!" she shouted as she punched the send button. In the kitchen, Buddha-Belly rolled his stone-blue eyes skyward.

"Ho!" he replied.

Three dead women live in my attic.

It was the end of a very long day when Eunice McTavish came out of her study and poured herself a glass of wine. The envelope that Mercy had dropped when she huffed off glared at her from the granite countertop. Eunice considered phoning Mercy to let her know she'd left the envelope behind, but for now, well, it flopped open, a gaping invitation. It was too tempting, even for the ever honest, earnest Eunice. She reread once again:

Dear Ms. Hawkes:
Three dead women live in my attic. I'd like to let them loose. Enclosed is a proposal for a book tentatively titled, "Healer, Hooker, Homeless: Three Women of Old." I envision a kind of fictionalized biography of three incredible women—two from the east coast of Canada and one from the Yukon/Alaska. These women have fired my imagination and creative juices. The work is based on fascinating, trailblazing, historical women whose stories have not been told.
Let me introduce them to you and see if you find their lives as intriguing as I do.

Marie Henriette Lejeune Briande Ross, or Granny Ross, as she was fondly called, was reportedly born in France in 1743 and sailed to the New World, arriving in Louisbourg after losing both a child and a husband. She married again and was widowed once more. Eventually she would marry a Scottish man, James Ross, and settle near Bras d'Or, in Cape Breton.

She became the local midwife and healer, and saved an entire community from smallpox by vaccination. "She used serum brought from France in a small, glass vial, and she renewed her supply with serum from the sores of the ill," wrote Elva Jackson in an article for the Cape Breton Post *in 1956.*

Gregoria Remona Antonia was a vivandière on the battlefields when Napoleon and Wellington fought for supremacy. When she was taken prisoner at one of the sieges, the duke befriended her and had her married and sent to the remote Annapolis Royal. She was a popular hostess and raconteur, wore turbans, befriended natives, raised poodles.

Kate was born in a village located on the Athabasca Trail, to a Tagish mother and Tglit father. As was the custom, her marriage was arranged. Her first husband died and in 1886, she married his brother, prospector and trader George Cormack, becoming Kate Cormack. She had a daughter named Graphie Grace. They travelled to the Forty Mile area and with Kate's skill and knowledge of the wilderness, they lived off the land.

Kate sewed and sold mukluks (kamiks) and mittens to other miners. Eventually, her brother Skookum Jim and another man, the infamous Dawson Charlie, found them and joined their camp. In 1898, in Rabbit Creek, they discovered gold. The men staked claims and took out hundreds of thousands of dollars, while Kate Cormack cooked, chewed caribou skin, sewed their clothing, and kept camp.

A move south to Seattle proved disastrous. Kate was overwhelmed by the city and missed the land. One source says she was found drunk on the streets and thrown in jail. Eventually divorced by George Cormack and abandoned by Graphie Grace, Kate Cormack returned home penniless. She died in the influenza epidemic of 1920.

Ms. Hawkes, I am a journalist for the Odell Observer *and have received numerous accolades for my work.*

Is there a convenient time I can call to discuss the possibility of working with you, before I approach an agent? I am a great admirer of your editorial work and the quality of books your press has produced in recent years—as you might know, from my reviews.

All best,
Mercy Beth Fanjoy

Eunice sighed and shovelled the papers back into the envelope. Poor Mercy, whose reach seemed to forever exceed her grasp. How would she ever find rest in that tangled head of hers? Just then, Gerald burst in the door, smelling of wet leaves and earth and like a man who knew his way around glaciers and rocks. Eunice forgot about Mercy Beth Fanjoy entirely and went to greet her husband with full warm lips and guiltless, naked glee.

If a person were to commit the act of adultery in the small city of Odell, it would be as desperate and passionate, as sweaty and crotch-tingling, as unbearably pleasurable as the pulsating cadence of a Leonard Cohen song or the sultry streets of New York in summer. Clandestine rendezvous in the Odell Hotel could be every bit as steamy and experimental between two plain-faced octogenarian lumpen-bodied souls as among those who were young and in their prime or those exquisitely small-jawed, thin-wristed women and tapered-fingered men wearing matching windbreakers, creased trousers, and genuine leather deck shoes in complementary colours.

Many a furtive Odellian lover could put to shame those airbrushed, spray-tanned actors with bad hair and giant mango breasts, penises hard as stalagmites, grunting with fake lust and performing tongue-defying, finger-fluttering acrobatic acts before the cameras. Not that Mercy Beth Fanjoy had ever watched anything close to a pornographic movie, except by mistake, that once, pressing the wrong button on the remote in a hotel room. Still, Mercy knew Odell had its fair share of philandering husbands and wives mixed in with the rarer breed of the steadfast and true. If anything, she felt compassion for the transgressors. She often pondered how it was, in a city the size of Odell, almost as transparent and quiet as a snow globe, they managed not to get caught.

Midnight found Mercy listening to the best of Leonard Cohen and contemplating sex. The subject of sex. The possibility of sex. The impossibility of sex. The distant memory of sex. She was ready to tackle item number four: *Destroy incriminating evidence (RP letters)*. She started a fire. She would read each letter one last time, tear them up, burn them all, forget the man, erase the history.

Dr. Raymond Piper was a small, bearded, bespectacled man. His students referred to him as Professor Pepe Pee-u, because of the crescent moons of perspiration that rimmed the armpits of his beige dress shirts. For the problem, he took baths in Epsom salts, tried acupuncture, shaved his armpits—his wife's suggestion—and received mail-ordered heavy-duty only-for-men roll-on deodorant. For the anxiety created by the problem, he meditated, swallowed pills, and drank far too much, especially when he went out of town.

He did not like travelling, he told his wife and others. It was hectic and exhausting on the road. But since the publication of his first book of poetry, *Home of the Beaver*, its subsequent short-listing for major awards, its positive reviews in the *Post*, *Globe and Mail*, and *Winnipeg Free Press*, he had new opportunities to embrace. He was in demand. He was being asked to do readings at universities on a fairly regular basis.

Normally, he taught The Poetry of William Blake, Myth and Symbolism, and The Bible as Literature. Dr. Piper studied under the famous professor and literary critic Dr.

Northrop Frye. This meant at one time he lived in Toronto—
"a necessary evil." Yes, he preferred small towns and staying
close to home, really, but an audience of listeners, however
small, was simply too hard for Dr. Piper to resist. It was such
an invitation that lured him to Mercy Beth Fanjoy's home-
town and the campus of Odell University. At the time, Mercy
was a part-time student on a long-term plan. The completion
of her degree was still years away.

Piper arrived in Odell one Friday afternoon and checked
into the Odell Hotel. He settled into his room, poured a gin
and tonic, and began to look over his notes.

"The selection of poems for a reading is often an organic process, and sometimes I will even change a poem if
the spirit of the moment moves me thus." That is how he
would begin. It was no lie. He still loved running his fingers
down the table of contents. The book was divided into nine
sections.

Land of the Silver Birch
Home of the Beaver
Where Still the Mighty Moose
Wanders at Will
Blue Lake and Rocky Shore
I Will Return Once More
Boom Diddy I Da
Boom Diddy I DA
Boo oo ooom!

"The book is really a lament," he would begin, "a lament
for the deterioration and erosion of the human imagination
and spirit. The external world is but a manifestation of our

internal life or lack thereof. So yes—pollution, toxic waste, land mines, terrorism, and the annihilation of the planet are recurring themes. But so, of course, is the quicksilver chance for redemption."

He sipped his gin. He read his favourite poem lugubriously, testing out various inflections of voice, looking at himself in the mirror.

That same day Mercy attended classes, finished an essay, shopped for groceries, plucked her eyebrows, cooked up a pot of spaghetti, washed and dried and folded three loads of laundry, dashed off a first draft of a "Mercy's Musings" column, and fulfilled her obligation as Tuesday's Storyteller at Thumbelina's Tots 'n' Toddlers Day Care. All this before, during, and after an entire house and toilet bowl cleaning at Mrs. McGrueter's. By evening she was exhausted. The last thing, the very last thing she wanted to do, was go anywhere or have to think about anything.

As fate—or was it destiny?—would have it, her mother phoned at suppertime offering to take Belle overnight, something she did on a regular basis, and this night Mercy accepted eagerly. She planned on sinking into a luxurious bath and studying. At seven o'clock she opened *The Canterbury Tales* and a sheet of loose-leaf, with the slow grace of a paper airplane, glided to the floor. It was a handwritten note from Dr. Wyndham, the head of the English department, her Chaucer and Shakespeare professor.

Mercy, I think you would enjoy this poet. Hope you can come.

Mercy had already read the notice in the student lounge. There was also a picture of The Distinguished Visiting Poet.

Dr. Piper's unexceptional face was pinched, sad, closed.

Mercy would never know why, worn out as she was, already cosied up in her flannel pajamas, she'd changed her mind.

Mercy had never been to a poetry reading before, and this was somewhat of a problem. She wasn't sure what to wear. She chose a burnt-orange sweatshirt, jeans, and turquoise sneakers. As she entered the theatre she noticed everyone was in black. Mercy was a walking, talking comic book, a garish advertisement for unfashionable mature students.

"Dr. Piper is of Irish descent," said the leaflet she was handed at the door. He lived and taught in Antigonish. He had a wife and two children. His book sold for seven dollars and sixty-nine cents. He also had a Ph.D. His thesis, on the illuminated works of William Blake, had been entitled, "Urizen's Endless Horizons."

Irish! Mercy Beth hoped she might hear the echoes of Yeats, perhaps Joycean rhythms, or enter Beckett's landscape, one she still could not fully understand but loved nonetheless. She was quickly disillusioned. She was not transported. Dr. Piper took more time explaining his poems than reading them. There were a lot of references to both male and female body parts. Not aching loins exactly, more like: "Your hand cups my scrotum/my tongue licks your breast/A taste of rhubarb." Rhubarb? Was he licking a goat's tit? she laughed silently. This was art? She snorted. Well, maybe, when it all came down to it, it *was* simply a matter of taste, as Cogswell had said once.

Like rhubarb.

Mercy suddenly laughed out loud, hyena style. No one else did. They were looking at the podium with solemn faces, heads all nodding. Fascinated. Riveted, as if to say, ah, yes, the rhubarb flesh of breasts. Mercy smothered her laughter by breathing through flared nostrils and widening her eyes— a trick learned in grade school. She was eager to be a good liberal arts student, to remain open, to get past her own biases and presuppositions, as her philosophy professor had urged of them all. So she sat there and thought, "Well, it is symbolism, after all. It's that yin/yang, female/male, anima stuff that Jung was on about."

Anima. But that word made her think of enemas. She free-associated far too easily. She giggled again and tried to remain attentive by guessing what themes were underlying it all. Fecundity, she thought, and fertility—maybe he is really trying to talk about the cross-pollination of souls, and sex is but a metaphor. She simmered down and began to take notes. It was after the reading, with Dr. Wyndham fielding questions, that Mercy's lack of erudition became painfully apparent.

First, everyone was talking a language she did not understand. Deconstruction was over her head. Mercy often wondered if she would ever obtain that coveted English degree.

"Yes, that is correct," Dr. Piper nodded in response to some gobbledygook question. "It's not what I've said; it's what I haven't said."

"Are you deliberately working with absence?"

It was the star graduate student asking, his eyebrows jumping and twitching, pleating his never-ending forehead, which Mercy Beth knew was a physical attribute indicating a mammal of higher intelligence.

"What didn't you say?" she muttered. The person next to her appreciated the sarcasm and laughed.

"Excuse me?" Dr. Piper looked at Mercy Beth. "You in

the orange? Did you have something to say?" Everyone looked then, some straining their necks, some hoping, perhaps, there was an upstart, or as she most feared, they were all detecting a fraud in their midst.

"No," she stammered. "I mean, nothing that hasn't been said."

"Clever," he replied, much to her alarm. Even worse, some were smiling at her appreciatively, as if her cleverness were profound. Mercy Beth smiled back. "Heidegger's 'nothing,' you mean?" Piper continued. Mercy Beth's smile stuck as if her lips were Varathaned shut. They were all waiting for her response.

"Heidi who?" she finally mumbled, imagining a crackle sound of skin as her lips broke free of their seal.

There was a long silence then a muffled giggle, an embarrassed cough.

Another hand shot up. Mercy was saved.

"Which poets do you admire?" Finally, a question she could understand. Again Dr. Piper disappointed her.

"None," he replied smugly. "Poets do not want to be admired. The true poets seek only to create and in so doing seek truth and beauty."

I have yet to see a beautiful scrotum, Mercy Beth thought. Even the word was ugly.

"So you have no influences you draw upon?"

"Now that is quite different. Certainly. From Homer to Dante, from Chaucer to Shakespeare, from Blake, the harbinger of the Romantics, to Rilke, Larkin, and of course, Neruda."

Mercy Beth wrote down in her notebook: *Who is Neruda? A Mexican?* She pictured margaritas and poets in sombreros, an outdoor old-style poetry reading. Lanterns blinking on and off. Guacamole. Ceviche. Her stomach growled. Folks glanced her way and shifted in their seats.

"But you, you are English students. If there is one aspiring poet amongst you I say this, draw on what is excellence, but above all else create your own mythology or be enslaved by another man's."

"Or woman's?" Mercy Beth yelled it out.

"You again?" his mouth puckered up. His lips disappeared in the bush of his beard.

"Yes," she said. "And I do have a question now."

He shuffled his papers and glanced at his watch. "Yes?"

"How would you feel if someone used a line from your writing and didn't give credit where credit was due?"

"Why, I guess I would consider myself plagiarized."

"So why didn't you give Blake credit when you used that line about creating your own mythology?"

A distinct gasp came from Wyndham, and others, eager for confrontation, looked at Dr. Raymond Piper accusingly.

"Well, he's dead, I suppose. But you're right. That's Blake. Sometimes you just forget."

Dr. Wyndham, who had appeared pleased when he first saw Mercy in the audience, now looked at her as if she were a Komodo dragon. He jumped up.

"One more question?" he blared into the awkward silence.

"Yes, good. Samantha!" he pointed.

"I have two. Can you make a living as a poet, and are you working on anything new?" Samantha was the editor of the student newspaper.

"Number two first. Yes, I'm currently working on a new collection of poems entitled, 'The Anguish of Angels in Antigonish.' As for making a living—actually, no! Which is why I teach and have to give these readings. A hard way to make a living, but, I hasten to add, a wondrous way to make a life."

Mercy shivered with pleasure at the sentence, and clapped with the rest of them. It wasn't every day you met a man who used the word "wondrous." There was a wine and cheese reception after in the English lounge, compliments of the Arts Council.

"Good use of taxpayers' money, I'd say," said Dr. Wyndham, raising his glass in a toast.

In the way women love kind, wise, asexual men, Mercy loved Dr. Wyndham. He had a wicked sense of humour and often used Huey, Dewey, and Louie, his three favourite cartoon characters, to make certain literary points in class. Dr. Wyndham whispered to her, "Good questions out there!" But he tried to make things right with Dr. Piper by introducing them formally.

"Mercy Beth is one of our mature students."

"Is that so?" asked Dr. Piper. "It doesn't show. I mean, you'd never know. What I mean is, you don't look older. What year?"

His face was a kaleidoscope, thought Mercy, his expressions shifting, rearranging, shifting again. It was hard to tell whether or not he had just insulted her.

"Second. Sort of. But I am considerably older than most of my classmates." She towered over him. David and Goliath.

"Considerably taller, too," he said. His laugh was deep and resonant. Pleasant.

"Well, you're not as shortsighted as I thought," she quipped. Her voice was tinkly. Peanut brittle.

"With a name like Mercy, why ever are you so hostile?" He looked past her at another student, as if he wanted to get away.

"Hostile?" She decided she did not like him then but smiled again, hoping to mask her true feelings about the pomposity of persons who used phrases like "why ever."

"Defensive, then. You seemed so confrontational out there. I was getting uneasy." He accepted a glass of wine from Wyndham and re-met her eyes.

"I just don't get it sometimes," Mercy sighed. "I mean, what a game, right? And only those who have some special access code get to play. It's a monopoly of knowledge."

"Who are *you* plagiarizing now?" He was focused on Mercy's breasts.

"Touché. I forget the author. I'm reading a book on literary criticism by a socialist." She sipped her wine.

"Oh, dear. Eagleton? But you make a good point. You are talking of course about intellectual elitism." He reached for a cracker.

"I am? I mean, I am. Yes." Mercy watched as his cracker disappeared, swallowed in a gulp. His thick pinkish lips, hidden by his beard, had made a brief appearance.

"I don't want to quibble with you. But who can analyze a Harlequin romance? Who wants to write one, for that matter?" He talked as he chewed, his mouthful of crackers, muffling his words.

"I would if I could," Mercy shot back, not following his logic. "I've got a daughter to feed."

"Have you seen the film *Educating Rita*?" Piper asked then, indulgently. "It's British. It's about a woman sort of like you, I wager, back to school after the school of hard knocks."

"And an alcoholic English professor with a board up his arse?" she retorted, edging away. Piper gaped. "No, I haven't."

Mercy went to eat a devilled egg. Piper was swarmed by a group of youngish bohemian types wearing their black and holding out pens and books for signatures. None of them appeared to have hands, their sweater sleeves pulled over their knuckles—like they were all members of a sock puppeteer troupe. Mercy would never understand fashion.

Forty-five minutes later, as Mercy was leaving, Dr. Piper rushed over to her, extending his hand, and said, "A pleasure." Then, as he shook her hand, he squeezed it several times. "Room 222," he whispered.

"Yes, I liked that book. I forget the author," she said.

"No!" he hissed. Then winked. "Not *Catch 22*. Room 222. At the Odell Hotel. If you want."

Mercy left in a hurry, with one arm through her coat sleeve, her face the colour of boiled beets. The nerve of that scrotum face, she bristled.

In the blue shadows of room 222 of the Odell Hotel, just a few hours after the poetry reading, Mercy Beth Fanjoy and Dr. Raymond Piper wound around each other, arms, legs, sheets, bedspread, socks, undergarments, and radio alarm clock. Clockwise. Counterclockwise. A fast and furious spinning.

Mercy thought of the huge dryer at the Spin and Grin Laundromat on fast-forward tumble. Then she thought the thought of thinking that thought. No matter what, there was no escaping the laundry.

Dr. Piper, it turned out, had an appetite for all that *was* there. He circled and spiralled above her like some kamikaze pilot, nose-diving into her navel and fleshiest parts, as if he wanted to suffocate himself. It turned out she needn't have worried about her lack of sexual prowess.

After an hour or so, she discovered a need to feel that pushed every thought, even the laundry, far from her mind. Her body did have a mind of its own. Now a lick here, now a kiss there, it arched itself up and forward, thrust itself back and twisted. She was...Nadia Comaneci! She was in a corner of the room looking down at herself, marvelling at her newfound athleticism. She was shocked if not delighted to discover she was something of a porn star in hiding.

Lust was a little like nibbling chocolate, she thought; you wanted more until the craving was satisfied. Once started there was no stopping it. The salty taste of her own sweat aroused her. The Ferris wheel kept spinning up, up, up and finally over the top! And came gently rocking to a slow, shuddering halt.

When the good doctor fell asleep beside her, his penis limp and shrivelled on his inner thigh like one of Belle's party balloons, she tiptoed to the bathroom. Her eyes were the same eyes that had looked at her a few hours back, though now overly bright. But the woman who looked back at her smiled and admired the full length and contours of her Amazon body in the mirror. "Friend," she said to her reflection. She gave herself thumbs up, washing between her legs while humming "Land of the Silver Birch, Home of the Beaver."

She walked home, a yawning cat, drifting in the early light of morning, stopping once in front of the statue of Robbie Burns. In the muted grey and neon pink of shadows reflecting off River St. John, she was sure the poet winked at her.

Scullers in the river appeared from nowhere, bronze silhouettes against the sun. So it was on the green, near the Christ Church Cathedral where all things holy were pronounced, Mercy experienced her first aftershock full-bodied orgasm.

Belle was still at her grandmother's. This meant Mercy had a Saturday morning stretching out before her. She put on a faded denim XX-large shirt and men's work socks. She sang with Leonard Cohen as she brewed Melitta drip coffee and made herself a grilled-cheese sandwich. Then, mummy-wrapping an afghan around herself, she settled on the sofa. The book fell out of her hands as she drifted into the kind of sleep only the deeply satisfied can have.

D. H. Lawrence was right, after all. This was her last thought before she faded finally: It wasn't hyperbole—sex really was slippery business.

The affair lasted four years, all told. Mostly, it was long passionate letters filled with the poetry of William Blake, but almost every other month Dr. Piper made the five-hour trek to Odell. A few times they'd risked it and met in Halifax. They even went out in public once, for supper, and though he was nervous the whole time, afraid of bumping into someone he knew, Mercy spent the evening pretending she was part of a couple, that she had a life she shared, that she was a soulmate to a man who told her if she were his wife, he knew that she would be willing to go into the garden with him naked and talk to the angels.

And she would have. Oh, she would have. Mercy Beth had truly loved Dr. Raymond Piper. At least, she loved imagining she was being truly loved.

It ended because of slingback shoes.

As was their usual routine, Dr. Piper phoned a day ahead so she could cancel her next day's plans and get a babysitter. Mercy was just getting out of the tub when he'd called, hissing into the phone.

"Sweet Mercy"—that is what he always called her— "change of plans, you can't come tonight. My wife paid me a surprise visit. She said she wanted to hear me read, it had been so long. I don't know…I think she might…suspect. Later."

The line went dead. Perhaps Mona was in the shower after having had sex with her husband. Or preparing to.

Mercy was livid.

That night she took great pains with her appearance: a long grey tweed skirt that flattered her hips, a heather green sweater. Black leather boots. With heels. She would show up just to make him suffer, just to sneak a peek at THE WIFE who may or may not have sensed something was up in Odell besides research on the United Empire Loyalists.

Except Mercy didn't make it to the reading. As she turned down the hallway towards the lecture theatre, Dr. Wyndham came out of the English lounge, his arm protectively around Dr. Piper on one side and Mona Piper on the other. Mona Piper had on slingback shoes. She wobbled when she walked, her feet spilling over the shoes, ankles rolling outwards slightly. She waddled. She reminded Mercy of Belle's little Weeble people. *Weebles wobble but they don't fall down,* the television jingle promised. Only Mona Piper looked as if she might. Mercy wondered why Raymond had never mentioned his wife's size.

Bare feet in slingback shoes in the winter. It was the sight of her heels—so bare, so inappropriate, that did it. The woman became a real person to Mercy then, and she realized in that split second she would never be able to enjoy Piper guilt-free again. She ended the affair.

Piper sent her a few sad missives. *Sooner murder an infant in its cradle than nurse unacted desire.* Mercy had that one in her quotebook notebook under "extreme quotes"—ones she did not agree with mostly. In this context, the quote even seemed menacing. Dr. Piper also called her three times, so heartbroken that once she almost caved in and ran to the hotel. The sound of his voice tested Mercy's resolve. But she closed her eyes and saw Mona Piper's wobbly walk and navy blue trench coat, and she even added dandruff like a rim of salt around the collar. The poor woman—psoriasis on top of everything else! When she really felt her resolve weakening, she pretended she was a member of the R.A.N.T.S. and used the solidarity argument. *Mercy, you simply cannot betray a sister—no, nay, never—not if you are going to be a good feminist.* But she had never wanted to be. She was a complacent underdogmatist. Still, the little blame game, the self-imposed, self-righteous scolding seemed to work. Mercy stayed away from Raymond Piper.

Mercy saw Piper once, many years later, in Halifax. Lulu wanted to do some early Christmas shopping and there was a reading and book signing. Jacinthe Irvine, one of Mercy's favourite authors, was appearing in the ballroom of the Lord Nelson Hotel. Lulu bought tickets as a birthday present for Mercy and booked the room. They shopped all day, barely making it to the reading on time. As tired as she was, Mercy Beth was elated to be seeing Jacinthe Irvine in person.

As always, Mercy was hungry for words, especially words that were not her own. Words that made meaning and created beauty; beautiful words that painted worlds where the landscape was a character you fell in love with and sank into, as if in a dream; words that cast a spell, and made her think, always, of her father, though she could not ever define why. Words that were an infusion of some sort.

The bookstore owners responsible for organizing the event were a couple named Jim and Melly York. Melly was a woman with wild auburn hair she wore in a thousand-petal lotus ponytail sprouting from the top of her head. She sported bright red, cat-eye glasses and burgundy lips that matched the cover of Jacinthe Irvine's latest book. Melly was holding it up as if it were a Bible and giving an eloquent introduction.

"Winner of the Ordre des Lettres in France..." and the list of accolades went on. But then, Melly stopped reading. Her voice got wavy with genuine emotion. She clutched her heart and looked skywards and said, "That aside, Jacinthe is simply a writer who transports us..."

"Yes!" shouted Mercy. Lulu jabbed her in the ribs. Luckily, her shout was drowned out by applause. Porcelain-skinned, ruby-lipped Jacinthe glided to the podium. She smiled and made a down-to-earth joke about how she was glad her fiction was transporting because transportation was so difficult that evening.

"So clever!" murmured Mercy. Jacinthe thanked them all for showing up. "And gracious, too." Mercy always felt that a writer should feel indebted to readers. As the reading began, Mercy ascended to heaven.

Afterwards, she stood in line for almost an hour. Her intention was to get her collection of Jacinthe Irvine books personally signed. Lulu waited patiently for a while then finally hand signalled she would be waiting back in their room. The closer Mercy got to the front of the line, the more her heart beat and the more her hands trembled.

"Would she mind signing them all?" she asked Melly. Besides the whole collection, Mercy had purchased three copies of the newest one. "I'll make sure she does," said Melly, and reached out, hugging her in, as if inside a very special circle. Mercy was touched by this touch and this woman's obvious empathy with how she must be feeling.

"Jacinthe, we have a real fan here," chirped Melly in her nightingale voice. Mercy nodded. Jacinthe smiled. Up close, she was even more ethereal. Mercy was so nervous she actually began a juggle with her armload of books. One popped into the air and dropped to the floor with a bang. Jacinthe blinked and waited. Mercy could have died. She almost cried out: Forgive me! I am nothing but a flustered, bungling idiot.

Finally, with Melly's help, she put a book on the table.

"Whom do I make them out to?" Jacinthe asked.

"All of them are mine except for two, and you just have to sign your name to those." Mercy's voice crackled like wrapping paper.

"Your name?" asked Jacinthe.

And so patient, thought Mercy, wondering if she should tell her she kept her books beneath her bed alongside Alice Munro's.

"Oh. Right. Mercy."

Jacinthe's hand stopped in mid-air. "Mercy?"

"Yes. Well Mercy Beth, really. Mercy for short."

Was it her imagination or did Jacinthe Irvine's eyes gaze deeply into hers, Mercy wondered. "As in lord have...?" asked Jacinthe.

"Yes, as in Christ have...etc., etc.," nodded Mercy, warming up. "Have Mercy upon us! Imagine how the boys used to tease me in high school."

Jacinthe Irvine giggled like they were back in high school. *To Mercy, keep on! Jacinthe Irvine.*

"I'd like to write a book," Mercy started in.

"Next!" said Melly, kindly. But still, Mercy had overstepped herself. She had taken up enough time.

"Thank you for your words!" she said, too loud, too grateful, as Melly steered her away. Mercy felt ridiculous. She hoped Jacinthe Irvine had not heard her, even though the whole lineup had.

Mercy hurried back to the fifth floor of the Lord Nelson,

woke Lulu up, and showed her the autograph and read her a paragraph from the new book.

"Nice. I'm hungry," said Lulu, yawning, as if suddenly bored. They did not share the same taste in books.

"I know just the place. Hurry up, then. Get dressed." Mercy smiled, continuing to read Irvine aloud as Lulu showered.

The Birmingham Bar and Grill on Spring Garden Road was perfect for a late supper. They ordered martinis and relaxed in the dim blue room. A pianist and saxophonist played light jazz.

"This is why I sometimes want to live in a bigger city," said Mercy. "Restaurants with live music."

"Mercy, we have live music in Odell too! You just never go out. The Odell Blues Band is every bit as a good as any blues band anywhere. You really have got to get out more."

"I know. I know." Mercy looked around the restaurant and sighed. Then, she spotted him.

"Oh my God, Lulu. It's him."

"Him?"

"Dr. Piper!" Lulu's gaze followed her friend's head tilt.

"Don't look obvious. To the left," she hissed. "Red sweater."

"Really?" Lulu seemed unimpressed.

"Yes," nodded Mercy. "I know. You are wondering how that wee leprechaun was the object of your best friend's only true love and passion, aren't you?"

Lulu covered her mouth. "Well, he's not the kamikaze pilot type you led me to believe."

"Oh my God," said Mercy again. "He was probably at the reading!" As Mercy remembered, however, Piper was a man almost viciously jealous of successful, attractive women writers.

"Are you going to at least say hi?" asked Lulu.

"God no. Let's leave." Mercy grabbed her purse.

"Why should we? No way." Lulu shook her head and clinked Mercy's glass. "Cheers."

Lulu was right, thought Mercy. There he was, with the secretary from the English Department from another university, she would find out later. There he was, in the same restaurant on the same Spring Garden Road in the same city where they had once dined. It was some weird Divine Calendar Time Warp. The man was brash. And so redundant.

"You are so right, Lulu. In fact—" Mercy stood up.

"Mercy what are you—" Lulu watched, mortified, as her best friend, who could be an imposing woman, moved with purpose across the room to Piper's table. The table happened to be directly in front of the stage and in everyone's line of vision. The pianist was singing his heart out in a duet with a woman who'd just joined him—a good imitation of Ray Charles and Bonnie Raitt singing "Do I Ever Cross Your Mind?"

For not the first time in Mercy's life, the perfect soundtrack appeared at the most synchronistic of times.

Piper rose to his feet and thrust out his arm, as if it were a sword, and shook her hand, pumping it up and down with enthusiasm. "Have we met before?" The secretary was scarlet-faced. Mercy frowned.

"Not exactly. I once went to a lecture you gave when I was in university. It made quite an impression on me."

"Thank you." Piper's eyebrows were like black pipe cleaners jumping. He was scratching his beard and sucking in his lower lip with his upper row of teeth.

"And I have a question for you." Mercy was enjoying his discomfort.

"Yes?" Now Piper's voice sounded like an apologetic child's.

"What would make William Blake cry?" It was something she had always wanted to ask him.

"Excuse me?"

"No, there is no excuse. But I hope you figure it out." She then took a water glass from the table, took a sip, and ever so lugubriously poured it into his lap.

Mercy and Lulu left the restaurant on cue, as the last line of the song trailed off. Lulu was still laughing when they took the elevator back up to their room. There they were, doubled over laughing, banging against the walls of the elevator in the Lord Nelson Hotel, gasping for air, singing to one another, "Do I Ever Cross Your Mind?" It was the last really good belly laugh they'd have together for a while.

Some who knew her well said it was shortly after that trip to Halifax that Mercy Beth Fanjoy had a borderline break-down. Most thought it was about Belle. Stress could be cumulative; maybe those years of Belle's various issues had simply caught up with her. Whatever the cause, it was evident she was not herself for the better part of a year. Dr. Wiggins suggested medication for depression, but Mercy talked it over with Ann the pharmacist, because "pharmacists, as everyone knows, are more informed about drugs than any doctor." (My Darling Drug Dealer! "Mercy's Musings," *OO*, Sept. 01.) She decided not to experiment. Instead, she smoked more.

If she had not had work she loved, who knows what may have happened?

Actually, Lulu Lutes and Hap Kunkle had a pretty good idea.

On a Sunday in mid-winter, a thick blue greyness covered the city, as if the sky sagged over their heads. This texture to the sky should have been a warning, but Odellians, in the midst of their Sunday rituals—going to church or nursing a hangover or walking the green or sweating at the gym—did not lift their eyes to the gently rolling hills on the other side of River St. John, let alone out to the horizon or up to the sky. The local weather station (inaccurately) reported possible flurries. Miniature cyclones of snow swirled along the streets of Odell. This all seemed benign, almost playful at first, flakes like a swarm of white butterflies herding together. Within an hour, dervish-spinning snow pellets were whipping into a monster cloud. It was a whiteout. A violent squall turned into a relentless blizzard. Odellians were blindsided by nature's frenzy. Power outages were reported along Electric Street and the entire downtown vicinity. Mercy lit a fire and began to drink. Irish cream. Brandy. Grappa. Crème de Menthe. Raspberry coolers.

At eight o'clock that evening, when repeated rings of the doorbell went unanswered, Lulu Lutes and Hap Kunkle, who had cross-country skied over, broke into Mercy's house, smashing the glass on the back door.

Mercy was sprawled on the sofa, covered in a Nova Scotia tartan blanket and bright green vomit. On her head was a toy tiara. Her socks, one green, one blue, were on her hands. A game of Scrabble was underway. The cat meowed as if to tell them to hurry.

"Hap! She's dead! She's drowned in her own puke. No. She's slit her wrists. There's blood!" screamed Lulu.

"She's passed out. It's just wine. Help me." They dragged one very drunk friend into the shower.

"Wwwo-wwo. Happy," were Mercy's first coherent words.

Hap left after she'd stopped vomiting and they'd sobered her up some. Lulu stayed the night, sitting on the edge of Mercy's bed, laying her hand on Mercy's forehead and patting her back. "Don't you ever goddamn go doing something so insane again," she scolded. As Mercy rambled on, Lulu, sometimes nodding to keep awake, wondered if

Mercy would ever stop. She was not able to answer when Mercy kept repeating, "You just don't know, won't ever know, I don't want you to know, really know, what it's like to feel so alone. I'm so lonely, Lulu. I'm so lonely I want to die. But Jacinthe-Irrrvine, remember. See here, she wrote 'Keep on.' Why did she say keep on? Why, Lulu? I miss Belle, Lulu. And look, inthisssone, Margaret Atwood she shhhhaid 'Don't let the bastards grind you down.' But I'm tired, Lou. I so f-f-f-uckin tired! I said the f-word! I must be d–runk. I sound like Teeny Gaudet."

In the morning, Mercy woke up and saw her friend slumped in the chair at the foot of her bed, her hands in mittens tucked under her armpits, her lips parted, snoring slightly. Lulu's ponytail was sticking out like a lopsided unicorn's horn. Mercy remembered Hap shaking her then, both of them towelling her off. They had seen her naked.

If only I could marry you two, she'd written to them a few weeks later. *Such unconditional love. You have it. You share it. You saved me. Mercy.* Hap called to tell her it was no big deal.

"Mercy, I noticed you needed a new tub."

"I do?"

"That jeezlzuz old porcelain thing's gotta go. I've got a great second-hand model of a whirlpool in the showroom. I can give you a great deal. Want it? Installation free if you make me some of your beef stew with dough boys."

So Mercy said yes, and had them over the day Hap, owner of Kunkle's Plumbing and Bathroom Supply Company, installed her whirlpool tub. Mercy was inspired to redecorate. As they were leaving, Lulu took her aside.

"Hap says Virginia Day says all women need is this tub, and they'll be fine forever."

Mercy was puzzled. "Really?"

Lulu coughed awkwardly. "The jets."

"The jets?"

Lulu looked down at the floor. "Mercy, do I have to say it?"

"Say what? OH!"

"Yes. O!"

Friends, indeed. The whirlpool jets brought her salubrious joy, as is usually the case when women of Mercy's predisposition learn they can pleasure themselves without guilt.

But even tonight, Mercy still had a great deal of guilt as well as shame over that black Sunday. "I'm just a little angry and sad," she told Goldbloom the therapist on one of her visits.

"Welcome to the club," was all he said, sniffing and fiddling with his suspenders. "You are not alone. What else?"

★★★

Sometimes in the dark, in the middle of the night, even now, when they could not sleep, Hap or Lulu whispered: Do you suppose Mercy is doing okay? Then, as if for the first time, Lulu would tell Hap how that night as they skied over, snow pelting them, almost suffocating them, she'd thought of those Canadian stories she'd read in university, like the one about the man who froze to death a few feet from the house, coming in from the barn. Then she would ask him to make love to her because she was glad she was alive. Hap complied. He was filled with gratitude and relief. He never admitted that he too had felt panicked in the storm and thought Mercy was dead. After all, things turned out fine.

After they made love, they often talked about the kids, sometimes argued about them, but not often. And more than once they said how great it was Mercy had agreed to see a therapist, finally.

Actually, Mercy only went a few times, telling everyone the therapist said it was no longer necessary because she had everything she needed inside of her to be okay. But the truth was, Mercy just did not have the time or inclination, the money or the stomach, to pick at old scabs. She read *O* magazine and listened to Oral Speakman instead.

Mercy reread her favourite part of Piper's last letter several times. He'd written to her after the encounter in the restaurant.

"Blake's tears?" he had scrawled, as if angry. "Well, Mercy, Blake cries for his mythical creatures Thel and Oothoon because of their corrupted desires. He cries for chimney sweeps and the sick rose, for all those oppressed, for the stale marriage, for lack of joy." Mercy pictured Piper resting his cheek against the paper, kissing it perhaps, thumping his head down on the antique mahogany desk. He was deeply remorseful, not seeing that forgiveness was an angel that danced on his head.

And what was he doing tonight? Perhaps, yes, after a night of vigorous lovemaking, Dr. Raymond Piper was being rushed to intensive care, a woman by his side, the woman he loved more than any other. Mona. He survived, and they lived a happily ever after. Well, Mercy sniffed, maybe they just lived.

The fire was out. The Piper letters were ashes. *Ashes to ashes*. Mercy reached in and rubbed her fingers in them, careful of the hot embers beneath. She applied ashes to her forehead, making a cross.

"Remember you are dust, and to dust you shall return."

Mercy made another cross—she crossed off number four on the list of things to do she'd left undone. Progress. Tonight, at least, she'd done what she'd intended.

As Mercy took a whirlpool bath and got ready for bed, in Antigonish, Dr. Raymond Piper woke up harder than a bed post, laughing, having dreamt of Mercy Fanjoy, a woman he'd long forgotten. He could not fully remember the dream but Mercy was there, bobbing up and down, like the Popeye inflatable punching bag he'd had as a kid. It was the two hundred and fiftieth anniversary of William Blake's death next year. He was organizing a conference. He wondered, were he to phone Mercy, even now, after all these years, would she agree to see him for old times' sake. Perhaps he would write a letter. Paraphrase, not plagiarize. Cohen, not Blake:

I've asked the angels and they've granted me the voice to sing. I beg for you, Mercy. I bargain with you. I offer what I can of love. We could begin again.

"Sweet, Sweet Mercy," he whispered out into the dark. His wife turned in her sleep and passed gas. "Sweet, sweet Mona," he said and hugged her close.

And Mercy? She continued talking to BB about metempsychosis, the transmigration of the souls, and reincarnation. She dug out an old essay on Book Seven of Virgil's *Aeneid* entitled "Towards an Understanding of the Underworld." For her essay, she'd even sketched a pictorial map. It was not comforting bedtime reading. Then she phoned her mother. "I want the note!" she said into her voice mail. "The note!" And slammed down the phone.

Cassandra Fanjoy-Rutherford shook Hubert awake. He checked the message and made them both a cup of tea. Cassandra reached inside her lingerie drawer where, stitched inside the cup of one of her bras, there was a small piece of paper. She ripped at the stitching with her teeth. She read the note. The note that never was. She hummed louder as she rocked back and forth. Hummed until she burst into song. "You've got to accentuate the positive and eliminate the negative..." Cassandra threaded a needle and tucked the note back inside the bra. She was grateful for her God-given talent, her gift in handiwork, the miracle of evenly spaced stitches. The activity was almost as soothing as prayer. Singing also brought her peace.

Mercy could neither sing nor sew. At the moment, she almost wished she could fall on her knees and pray or even vibrate like her mother did—anything to calm her nerves. Yet she felt that would be cheating somehow. To make a wish for her own health, suddenly, after a lifetime as an underdogmatist, would be hypocritical. The closest thing to divine guidance she'd ever known was whispering to the dead when she was a child, when she thought her father might hear. Now, she considered the possibility again, but it wasn't her father she wanted.

Three souls were locked in research boxes in her attic. The healer. The hooker. The homeless. The Godmothers. She would go now and make a plea to those intrepid spirits of the past. "It can't hurt," she muttered to BB, who shot her a detached look and refused to follow. She tucked Gladys' statue of Faustina under her arm and climbed the stairs to the attic. She lit a candle and with great ceremony placed Faustina on top of the boxes.

"Marie Henriette, Gregoria, Shaw T'laa," she whispered. "And Faustina, yes, you too. Any words of wisdom? How to keep a daughter from deserting you? How to get a man to say yes? How to shrink a tumour? How to find that note?" The candle flame flickered. Mercy beat a hasty retreat downstairs. The cat looked at her, bemused. Back in bed, Mercy pulled the covers up to her chin and finally drifted off.

When she was deep asleep, the Three Scary Godmothers drifted out of their cardboard coffins in the attic and danced around her bed, the cat the only witness. Mercy slept peacefully, curled, like a newborn woman.

Amazing. There I was. Among the one-breasted, two-breasted, flat-chested, Mae Wested. Feathered, leathered, tethered, gathered together. No one is alone. We are united. and... delicious? One woman just walked (jiggled?) by me in a bra of M&Ms. Is this chewable, wearable art? Will she have a melt down? The room is abuzz. An over-the-top giddiness. Maybe it's got to do with being allowed to be proud to be a woman and vulnerable at the same time. To be naked in public, and there's no beach nearby. Is there an exhibitionist in every woman?

—Mercy's Journal notes for feature article in *OO*.

Mercy wept. She reached for the knife. She let the tears drip down her cheek and off her chin. This was better than the Chinese-torture kind of tears, ones that dripped into her eardrum when she cried lying down, tears that leaked so far into her brain cavity she had to do an after-swimming head shake. Soon, very soon, what she liked and did not like would not matter.

Surely death did away with perpetual desire and hope, suffering and hangnails. Sniffling, she widened her red-rimmed eyes, put the knife down, and picked it up again. Mercy knew full well that if she didn't want tears, she could cut the onions under cold running water.

But she did want tears. Today, she did.

It seemed these last few days, she wanted to feel everything and sniff everything. Just an hour ago in her journal she'd written:

Friday. Morning. Heaven? Is there? If so, are there? Smells. Are there smells in heaven? If a soul goes to heaven, would it/her/whatever have memory/recollection? Forget the smell of onions, for example? Would the soul, the disembodied spirit, long for roast beef dinner with Yorkshire pudding and gravy? Why deny myself any longer? Go have Yorkshire pudding. Why does not smelling and tasting seem even more tragic to me than simply dying?

Mercy envisioned a fresco of her own Last Supper, of sitting around the table with her family, maybe Lulu and Hap and their children. There would be a lot of royal blue. Mercy would look pale, almost translucent, and, for the first time ever, thin. They would all be saying extremely nice things about her on the eve of her death.

"Mercy, is this useful thinking? Go to an oasis of calm." Buddha-Belly rubbed up against her shins. Mercy nodded, and concentrated on making soup.

The onions sizzled and turned a soft, transparent yellow—fine green veins appearing, striped and even. Art in a pan. The phone rang. She'd been waiting for the call and dreading it at the same time. But it wasn't Belle. It was the other call. *The Call.*

"Mercy? Doc Wiggins. Good news! Linda slipped you in for surgery at ten next Thursday…"

"Good news? This next Thursday? Dr. Wiggins, when it happens this fast in this health care system, it kind of makes a person nervous, you know?"

"The sooner, the better. Besides, I'm going on vacation in a bit, and I'd like to know before I go away."

"See? You're worried about me."

"Concerned is a better word. Yes. But mostly because I'm thinking about that list of yours. How's it going?"

"Slow but steady. Best get cracking now, though! And I'm not sleeping very much."

"Do you need anything to help you sleep?"

"No."

"Okay then, dear. Linda will call and give you instructions and details. I'll see you morning of."

Mercy swallowed back a sob. She wanted to be ten again with Walter Wiggins by her bedside, shaking his head saying, "You, young lady, have the worst case of chicken pox on top of measles I've ever seen."

Mercy pencilled the date in her daytimer as if it were any other item of her agenda in any other week. *Surgery. Be there.* The phone rang again.

"Mum! I am soooo sorry about not meeting you at the Coffee Mill. I totally forgot I promised Aislin I'd substitute teach her yoga class. I wish you'd get a cellphone. I could have called."

Mercy almost began to apologize until she realized once again Belle had managed to twist things around so Mercy was somehow to blame.

"But why not phone last night?" Mercy retorted, trying to sound merely curious, not agitated. "And did you get the envelope I lef—"

"I was helping decorate and we are still not finished. Is there something wrong with your phone? It's all staticky. So've you got your speech all ready? Sage thinks it is so awesome you've agreed to do this."

"What?"

"Your speech! Hello! For the Boobs & Baubles Ball. In a few hours? Hey, I actually said it! If I say it five times tonight after three glasses of wine, CHJO will donate one hundred dollars. A new contest this year. Maybe I'll enter."

Mercy clenched up. "Damn it!"

"What? Have you *forgotten*?"

"I have *not* forgotten. I just got home from seeing Doris."

Mercy looked at the knife in her hand. "How long does it have to be? I'm...I'm just in the middle of cutting."

"No big deal. Five–ten minutes."

That would mean at least three hours of writing—time Mercy did not have.

"I'll be ready."

"So you gonna wear a bra?"

"Belle!"

"Chick—aaaaan."

"Belle, I told you before, that is not an option."

"Chill out, I was only teasing. Sheesh."

"Well, it's not funny to me. You know I'm self-conscious."

"You could wear a bra on the outside of your clothes. A lot of women do."

"Belle!"

"Well, I can't help it. I think you could have decorated a bra with, like, Bic pens and stickies and called yourself 'Her Nibbs.' Get it? You're a writer, nib of pen? Her nibbles? Or feather quills. Nice! Or just a kind of female knight in armour, carrying a sword, pen is mightier than the sword—"

"Belle! Cut. Time out. Did you get the let—"

"Power, telephone, Mastercard—pardon?"

Mercy saw her daughter clearly then. A lycra top molded over small, flying-saucer shaped breasts, capri yoga pants with a drawstring cinching her tiny waist, her ponytail bouncing in time with her catlike padding around the apartment. Mercy saw her bare feet, toes polished silver, rings on at least three of those toes, toes she used to kiss and nibble. She saw her, the chin-tucked cellphone, shuffling the mail in her hands, closing the door with the sole of her foot. Mercy could almost smell the patchouli. And taste the soy chai latte.

"God, what's this? It's from…you! Is this that book you always wanted to write? The envelope weighs a ton."

"No. It's a letter."

"Mum! You haven't written me for ages. That is so sweet."

Mercy wrinkled her nose, not knowing whether Belle was genuine or if she was being humoured. Either way, she felt patronized.

"I'd like you to read it and get back to me. Tonight."

"About what?"

"You'll see when you read it."

"Can't it wait, Mom?"

"No."

"Pardon?"

"I said no. I dropped it off Wednesday. This is Friday. No."

"Oh." Mercy heard her take a deep inhale and a long exhale. "But I only got it now. Geez, you are acting weird, Mum. It's not like it's a matter of life and death or something. You are not the only one with deadlines." She did the breath thing again.

Belle explained to her not long ago that this breathing technique was used to help quell anxiety. "A calming breath," she'd said.

Little Miss Yogini, thought Mercy, who was growing more agitated the more she heard the calm coming through the phone—like a tornado through a wind tunnel.

"I just need you to read it. It's fairly urgent." Mercy inhaled and exhaled so Belle could hear her.

"Okay. Okay. Okay." Belle was pouting. Mercy could hear that too.

"Thank you."

"Well, so...go finish your speech! Toodles. Love you. Eeemeupp!" Belle smooched into the phone.

"Love you too," said Mercy. All she got was a dial tone.

"Right," Mercy fumed, wiping her hands and going to the computer. "I'm accused of weirdness every time I say no. Saying no is something I might have done more of when Belle was little."

"And a little swat on the behind every once in a while doesn't hurt, either." She remembered her mother's words of advice. Her mother was right on that one. Mercy saw that now. Mercy had not only spared the rod, she'd been far too permissive—spoiled that child rotten as a tooth. She even had half a column written on the subject.

Stop and no are good words. Don't beat but swat if necessary. Example: Child runs out on road? Spank! Child bites other child. Bite softly back. Be tender mother bear teaching cubs.

But the discipline of children was a far too controversial subject for Mercy to tackle. *Do the best you can,* she longed to write. *But do better than me.* Mercy had an inkling that other mothers, even the ones who on the surface appeared to have gotten the results they wanted, felt like that as well. She felt better knowing she was not alone.

Mercy resented being called weird by her blue-haired, navel-pierced, tattooed, raindrop-therapist, ritualistic-fasting daughter who planned, in a few hours, to wear only body paint from the waist up and attend a fundraiser with her lesbian lover, Sage. They were calling themselves Beauty and the Breast. "If that is not weird," Mercy muttered, "it is still hardly normal."

"Let it go, Mercy!" said Buddha-Belly just then.

Smoke was coming from the kitchen. The onions were burnt, curled like scorched toenail clippings. Is this tonight's personal metaphor? she thought. "I am a house on fire," she said then, in Jan Muir's most earnest voice, running to the bathroom to shower. "I am a scorched pan," she shrieked, laughing, as she towelled herself off. "I am a hot mama!" she giggled as she shook naked in the mirror. "Okay. Not. I am dead as a clipped toenail."

She flung herself on the bed and screamed into the pillow.

Buddha-Belly yawned and leapt mindfully from the bed, not offering her one word of comfort.

Boobs, jugs, ta-tas, bazookas, bosoms, peepers, puppies, ladies, headlights, titties. How many words were there for breasts?

The women of Odell, the ones who could afford the tickets or were given them free, were assembling in teams in the lobby of the Odell Hotel, waiting for the doors of the River Room to open. Women in their outlandish, funky, painted, cross-stitched, staple-gunned, plastered, velcroed, pasted, macraméd, hot-wired, iridescent, decent and indecent, amazingly decorated bras, bustiers, and brassieres. Women, stripped to the waist and stripped of inhibitions for "one wonderful gala galpal night," the posters promised.

Mercy, however, could scarcely breathe let alone relax. Not only did she have to deliver a half-finished speech, she'd gone and done it: At the last minute, she'd thrown caution to the wind and worn the belly-dancing outfit, a present from Belle last Christmas. What on earth had possessed her?

There she was, a deep purple scarf with its hundreds of shiny gold coins tied around her waist. She made music whenever she moved, for the bra was sequined as well as spangled. It matched the glitter of her harem pants. She'd wrapped another sequined scarf around her head in a turban. Mercy used other scarves to wrap herself, sari style, hiding the fleshiest part of her belly and covering any stretch-marked cleavage spilling out. Or so she hoped. She was a jangle of nerves, not just gold coins.

She was also on assignment. She had an article to turn in by morning on the fundraiser. She hauled out her notepad. As she flipped to a new page, she saw the word "Zanzibar." *Book tickets,* she scrawled. There was so much to do before the surgery, she realized.

"Mercy? Mercy, is that you? Oh my lord! You look amazing!" Lulu and a group of teachers from Odell Elementary surrounded her. "Can you guess?"

Last year they had all worn bright red headdresses and matching bras made out of apples. They'd called themselves Breast in Class. This year, they appeared to be caricatures of private school mistresses—grey pleated skirts, sheer white blouses bursting at the buttons. Their exaggerated bosoms were shaped like light bulbs and padded with yellow foam. Their breasts blinked on and off like giant light bulbs.

"Bright ideas?"

They laughed. "No, but not a bad try."

"I give," said Mercy.

They held up a sign. Wanda—"Whining Wanda"—Lulu called her—tapped the sign with her wooden pointer and yelled, "Girls! One-two-three!"

"We're the Learning Curves!" they chimed, and started singing "School Days."

O dear god in heaven, thought Mercy. A whole night of this? She looked around for the nearest exit.

In one corner was the Victoria Public Hospital team: Nursing Nurses. Dressed in starched white nurse uniforms, they sported breasts made out of pantyhose, spilling out of unbuttoned fronts, and Cabbage Patch-like dolls suction-cupped to their plastic-soother nipples.

In the other corner, Mercy recognized female members of the Odell police force. They had pointed steel cone bras on over their bulletproof vests. Handcuffed together, they turned around and raised their arms. Mercy read: You. Are. Under. A. Breast.

Fitty-titties was a team of personal trainers from the Y. They stood next to the region's few television journalists, who were sporting cube-shaped bras and had come as the Boob Tubes. Then there were the professors. They had come as archetypal goddesses—Aphrodite, Athena, Demeter, and the rest. In flowing medieval velvet gowns, they were gorgeous.

"Can you take our picture, Mercy?" It was Lulu again.

"Sure. Say cheese."

"Tittees." They giggled. Lulu hugged her friend and went back to her colleagues. Something I don't really have, thought Mercy in a sudden puddle of self-pity.

"Mum! Oh my Gawd. Look at you! Wowee."

It was Belle, behind her somewhere, her voice chirpy.

"Belle!" Mercy turned and gasped. Belle had blued her entire upper body. Her breasts were covered with amazing swirls of painted purple butterflies.

"Who did the artwork?"

"Rio!"

"Oh my God. He must have been in heaven. It's…you're stunning!"

"I know. So are you, Mum. You are gorgeous!"

"Has Lulu seen you?"

Belle nodded. "She supervised." Rio was Lulu's young-est son.

"Hey, Mercy." It was Sage. Mercy inhaled. Sage was bare from the waist up, too—but naked. No art on her flesh. She was white and pale as fillet of sole. In the place where her breast used to be was a long, puckered scar. It reminded Mercy of an old woman's mouth without dentures, as if something had swallowed the breast.

"I know," said Sage. "It's not one of the best boob jobs you'll ever see." Mercy hugged them both.

"It's Gram!" Belle shouted. "Over there, see?"

"With the...Mamo-Grammies!"

Mercy recognized her mother in the midst of some older staff from the Rehab Centre and some of her bridge club. This included Mckenzie Wells, the psychologist who dealt with chronic pain patients. Someone, Mercy feared, she might be needing in the not-too-distant future.

The Mamo-Grammies were glamorous movie stars. They wore matching feather boas and Oscar-type statuettes on the points of their bras. The hubbub was rising.

"Belle."

"What?"

"The letter! Did you—"

"Tonight, Mum. I promise. I'll read it later tonight."

Then she was gone, carried off by a member of the planning committee dressed only in bubble wrap who was helping Belle work the bubble-making machine. The doors opened, the music began. Bubbles floated out and the sea of women flowed into the River Room.

Mercy escaped through a side door. She didn't have to go on for a while, and she needed air. In the old days, she would have reached for a cigarette—even if it was a fundraiser for cancer.

It was a beautiful night, still unseasonably warm for mid-October. Mercy trudged down to the trail along the river, jingling every step she took. She sat down on a bench to go over her notes before it was time to speak.

An hour earlier, a hotel guest left the Coffee Mill dining room only to find he had stumbled into a bizarre paradise in the front lobby of the Odell. He was surrounded by half-naked women attending some sort of Halloween party. Two women in jeans and bras of peacock feathers, with peacock half-masks hiding their faces, brushed up against him.

"You're not from around here, are you?" one of them smiled.

"*Mais non.*"

"Will you donate to the cause?"

"What deep dimples you have."

He forked over twenty dollars and decided to take a trek along the river on the trail behind the hotel he'd noticed from his window earlier that day. He'd hiked for an hour and was heading back to the hotel when he heard a jingling nearby. A curious man, he followed the sound.

Caught in the spill of light from the Odell Lighthouse, at exactly the right angle, Mercy Beth Fanjoy was a vision. A golden goddess. The man stood, transfixed as she sparkled, gold coins shining out in the dark, like stars flung to earth. Mercy's turbaned head was down. She was scribbling furiously.

"*Excusez?*"

She did not hear him. He inched closer.

"*Excusez, madame?* Would it be poseebal for me to take your pho-toe?"

Mercy jumped and jangled, then recognized the blue-eyed, dimpled French man. "My what?" Her heart walloped, its wild drumming filled her chest and travelled to her head. Inside her turban the thumping magnified. She clutched her notepad to her bosom.

"Your picture." He pointed to the digital camera around his neck.

"You want my picture?" She looked around, as if he might be talking to someone behind her. "Why?"

"Madame, it is not every night I see dressed a woman such as this in the moonlight glowing."

"There are more glowing women in the lobby of the hotel such as this and better—all night long." She was shocked at how sarcastic she sounded to herself.

"But it is you here now I would prefer."

Mercy laughed, the gold coins on her outfit tinkling as she did. Why did he suddenly sound like Peter Sellers in *The Pink Panther*? she wondered. *Oh oui oui it eez you here now I would prefer.*

"Go ahead." Yes, he was a complete stranger, she told herself. Yes, he might indeed be a pervert and post her photo all over the web for other perverts. But where had a life of modesty gotten her? And if he were to kill her after, strangle her with the scarves, would it not spare her months of suffering a slow, painful death?

He rushed over and positioned her. His hands were small for a large man.

"Tilt your head thees way. Ah yes? No, thees way. Oh *oui*."

Mercy Beth Fanjoy became, in a flash, a supermodel with her own private paparazzo. She posed. She pranced. She glittered and chimed. She did yoga positions Belle had taught her. She waved her legs like magic wands and the harem pants billowed in the soft night breeze. She turned the scarves into veils and danced. She was a belly dancing seductress.

"*Enchanté.*"

The deeply dimpled French man had only wanted one picture. He was taken aback. He now recognized the woman beneath the heavy makeup as the same strange one he'd watched yesterday in the coffee shop. "Is she not right in the...*tête*, head?" he'd asked the waitress after she left.

But the waitress had only laughed and said, "Who is, mister? Who is?"

Now, not wanting to dampen her apparent exuberance, he continued snapping pictures.

"Are you a professional photographer?" Mercy asked, breathless, shaking her head the way she'd seen it done in the movies. She wondered if she'd qualify for one of those new beauty product commercials. Real-sized women with real bodies, unairbrushed.

"No. No. Are you a belly dancer?"

"No! No! I'm a...I'm...late!"

She heard the swell of music coming from the River Room. "I have to go!" She turned and ran up the trail.

"Wait. What hhhhhis your name?"

But Mercy couldn't hear him over the tintinnabulation of the medallions on her costume and the clang of the bracelets on her wrists.

The mistress of ceremonies was CBC morning show anchor Eleanor "Ella" Lutes, Lulu's older sister. She had that older sister air of superiority about her, though she'd always been cordial to Mercy. Still, Mercy resented her pixie-like features, her delicate bones, her upturned nose, and felt she never really measured up to Ella's standards. After all, Mercy was a girl from Doonan Road. Ella was very much a south side Odell girl, an accomplished singer as well as a broadcaster.

"Just makes me want to gag!" Teeny used to say. Ella studied journalism in Ontario and worked in Toronto for years before returning to Odell. Now, she did have that "gone way back-agin" air about her, a fact even Lulu would be forced to admit. So Mercy was surprised, really touched, by Ella's introduction, which ended, "and not only has she been a wise friend to all of us who've read her column over the years, but she's my sister Louise's best friend. I happen to know first-hand that Mercy is a loyal friend and woman who truly lives up to her name. Please join me in welcoming Mercy Beth Fanjoy!"

Ella hugged her. Squeezed her. Mercy was struck with the possibility she'd been reading Ella wrong all these years. All week long this growing sense of her own wrongness—about everything—had increased. Now, suffocating with uncertainty, Mercy stepped onto the stage.

The room grew still, save for a few drunken giggles coming from the very back.

"Thank you, Ella. I'm going to keep this short. Tonight it is the words of the survivors, the stories of families and friends of survivors, and of those who have lost the battle that are the words of truth. As the daughter of a survivor, I celebrate the courage and faith of my mother and all our mothers. As a mother myself, I hold hope for all our daughters."

She glanced over to where Belle and Cassandra stood arm in arm. The night before her mother started chemo they'd had a head-shaving party. "Let's get it over with from the start," she'd insisted. "I don't want to have it falling out in fistfuls." Mercy had never seen anyone so brave. Even her mother's bald head was perfect and beautiful. Cassandra had modelled every hat and set of earrings that evening. Her many friends had come bearing gifts. They did not get just a little tipsy, they got drunk, plastered, pissed. The following months were scary and hard for everyone. Cassandra had refused to stop working. Mercy would not have been so brave, she was sure of it. Now, unexpectedly, she felt her voice breaking with emotion.

"There has been progress on so many levels. Breast density, for example. Just last month in *Maclean's*, an epidemiologist with the Ontario Cancer Institute in Toronto said that breast density is now a risk factor beyond a doubt. This means early and different screening methods for women identified with breast density. That is just one example." She cleared her throat. The whole room appeared on collective inhale.

"Every year, the proceeds of the Boobs & Baubles Ball—hey, I said it!" There was a ripple of congenial laughter. "... goes directly to women who are suffering hardship as they undergo treatment. The funds go to transportation costs, drugs, day care, and housing, especially for those who cannot work and lose income. This year, one of the members of the planning committee did a wonderful thing. A portion of proceeds will also be donated to help support women of the north. Thanks to Eunice McTavish, who has long been in touch with women in northern communities. Eunice, are you here?"

Eunice waved shyly from the sidelines. The whole room vibrated with applause.

"Well, I'd like to end with a message from breast cancer survivors from the north, via a documentary filmmaker who followed the stories of Inuit women as they travelled miles from their communities, away from their loved ones, in order to receive treatment. Her name is Tunnuq.

"'If I was there tonight, I would want to say to everyone, all genders, *sapiliqtailigit*—don't ever give up!' So join me—in Inuktitut? *Sa-pi-liq-tai-li-git!*"

"*Sa-pi-liq-tai-li-git!*"

"Louder. Three times!"

And they did. And the sound of those syllables, so unfamiliar to the ears of most, became a chant, a mantra, a deep heart prayer.

The melody travelled out of the room, vibrated in the hallway of the Odell Hotel, where a French man stood, having watched as a woman in a purple belly dancing costume spoke and shook her fist in the air. He needed a drink.

After the auction, Mercy was asked to go back on stage and draw numbers for the door prize. She was standing with her mother, waiting for Ella to finish singing "The Rose," when Sage and Belle, arms linked, drew her aside. Belle's eyes were shining so bright that for a second Mercy feared she'd been smoking up again.

"Mum, tonight's our anniversary. This is where we met last year."

"Oh! Happy—anniv—"

"And," Belle hopped up and down the same way she did when she was a kid. "We wanted you to be the first to know. We're getting married!"

Mercy blinked. "Pardon?"

"Married! We're getting married!"

"Can you do that?" One look at Belle's crestfallen face and Mercy knew she had reacted all wrong. "I mean...you know...legally. I mean, as an almost Buddhist? And what are you, Sage? Religion wise, I mean?"

"Actually, I used to be a Sufi. But now I'm focusing on centering prayer in the contemplative Chr—"

"A Sufi?"

"You've never heard of Sufism? But like I said that was—"

"Of course, I have. Rumi, the poet. He was Sufi. Aren't Sufis Muslims? I just never knew there were Sufis in Odell. But you come from Ontario, don't you? But you're not a Sufi now you said, so okay, married...I—well, my goodness."

"Mum!" Belle was pouting. "Mum, all we wanted was congratulations."

"Honey! Sorry! Congrats! I'd hug you, but I don't want to smudge your paint!"

That's when they called Mercy back up on stage. She walked up so thoughtfully, it seemed as if she may have been deeply stirred by Ella's song, when in fact she was thinking: I'll finally have a reason to buy a fancy hat. Will I be mother of the bride or mother of the groom?

Up on stage, she looked down into the crowd once again. It had thinned out; the women still there were starting to look a bit worse for wear. Cinderellas fading, even before the stroke of midnight. Their makeup needed touching up—mascara was smudged from laughing, crying, dancing, and sweating; feathers had fallen; glitter had rubbed off; the M&Ms had indeed melted; and balloons had deflated. The bubble machine was empty. Someone found a soother on the floor and was flouncing around asking, "Is this your nipple?"

Mercy watched as three jellybean shapes of blue light floated into the room, flickering from woman to woman. Laser-like, they danced, slipped back out a window, leap-frogging fireflies flying towards the river. She was not surprised on such an unusual night as this that spirits, maybe the spirits of sadness and beauty and hope, were manifest in the room. Such sad beauties, all of them. And really, how privileged they all were.

"You'd never be able to celebrate quite like this if you had say…colon cancer," she said to herself but, unfortunately, also out loud and over the microphone. "Poor Harold, my old landlord. That's what he died of. Or bone cancer. Hey, how about coming all dressed up to the Pancreatic Ball? And where would a woman with, say, ovarian cancer go to dance and celebrate? How about to the Men's Prostrate Fundraising Gala? Picture that one!"

There was a collective gasp. A pregnant silence. Humourless, all of them. All of a sudden they were utterly joyless. This was another of Mercy's greatest fears. That she would grow old and bitter, as grim as the grimmest among them, especially those who confused seriousness and intellect with intelligence, kindness with weakness, heartfulness with soul, joy with happiness. "Well, there are other people dying," she protested, but the sea of faces continued to look rather appalled.

"The winning number is…KERCCHHHwhohoh." The laughing gremlin seized her by the throat once more. "Kerch—whooooh."

"Mum! Mum!" Belle hissed from the side of the stage.

Ella took over, as she elbowed her offstage. "Mercy Fanjoy—in good spirits! Hahaha."

Mercy simmered down long enough to collect the painting she'd bid on and won. Called *Self-portrait*, it showed a single breast, an impossibly perfect breast, done by local artist Judy Sullivan, sister of Ellen Sullivan. Benjamin, Ellen's son, was a friend of Belle's. In Odell, it seemed everyone ended up connected or tangled together somehow, eventually.

As Mercy traipsed through the lobby carrying her breast, the pervert photographer was leaving the James Joyce Pub.

They stared at each other and then at the breast.

"Are you okay to drive?" asked Lulu, who had followed her.

"Yes, I'm not drunk. I just got…you know…giddy."

"Give me your keys, Mercy."

"Lulu!"

"Mercy. Friends don't let friends drive drunk. Or even tipsy."

The man nodded to Mercy and passed them both, hurriedly, as if the last thing he wanted to witness was two women wrestling.

"*Bon nuit*," he said.

"Did that guy just say something to me?" asked Lulu.

"No, he didn't!" snapped Mercy. She normally did not resent Lulu's natural born looks, but she wished her friend just once might consider that an attractive man could possibly prefer a tall, ample-bosomed brunette over a petite raven-haired beauty.

Five minutes later, at the stroke of midnight, Mercy Beth Fanjoy sat in her muffler-roaring gas guzzler at a red light on the corner of Electric and Regent streets, absent-mindedly unwinding her turban and shaking out her hair. The street light ignited the golden medallions she wore, and this in turn illuminated Judy Sullivan's painted breast, which Mercy had lovingly propped up and belted into the passenger seat.

Mercy hadn't noticed, but a black, mud-splattered truck had pulled up alongside her. The man glanced over and did a double take. He honked, winked, and waved. Mercy waved back, smiling.

The man, wearing a black baseball hat, curled his tongue and, snakelike, slithered it out of his mouth, then quickly darted it in and out, in and out, and rubbed it back and forth over his upper lip. He rolled his eyes skyward and appeared to be growling or maybe barking.

"Pervert!" she screamed through the window.

He nodded his head in agreement.

The light turned green, and Mercy sped through the intersection, terrified he'd follow her, but he turned onto the bridge. She turned on the radio, having forgotten the last person in the car was her mother, who had of course changed the frequency to pick up the Finding Faith network.

A gospel song ended and a commercial came on advertising a special offer of a children's bible on DVD. "Watch Shadrach, Meshach, and Abednego stand fast in the fiery furnace! Watch Daniel in the lion's den. Hear the lion roar! And make a journey with the shepherds as they make the pilgrimage towards Bethlehem."

The next commercial Mercy had heard before. Still, it made her sit bold upright.

"Did you know that the People of the Church of Faith and Light and Celestial Vibrations have been practising what New Age spiritualists are now calling 'the secret' for at least the past fifty years? But we don't package it and sell it. We give our truth away! And we keep it simple and true. Sit down, be quiet, and listen. Hear the voice of God! Once you do, you can create the vibrations you need to find a deep and lasting harmony and path to inner peace.

"Sit down, be still, and listen! God's there. In the silence. This is Cassandra Fanjoy-Rutherford for the People of the Church of Faith and Light and Celestial Vibrations. Join us for Sunday worship and music." Mercy, pulling in to her driveway, switched the frequency and turned the radio up full blast. Then, Mercy Beth Fanjoy belly danced in place. She opened the window. In her strong off-key voice, she belted out the lyrics and imagined they travelled up and away to the man in the moon.

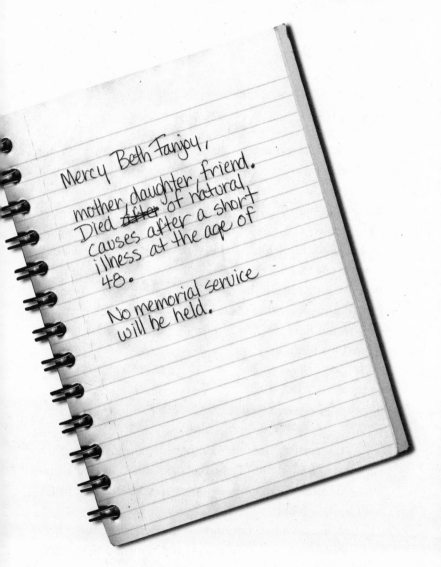

Mercy Beth Fanjoy,
mother, daughter, friend.
Died ~~after~~ of natural
causes after a short
illness at the age of
48.

No memorial service
will be held.

—first draft advance obit.

On Saturday morning, as she had every Saturday morning for twenty-two years, Mercy woke up early, did forty-two jumping jacks, listened to Saturday morning radio, and lifted ten-pound barbells. Determined to erase the previous evening's fiasco and not let it dampen her day, she showered and dressed. Basket in hand, she made her way to the Odell Farmer's Market, where she bought a week's worth of fresh produce and a bag of hot curried vegetable samosas, strolling the aisles, nodding good morning to those she knew. As luck would have it, she ran into a few people who had attended the fundraiser.

Are you feeling better?

How's the hangover?

Not to worry, we've all made fools of ourselves. Just not so… publicly.

A week earlier Mercy would have been mortified. Now she floated in a cloud of nonchalance, a nonplussed ballerina. She smiled the smile of a woman very much at peace with being a fool.

Then, like on other Saturdays in the past, she bought herself some flowers—purple ones—and returned home. She fed the cat and ate, washing down the vegetable samosas with freshly squeezed orange juice. She brewed coffee, put her flowers in a vase, changed into a skirt and matching sweater set—today it was the blue one—and took extra care in the application of her makeup. On Saturdays, Mercy Beth Fanjoy even wore red lipstick. Weekdays, she preferred a shade called Naturally Neutral. Today, before she went in to work, she would sit in a corner of the kitchen in a warm puddle of sunlight (if the sun was shining) and look at her flowers or read the one-page literary section of the *Odell Observer*. This morning there was a poem by a dead Odellian whose family would publish his collected poems in the near future.

Green Water Death
Late last night I walked by River St. John
Was joined by a shadow which sang to me softly
The toll song of a death bell. A phantom's opera.
Death smells green; cracked as my stained glass heart.

Mercy read the poem a second time, out loud and with feeling. She glanced at herself in the mirror on the wall beside the chair, placed there to make the room appear larger. She looked small in that mirror, suddenly, and at this moment, like a raccoon, mascara smudged beneath her eyes and down her cheeks.

It was getting late. She splashed her face with cold water and wiped it on a dishtowel. There was no time to reapply her makeup. There was, however, time enough to leave a message on her mother's voice mail. "Mum. It's me. I want the note. You have until Thursday. Meet me at twelve sharp on Wednesday at the Coffee Mill, if not before. I will also phone you every two hours with this same message. I want the note." Racing upstairs, she then sent an email message to Belle.

To: belleoftheblog@sympatico.ca
From: mercymuse@hotmail.ca
I've been thinking about you. I am sorry my response to your big news last night was not more enthusiastic. I'm a little off this week. Deadline pressure. I am so happy for you both. RE-ALLY. And I wondered if you and Sage wanted to come for supper at my place soon? Xoxoxo mama filled with pride—ha ha. Little joke?
ps In case you wondered I was not drunk.
pps Have you read the letter?

Then Mercy kissed the cat and left for work.

Occasionally Yours Stationery, founded by one Horace Manley, began as a mercantile store in Odell at the end of the nineteenth century. Manley's Mercantile was then Manley's Shoe Store, Manley's Wedding Dress Boutique, and Manley's Yarn Shop. A final name change transformed it into a stationery and office supply store that had been doing a decent business for over twenty-five years. Ewart Little, great-great-grandson of Horace, was the absentee owner and landlord. He lived in the Cayman Islands most of the year. The weekday management was left to a second cousin—Rupert Moore.

When Mercy was given sole charge of the shop on Saturdays, she and Rupert left messages on pink memo tablets for each other. Occasionally, they talked on the phone. Mercy earned just a little over minimum wage, but this job was not about the money. The job was life support to her.

First, it had a kind of pheromonal attraction. She very simply loved the way the place smelled. Paper, manila envelopes, fresh cardboard, poster board, Wite-Out, indelible markers, glue. Rupert had impeccable taste and the store was filled with miniature works of art, like scalloped, lacy-edged vanilla cream paper. Mercy loved to touch and smell, arranging and rearranging the shelves with something akin to devotion. Even the paper clips and stapler section held a utilitarian beauty. It suggested the possibility of organization and control, an illusion some people actually bought into. But the sensuality and optimism of the place was just a perk. Above all else, in this job Mercy herself felt useful and appreciated. Cherished even.

"Mercy—I'm in a hurry, help me find a card for my sister-in-law's birthday. Can't stand her, a conniving bitch, really, but it's the big 3-0. Mercy, my best friend's moving. Mercy, we are grandparents! Mercy, my son graduated. Mercy, my daughter's miscarried. Mercy, my brother's in rehab. Mercy, my sister's youngest left for college and she's depressed; my mother's going into a nursing home, anything cheery? Do you have a happy retirement card for someone forced to retire? Mercy, do you have any Muslim holiday cards? Happy Ramadan? Why not? Are you racist? Happy Menopause! Any post-vasectomy-surgery get-well-soon cards? Ha. Mercy, my Hungarian neighbour's pet shaker parrot died. She used to walk around with it on her shoulder and it shit all down the back of her sweater. Looked like boiled icing. But she loved it. Have you got a sorry about your dead bird card? Mercy, do you have a please come back to me I'll never cheat on you again card? Is there a Valentine's Day card I could send to myself?"

She felt like a cross between a consultant, a counsellor, and a confidante. Very often at Occasionally Yours, Mercy Beth found people in the aisles, overcome with emotion. She would usher them to the back room, make green tea, and leave them be.

No, this is no job. The world inside this shop is a link to the universe, to ebbs and flows, to celebrations, to rituals, a link to lives that make me realize no one comes through unscathed, that life is what life is. As a customer hands over a card to me and I ring it in, and hand it back, for one amazing connected split second in time I am transfused and flooded with a gratitude beyond what any words on any card could ever express. And I like to think they feel it too.

She'd written this in her journal just yesterday. She hummed as she pulled into the parking spot behind the courthouse. A small sign said: *This spot reserved for OY employees only.* She loved easing into the space.

Mercy rounded the corner, smiling as an elderly woman approached, picking her way carefully along the cracked sidewalk. The woman was dressed in a bright orange embroidered tunic and matching hat; a flaming matchstick against the grey of the cement. She nodded as they passed each other, and Mercy smelled lilies and noticed her skin, the relaxed suede cheeks of brown, the pleated flesh around her eyes. What a vision of beauty, she thought. "Excuse me," she said. "I need to tell you…you look so…beautiful!" she gushed.

The woman smiled. She had only three bottom teeth, spaced widely apart. "I eighty-three!" Then they stood looking at each other awkwardly. "Is nice. You very tall. Pretty eyes, too." They turned and walked away from each other, both smiling. Mercy purred with gladness of heart, jingling her keys in time to her humming, then stopped. A gaggle of about twenty women, carrying placards, marched back and forth in front of the entrance to Occasionally Yours.

She recognized two of the women at once—Vonda Kitchen and Victoria Curtain. Here they come, the kitchen-curtain girls, they'd teased in high school. These were the smart girls from Odell's conservative, affluent families, active in many good causes even back then, girls who'd become women who married young but well, women who gave up careers in engineering and medicine to devote themselves to family. Mercy thought this admirable and was in fact terribly envious. Up until a few years ago, that is. Vonda's middle son Carter had overdosed, some said on purpose. Vonda had gone religious and joined the People of the Church of Faith and Light and Celestial Vibrations.

Vonda and Mercy had a long discussion one Saturday about why Mercy did not attend church like her mother and why the shop carried inspirational as opposed to religious cards. This, after Vonda stood in the middle aisle shouting, "Mercy, where is Jesus? Why can't I find Jesus anywhere? Are you afraid of Jesus? I suppose next you'll have no Christmas cards, just happy holidays! Mercy, surely Jesus deserves some shelf space if Santa does!" Several customers nearby scurried out the door. Mercy suggested Vonda could find Jesus uptown at the Christian bookstore. "I know," said Vonda. "My question is: Why isn't Jesus anywhere here at Occasionally Yours?" Mercy said she'd ask Rupert but she never did. Maybe this is what the hubbub was about. Mercy read the placards.

M.O.M.S. AGAINST HATE LITERATURE
The Foxy Moxy Roxy Galpal Greeting Cards—Corny
PORN

SEXIST ROXY LEAVE ODELL
Mothers of Men Society says NO to Foxy ROXY

"She's here," squealed Vonda. The women were dressed in electric blue smocks. They crowded around her in a horse-shoe formation.

"What's going on, ladies?" Mercy inquired. "No one told me there was a party today." This was one of those times Mercy appreciated being so tall. She could look down on them and not panic. Even though they outnumbered her, they seemed like a fierce bunch of Smurfs, chins jutting forward, ready for a fight. She pinched the bridge of her nose as if holding back a sneeze and, fortunately, the urge to laugh left her.

"We have a petition, Mercy Beth, and we will be soliciting all day long for more signatures. We want you to remove the Foxy Moxy Roxy Galpal Greeting Card line from the shop and discontinue selling it."

"And just exactly who are we?" Mercy retorted.

"The M.O.M.S. We are the Mothers of Men Society. We are mothers who feel that white males are being discrimi-nated against in ways both big and small and this leads to feelings of impotence and depression and futility, especially amongst our youth."

Mercy raised her eyebrows. "I see. So you are taking of-fense to…?" Mercy shrugged and turned her palms up, as if in surrender.

"We have not been merely offended! Our sons are being attacked! We are standing against hate literature. The male-bashing has gotten way out of control. And if men complain they are accused of being males who are part of a backlash movement to The Feminists. So we think women's voices might be heard!"

"Oh. So. What can I do, exactly? Excuse me, I do have to open the shop." She held up the keys.

"We know you're an understanding woman, Mercy Beth. We thought you might sign the petition and get whoever orders to stop ordering the Foxy Moxy Roxy Galpal Greeting Cards." Vonda spoke with authority.

"Can you tell me, is it all the cards or one in particular? I should confess I like the Foxy Moxy Roxy cards, myself." Mercy's patience was waning.

"The 'p' card! You think the 'p' card is funny?"

"The 'p' card? Yes, there is a card about men peeing, but it's all in fun and men even buy it."

"No! '*P*' as in..." Vonda lowered her voice, "...penis."

"Oh." Mercy nodded solemnly. "You mean the one with the two apes on the front comparing bananas?"

"Have you read the inside?" Vonda wagged a card under her nose. "Here."

Mercy knew it well but acted perplexed. She read it out loud, slowly:

For years now we've been saying,
It doesn't matter about the size!

Mercy opened the card.

Surprise guys!
We've all been telling lies lies lies!

She looked at them, feigning shock. They looked at her, nodding in unison. Mercy pinched her nose. "Well, I see how some men..."

"And this...'good men are hard'...and then on the inside 'to find'? What kind of message does that send to our boys?"

"Hate! Simply Hate!" they chimed together.

"Vonda, I'm sorry but..." Again, Mercy felt a laugh attack coming on.

"I told you she wouldn't get it," Victoria snapped at Vonda. "She only has a daughter," she sniffed. "A lesbian daughter, at that. And obviously no empathy whatsoever."

Mercy sobered up then. She shot Victoria her special practised look of benevolence while placing a hex: Because you will so be reincarnated into a cockroach next life, Victoria Curtain, I therefore have great compassion for you now but if you say anything else about my Belle, I will stab you, mutilate you with my keys, drive them straight into your eyeballs back into your numbskull brain until you are dead dead dead.

"I'll talk to Rupert, Vonda. But now, you must let me through or—"

"Or...?" They began to chant. "Moms against hate! Moms against hate!"

"Or she will have to call the 'p'—for police, *n'est pas? Excusez.*" A man in a black beret emerged. The throng of women parted like waves of a blue sea, letting him through. It was Him. The dimpled French man. Mercy then remembered last night's dream. A sex dream. She remembered waking up, throbbing, her legs pretzel-twisted, wrapped tightly around each other. This was the man in her dream. She blushed as if he knew these things and had actually seen her naked.

"May I enter? I have business here. *Je m'appelle Valmont LeClair. Vous êtes Mercy?* You've been in anticipation of me?" He pronounced her name as *Merci*.

"No. *Oui?* Yes. Yes! I don't speak French much."

He smiled at all the women. "No problemo." He took Mercy Beth's keys, opened the door. "*Bien.*" Mercy ducked in.

On the sidewalk, the women began marching and chanting as the door shut behind them. Still, their protests echoed. "M.O.M.S. against hate! M.O.M.S. against hate!"

They could see their breath in the inky darkness. Mercy opened the venetian blinds and began snapping on lights.

"Who are you, anyway? You've been everywhere this week." It came out belligerent. "Valmont LeClair, is that what you said? I'm not expecting anyone! You're stalking me, aren't you?" She forced the gaiety.

Despite the barrage of questions, he just kept standing there with his impeccable posture and dimples. Then he reached into his coat and handed her his card. On it was a picture of the man in the moon.

Valmont LeClair, LC
Le Clair de Lune, Inc.

Quebec, Que.
www.leclairdelune.com
Member of IESNA

"Monsieur Rupert hired me as a consultant," he began. ConsoulTANT is how he said it. He followed Mercy into the back room.

"Yes, yes. Of course. I forgot. You're here to do an estimate for new lighting."

"*Oui. C'est ca.* Where can I put my serviette?" He held up a satchel.

"What is IESNA?" asked Mercy, clearing away some clutter on a desk and motioning to him.

"The Illumination Engineering Society of North America," he said, setting down his equipment. She watched as he withdrew items from his "serviette": a light meter, a protractor, a compass, a sheet of tracing paper, a chalk line, a level, a flashlight. A product catalogue.

Valmont LeClair didn't call himself a businessman and his company was not a franchise. He was not pretentious enough to call himself an artist, although others did. He was one of a dying rare breed of experts. He called himself *chasseur d'ombre*, a shadow hunter.

In a commercial space such as this, Valmont LeClair began to explain in his broken English, he liked to take time to study angles and figure out shadows from the time the noon day sun poured in until the last of the customers had straggled out the door. Whenever possible, he worked with interior sensors, so that a person's movement controlled the light. He did not waste precious resources or energy. By employing "tried and true lighting design principles and techniques and keeping up with the leading edge technology," he had built up a small but loyal clientele. These days, he was most excited about LED—light emitting diodes— for commercial markets. Energy consumption would be a tenth of what is used to be, he told customers. The light bulb as Thomas Edison knew it would disappear! As he looked around Occasionally Yours, he spotted immediately how accent lighting could enhance the vintage checkout counter and display cases.

Mercy just tried as best she could to understand. She nodded in accord even when she did not follow or could not decipher his accent.

"So, I am here most all today," he told her, almost apologetically. He was unrolling blueprints. Then he went to the window. "First. I have to go back outside and measure the distance of those trees from the store."

Mercy was now genuinely impressed. In the summer, though she loved the rustling sound the old elms made when she opened the windows, the foliage did make the place dark. But so many of the trees had died from Dutch elm disease in the last ten years, she was grateful the ones around the store and the one in her backyard had somehow survived.

She busied herself opening the cash, but watched as he made a few measurements. Mercy admired this kind of attention to detail, loved to watch people focused on their work. People like Bee, for example. Or Doc Wiggins. Or her mother. Or Lulu. They were all so thorough, but not caught up in a crazed, overcompensating, frenetic mode. They appeared relaxed. If only she could learn this habit of being, of not trying so hard.

"They are still out there. The M.O.M.S.," she warned, as he headed towards the door.

"I am a man. They like men, remember."

"I do too!" She cringed when she realized how defensive and eager this sounded.

"That is good to know," he grinned back, and for a second Mercy considered the possibility that he was flirting with her.

A bell jangled, announcing the first customers.

"Well, anyway, you can use the desk, but just so you know I might have to go on the computer from time to time. And I'll be locking up for half an hour for lunch."

"Merci," he said, but did he mean "thank you" or was he saying her name?

Mercy checked her "Mercy's Musings" email. A few lukewarm responses to "Home Remedies." No answer still to the email she'd sent Tuesday evening.

For years you have been the faithful reader who has praised me and encouraged me as loyal fan and secret admirer. It's time we met. Don't you agree?

She re-sent it then dialed Noah.

"Hello. Glooscap Animal Shelter."

Even his voice made her weak. She pictured him, standing tall as Glooscap himself, the sandpapery but gentle hands, the long black braid down his back, tied with leather. *Eyes deeper than Kubla Khan's caverns*, she'd written in her journal. Noah had gone to her mother's grief support group for a while a few years back. He told Mercy he thought the PCFLCV-ers had a very intercultural approach to healing. Sometimes, he drummed for them at funerals.

"Noah. It's Mercy."

"How are you, Mercy?"

"Um. I'm okay, Noah."

"Bird's okay. Cage is cool. Sorry I wasn't here when you dropped in."

"Me too. Could I come over on my lunch hour? I have something to ask you." *Will you have sex with me before Wednesday?*

"Sure, Mercy."

"It's no big deal. It won't take long. Just a few questions, as I know you're coming up to the anniversary of the Glooscap shelter. Thought I'd do an item on you. I wanted to talk a little about your participation in the October fourth feast of St. Francis of Assisi and the Blessing of the Animals service at the Church of Faith and Light and Celestial Vibrations."

"Oh yeah. It was good, Mercy. Your mother sang 'All Things Bright and Beautiful.' It was really nice, eh? And when Hugh turned on the audio generator and fiddled some with the sound waves, holy, Mercy, the dogs and cats went crazy like. We couldn't hear nothing, right, but they were howling and singing like some choir praising the Creator."

"I heard it was pretty impressive."

"I've got pictures too, if you want."

"Terrific. I'll be there around 1:45."

She hung up the phone just as the little bling on her computer told her she had mail.

From: Belleoftheblog@sympatico.ca
TO: mercymuse@hotmail.ca
Mum. Sorry about not reading the letter. Will soon—love ya. Sage said you're welcome to come out to Mystic Stables. I need to practise-teach some yoga. You can be my guinea pig again. Nothing strenuous, I promise. Just some seated flow poses maybe and pranayama, a little ujjayi breathing. Tomorrow?

FROM: mercymuse@hotmail.ca
To: Belleoftheblog@sympatico.ca
Okay. But please read the letter? Why do seated flow poses make me think of having to go to the bathroom and ujjayi make me think of candy?

From: Belleoftheblog@sympatico.ca
TO: mercymuse@hotmail.ca
HAHAHA. Jujubes maybe? xoxobelle. As for how—yoga helps your bowels and innards! Check out my latest blog!

Mercy sighed. The B-word again. Ted Dawkins, senior editor of the *Odell Observer*, had been pestering her to get a blog if she wanted to keep current. But he really meant, if she wanted to keep her column. He'd hinted to Mercy more than once in the last two months that she was becoming stale. Little hints like: "We need new blood." Or, just this week, "Home remedies? Mercy! Isn't that a bit passé? Fiona, my brother's niece, just phoned to tell me she had written a piece on iTunes, iPods, iPhones, Photoshop, and YouTube, and how keeping up to speed and needing to know technological abbreviations is essential. So she'll pinch hit for you, okay?"

Blogs: a word that reminded Mercy of a bunch of bloated frogs, of ribbiting toads. Blogs: proof that anyone can write (and much better than, say, Mercy Beth Fanjoy of small-town Odell's "Mercy's Musings"). Cell phones: as yet unproven major cause of brain cancer. E-cards: destroying the old-fashioned greeting card industry. Occasionally Yours was suffering as a result of e-cards and the new office supply chain store up the hill at the Odell Mall. They had some loyal customers among those who lived downtown and had no uptown transport. They also had their share of loiterers. Like the public library, OY had a few regulars—like Old Stinky—who just wanted to get in somewhere for awhile to stay warm. Mercy kept a close eye on Old Stinky. He didn't shoplift or do anything sinister or perverted but he sometimes left greasy smudge marks on the most expensive envelopes. Mercy often feared he might be trying to sneak some glue to sniff. She tried to always have a pot of tea on and animal cookies out on a plate on the counter.

Soon enough, the store was humming: a handful of regular Saturday-morning customers browsing and scanning, in to buy their *Globe and Mails* and *New York Times*. Five people in all of Odell special-ordered the *New York Times*—three professors, one cab driver, and a petrologist, Eunice McTavish's husband, Gerald. Mercy showed one person down the aisle to the birthday invitations and another over to the padded envelopes.

"Mercy. Hi!"

"Hanna, hey." Hanna Davis had moved in just around the corner from Mercy Beth a few years back.

"What's with the nutcases out front?" Hanna said, pointing to Vonda and Victoria.

"Oh, well, yes, tell me about it. They're exercising their right to free speech, I guess. I'm just going to ignore them and maybe they'll go away. But, just so you know, a few of those nutcases used to be on your board." Hanna had just taken the position of executive director of Ferguson House.

"Scary." They both laughed.

"Anything I can help you with?" Mercy was trying to

keep her eye on Valmont LeClair. He had secured a string around an elm and was attaching it to the window at the left of the door.

"I want to order some wedding invitations!" Hanna squealed like a teen.

"Hanna! How exciting!"

"I'm still in shock," Hanna gushed. "And the kids love him."

"Who's the lucky man? Anyone I know?"

"As a matter of fact, I think you do. It's Noah Perley." Hanna hugged herself as she said it.

Mercy's grin never wavered, not for a second. But she sucked in her breath, as if someone had just socked her in the belly.

"Noah!" she finally said. Her grin widening, rising, extending from ear tip to ear tip, in fact, filling her face, her eyebrows jumping in mock delight. She could have won an Academy Award for that performance. She clasped her hands in front of her chin, against her lips, as if ready to say a prayer.

"Noah? Oh, Hanna! That's—"

Hanna stopped hugging herself long enough to hug Mercy. "I know! I know! Unbelievable. It just all happened so fast. You know, our shelter is next to his shelter. We kept bumping into each other. I'd never seen Noah with anyone and for a while there I thought he might be…you know." She flapped her wrist in the universal signal for "gay." "Not that I judge! But he's not—let me tell you! He is so damn shy, but once you get through that…well! Come to find out, he told me, after jail and all, he'd sort of given up on women. He said he only ever really loved one woman in his life. Wouldn't tell me who, and that woman never noticed he was alive. But that was long before I moved to Odell. Then he had his work and his nephew. And so... Anyhow, you're invited to the wedding, you and Lulu and your mother, of course."

"Wonderful," Mercy stammered, smiling even wider.

"I know! I know!" Hanna gushed. "Enough to make you believe in miracles. Mercy, are you crying? You are such a tender heart." Hanna tilted her head in a look of extreme gratitude.

"Oh well, squeeze me and I wring out like a sponge! I-I-I have just the perfect invitation for you," she said, reaching underneath the shelf. "Still, I'll give you the binder to look through them all."

"Ow!"

"Oopsie! Sorry. Are you okay?" Mercy, unintentionally of course, had slammed the sample binder down a little too soon, and a little too hard.

Hanna shook out her hand and rubbed her fingers. "No. I'm fine. I think."

"Here. This is the one." Mercy pointed to a delicate grainy parchment.

"Almost like birchbark."

"It's called Silver Birch," said Mercy. "It's our top of the line but...hmm. Wonder if that might be a good wedding present?" She flashed a beneficent smile.

"I think Noah would like this very much."

"I know he will," Mercy laughed. It was a melodious laugh, she hoped, a tinkly, oh the gods are laughing at me aren't they Sweet Jeezuz, carefree, reckless laugh. No one would have guessed at that moment that Mercy Beth Fanjoy was wondering just how deep a cut could be made by an edge of silver birch parchment paper number 005 and that, even more shockingly, she was as yet undecided as to whether to try it on her own wrist or the small-boned wrist of the hand with the finger bearing an engagement ring made of whalebone belonging to sweet, kind, hardworking, inspiring, advocate-activist Hanna.

Luckily for Hanna, Mercy was not the murdering sort.

She called Noah as soon as Hanna left the store to cancel the interview. "Congrats!"

"Thanks. I sent Hanna over after you called. Knew you'd give her special treatment."

"I did indeed." *Was it me? Was I the one you thought didn't know you were alive?*

"Look, I won't make it over."

"Ohh. Too bad. And Mercy?"

"Yes?"

"I was just going to call you. Um. Well. You can come get your cage back. The bird died."

Noah took a deep appreciative whiff of the Glooscap shelter's earth perfume: a mixture of flea shampoo, sweetgrass, and the thick wet-fur smell of happy, healthy animals. There was a different, sour, sewer-backwash smell when animals were sick. Today there were five cats, five dogs, and a ferret. Noah adjusted the framed prayer poster of Saint Francis and the Mi'kmaq prayer beside it. He whispered it to the animals, went to the window, asked the sun to erase all past sadness, future worry, and utility bills, and closed his eyes. When he opened them, he saw Hanna trotting up the street, her blonde hair blowing out like sunflower petals, fanning her face. She waved at his silhouette, and broke into a run. He waved back, perhaps realizing in one of those shattering moments he'd had often enough in life that it was this Lab-happy eagerness and Hanna-esque light he'd yearned for most of his life. This was what he needed more than reluctance and shade, and only now, at the age of fifty, was he blessed enough to receive and inhabit such bliss.

Noah reached for his drum. As he'd been taught, there was no shame to a warrior's tears, and so he let them fall in sync with his knuckle rap, hand tap on the drum skin.

Before Hanna came bursting through the door, he drummed out a prayer to the Creator that some day Mercy Beth Fanjoy might find her spirit's match. Mercy, the woman eagle from a dream, was a twin soul, not a life companion. That was now clear. The spirit world had its own biorhythms, mating and migration patterns. As the elders taught, it often took years, if not lifetimes, for a vision to be fully understood.

Mercy put a CD on the store's stereo system and reached for her spiral notebook.

Hanna is marrying Noah and Belle is marrying Sage. Sage, the horse owner and entrepreneur. Sage of Mystic Stables. I like Sage. I really do. Marriage? A good thing! And Hanna and Noah: Perfect. At least this time I was spared the humiliation of rejection. I wish them such a good life. I so do not mean that. And the bird. My blue jay, my hope, died today.

The bells jangled and a customer came into the store. Mercy flew to the back room to wipe her eyes and blow her nose. She managed to look almost perky when the customer purchased some Foxy Moxy Roxy greeting cards. "Controversy will be good for sales," said the woman. "Phone the media."

"Thank you for the suggestion," Mercy said, then went searching in the animal sympathy card section. There was one card for birds: A yellow canary with an empty cage. Just seeing the words "I am sorry for your loss" brought her comfort. She opened the card, which was blank inside. Swallowing with difficulty, she wrote:

William Blake wrote, "For everything that lives is holy." Maybe everything that dies is holy, too.

She closed the card. The one man she'd always been able to count on was none other than a long-dead poet named William Blake.

Death knocking at Mercy's door was one thing. Parading, angry members of the Mothers of Men Society outside her shop door was another. After learning Noah and Hanna were to be wed and that no night of soft chants or sacred sex awaited her, and that the blue jay, her small feathered kindred soul, had indeed succumbed to death, Mercy crashed. She'd considered cancelling dinner plans. But here she was, showered and on her way out, ready, finally, to confide her fears of impending surgery to Lulu. And maybe Hap. Above all else, Mercy longed to forget the humiliating events of the afternoon. As if stuck in place, she'd stood, transfixed, endlessly thumbing through the sympathy card section, seeking some kind of morbid comfort.

When days ahead are dark and pain
Overwhelms you once again
We are here in time of need
You have friends. True friends indeed.

The verse she was lost in was enough to make anyone weep. Yet it made her think of Lulu and Hap and how dependable she knew they'd be in the days ahead—however numbered those days might be. There she was, glued to glucose-dripping words, snivelling, her eyes rimmed an un-attractive orangish soda pop colour, pupils like pinpricks, when Valmont returned from his lunch. Mercy, doubled over in a panic attack, was hunched in the aisle as if in pain, hyperventilating into a brown paper bag.

"Allergies," she'd lied when he asked if she were "ho-kay."

For a few minutes, she locked herself in the restroom and ignored the urgent *ping* from the nipple of the service bell on the checkout desk. When she finally emerged from the restroom, customers were lined up. Rudolph-nosed and with miniature airbags inflating the skin around her eyes, she took her place at the cash and, with her usual air of efficiency, did her job. *I'm a stationary woman at a work station in a stationery store,* she'd scribbled in her diary one boring Saturday night a few weeks ago. *What an exciting life I lead.* Today, she realized she'd settle for life period, boring or otherwise.

Valmont asked her again, as soon as they were alone, in a voice as soft as chalk, if she was ho-kay.

She'd imagined grabbing him by his blue denim shoulders then, and drawing him to her. Non non. I am not okay. You see, Meessuurrrr Meessuurrr Leclairrr, I wanted sex before I die from ovarrrian or cerrrvical or uterrrine cancerrr, but the man I longed to do that with is now and just recently as it happens engaged to be MARRIED and unless you'd like to be the pinch hitter and jump my bones before Thursday, you cannot help me. I am almost positive I'm going to die an almost-virgin. No regular sex my whole life. No irregular sex much, either.

Instead she said pleasantly, "Are you married, Mr. LeClair?"

"Widowed." He looked away quickly.

"Oh, that's awful! I'm sosorryforyourloss. A friend of mine died today, actually." She skulked back into the restroom, slamming the door in his face. They'd hardly exchanged glances the rest of the day.

Now, as Mercy parked the car, grateful for the comfort of old friends like Lulu and Hap, she felt a surge of relief. Why had she kept herself in an isolation chamber since Tuesday? Why not ask for the support of her two best friends? Lulu was making Caesar salad when Mercy let herself in through the sliding glass doors, brown paper bag in hand.

"White wine's in the fridge. Pour me some, too?" Lulu gave her a quick hug.

Mercy set her bag down.

"Can I do anything else?" She lifted a lid from a pot on the stove.

"Not a thing. Just pour and sit." Lulu wiped her hands on her apron. Mercy poured the wine and perched on a wooden stool.

"Lulu, about the visit to your class," Mercy began. She swirled the stem of her glass. She hesitated, unsure how to continue. Lulu would be disappointed, but she'd decided to cancel the classroom visit they'd arranged for Monday morning. "I need—"

"Tell me anything you need. The kids are so excited. Oh Mercy, after you interview them, they want to interview you for their classroom podcast. Isn't that amazing? It was their idea, not mine. Did you check out the classroom podcast link I sent you? So anyhow, I said I'd ask you first but I told them they had to be prepared. After all, they were interviewing a *real* writer. As for you, well, I assigned them each a task and a fact and made them all mummichog experts.

Can't you just see them practising all weekend? 'My most favourite thing about mummichogs is...' They also wanted to know if they'll have their pictures in the *Odell Observer*. I sent home release forms just in case. I said I wasn't sure. I hope you can get all of them though, if you do. I don't like anyone singled out, but it would be nice if the paper covered a positive educational story. So don't worry—we are all set. Anyhow, was there anything else you wanted to ask?"

Lulu looked up, smiling. Mercy never figured out why, given Lulu's gamine beauty, she didn't resent her. But right from the start—the start being elementary school, when Mercy looked across the classroom and noticed the uneven splashing of freckles, and Lulu's distinct beauty—she'd seen only kindness in that wide open face. The pouty lips suggested Lulu might be a bit of a mischief-maker. But Mercy knew that Lulu was safe, and she would never hurt her knowingly for anything in the world.

"Mercy? Mercy? You said you needed something? For Monday? I sent you some links today with useful information on mummichogs."

Every year, Lulu fell in love with a different creature or ecological wonder of the world. She'd hatched butterflies from cocoons and chicks from eggs, filled aquariums with slugs and spiders and snakes, and infected her students with a love of the natural world she hoped would last a lifetime. Each day was a field trip and the classroom a theme park where learning of all subjects from geography to math to English was informed by her current passion and obsession. As Mercy understood it so far, this year's class mascot creature was a bottom-feeding fish with the unlikely but adorable name of mummichog, which Lulu pronounced "mammachug." That was the extent of Mercy's knowledge and enthusiasm. In truth, it sounded like a good name for a funky bluegrass band to Mercy's ears. Now, Lulu was telling her, politely, to do some homework on her beloved mummichogs before the classroom visit.

"Great. Mummichog links! And a podcast! How do you find the energy? I'll look at them tomorrow night. As usual, you seem to have everything all covered. Thanks. What time do you want me there again?" Mercy inspected the shelf of pink geraniums blooming in the window, poked around in the soil, rubbing her fingers against the fuzz of the leaves, smelling her fingertips, dabbing the scent behind her ears.

"Ten would be great. We can have coffee in the staff room and begin after recess." Lulu crunched a carrot and reached for the cutting board.

"Can I at least chop something? Toast the croutons? Where's Hap?"

"Ran out to get rolls. Here, okay, put out some cheese and crackers. What's in the bag? I told you not to bring anything!" Lulu rapped Mercy's knuckles with her wooden spoon.

"Ow! Hope you don't use the ruler like that on your poor students. Lulu, you're going to think I'm crazy maybe but—"

"Not think, I *know* you're crazy. Bonafide fruitloop. What got into you last night, anyhow? Going off on that tangent like you did. I really thought you were plastered but I know you're trying to go easy on the wine. Just like me," she laughed, taking another sip of chardonnay.

"I was overtired, Lulu. No. Well. That's only partly it." Mercy hesitated. "You might say I've had a revelation this week."

"Heavens, revelation. Sounds serious. You? Religious? HA!"

"Not that kind of revelation. It *is* serious. I need to clean up my act. Tuck in the edges of my life."

Lulu turned and stared at her. "Mercy, you are talking in that weird coded way of yours. It sounds like you are doing the laundry or making a bed or something. What does this mean in plain, non-metaphorical language please?"

"I want to clear the clutter in my life. My house. Because—"

"You've been watching the Home and Garden channel again, haven't you?"

"No. Actually, when I was at the doctor's—"

"The other day. Yes, you told me. Is this a perimenopausal sort of revelation? New-found crone wisdom? Mid-life madness?" Lulu talked with a mouth full of cracker. "The red pepper hummus is great!"

"Well, the thing is. The thing is…" Mercy decided the bad news about her lump should wait until after dinner. "Actually, do you remember that toy you got me for my forty-fifth birthday?"

"Toy?"

"The Horny Little Devil Vibrator, it was called. To be specific."

Lulu rolled her eyes and frowned. "Yes. You didn't talk to Wiggins about that, did you? You did *not* say who gave it to you." Lulu was clutching her throat.

"No. No. No. Of course not. Well, anyhow, I never used it. It seemed a shame to throw it out. Who else would I offer it to? I've got it here, in the bag."

"You want me to have it? Mercy. That's a little…intimate, even for us, isn't it? My God, Hap would die of humiliation.

Lemme see." Lulu wiped her hands on her apron.

"Haven't you ever seen one?" Mercy reached in the bag.

"Hardly. I just ordered it online, wrapped it, and gave it to you. Getting it for you was an act of courage. Actually, it was Teeny's suggestion."

"What? Teeny? Sweet Jeezuz. You and Teeny Gaudet—the nymphomaniac slut husband stealer alcoholic—sat around and discussed my lack of a sex life? Lulu!"

"Mercy! She is not and Teeny never hit on Hap!"

"Well, I wouldn't leave him alone in a room with her for a split second."

"We better not get started on Teeny. You know I love you both."

Mercy wrinkled her nose, twisted her mouth, then bowed. "Of course you do. Namaste to you, too." She yanked the vibrator out of the box.

Lulu looked alarmed. "It looks so *big.*"

Mercy ignored this, knowing Lulu had no idea how the statement revealed far too much information about her husband.

Then Lulu leaned forward, her chin jutting out, lips sucked in, trying not to laugh. "How does it work, exactly?"

"Like I said: How would I know? Here are the instructions. It has two 'on' buttons and different vibrational speeds. You turn it on here. And if you want to…then this thing-a-ma-do is for like the, you know, the outside."

The Horny Little Devil started rolling and spiralling in her hands. Lulu started shrieking hysterically. "Mercy! Oh my god!"

Mercy laughed with her. "It looks…like it's alive, eh?"

Lulu shook her head. "No, it looks demented. Maybe I

could use it as an egg beater."

Mercy wagged it around. "Hand-held Mixmasters like you've never seen before! A martini shaker just for you!" Lulu was clutching her stomach, laughing. Then the expression on her face changed. She was gazing past Mercy. Her eyes widened and her face froze in an expression of utter horror.

"Mercy? Lulu? Louise! Look who I bumped into in the parking lot. Some old friends."

Hap Kunkle's voice was like a truck rolling over gravel. Mercy turned around, the Horny Little Devil wobbling right in front of her face.

Hap stood in the doorway, gaping. With him was Cassandra, smirking. Hubert Rutherford, beside her, swirled his brown fedora in front of his heart. And trailing after them all was none other than Valmont LeClair. The very last person Mercy ever wanted to see again. Now, here he was, his head cocked sideways like a French poodle, looking at her in that same concerned way he had all day. And there she was, with a whirling dervish sex toy in her hands and once more a clueless if not insane look on her crimson face.

"Come in!" shouted Lulu. "Make yourself at home!" Mortified, she bustled around them all, giving Mercy the opportunity to stuff the Horny Little Devil into the box. This Mercy did, but the box began to dance along the countertop back and forth in a mechanical shuffle.

"So glad to see you, Cassandra, Hubert. And you must be Val." With one arm extended towards Valmont, Lulu grabbed the devil and the box with the other, and threw them into the bag. On cue, Mercy fanned the bag with a dish cloth, as if she were putting out a fire. But there was no stopping the little bugger. All of them, in a kind of semi-circle, stared curiously at the bag as it hopped five times and then—all of them heard it—let out a distinct shuddering gasp. There was one last triumphant swirl and the bag slouched down, next to a bowl of bananas, satiated, exhausted, and ready to rest.

"So, where are those ribs?" said Hap. "I'll fire up the barbecue."

"What was that thing?" asked Hubert.

"Like I love to say, Hubert, there are some things you just do not want to know," replied Cassandra. She winked at Mercy. Thank God for celestial vibrations! Alleluia and Sweet Jeezuz!

Arriving home as supper started, his hair still wet from showering after soccer practice, his handsome face scrubbed shiny, fifteen-year-old Rio Lutes-Kunkle grabbed a plate with enough food for a small army and pulled up a chair beside Mercy. Rio's presence somehow transformed the spirits of the awkward, confused adults gathered together in that cozy kitchen on Allan Street.

"Can you believe we're still barbecuing in October? Mercy, where were you on Thursday night?" He reached over and hugged her, a forkful of potatoes in his fist. "Seven three-pointers. I kid you not. I was hot. Swish! You weren't there…"

"I read it in the paper. Congrats! Sorry, but I had to work." Mercy high-fived Rio's open palm. Cassandra's ears perked up, catching the tone of a lie in Mercy's voice.

"Swish?" Valmont smiled at Rio. "Can you explain?" Rio became a sportscaster, launching into a play-by-play description of every move in the game. The adults watched and listened, delighted by the exuberance of youth, the animation of a soul not yet jaded by life. Cheerfully, they passed the bread and refilled their glasses.

After Rio left, Valmont talked charmingly in his broken English about his work and Hap explained how they'd met at a home and garden expo back in the eighties. Cassandra only half listened. She was much too conscious of her daughter. Despite the embarrassing outburst at the fundraiser the previous evening and Mercy's borderline psychotic phone messages, and perhaps a strained look around the eyes, she appeared normal. She had no cough, Cassandra observed. Could it be her breasts? she fretted. The same cancer as mine? she wondered. Or was it at too advanced a stage to cure? Perhaps it was her heart. Cassandra's own heart was on a drum roll of anxiety. She snapped and unsnapped the compact in her pocket.

"Isn't it just an amazing coincidence how you met Mercy today and ended up here tonight?" Lulu asked Valmont just then, interrupting Cassandra's stream of worry.

Cassandra looked up and caught Hap wink at his wife.

"Maybe it's one of one of those Divine Gongs. You know, there are no coincidences, just those things meant to be. Ding dong clang! GONG! In case we forget we get slapped upside the head now and then, or pleasantly surprised and then, well, we remember everything is just all as it should be, all part of God's plan," suggested Cassandra brightly.

Hubert nodded and murmured, "Amen." Mercy winced. Hap reached for more wine. Lulu rolled her eyes at Mercy. Valmont appeared even more confused.

"Well, I am appy to see Merci so appy tonight." Valmont turned to Mercy then. "Who was your friend who died?" He looked at the others, his hands fluttering in front of his face. "Merci? She was...so sad today she made herself...*malade*."

"*Malade*? Sick? You were sick at work? A friend died? Who?" demanded Cassandra, immediately on alert. The word "death" sent a chill through her.

Mercy smiled at Valmont with great difficulty and fantasized kicking him in the shins.

"No one you know, Mother. A friend from university— Isaiah Livingstone." Of course, she would not tell anyone the real source of her distress: that her blue jay had died, that her unrequited Noah lust would forever be unrequited, and that she herself heard faint steady echoes of Death's gong.

"God rest his soul," said Hubert out loud.

God heal my daughter from whatever affliction has got her going on again about the note, prayed Cassandra silently.

God may have been busy elsewhere, for as they cleared the table after supper, Mercy leaned down and whispered in her mother's ear, in that ever-hopeful tone.

"Mum, did you get my message? I left several reminding you about the note."

"What note?"

Mercy nearly stabbed her mother with the fork she held in her hand. She rushed to the sink and shook crumbs from the placemats.

"What note?" her mother had the nerve to ask again.

Mercy dropped the fork. It went down the garburator.

"MUM! Would you please—"

Lulu came in from the dining room, juggling stacked plates. "Help me out, Cassandra?" Mercy stomped out of the kitchen.

"Thanks for saving me," Cassandra whispered to Lulu. Mercy was pacing in the hallway, trying to calm down.

"From what?"

"Lulu, she's asking about the note. I'm worried about her." Lulu was about to reply, but Mercy re-entered the kitchen.

"He's so handsome, don't you think?" Taking some plates, Lulu pointed with her chin outside to the deck, where the men stood. Valmont and Hugh talked to Hap as he scraped crispy grunge from the barbecue tools.

"He is. I remember a little French. I think I'll go have a smoke with the boys," Cassandra replied saucily as she plunked the dishes down.

"Cassandra, I'm shocked! You—a married woman." Lulu and Cassandra giggled conspiratorially. The way only two married women who have sex on a regular basis could giggle together, thought Mercy.

"And don't you dare give Hap a cigarette!" Lulu warned. "It's been three months. Longest ever."

Cassandra was already out the door.

"Lulu, do you know it was her cancer that made me stop smoking? And she's still puffing now and then, the witch." Mercy began rinsing dishes.

"Mercy! You are the worst reformed smoker I have ever met."

"I want the note and she's refusing. Again."

"The note? As in The Note? Why? I knew there was something up with you. Was this part of your revelation?" Lulu stopped loading the dishwasher and looked at Mercy. "Talk to me."

Mercy grabbed her friend's hands and nodded. "Let's go into the living room, okay?"

Rio was back in the living room practising his cello. As he played, the notes wrapped around the Lutes-Kunkle household in ribbons of sound, protecting the heart secrets and necessary lies they knew or thought they knew about each other.

In the end, Mercy didn't tell Lulu about the surgery. Nor did she bother to point out to Lulu that Rio now looked a little stoned and his hair smelled of pot. Instead, she railed bitterly about her mother's pertinacity.

★★★

"If only my mother were still alive and that stubborn. Why doesn't Mercy realize how lucky she is to still have her mother? And why the sudden obsession with the note again?" Lulu said to Hap as she brushed her teeth and got ready for bed. "Do you think she and Valmont liked each other?" she added.

Hap shrugged, getting into bed, reaching for a magazine on the bedside table. "I know he found her physically attractive. I guess he ran into her all week, not just today. He said he met you briefly, too."

"He did?"

"In your bra."

"Oh lord!" Lulu choked on the toothpaste.

Hap's hearty laugh boomed out. "Lulu, Valmont also said he thought she was troubled." Hap hesitated. His voice sobered. "About this note business, do you think there was a note?" he asked, looking over his reading glasses.

Lulu spit into the sink and closed her eyes, "How on earth would I know, Hap? Do I look like a mind reader?"

"It was just a question, Lulu. Relax. And what on earth were you two doing when we came in?"

Lulu giggled and skipped back into the bedroom. "Let me explain." In her hand was a brown paper bag. In the bag was the Horny Little Devil.

At that same instant, a few streets over, Cassandra Fan-joy-Rutherford was vibrating in prayer, recalling the conversation she'd overheard earlier.

"Mercy, will you be coming next week to the Odell Youth Symphony recital?" Rio asked when the after-dinner cello concert was finished.

"If I live that long," Mercy replied flatly. Rio and Lulu, thinking this was a joke, laughed. "I wouldn't miss it for the world," Mercy added quickly.

Cassandra-Fanjoy Rutherford, mother of Mercy, keeper of the note, lover of Hubert, concealer of truth, had at that moment been pouring herself tea in the kitchen. *If I live that long.* Mercy's words settled like ten-ton bricks in Cassandra's stomach. Her beautiful mouth quivered as she bit her lower lip hard. She'd poured her tea without spilling a drop, but the cup rattled in its saucer. Now, as she prayed, she knew that she was hearing the rattle of death at her stubborn, selfish, odd, beloved daughter's door.

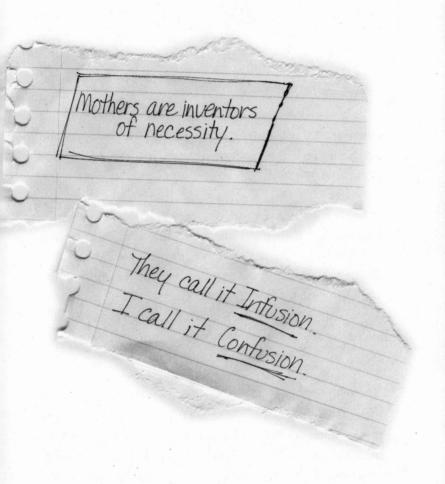

Mothers are inventors of necessity.

They call it Infusion.
I call it Confusion.

—Mercy's quotebook notebook

"Find your mountain." Belle's voice was firm and melodious.

Twenty people floated to the front of their yoga mats like synchronized swimmers in the belly of a pool. They stood straight and tall, their necks long, arms by their sides, palms like small cups from which they were gently, slowly, releasing water.

"This is Tadasana, or mountain pose, Mum. Now inhale, pushing your belly out. Exhale, pressing your navel to your tailbone as you do. Repeat three times. Mum, the exhale is through the nose not the mouth for now. Keep your mouth closed, lips parted slightly. Relax your jaw. Don't grind your teeth. Mum? And exhale. Keep your eyes closed or slightly lowered, gazing at a point in front of your mat. Now, thank your body for showing up."

"Thank you!" shouted out Mercy.

"Silently, Mum." Belle shot her a look of practised patience. "Set your intention for today's practice. What do you need? Stillness? Resolve? Strength? Emptiness? It is your time. This is your choice. Whatever your intention, be mindful as we work through each pose. Keep breathing. That, too, is your choice."

Mercy grimaced, wishing Belle would pick up the pace. How could you be empty and have a full mind at the same time? she wondered. And why would anyone choose emptiness? Mercy's breathing was rapid and uneven. She was hyperventilating. How did she end up here anyhow?

Mystic Stables, 123 Agape Way in Lower Ferryville, was a thirty-minute drive south from Odell, if you took the new highway and skipped the ferry, which Mercy did that morning. Belle was pacing in the driveway as she drove in, pointing at her wristwatch and beckoning Mercy to hurry up. Mercy hastened out of the car, puzzled at Belle's impatience.

"I didn't know you meant eight on the dot!" Mercy rushed towards the yoga studio, a recently renovated stable. A tight hair band of pain arched over her skull. She was hungover from the barbecue at Lulu's.

"Well, I did. We're waiting!" Belle carped.

"We? Who's we?" asked Mercy.

"Oh, just a few who gather on Sunday mornings to pray with our bodies." Belle smiled.

"But I thought it was just going to be you and me. Yoga." Mercy pouted and almost stomped her left foot. "And have you read my letter yet?"

"There's a mat all ready for you, Mercy," Sage said, appearing at the door. As usual, her face was a mask, impossible to read.

The inhabitants of the small room, sitting like Buddhas, were silent and rather constipated looking, observed Mercy. Breathing was apparently serious business. There was not one familiar face. Music was playing. Incense was burning. All Mercy had come for was to see if Belle would agree to meet her father. Now she considered how she might leave.

This was exactly the second Belle hit a bowl with what looked like a meat tenderizer, and told them to find the mountain.

If contorting her body for an hour was the price she had to pay, so be it, Mercy told herself. She placed her palms at heart centre, her mind whirling. Now, as she swan dived down, she stifled a giggle. She was not at peace. The only thing her inner voice chimed was *letter letter letter Belle did you read the letter?*

"*Namaste,*" Belle said an hour later. Groggily, they rose from corpse position, which Belle called *savasana,* and bowed to one another. "Today I won't join you for tea. My mother and I are going to have some time alone." Mercy, who had not relaxed much as a corpse, suddenly leapt to her feet. "Terrific!" she squealed.

The farmhouse was old. It had been lovingly restored beam by beam by Sage and a few friends. The kitchen was a large communal room; a cooking area and island led into a family room with a pine dining table and high-backed, distressed wooden chairs painted in faded primary colours. A tartan sofa and wingback chair were angled in a horseshoe in front of a fieldstone fireplace.

"Tea, Mama?"

Mercy nodded, gazing out over the pasture where three majestic horses grazed. The leaves on the trees beyond the pasture were brilliant—oranges and burgundy and maple leaf crimson. Mercy almost relaxed until she remembered why she was there. Belle clattered away. "Are these Sage's nieces and nephews? Sweet kids," said Mercy, looking at photos on the refrigerator.

"Those are her children. They're quite a bit older now." Belle put a plate of cookies on the table.

Mercy was dumbfounded.

"She'll explain sometime. Those are carob chip oatmeal

cookies. Try one. Delicious. Soy milk okay?"

Belle's head disappeared into the fridge. She was at home here, thought Mercy, feeling a pang of territorialism. "I am your home," she wanted to say. "Me. Remember me?" Sweet Jeezuz, she rebuked herself. Have I become one of those mothers resentful of their daughters' lives because they've never had a chance to live their own?

"By the way, I haven't read the letter, but I will. I promise." Belle spoke offhandedly. Mercy began biting her right baby fingernail, her head tilted to the left as she munched.

"I see."

"Do you want me to read it now and then we can talk?"

"Yes—No. Yes. No. Fuck it. Belle, actually, just give me the letter back."

"What? Did you just say 'fuck it'?" Belle wheeled around, her eyes wide.

"It's just some old stuff, anyhow."

"Oh, Mum, please. I want to read it. See, it's right here, I just haven't got 'round to it." She held up the envelope, the milk under her arm.

Mercy snatched the envelope out of Belle's hands, and the milk went flying. Ignoring the mess, she stuffed the envelope into her bag. "And forget the fucking tea. I would not want to inconvenience you any further. This has been—was just lovely, Belle. Thanks. Now I'll just get out of your way and let you get to all that stuff you have to do. *Namaste*. Have a great day!"

"Mum. MUM!" But Mercy was already out the door, and before Belle could blink, Mercy was in the car, roaring out the driveway. The Deville spewed toxic, caustic exhaust in Belle's face.

Retreating to the safety of the farmhouse, Belle paced frantically in front of the fireplace.

"Find your mountain." It was Sage. Belle stopped and went into tree pose instead.

"What happened?" Sage asked.

Belle, her hands extending out like branches, became a tree in the wind, swaying from side to side. "We sure didn't plan on this one. She took the letter back."

"What? Shit."

"I know," said Belle, unravelling herself and pacing again.

"She took it back? Well, I never, we never—" Sage had her hands to her cheeks.

Belle nodded again. "I know. I know. What have we done?"

Sage reached for a cookie. "What now?" she munched.

"Well I'm sure I don't know. I followed your advice. I should have—well, no matter. Anyhow, maybe Grambo will know what to do," Belle said over her shoulder, jabbing the numbers on the phone. "Breathe, Sage," she added.

"Okay. Right, good idea. And consulting an elder. Very good. Yes. Good idea." She woofed down another cookie, took a gulp of water, and lit a clove cigarette.

"Give me one of those? And try to relax." Belle had never seen Sage this shaken. "Put on some k.d. lang."

"Relax? You are telling me to relax? This is a disaster. Oh, Belle—what are you going to do? Holy Mother Mary of God!"

No matter how many years she'd meditated, in times of crisis, Sage, formerly Karen Riley from Flin Flon, Manitoba, sounded a lot like her good old Flin Flon Roman Catholic self. Now, she was wringing her hands, concerned for Belle. But as a mother herself, she was equally worried for Mercy. She watched as Belle waited for an answer, then went to put on the CD.

"Hello Grambo. It's Belle. I...um...need to talk. About Mum. She's acting really strange. And I need some advice. Call me. Love ya."

Belle disliked voice mail. She would keep trying until she got her grandmother in person. How easy it was for messages to get missed. Or ignored. Or erased by accident. Or forgotten, for any number of reasons.

After her father's suicide and her mother's subsequent conversion, Mercy was never confirmed and therefore had never taken communion in any church, certainly not in the church of the People of the Church of Faith and Light and Celestial Vibrations.

When Hubert first moved in with Cassandra, Mercy was thirty years old, and she'd learned all she ever wanted to know about the Vibrationists already. Nonetheless, Hubert had proudly invited her into his "office," converted from her mother's back shed. He wanted to give her a tour and explain the Vibrationists' version of communion. "Just tell you a wee bit about Infusion." Out of politeness and curiosity, Mercy had accepted the invitation. She took along her notebook for comfort and protection.

The office was actually a workshop—metal shelving units and racks of high-tech equipment on one side of the room, a honeycombed wall of Tupperware containers and small jars holding screws, bolts, adapters, sockets, and plugs on the other. Extension cords and connector cables of varying lengths and thicknesses, in hues of orange and black, purple and green, hung in tightly wrapped coils from every rafter, nook, and cranny, like waiting serpents ready to uncurl and strike out at any moment. Hubert's long narrow workbench, flush against the end wall, was littered with gadgets, familiar tools like screwdrivers and pliers, and uncommon others. This miniature electronic scrap yard was Hubert Rutherford's world. There was usually something dismantled or broken in the process of being assembled or inspected or tuned up on his workbench.

"The man is always tinkering with something in there," Cassandra had said many a time with pride and affection. Hubert's machines made high-pitched sonar sounds, making Mercy wonder sometimes if he was a ham operator attempting to receive secret signals from UFOs.

That day, by mistake, she'd reached out and touched a knob. A slight electrical shock had surged through her.

"OW!"

"Look, don't touch!" Hubert laughed.

"Sorry, I'm a tactile learner," Mercy said.

"This means you have a lot of vibrational energy yourself, Mercy Beth. Did you know that?"

"No." She'd wondered if Hubert was referring to the chakras. Even as a teenager, Belle had been trying to tune her into some chakra-centred swirling energy concept. "How did you become a Vibrationist, Hubert?" she asked. "I'm fascinated." That was no lie. Mercy was deeply fascinated with how people ended up being the people they were.

"Well, my excess vibrational energy, until I could identify and harness it as such, was leading me to drink. Many Vibrationists are ex-addicts. Are you suffering from any compulsions or addictions? Addictive patterns of behaviour?"

"I quit smoking. *Again.*"

"Alleluia," Hubert smiled, crossing himself.

Mercy was encouraged. "Then there's nail-biting, obses-
sive worrying, and reading in every room of the house. And
well, okay, I actually do have a diagnosable condition…"

"Feel no shame with me, Mercy," Hubert nodded, urging
her on.

"I've diagnosed myself. Do not tell my mother. I have hy-
pergraphia. I'm a…a…hypergraphic." She began scribbling
furiously, as if to punctuate her point.

"I'm not familiar with this…uh…condition." He clasped
her hand.

"It's an obsession to write. I can't stop myself. Where
there's paper…"

"Well, Mercy, it's not hurting anyone, is it?"

"Other than trees? Well, sometimes I think, stop writing,
Mercy Beth, and get doing."

"Do you want healing from this?"

"No, heavens, no. I'm more comforted by it than both-
ered—really." She flipped to a new page. "Besides, I get a
little something for my column every week."

Hubert proceeded to show her a machine called an oscilloscope. He owned several, ranging in size and versatility.
He used a portable one for communion—or Infusion, as it
was called.

"I'd be more than happy to show you how it all works, if
you come to just one service."

"Perhaps I will sometime," she'd lied.

Now here she was, at Sunday Evensong Vespers, eighteen
years later.

Her mother was surprised to see her. Mercy reached for
her hand. "I know why you're here," she said, giving Mercy's
hand a quick squeeze and letting it go. "To pressure me

some more. Your phone messages are getting downright hostile. There was no note."

"I came to take Infusion. Hubert said I could. I'm sort of praying—that you will find it in your heart to give me the note."

"You don't 'sort of' pray, Mercy Beth. You do or you don't. And I'll pray you'll come to your senses."

The service began with a vibrophone solo and the psalm of the day.

The formal prayers were short and, Mercy felt, rather honest. Then there was a sermon, which was a cross between performance poetry and an evangelical television special. Today's sermon was on the theme of harmony. "Do you see the word harm in harmony?" began Hubert. "Harmony does not come easily. We so very often struggle towards it, especially when we don't listen to each other's beating hearts. Or when we think we can do it alone."

Mercy didn't fully understand the Vibrationists' metaphor of The Great Conductor God. Supposedly, humans and all other living things generated the vibrations and the Conductor got to orchestrate. Therefore, the state of the individual—indeed, the world—had everything to do with the vibrations the Conductor was receiving; this, in turn, determined the melody one heard, the key to be lived in. God could only work with what he was given. Therefore, everyone sought to achieve inner equilibrium in order to position themselves to hear God. It was all very convoluted.

"So can you create harmony without harming an other? Is it harmony at all costs? And don't we sometimes *need* discordant notes? As the weeping philosopher Heraclites once said, out of discord comes the fairest harmony."

Mercy looked up at the mention of Heraclites and thought of Raymond Piper talking to her navel about the beauty of how beavers built their homes. Mercy erased the memory immediately; it was not the right place or time for remembrance of one's sexual past.

Hubert must have composed the day's sermon to soften the hardness of her mother's hard heart, Mercy thought as she listened. What a wonderful man he was. She glanced sideways at her mother, who looked oblivious to any subliminal message or subtext in her husband's words about the note. When the sermon was over, a hymn was sung.

Mercy tuned out and wondered, were she to leave now, if there was enough time to break into her mother's house, ransack it, and find the note herself. She pictured herself handcuffed and in jail before the sermon was through.

"Mercy, you are welcome to join us," Hubert was saying, rousing her with the mention of her name. Mercy had almost fallen asleep. She stood and positioned herself for Infusion.

The People of the Church of Faith and Light and Celestial Vibrations shuffled to the front of the room in single file. In horseshoe formation they gathered around the altar. Reluctantly, Mercy joined them.

Hubert cradled the hand-held oscilloscope. He arranged a small metal box resembling a vintage radio on the altar and connected the two machines with a thin blue connector cable. This second machine was an audio generator, a device that could generate sound waves, measuring the frequency in cycles per second. This was the machine that hummed and registered static, and made wizardy radar sounds. In the left corner of the generator, a small black knob set atop a silver protractor-like disk shielded in plastic controlled the frequency. "Anything beyond 20,000 hertz or 20 kilohertz, the unit of measurement, was out of range of what the average human ear could detect," Hubert had told her that time in his shop.

Infusion went like this: with one hand over the heart, the other hand on the knob of the audio generator, each person generated a sound. The sound registered graphically on the oscilloscope in green phosphorescent light— etching lines and waves and patterns like an electrocardiogram. This sound from the audio generator was then transmitted through a small, black, portable speaker, the top of which had a hole in it. The vibration could be felt almost through the palm of the hand. Then came a spurt of air. One could hear, see, feel the vibration they were generating. All of this was sent by computer to Hubert, who printed out what he called The Evensong Symphony. When Infusion was over, he went to the keyboard, usually set on vibraphone, and played the readout as if it was a musical score.

Now, Mercy took her turn. "Gggggreeeeek?" She sounded like a dead bird. Then she returned to her seat, and with the rest of them, waited for the feature presentation. Lunatics, she thought, shifting in her seat. All of us.

Hubert began to play. The Vibrationists began their vibrating.

Mercy did not vibrate, but she was, surprisingly, deeply stirred by the music. Her mother reached for her hand.

"See. It's worth it, honey, even if it's just for the music that opens up your heart. And the people."

The music, yes, okay, thought Mercy.

After church, Hubert invited Mercy back to the house for a drink. Cassandra lit a fire. Mercy fidgeted and waited while Hubert poured himself a soda and the women a gin and tonic. Mercy was hoping for an opening, an appropriate moment to ask about the note. But her mother was on a roll, lecturing her on how music and vibration settled the soul and cooled the spirit.

"Mum, please, there *was* a note, wasn't there?" Mercy finally interrupted.

"Mercy, lord—so off topic. No! No! Let's not fight, okay? Especially so soon after Infusion."

"Don't you have the 'Thou shalt not lie or bear false witness' rule?" Mercy was towering over her mother.

"Mercy, please?" It was Hugh. He winked as he handed her the gin. "Patience," he whispered. Mercy placed the gin on the table.

"Okay," she said, sitting back down. "No fighting now. But Mum, there was a note. I know it. Before Thursday you will give it to me."

"Why Thursday? What is going on with you, anyhow? You're not telling me something, Mercy Beth! Are you sick?"

"What makes you think that?" Mercy clenched her fists.

"I knew it. Like me. Oh Mercy, honey, it's your breasts, isn't it?"

For one crazy slice of a second Mercy considered blurting out the truth: No. It's in my belly. An unusual cluster of *cells*. Picture mini terrorists in my belly ready to detonate. Instead she smiled and said, "There is nothing wrong with my breasts."

"Then what has gotten into you?"

"Didn't you want some lemon in your gin, Mercy?" Hubert asked politely and smiled over at Cassandra.

"Right, I'll go get some," Cassandra huffed off knowing she'd been dismissed. "Go ahead, you two, talk it over!" she shot back over her shoulder.

"Hubert, did she tell you if there was a note? I mean, I know there was but did she lie to you too?" Mercy leaned forward, searching his face for truth.

Hubert turned to stone. Finally he spoke. "Mercy, the truth of the matter is, the truth is, well, dear, I'm not sure the truth will set anybody free."

Mercy began to hiccup. Cassandra bustled back into the room. Mercy's hiccups continued, small claps of thunder breaking into the tense silence among the three. The fire roared. Hubert's eyes closed.

If only, they all were thinking, some things could go away as easily and eventually as the hiccups.

"The mummichog, otherwise known as the *Fundulus hetero-clitus*, is a small but heroic killifish found in estuaries along the eastern seaboard of Canada and the United States. In 1973, the mummichog became the first fish in outer space when it was carried on Skylab 3 as part of a biological experiment," Mercy read out loud and sipped her wine. *Talk about a fish out of water*, she scrawled in her journal, feeling she'd nailed the title of the "Mercy's Musings" column she would write after the visit to Lulu's classroom tomorrow. Then she continued to scan the information on the website links Lulu had provided.

Tonight, perhaps because she was still somewhat tenderhearted from the notes of Hubert's Evensong Symphony, Mercy found herself captivated by the beauty of mummichogs, their place in the universe as well as the miracle of their resilience. They were such survivors, she was discovering, sometimes the only species remaining in severely polluted, oxygen-deprived waters. They could live in cold and brackish water. Chameleon-like, they blended into their surroundings to protect themselves from enemies. In winter, they burrowed into mud. They spent their entire life cycle in the same place, in a radius no bigger than the size of one football field. The female mummichog outnumbered the male by a ratio of three to one. They were easily baited because they ate almost everything.

Such romantics they were. Lunar or semi-lunar spawners, they spawned by moonlight only. *Lunarsexuals*, wrote Mercy in her coiled notebook. On one website Mercy learned their name came from an unidentified Native American tribe, and meant "ones who travel together in groups."

"But isn't that just like all of us, BB? Sojourners in the school of life? Thriving best when travelling along with others?" Mercy's tone was shrill and her voice thick. "At some level we are all just a school of little mummichogs, trying our damnedest to survive. We need each other, right old cat?"

The cat only purred.

Caught in the trap of her own melodrama, Mercy was mesmerized by the mummichogs, fish so transparent it seemed she could see their teeny tiny beating hearts.

It was in this somewhat histrionic frame of mind, with images of fish floating in her head, that Mercy, with BB curled up on her belly, settled into bed.

"No nightmares tonight," she whispered. "I need my sleep." It had been almost a week now of hellish nightmares—the three Godmothers, like Bob Marley's ghosts, leading the way every time. Night after night she'd seen herself descending to—was it hell, or bardo, or limbo land, purgatory? Or just some never-ending back alley? She'd floated into tunnels and empty, cave-like chambers until finally she emerged from the darkness to find herself at the river's edge. Always, the river. For as far as she could see, fish leapt and splashed, like sparks igniting in air, frolicking and kissing the water. Somewhere a child called out, as if in distress. Then, a gurgling sound—was it laughter? "Belle?" Mercy had screamed. Then there he was, her father, wading into the waters of River St. John, his hands swinging by his side. She'd wake up, flooded with relief, her heart doing triple time. But tonight Mercy had a plan.

Tonight she would have her very own Death Rehearsal. She would visualize her own death, but instead of going down, she'd go up. For a few moments, she'd suspend her disbelief and pretend that there was a heaven. Perhaps no streets paved with gold, but a place of light, and she would have her seat in the clouds, along with all those worthy ones. Earlier, to be prepared, she'd listened to the tape her mother used in the death workshops she once gave.

"Okay BB," she said. "Here I go."

She relaxed her eyelids. She pictured herself on a gurney, caged in by rails of steel. Tubes snaked above her head. An intravenous pinched her arm. She was alone. Where was Belle? Her mother? Lulu? Why had they left her bedside? Her beloved radish-nosed Dr. Wiggins kissed her forehead and pulled the plug, and left. *Come back.* But she did not have enough breath left to say it. "Three, two, two and a half, two and two and two and sixteenth millions...one." She exhaled.

It was dark at first. A cavernous darkness. She felt light. Spongy. She did not walk. She floated. In the distance, a light. Three flickering lights. The Godmothers holding their lanterns. Mercy followed the light and came to a place that was like a clearing in a forest. Everything was indigo blue. There was The Glowing Tree, just the way she'd told it in stories to Belle. Leaves were being transformed into stars in a funnel of light. In the distance, a dirt trail spiralled up a mountain. Ahead on the trail, the Godmothers waved and beckoned. Above them were others. Some were skipping. Some singing.

Then she saw those she knew, Stirling Cogswell, Harold Hubbley, and others, cheering like spectators at a parade, calling, "Hurry, Mercy!" Near the top she saw her father. "Sweet Pea. Mercy. Great job! You did it!" Behind him was Gladdie. "Gladdie! I've missed you so!" shrieked Mercy. She looped up the trail, running at full speed. The Godmothers stepped out from behind a boulder and stopped her. Granny Ross spoke sharply. "First, Mercy Beth, you have to look back and say goodbye."

"What?" The three women pointed downwards.

There, at the foot of the mountain, were Cassandra and Belle and Lulu.

Mercy looked up to her father and then back down at her mother. Then her daughter.

"Tell them good-bye, Mercy Beth," whispered all three Godmothers, their voices terse and firm.

Mercy Beth could not breathe. "I just can't."

"But you must," they answered and placed their hands on her arms.

"No," Mercy said out loud. She managed to pull away. Then she saw the trail had vanished. There was no way down.

Mercy bolted up out of the reverie, clutching her heart. "Belle!"

Eventually, Mercy reached for her bathrobe and slippers. Settling by the fire, she sipped tea, nibbled toast, and wrote in her journal until early morning. *Going up to heaven was no better than going down to hell. You still go. Going. Going. Gone. Dead. Died. Done.*

Raindrops like small footsteps in a slow dance beat a steady rhythm against the window. Buddha-Belly wrapped around her ankles. Suddenly, Mercy was grateful for the life she'd had. She was grateful for cinnamon toast and green tea and old cats and postcards and amazing bottom-feeding fish. It was a good feeling, a feeling that lasted until she realized it was Monday. She had to live her life, visit Lulu's classroom, get the suicide note, work on her obituary, and have blood work done—all before lunch. She stretched and shrugged herself awake. As soon as she was done, she would come straight back home to bed, pull the covers around her and read or write or do absolutely nothing but sleep the day away. This was only one of many things she'd always longed to do but had never quite gotten around to. Well, *carpe diem*! She'd seize this day and sleep.

To the Editor:
I have been overwhelmed this past week. The well wishes and emails from the readers of your paper and the people of Odell after your recent interview with me on living in New York these days have made me quite homesick. Thank you for all who sent their prayers and well, just continue to be kind to each other.

Sincerely, Christina Gaudet

—pasted in Mercy's quotebook notebook

On the seventh day after Mercy Beth Fanjoy was told she needed exploratory surgery, just when she was feeling runny as egg yolk with an overflow of jagged emotions, just as she realized she might never get through all the things she needed to do on her list of things to do and with only two days left before her date with the scalpel and maybe even death itself, she arrived home to find a letter postmarked from New York. It was, she knew at once, a letter from Christina "Teeny" Gaudet.

Mercy wasn't surprised. They'd always had a strong telepathic connection. Teeny had simply "heard" Mercy thinking about contacting her. And like always, she made the first move.

It was a blue letter in a purple envelope decorated with *Wizard of Oz* stickers. Mercy remembered the joke, the shared mythology: Mercy was the scarecrow; Lulu the good witch. Teeny was the Wicked Witch of the West and Dorothy and whoever she damned well wanted to be. The ink was turquoise. Teeny's handwriting was loose and generous and full of curlicue S's and swirls.

Dear Oldest Galpal:
It has been a while.

Twenty-seven years exactly, thought Mercy.

Whenever Teeny visited Mercy on those long-ago Saturday nights, she always brought three things: a forty-ouncer of Southern Comfort, a box of Bits & Bites, and whomever she was sleeping with that particular week. "The more, the merrier," she loved to say. Sometimes, Teeny would bring two boys, hoping one of them would linger and take mercy on Mercy. A Mercy fuck, she'd joke. Mercy was never amused.

Mercy didn't remember many of them by name or face. Probably Teeny wouldn't either—they all blurred into one after a while. A composite man remained in Mercy's mind, a shadowy figure eventually magically blooming into focus, like a Polaroid photo.

Except for Dave Ferguson, Mercy remembered him. He smelled like Brute aftershave and had a smile that revealed perfect Chiclet-like teeth. His jaw was square and, at first glance, it looked like he had no neck. His shoulders and chest were muscular; his T-shirt looked like it was shrinking on him by the moment. His buttocks were round and as hard as two halves of a cantaloupe. The crotch of his Levi's bulged conspicuously, reminding Mercy of the denim pouch of marbles she'd had in sixth grade.

He followed every move Teeny made through heavy-lidded eyes. His eyelashes were long, curled up and under, moving around his eyes like a spider spinning. He had the habit of slapping Teeny on the butt when she got up to get him another beer. Mercy didn't like him for this but then, Teeny Gaudet was no victim.

Whenever Mercy began nursing Belle, Dave smiled a shy, secret smile and blushed. He tried to avoid looking but didn't succeed. This shyness made Mercy halfway like him.

I am in AA. I am writing to you to make amends. But first, how are you? I heard you went to university and got yourself edjabacated. Go gal. Are you still working with the elderly in some kind of literacy education program? And are you doing a little writing of your own now? An advice column or some such? Good for you! News from home trickles in from good old Lulu. How is Belle? I'd love to see both of you some time I'm home. I cherish memories and fun of the good old days.

The Teeny Gaudet of the good old days had her faults. Her breath always smelled like Bits & Bites, and she was, even back then, an alcoholic. And she was sexually reckless. Not that Mercy should judge. But she did.

One Saturday night they were in the bathroom together, the place they always ended up by the third period of *Hockey Night in Canada*. They sat side by side, backs against the bathtub, legs halfway up the door as if barricading themselves against the hoots of "He shoots! He scores!"

"I'm pregnant," Teeny said, just like that.

"Oh my god...wh—?"

"I haven't got a clue. Maybe Mike. Maybe Dave." Teeny lit up a cigarette and passed it to Mercy. "You're leaking," she said.

Mercy looked down at her blouse and saw the circle of wet like a sunburst around her nipples. "I thought I'd go without my breast pads and look what happens."

Belle was four months old. Like a four-month-old herself, Mercy was only slowly getting the hang of things. She hadn't gotten over always feeling a bit lopsided.

She took off her shirt and started to express some milk into the tub.

"Holy shit," said Teeny, "you're like a goddam cow."

"Watch this," Mercy said, and sent a spray of milk across the bathroom. It splattered against the mirror then streamed down, slick as raindrops against a window. This sent them into fits of hysteria.

"I can't go through with it," Teeny said.

"What about adoption?"

"I'm too selfish. I can't see me being a single parent, either. Belle's sweet and everything, but I mean, I'm not like you. You love all this, right?"

"Yes. I love it," was what Mercy said to Teeny Gaudet that night. "I do, except, it's not like they try to tell you. The pregnancy, the delivery, the breast-feeding and stuff. God, all those books I read made it sound like some sort of organic spiritual experience."

"Orgasmic," Teeny corrected.

"Look, this is the reality." Mercy lifted her shirt again, this time to show her friend her chaffed nipples. Then she rolled down her pants and showed Teeny the stretch marks and belly ripples.

"Cracked nipples and belly ripples," Teeny shrieked. "You should write that in a book, Mercy. Bet it'd make you a mint."

That's when Dave exploded into the bathroom. "What, are you two lezzies or something? Your baby's crying, Boston just scored, and I thought you were getting me a cold beer."

"Get it yourself," muttered Teeny. Mercy high-tailed it to the bedroom to soothe Belle. Teeny kept drinking.

So. I'm two years sober. It's sobering in more ways than one.

You have to take a look at the mess you've made of your life, believe in some sort of higher power, and accept things as they are. I go to meetings every Tuesday at a Unitarian church these days.

When I think about what happened between us, I think maybe I was so envious of who you were. I was the hard boiled egg. You were such an innocent. I longed for that.

"Would you come with me, to have the abortion?" Teeny whispered that evening as they left. Mercy froze.

"Please. Your mother would take Belle. We'd only be gone overnight."

"Of course I will."

"You are ssssuch a good friend," slurred Teeny. "I don know what I'dever dowithoutyou."

They left Odell at daybreak. It was a five-hour drive to Sandy Harbour, described in tourism brochures as "a charming coastal community." Abortion Bay. That's the name the Canadian girls on the east coast knew it by.

As the sun rose, light smeared the sky deep red and Cat Stevens crooned "Morning Has Broken" on the eight-track cassette player. Teeny snapped gum and played hand drums on the steering wheel. Mercy navigated. The directions were clear. The trip was uneventful save for three roadside stops. Mercy's carsickness was triggered by Teeny's perfume, yet as her sense of misgiving increased with each mile travelled, Mercy worried her nausea was a gut reaction, an omen, a signal to turn back to Odell. She said nothing of this apprehension and sipped ginger ale to settle the heaving. Teeny burbled on about nothing in particular. "Feeling better yet, Mercy? Stick your head out the window and get some fresh Maine air."

They drove into town, such a small sleepy town, especially at that time of year. They reached the modest brick bungalow where a small sign out front flapped back and forth, squawking a rusty hello. Dr. Franks. M. D. "Frankenstein," Teeny whispered. "Murder Doctor," Mercy almost replied.

The house was clean and respectable. On the front stoop beneath a striped awning, flowerpots contained purple petunias. A toll-painted gingerbread man with "Welcome" painted on his chest twirled on a string by the doorbell. What had they expected? A back alley walk-up? A flowerpot of coat hangers? A sign instructed them to ring and wait. Mercy pressed the doorbell.

A voice floated out of nowhere. "Please state your name."

Teeny clutched Mercy's arm. "Christina Gaudet." Mercy had to say it for her.

A buzzer sounded. "Enter," commanded the voice.

The living room had been converted into an antiseptic-smelling waiting room. The nurse talked to Teeny in a low voice, soothing as honey and lemon on a sore throat, then gave her some forms to fill out—multi-coloured papers the colour of mint pastels. Her uniform was a faded mint green as well. Operating room colours. Her shoes squeaked on the tile floor every step she took. Mercy surveyed the empty room. Where were all the women with bellies starting to show, or mothers and daughters clinging to each other, or strained, skinny, acned teenage couples? she wondered. There wasn't another soul in the place.

Teeny's entire body vibrated. The smell of her fear was hot and spicy, like pizza left in a cardboard box overnight. Mercy smelled it through the layers of her perfume. A door finally opened on the far end of the room. A woman with a stethoscope necklace lumbered towards them.

"Which one of you is Christina Gaudet?" She looked like a wax museum sculpture. For a second Mercy thought Teeny was going to point to her.

"I am," she said finally, in a voice small and soft and unlike hers.

Dr. S. Franks glared at Teeny over the top of reading glasses. She was in her fifties, her hair chopped short and ragged. There was something martyr-like about her, thought Mercy. She'd never seen a physician wearing a navy blue track suit and sneakers.

Dr. Franks asked if there were any questions. Teeny confirmed her intention, filled out the final consent form, paid the money—three hundred in cash, a hundred of which was Mercy's. Then the good doctor left the room. "Did you get a load of those sneakers?" said Teeny. The nurse came to take her away.

When the door clicked behind her, it was the same metallic twanging as a prison door slamming shut, like in the movies, a reverberating sound meant to accentuate the theme of imprisonment, heighten the drama. Mercy breathed a sigh of relief and started to read an article in *Good Housekeeping*. It was one of those personal anecdotes. Widowed at Twenty-five: How Friends Helped Me Through. The article reminded Mercy of her mother and she worried how Belle was doing. She remembered the moment of giving birth, how it felt when the baby was in her arms that first time. For a second, she considered how she could write a story about what was happening to her that day. How I Helped My Best Friend Get an Abortion Even Though I Chose to Give Life. For about two seconds she entertained the idea of barging in there and saying, "Stop. I'll raise your baby, Teeny."

As it turned out, Mercy did have to go in.

The nurse came out, her velvety brown eyes clouded with anxiety. "We need you," she said. "Your friend didn't know…didn't realize she'd be conscious. We think you being with her might help calm her down. So if you wouldn't mind?"

Mind? Mercy would never again be able to grind coffee beans in those machines at the grocery stores. It reminded her of that sound, that vacuum sucking sound.

All she could see, past the tent of sheets made by Teeny's knees, were her friend's feet. Someone had made quilted gingham covers that fit over the metal stirrups, to warm them. Like oven mitts for a baby.

They held hands. Teeny squeezed so hard Mercy's birth-stone ring left a dent in her baby finger for a day. Mercy tried to make eye contact, but Teeny kept her head tilted backwards, studying the clock on the wall behind her. Mercy wondered if it was like a focal point you find when you're in labour. Teeny whimpered once or twice, and it was over.

That afternoon, they checked into the Bootlegger Inn. It was a tacky place with a skull and crossbones flag flapping in the parking lot. There was a plaster of Paris hull of a ship marooned on a rock in the front lobby. Someone artistic had taken the trouble to glue green felt over the rock and varnish it. Mercy was amazed at how much it looked like slimy algae.

The desk clerk looked them over and smiled. "Oh, you're Maritime gals," he drawled. Only he said it slowly, making the "i" a long "e" so it came out *merry*time. Merrytime guhls. His smile turned into a sleazy grin. "We get lots of yous down here. Wild women, all of you. Real good-time guhls. Welcome to Sandy Hawbuh."

"That Maine accent. So attractive," said Teeny as they turned away. "I feel like I'm in a Stephen King movie."

At around six o'clock, Teeny took the pill they'd given her at the clinic and slept fitfully through the evening. Mercy ordered from a Chinese takeout and watched a game show with the sound turned off. Teeny jumped when, by mistake, Mercy shouted out, "What is *Moby Dick?*"

In the middle of the night, Teeny woke up with cramps. She only settled back down after Mercy rubbed her belly and reassured her it was the right decision, one of those times, Mercy figured, you tell a person what you know they want to hear.

They went through Bangor on the way home. It was out of the way, but Teeny insisted they drive by Stephen King's house. She had directions. The house was palatial, almost gothic. The pink colour most unusual, a bloody rag in water. It triggered for Mercy the trauma of the previous day.

"Let's go, Teeny. Now!" she'd demanded. "The place gives me the willies."

Teeny insisted Mercy take a picture of her standing in front of the mansion before they left.

"I'm going to be a writer, Mercy. I am," she proclaimed. "Maybe someday I'll even meet Stephen King."

"I'd like to write too," Mercy admitted.

"No, but I'm serious," Teeny said. "I even enrolled in a course in writing for children. I'm going to start with something easy. Work my way up."

They were stopped at the border by customs officials, who rifled through their suitcases for over an hour. "Sick," said Teeny. "They only want to see our underwear. I should have opened my thighs and said 'Look, no hidden babies, either.'"

Mercy stared straight ahead.

"Lost your sense of humour, have you?"

"It's not something to joke about, is all."

Teeny turned the music up. If they talked after that, Mercy could never remember what was said. Teeny mumbled thanks when she dropped Mercy off. Mercy raced into her mother's house. She snatched Belle up, sniffing her baby oil and Ivory smell, sniffing long and deep, sniffing and kissing every inch of her daughter, as if the feel of her flesh against her lips and her smell, the smell of one baby who swam to shore, would reassure her they were both still breathing.

So we both know what I have to make amends to you for. That night. That awful night.

Mercy put down the letter. About two months after their trip to Sandy Harbour, she'd left Belle with Teeny to go out on a date, one of the very few she'd ever had. His name was Evan McArthur, a boy with high cheekbones and almond-shaped eyes, a quiet boy from high school, home on vacation. They had ended up in his bedroom in the basement of his parents' house.

It was well after midnight when Mercy got home. She tiptoed in, her shoes in her hand, not wanting to wake the Hubbleys, not wanting them to know she'd been a loose woman and a bad mother, out so late. But Teeny and Belle were nowhere to be found. Mercy thumped a wild woman roar upstairs, pounding on her landlord's door. It was when Harold came squinting into the kitchen that Mercy heard the music blaring from across the street. And she heard Belle, screaming in that terror-stricken way that babies have, the kind of shriek that always made Mercy think they were being pierced by a diaper pin. Or worse.

Mercy flew through the front door of the house. There was Teeny in the smoke-filled front room, on the couch, draped over a man dressed in black leather. "Oops!" she said, belching in Mercy's direction. "You're home! She's having a ball." Belle was eyeing her mother and smiling. She was saying "Mummumumum" as she cooed from the lap of a Hell's Angel.

You drunk, you whore, you fucking idiot. Had Mercy said it? Or only thought it? Did it matter? It was enough to discover she was capable of murder. She smacked Teeny on her shoulder. Teeny curled into a fetal position and held her hand up. Mercy pounded her back once with her fist. The second her fist made contact Mercy wanted to hurl. Teeny cowered, but tried to laugh, as if it were a game.

"Oh. Girl fight! Let's get out of here, could get nasty," said one of the bikers.

Mercy snatched Belle up, walked slowly out the door, and never, not once, talked to Teeny Gaudet again.

After Teeny moved away to the States, she became Christina Gaudet, pronounced *goday*, and began writing children's books. She bought herself fur coats and jewellery. She wore hats. She did good deeds. She made a lot of money and knew many "C list" celebrities.

Celebrity is so not what it's cracked up to be. I've got money and a career and a lot of regrets. Burt the Burping Bear has made me a small fortune. And the TV gig was good too. So that part of life is good. Well, if you like being a kind of factory supervisor. I don't even write the books myself anymore. Actually, I feel I am in a transition. I'm hoping the next twenty years will get better. I have just met a very nice man. At—get this—an S.A.A. meeting. Sex Addicts Anonymous. I'm sure you won't be surprised by that. Usually most of us addicts have more than one…compulsion. A nice man, Mercy. Me and a nice man? Maybe I'm ready.

There was a phone number and an email address. Mercy pressed the letter to her forehead. Then she folded it carefully, put it back in the envelope. What was she supposed to say? I received your letter. You are forgiven for being young and wild and free and wounded. You don't seem to understand, Teeny. I should never have trusted you with my child. You remind me of my biggest failure. My poor judgments. I've missed you at times. Good luck facing life sober. It pretty much sucks. Except when it doesn't and, yes, my life's been decent if not as exciting or luxurious or glamorous as yours. But I'd rather have my life than yours any day. I do have a column and some people even think I write fairly well, if I do say so myself. Also, I might have ovarian cancer.

Mercy threw the letter in the garbage. Belle called a half-hour later.

"Mum, will you go with me when I meet him?" she began, tentatively.

"Pardon?"

"I need you to come. When I meet him, okay? I called him. Isn't that what you wanted?" Now Belle's voice was pulled tight—a string ready to break.

"Wha—?" Mercy gripped the phone in one hand and her throat in the other.

"You wanted me to call. I called. And—"

"Call who? Meet who?" Mercy massaged her neck.

"Mum, I read the letter, okay. I read it the day I got it."

"You read it. Almost a week ago? I don't understand."

"I…lied. I was just uncertain. I guess I tried to avoid making up my mind. Anyhow, so yes, I called him. He's coming to Odell tomorrow."

Mercy was going to be able to cross out number two on The List. The hoped-for reunion between Belle and her biological father had been arranged. She felt as if someone had just pushed her to the edge of a cliff and she was looking down. She felt the ground at the cliff face giving way beneath her feet.

"Tomorrow? Belle, are you sure?" *I would rather not but I will.*

"Yes," Belle said. *I need you Mum I cannot do this alone.*

"Well, of course, then. Yes." *Anything for you my own small fortune.*

The next day would be a busy one, but Mercy had made progress. Cassandra had called to say she and Hubert wanted to have breakfast. Mercy's most loyal fan had replied, so she had scheduled a blind date for three o'clock. As well, she had to go to the travel agent and get more blood work done before the surgery. The windshield wipers were acting up—the car needed to go to the garage. Mercy called to BB. She went to bed early, perused her tattered list, turned off her light, and hoped for a parachute.

Fanjoy, Mercy Beth. (Aug. 15, 1957–)

Mercy Beth Fanjoy, a lifelong resident of Odell, died on [...] from [...] cancer.

Self-employed for most of her life, Mercy Beth was part-time assistant manager at Occasionally Yours Stationery and Office Supply store, a part-time instructor with Odell University's Department of Extension Services, and a freelance contributor and regular Spice of Life columnist for the *Odell Observer.* "Mercy's Musings" was nominated three times for the East Coast Community Journalism Award. After seven years as a part-time mature student, she graduated with honours from OU. Her hobbies included rug-hooking, collage, gardening, making soup, and reading the poetry of William Blake. She also had a fine collection of vintage self-help and fitness books and nineteenth-century postcards.

A devoted single parent, Mercy Beth was loved and will be missed by daughter, Belle Fanjoy, mother, Cassandra Fanjoy-Rutherford, and stepfather, Hubert Rutherford. Her cat, BB, will need a good home. In lieu of flowers, donations to the Millennium Riverbank Revitalization Fund or the Glooscap Animal Shelter would be welcome. Alternatively, donations for daughter Belle will make Mercy Beth rest easier. A memorial service will be held in the Coffee Mill Restaurant at the Odell Hotel; Bee Godwin and Eunice McTavish presiding. Refreshments at the James Joyce Pub to follow. RSVP Louise Lutes and Hap Kunkle at 454-7803.

"She laughed She loved She really lived.
She cried She tried She died She did."

"This is not about sex," Mercy explained over a dessert of tiramisu. "This is about death. Do you understand?"

"*Non*, but I am fascinated. Enlighten me."

Mercy was in bed, snuggled up to Valmont LeClair. It was no dream. They were in a king-sized bed in Room 333 of the Odell Hotel. It was three in the morning and they were still talking. Rather, Mercy was talking. Valmont was valiantly trying to keep his eyes open. Not only could he not understand English very well, he was exhausted from the effort he'd exerted in *not* kissing her, as promised. And he wanted to kiss her, if for no other reason than it might possibly shut her up.

They had bumped into each other again—literally. In the hotel foyer, Mercy was walking backwards, waving good-bye to Bee as if it were the last time she would see her. The tile floor had just been mopped down. Valmont did not have a chance. Mercy slipped and came down hard, knees first. He bent over her in concern. "I'm fine, just fine," she said, jumping up. But she wasn't fine at all. With the help of the hotel manager, Valmont assisted her to a sofa just outside the James Joyce Pub.

The manager left when his walkie-talkie began making urgent static sounds. Valmont kept holding her hand, then invited her to dinner. Mercy accepted, realizing with a pang that she'd like nothing better.

Of all people, it ended up being Valmont LeClair that Mercy chose to confide in about the next day's surgery. They drank some wine and Mercy blurted it right out, ending with, "So I just don't want to be alone tonight. I'll leave before the sun comes up."

As they waited for the elevator and Mercy watched the numbers light up, she wondered if, when her life was over, she'd find herself going up to heaven or down to hell and either way, when the doors opened, if it would all look like the lobby of the Odell Hotel.

Valmont passed Mercy a glass of wine. She sat on the edge of the bed and watched a news channel as he packed his suitcase. "I 'ave an early flight," he explained apologetically. Mercy fidgeted and changed the channel.

It was only as they undressed, with their backs to each other, that Mercy realized what she was wearing: her Maidenform underwire support bra for the full-figured woman, which she realized was about as sexy as a body cast. She decided to keep it on.

They crawled under the covers and curled into each other. Mercy rested her head on Valmont's chest, which was not overly hairy. The hairs that were there were greying. She checked quickly, relieved to find he had none on his back. Resting her head on his chest, it felt cushiony, as though it had been custom-designed for her. He stroked her forehead.

Soon they slept, two chaste, intimate strangers. When Mercy woke herself up with her own snoring around midnight, she found Valmont staring, unblinking, up at the ceiling, his hands under his head, elbows out at the side, as if ready to do sit-ups. Mercy had drooled a puddle on his chest.

"I'm so sorry!" She jumped up and ran into the bathroom, wet a towel, wrung it out and slapped it on his chest. "I'm sorry. I do this all the time, drool, I mean. I can't keep my mouth shut even when I sleep, ruin all my pillows...I'm so embarrassed. Was I snoring very loudly?" She finished mopping him off.

"Like a tractor. It's ho-kay. *Pas de problème.*" He took the towel and finished the job. He was staring at her breasts. Her nipples poked like strawberries ready to pluck right through the cups of her plaster of Paris bra.

"Those are powerful nipples," he couldn't help saying. "Candies for a baby." Mercy jumped back in bed and rubbed against him.

"Oh. My."

"Sorry," he said.

"It's all right," she said. "I'm flattered."

"It's been a while," he said.

"When did your wife die?"

That certainly took care of Valmont's lust surge.

***

Sometimes in life, sometimes in those rooms of the Odell Hotel and places like it, people, mostly lonely or insatiable people, find themselves cozying up to other people, ones they scarcely know, confiding secrets and truths they cannot utter to their best friends or closest relatives. There is sometimes great joy in the perceived wickedness of the act. Certainly, there's the illusion of safety and a lack of accountability, and true confessions become whispered foreplay.

Valmont told Mercy about his late wife, the suddenness of her heart attack. He admitted that every morning he leapt from his bed to go running. He feared if he lingered there was a real danger he might be swallowed by the hole that was still there in the middle of his mattress, the middle of his life.

After Valmont confided so honestly, there was a tender silence in the room, accompanied by the laugh track on a comedy show from the next room over. In the cocoon of this unexpected undercover liaison, Mercy had been granted permission to speak. After almost a week of pent-up thoughts and bottlenecked emotions, a floodgate burst open.

"Well, Valmont—can I call you Val? You would not believe what my day was like."

Mercy woke early that pregnant Wednesday morning, determined to remain focused, clear, and detached in order to proceed with intention and clarity and do what needed to be done with the least amount of pain and drama. She was in enough pain. Belle's easy seated flow poses had done something, all right—they'd sparked her sciatica. It was like having a toothache in her leg, hip, and lower back. But it was worth it, after all. At least one thing on the things undone list would be achieved today, she thought. Belle's meeting her father! Maybe her mother would hand over the note.

Mercy rose, washed, ate, brushed, flossed, flushed, dressed, scrunched, lip-glossed, smacked, smiled, dabbed, patted, changed, fluffed, fed the cat, and left.

It was raining. At first, it was just a drizzle, but soon it was a pavement-splatting downpour accompanied by a howling wind. Mercy held the edge of the umbrella as she hurried towards the Coffee Mill. Again, she was a bit hungover. After Lifelines last night, some of the class had gone to the James Joyce Pub. The obituary assignment had been a huge success and everyone was in the mood for celebrating. Ernestine left with Lincoln and Jan left with head-twitching Trevor. Funny how the contemplation of death got folks excited about living.

· Bee was at the Mill early this morning as well, bustling from table to table as usual.

"You're the early bird today. Some wicked out there, eh?"

"Crazy wind. I'll be here all day," Mercy replied, shaking out the umbrella and setting it against the wall.

"Fine by me. Breakfast then?"

"I'm waiting for Mum and Hubert."

"Well, sit over there then—that's their booth."

"She's fine where she is. We won't be long." Cassandra was dressed in a rich shade of brown. It really was a colour few could wear to such effect. Her lips were painted coral. Hubert hung their coats up and sat down opposite Mercy. Cassandra slipped in beside her. Mercy's heart thumped. Could it be, after all this time, that she would get the note?

"Mercy, please listen. Carefully." Mercy felt like she was getting covert information from a spy.

"I have decided to tell you…"

"Mum! Thank you. Thank you." Mercy grabbed her mother's hand. "Wait! That, yes, there was a note. Yes there was. You did not dream it."

"Go on." It was Hubert.

"And I have also decided to apologize for not telling you that long ago."

"Continue," Hubert reached for Mercy's other hand.

"And, I have decided in my wisdom and out of—"
"Love, truly a mother's deep love," nodded Hubert.

"That I cannot divulge the contents of that note. Not now. Not ever."

"Mercy—" Hubert began, his voice begging forgiveness.

But Mercy had stood up and faced them both.

"This is so cruel—the cruelest thing you could ever have done to me. Both of you." She was wagging her finger. People were looking.

"You have to—"

"Actually, I don't have to anything. Leave. Now. I shun you! Shun you both! Do you hear me? Shunned! Go," she said. "GO! Go. Go vibrate yourself!"

★★★

Mercy looked into Valmont's face. He was scratching his cheek, his forehead crinkled in confusion.

"That's what I said. To my mother! Poor Hugh."

"I don't understand. Shun? Vibrate? And what note?"

"My father's suicide note," Mercy said matter-of-factly.

"I'm sorry."

"Me too. So anyhow, they left and I left. I went to the Y. I had a really great workout and then a steam in the sauna. But then that's when the day went from bad to worse. My daughter and her biological father were going to finally meet. I have a twenty-eight-year-old—I know, I know, I don't look that old, but I started young—and anyway, she has never met her father. So you can imagine how intense that was. Well, maybe you can't—you're a man and not a mother. But trust me, I am telling you this was a day I had thought about and hid from since the day she was born…all her life…Anyhow, I sat there and Belle showed up, on time for once, with Sage, her partner. My daughter is a bisexual who has chosen to love a woman and I am happy she has someone she loves in her life so I hope you are not hung up about gays and lesbians or anything."

"Ung up? I do not understand. I hung up the phone. I hang on when someone want me to wait. Gays. No I like women very much many women. Hung up?"

"No, I mean…do you have a problem with same-sex marriage? My daughter is going to marry a woman."

"Oh. No. No problem. I have an aunt…she was a nun…"

"Good. Great. Not that it matters, I mean I might not ever see you again after tonight. You will leave and go back to Quebec and I will die. Anyhow. 'Oh honey, how are you?' I asked when I saw her. She said, 'Fine, you?' I said, 'I'm a nervous wreck to meet your father again after all these years,' and she said, 'Mum, I need you to listen.' I was really puzzled. And she said—are you awake, Valmont?"

"*Oui, oui.* What did she say?"

"She said, 'Mum, we were both going to tell you.' I said, 'What do you mean? Tell me what?' And she held my hand and she looked at me and said, 'Well, I've known my father for years.' Sage, that's her girlfriend, well, I guess I should say her fiancée. No, that's her name, Sage like the spice. She took my other hand. I felt like some sort of an invalid. Lord, I hate getting looks of condescending sympathy like they were giving me. Then he was there, her father, he appeared by her side—like they'd had this all planned and she'd cued his entrance.

"'You must be—I believe you are my daughter, Belle.' He was trying to fake the reunion still because he did not know Belle had changed her mind and had just blown the planned fake reunion. He was shorter than I remembered. And he was very handsome. No wonder I fell for him. No wonder Belle is so beautiful."

"Well, she might get some of dat from you, *non*?" said Valmont. Mercy blushed in the dark.

"Anyhow, Belle hugged him and said, 'Dad, it's okay, I

am going to tell her the truth. Mum, I've been a part of my father's life for six years now.'

"So, I come to find out that when she disappeared for those long, god awful months she'd finally called him and he'd been the one to 'rescue' her, she said. Those were her words. Rescue. He is an acupuncturist. Then, all those seminars and courses she said she was taking, all the times she disappeared and I never heard from her? She was off going to visit her father. And, oh. Not just her father, her sister and brother and stepmother, who is apparently 'wicked' in the best sense of the word. 'Why didn't you tell me?' I asked. 'You lied to me,' I said. And she said, 'Mum, I didn't want to hurt you and Dad agreed.' *Dad.* She calls him Dad! 'He said he honoured you and would rather we not bother you.'

"I was speechless. I mean, he never betrayed me either, never told her he'd tried to contact her when she was younger, never told her he gave me money. I let that cat out of the bag myself. Belle left the restaurant crying and told me I was the worst, most selfish mother in the world."

"I am sorry." Valmont reached out to rub Mercy's arm, but she was oblivious.

"I also got fired from my job today and discovered how much of a fraud I really am. Ted Dawkins, my boss, set up this meeting. He said no more 'Mercy's Musings' needed at the *Odell Observer*. Blogs and podcasts were the way to go. He gave me a brochure on a blog workshop and another on podcasts by a guy they call The Podfather. Then, well, it just keeps on getting better. To add insult to injury, Stella McBride comes in a half an hour later—at the same time I scheduled a blind date kind of thing with a loyal faithful reader. She tells me that my most loyal fan and se-

cret admirer was Stirling Cogswell. All those years Stirling
Cogswell had been my fan and secret admirer! Also my
most sarcastic, rattlesnake biting critic—the disgruntled
grammarian, trying to keep me on my toes. Imagine. I was
so insulted! I mean, was I that pathetic? I wonder if I have
any real fans. After Stirling died, Stella tried to keep it up.
Stella! I knew something had changed. What a hubbub.
What is the French word for that?"

Valmont was asleep.

Mercy got out of bed and got out her spiral notebook. She
sat on the floor in her underwear and wrote:

No note. Mother out of life.
Reunion between Belle and father. Daughter out of life.
Other Man of Letters burned. RP gone forever! Except he
emailed me today. What the hell do I do with that?
No book, a new query sent, but no response to query letter.
Belly danced by myself and gained five pounds.
Noah. The Animal Man. Never.
No secret admirer, really.
Teeny made contact—with me! I have not replied.
I DO have tickets to Tanzania.
I am going in to have a little procedure. In a few hours. Doc
Wiggins will be there. I am not going to sleep. In case I die
before I wake. And yes, I am afraid of dying. And pain. And
being alone. And all those unfinished dreams.

"Why are you on the floor?" Val was awake again. "Are you
praying?"

Mercy laughed. "I suppose I should."

"I have something that might help." He got up and went

over to his shaving kit. "Close your eyezz. Hold out your hand."

This was creepy.

He was wearing jersey boxer shorts.

She did as she was told. In her hand he dropped something cold and round. It was a shining medallion from her belly dancing costume.

"You lost this the night I met you on the river."

"Why were you saving it?"

He shrugged. "Good luck, I guess."

Mercy bowed her head and scribbled: *To do before morning: the dimpled French man.*

ZANZIBAH!

The sun is going down and the tide is coming in. It's like dreaming in fluorescent Technicolor. Like a mirage, a quivering dream. Here I am. Am I here? I. Am. Here. A merry time gal far from my east coast. I have Jackie O sunglasses and a scarf around my hair. No. Make that Sophia Loren. I'm sitting by the pool looking out at the Indian Ocean. Mango trees line the shore, sway like a fringe separating sea and sky. Something moves out of the corner of my eye. A giant crab, the size of a footstool. It's the same colour as the sand, and looks like a monstrous potato sprout. I think of Stompin' Tom singing "Bud the Spud" and I think of Stirling Cogswell reciting T. S. Eliot's "The Lovesong of J. Alfred Prufrock." Crabs really do scuttle sideways. Strange thing was, I was actually swimming in that very spot yesterday. It's a good thing I didn't know something with claws that big lived there. I would never have gone in! I would have been too afraid; too afraid of being bitten, of potential pain, infection, gangrene, and amputation. Going to the hospital alone. In a place I know no one. It's good to leave home and comfort now and then. We all have our thresholds for adventure. I'm homesick. Last night, I dreamt of men with machetes and snakes slithering in through the shutters. I woke up gasping as if being suffocated by a boa constrictor. I calmed myself by reciting a Shel Silverstein poem.

—Mercy Fanjoy, excerpt from Postcards from Zanzibar published in *Odell Observer*

After the little laser beam of light had zigged and zagged and explored her abdominal cavity and solar plexus region, upon first opening her eyes, all Mercy saw was a set of lips. Perfectly polished watermelon-coloured lip-sticked lips. Lips floating in the air, moving in circles, whispering lips, her mother's lips. As her eyes adjusted to the room, Mercy realized it was indeed her mother, leaning in to her, kissing her cheek, patting her face.

"Mum?"

"Mercy! How are you feeling, honey?"

"Why are you here? I'm dying, aren't I?"

"No. No, heavens no. The test results won't be in for days." Cassandra's familiar no nonsense voice seemed to melt somewhere, drip into the floor. Mercy closed her eyes. When she opened them, her mother was still there.

"Mum?"

"Why didn't you tell me? Here, water." Her mother put a paper cup to her lips. Mercy sipped gratefully.

"How did you know I was having surgery?" Mercy rested her throbbing head back on the pillow.

"Wiggins," Cassandra said, blowing her nose.

"That old—" Mercy winced as she realized the IV needle was taped to her flailing arm.

"He didn't want you to wake up in recovery alone," explained Cassandra. She flopped down beside the bed and stroked Mercy's arm.

"But that was my choice." Mercy shifted her arm away.

"He loves you almost like a daughter." Cassandra's voice was soft as dove feathers.

"Well, then. That certainly explains the problem," Mercy snapped back, bitterness in her voice.

"And...and he also said you had some idea of taking a trip?" Cassandra was fishing, Mercy realized. She took a breath as if girding her loins and nodded.

"Yes. I'm booked. Zanzibar, Tanzania. Africa." There. She'd said it, as if it were the most natural thing in the world to say.

"They must have you on some real strong drugs. For a minute there, I thought you said Africa." Cassandra gave a snort.

"Mom. Listen to me. I'm going to Africa in ten days. Wiggins says I'll be good to go. I've had my shots, my passport's in order, and I'm going."

"What? But you won't even have your test results!"

"Maybe. Doesn't matter. I'll call or maybe even wait until I'm home. I don't know yet. But I'll take the note with me. I still want it, you know." She flashed what she hoped was a forgiving smile.

"Africa? Alone? Don't they have Muslims there? Forget the note."

"Yes, Mum. They do have Muslims. Snakes, too. I still want the note."

"Hush. International travel? Terrorists, Mercy! Bombs on planes! A woman alone? What has gotten into you? You are being ridiculous."

"I'm leaving Odell. I want the note."

"No. No note. How long are you going for?"

"I haven't decided that yet."

"An open ticket? How could you do this to me? You know I'll be worried sick."

"Mum?" Belle's voice came from behind the curtain.

"Belle!"

"How could you do this to me? Not tell me you were going in for surgery? You are so so so so selfish." Belle leaned over the bed, her face puckered.

"I…just…didn't want to worry you." Mercy offered up her cheek. Belle kissed it lightly.

"Thanks one more time for treating me like I was three," Belle pouted.

"Belle. Your mother just got out of surgery. For heaven's sake, don't attack her, just shut up!"

Belle's eyes widened in shock. Mercy stifled a giggle. "Mum, you can't talk to my daughter like that."

"I just did! You shouldn't let her talk to *you* like that."

Mercy looked at them both, leaning over her, scowling. "No…I shouldn't let either of you talk to me like that."

"Here you are. Thank God." Lulu appeared behind Cassandra and Belle.

"Mercy, how could you do this?" Like Belle, Lulu looked like a scrunchy-faced infant readying to cry. "Valmont called me a few minutes ago, said he couldn't stop thinking about you and he told me about the surgery even though you swore him to secrecy."

"And I actually thought I could trust him. When will I learn?"

"Why didn't you tell me you needed surgery?" Lulu continued.

"Oh, she was playing the martyr. She didn't want anyone here," Cassandra said, accusingly. "Even me. How did Valmont know?"

"Who is Valmont?" interjected Belle.

"God, I'm your best friend, Mercy." Lulu rambled on, sounding more afraid than angry. "You said you were okay last week. Okay, fine. You out-and-out lied to me."

"Join the club," said Belle.

"Oh, Belle, please," Lulu said. "Your mother called me at school yesterday, upset after you finally told her about knowing your father. When I think of all the nights she was worried sick about you, well, I could just wring your neck!"

"Well," Belle protested, "that was Grambo's idea. To tell her I mean. That I knew him. We were going to fudge it."

Mercy jerked, tried to sit up.

"Mum, you knew Belle knew her father?" Mercy was incredulous.

Cassandra side-kicked Belle's shins. "Only recently," she confessed. "Isn't that right, Belle?"

Belle bobbed her head up and down, lying in agreement. "Yes, yes, recent."

"Mercy, what I want to know now is have you told Lulu or Belle what wild-goose-chase of an idea you've got in mind next?" Cassandra placed her hands on her hips.

Mercy just blinked.

"What wild goose chase? What do you mean?" asked Lulu.

"Go on. Tell her, Mercy," urged Cassandra.

But Mercy, tuckered out, fell silent.

"Well. I'll tell them, then." Cassandra took a drink of water and turned to Belle and Lulu. "She's about to go gallivanting halfway around the world—to Africa—after some man."

"Africa?" said Lulu "When? What man?"

"A black man I think. Not that I'm prejudiced. Soon."

"What? Mercy? Valmont said last night you two had dinner—"

"Who is this Valmont person?" whined Belle.

"Personally, I think after her father's suicide, she's always harboured something against white men," Cassandra muttered. "She babbled about this African man as she was coming to." Cassandra clucked her tongue. "Not that race matters, right Belle?"

"Actually, Grambo, race matters. A lot. Especially when you are in the minority."

"Please, let's not have a political discussion of race, gender, sexual orientation, religion, or the environment. Not now," protested Mercy, shutting her eyes.

"Mercy?" Lulu said suddenly. "Are you okay?"

Mercy winked open one eye.

"Are you really going to Africa? You didn't forget about our anniversary party, did you? You'll be here in a few weeks, won't you? What man? Did you go on edates.com finally?"

"You are encouraging Mercy to go online dating? That can be dangerous. Mercy is fine on her own, Lulu! She doesn't need a man." Cassandra was indignant.

"STOP! Would you all just shuuush. It's like this. Do you remember my friend Isaiah, from university?" Mercy began, but her voice was as limp as wet cardboard. Besides, they were no longer listening to her at all. All she heard was three squawking crows around her bed. Then, Dr. Wiggins walked in and they hushed. The women waited.

"Seat 19A. Have a nice flight, Ms. Fanjoy."

Have a nice flight. Those were the words she'd wanted to hear her entire life, having only ever flown over the ocean in her dreams. In fact, she'd only ever been outside her own time zone once before, to Windsor, Ontario.

Zanzibar. Zanzabah! Mercy loved the music of the word, the acoustical energy and arrangement of syllables, its mantra magic. The vibration of all those Z's.

The first time she'd heard the word she was ten—in Mrs. Justice's fifth grade class. There was a tickle she learned to call brain crackle, a small explosion inside her head that seeped down slowly into her chest. Snip. Snap. Synaptically, some special current fired up whenever she said it. It later became her code word for extreme aftershock orgasm of the most ecstatic kind, when her whole body was abuzz and ahum.

Mercy felt at those times like she was a human tuning fork. Maybe that was what the Vibrationists were all on about, she thought now as she opened her packet of peanuts. She'd never considered this before.

Zanzibar. After she'd met Isaiah, the word had a colour too. It was the distinct blue and green of the eye of a peacock feather. Mercy was on her way to Africa. Were there a heaven above, Isaiah surely would have been smiling and nodding his approval. Mercy should have been in fine spirits; instead, she was numb, her entire body on Novocain.

In her pocket, Mercy had The Note.

The night before she left, Cassandra had appeared unannounced, banging at Mercy's back door, as if there were a sudden emergency. Mercy opened the door to find one very dishevelled mother. Cassandra's coat was buttoned crookedly. She looked as ragged and unkempt as Old Stinky before his grease paint. Cassandra stood stiffly on the stoop, the wind tousling her hair. Her face was pale. Mercy saw her, suddenly, as frail. And afraid. Cassandra with no lipstick and no explanation. She continued to stand, silent, blinking, and wild-eyed. Mercy was alarmed.

"Mum?" They'd had one conversation since the hospital. Cassandra was still angry about Mercy's travel plans and she'd refused to say anything more about the note.

"I wanted to say goodbye. Properly."

"It's almost ten o'clock. I have to get up at five." Mercy shivered as a gust of wind blew in the house.

"You're still determined to go through with this foolishness? I still can't believe Wiggins is letting you traipse halfway around the world so soon after—aren't you afraid of…?"

"Mum, I'm afraid of everything, okay? Yes, including the terrorists and snakes. I'm afraid, okay. Terrified shitless. But I'm still going. Are you coming in? Tea?" Mercy toned down her voice. The last thing she wanted was such harshness of heart. She didn't want to leave Odell and all those she loved and carry such anger all the way across the world. "Please. Come on in, Mum. You can help me pack."

"No. No. I'm not staying. Hubert is in the truck waiting. With Sweet Jeezuz." Nonetheless, Cassandra stepped into the foyer.

"I came to give you this." She extended her hand. "The note. The goddamn note. And so you know, it's still not going to make much sense. So if you want me to stay while you read it, fine. I'll let Hubert know. If you want to read it alone, I'll go."

Mercy took a step back, as if zapped by a small electric current. She was staring at the note, stupefied. It took a few seconds to find her voice.

"Tell Hubert to come in then, Mum. I'll put the kettle on. Maybe, for now, put the note on the table."

To Mercy, that piece of paper glowed white hot. The note ticked, as if ready to detonate.

Hubert Rutherford tucked Sweet Jeezuz under his arm and stepped into the kitchen as if negotiating his way through a minefield. Mercy poured chamomile tea into small white cups and joined them at the table. Cassandra was praying with her palms open and eyes closed.

"Amen," she whispered as Mercy sat down.

All of them stared at the note.

"Go ahead, then." Cassandra sniffed. Hubert took his wife's trembling hands in his.

Mercy unfolded it. The printing was masculine, the letters large and, towards the end, crooked and spiking downwards.

Dear Cassandra:

I write to you not because you do not know the truth, but because you know it, and know that no lie is of the truth. You have never known the lie I am. The truth of many lies is soon to come out. Sweet Jeezuz is with me.

YOURS TRULY BEAUTY
Gabe

Mercy re-read the words three times. Cassandra finally broke the silence.

"Do you see what I mean? Tells you little unless I tell you

more. Fill you in. You have the missing note now, Mercy. Words. Words. Words. And what good are they, really? The words of your father you've wanted for so long. So do you have any idea what they might mean?" Cassandra tapped her fingers on the table.

"Was he...was he...gay, maybe?" Mercy's throat constricted.

"Hardly. Stud that he was with me. No offense, Hubert."

"A mental illness then, obviously. But I thought you told Lulu he wasn't crazy."

"He wasn't. He was a thief, Mercy. Even his note is plagiarized from the Bible—the first letter of John 2:21. And Mercy? Give me your hand. Are you able to take more?"

Mercy nodded, her tongue too numb to speak.

"Your father did not mean Jesus was with him as in the religious sense. The father you worshipped and adored, whose absence meant more to you than my presence, was a dog-murdering thief of a father. He took that sweet poodle of yours with him. I know—yes, go on, cry good and long. Cry not because your father was a thief and worse, stealing cheques from the mailboxes of the elderly and the poor, not because even though he had a good job, he wanted more, not just because he was a greedy man—a gambling irresponsible lying conniving pathetic bamboozling charmer con man. Cry because now you know—he can no longer be the father you wanted to remember. Yes, he sang great songs and laughed and was good to us in so many ways. That jewellery he was always landing home with? I never questioned. Why would I? I trusted him the way so many of us wives trusted our men back then—he worked and took care of finances, I took care of you. So yes, he got himself in a mess and they were on to him. It would have been jail for sure, but still, we might have made it through, maybe started over. I loved him that much. I did. Hector gave me the note so I'd be spared further humiliation. The post office never finished their investigation. People whispered, of course, they do in Odell, but with no note it was called accidental. Hector and of course eventually Dr. Wiggins knew; he knew after that time I near beat you to a pulp when you asked about the note. But tell me, Mercy, if it were you what would you do? Well never mind…What I'm saying is we all have our reasons for doing what we do, or don't do, about why we think we know what is best for our children. And yes, maybe ourselves too. I'll grant you that, but you have a daughter, so you know how it is."

"Sweet Jeezuz. He drowned my dog?" Mercy whined like a five-year-old.

"There's more. It is not only because you'd know the truth about your father that I kept this note all this time."

"God, what else?"

"Tell her, Cassie," Hubert commanded. "Tell her now."

"What?" Mercy yelled. "What?"

"Look at the note again carefully."

Mercy did and opened her palms as if in surrender. "What?"

"I was bowling that night, like I did every week. Your father always babysat. He was teaching you how to print the alphabet. You loved to write even before you could read. Mercy, the last time you saw your father alive you…"

Mercy saw it then. The "yours truly beauty" line was different—yes, a child's printing. She clutched her stomach.

The dim light of a kitchen. The smell of what…bacon?

Pencils on a tabletop. Dog barking. Her father in the doorway, folding the note.

"Thank you, Sweet Pea. Beautiful work. Give me a big hug. Come on, Sweet Jeezuz. Don't cry, honey. No, you stay here. I won't be long. Let go, Mercy."

"You're remembering a little, aren't you?" said her mother, clutching her arm at the elbow. Mercy nodded. "Wiggins always said that would happen if we talked about this."

"All right, then. You can come. We're going for a walk by the river."

The path was muddy. Sweet Jeezuz whimpered. Lights from the cars on the distant bridge pierced the dark. *Look, Daddy, falling stars.*

Mercy watched as her father took off his watch. He rolled his socks into a ball and stuffed them in the toe of one shoe. He tucked a piece of paper, the note, under the heel of the left shoe. He lifted her into his arms.

"Mercy? Are you okay?" her mother's voice funnelled into the kitchen. It was a strange voice, muffled—as if she were talking underwater. Under. Water.

In her ears, a splashing of water, a bone-shivering cold, a gulp of water, something on her head, holding her under.

"Mercy!" It was Hubert, shaking her gently and looking terrified, peering into her eyes.

"Mercy!"

"Dodie?" whispered Mercy.

"Yes. Dodie. I got home from bowling. The house was dark. I'd just called Gladdie and the police when Dodie arrived, quacking up a storm, holding your hand, pointing to the river. '*Allwetallwetallwet, Cassandra, quack. Gabe all wet.*' I think she saw him go in. I think....I think Dodie

Potts saved your life.

"You were hysterical. Shivering. I dried you off and rocked you until you stopped crying. Put you to bed. I waited. Gladdie came. We waited and waited."

Mercy covered her face.

"All I know is I've thanked God every day of my life it was just the dog, Mercy, and not you. I never gave you the note because I never wanted you to remember. I always hoped you would forgive me. Eventually." Cassandra stood and for several minutes cradled Mercy's head. Mercy folded into her arms.

Hubert rose then, kissed Mercy's wet cheek, and slipped out quietly. Cassandra stayed the night with Mercy.

Mercy put her hand in her pocket and clutched the note—its words still like raw paper cuts into her heart. She seemed unable to stop spinning the paper, as if somehow the words might twirl away like leaves to The Glowing Tree. Then? There would be no note.

"Prepare the cabin for landing."

The Livingstone Inn outside of Stone Town on the island of Zanzibar in the country of Tanzania was named after the famous adventurer David Livingstone, not Isaiah. Mercy's room had an ocean view and a canopy bed with mosquito netting. This was not Isak Dinesen's *Out of Africa*. Mercy was not doing anything in the least humanitarian—not saving gorillas or visiting babies in AIDS orphanages or anything philanthropic. For now she was staying in a four-star hotel with a pool, resting. She had been there two days and had written one postcard and emailed it to the *Odell Observer*. Ted had agreed to let her submit a travelogue of Mercy-style postcards. She was lethargic and still not sure her body had accompanied her. Everything around her seemed to vibrate, and was bathed in a haze of light. What if she were dreaming?

"Not bad for a girl from Doonan Road, eh what?"

She didn't know whose voice that was exactly. Teeny's? Or her father's. His voice kept coming back. It was one thing to remember he'd tried to drown her. The harshness of the truth was that every day since, it continued destroying—as her mother knew it would—the father she had created. Now, it was as if everything she'd ever held as true was wrong. She wrote a lot. But words seemed to betray her. Other times, she just cast a pleading glance towards the sky.

She had a book to write, things to consider, and enough money to stay in Africa for one month. She would go on safari, and then, it would all depend upon her test results. But for now, all she had to worry about was taking a spice trail tour after lunch.

Rasheed arrived in a truck bruised with dents. Although he spoke little English, the hoteliers assured Mercy that he was one of the best tour guides in the region. Mercy adjusted her backpack and climbed into the vehicle. Rasheed informed her that they would venture into "deep jungle" on a very special spice trail tour.

"Rasheed has friend who lives near…a famous runner, Olympics? Yes, Olympic champion." They could get fresh lychees there. "Miss ever eat fresh lychee?" Rasheed had stopped at the side of the road to consult his map.

"Are we lost?"

"Nomissnoworry." But Mercy was unsettled. By now, they were so far off the beaten track they hadn't seen another vehicle for an hour. Mercy got out to stretch. Wandering across the road, she read the weathered plaque on the muddied adobe hut. "Scheherazade? The real Scheherazade?" she shrieked.

Rasheed rushed over, confused, unable to understand. "Not clean, miss," he said. "No, miss." But Mercy had already entered the dwelling. Entranced, she walked down several steps. "Careful miss!" he yelled after her, his voice reverberating.

Mercy walked into the belly of the concrete room. Light seeped through an oval opening. It appeared to have been a bath house, once white. Now it was a perfect echo chamber. Her eyes began to adjust to the light.

"Snakes, miss. Maybe snakes." *Snakesnakesnakes*, his voice echoed. That did the trick. Mercy turned back. She emerged, smiling at Rasheed, wishing she had the language to share what she'd seen. For a second, she had glimpsed a long ago world, naked women and men bathing together. She heard the jingle of dancers and music so sweet, and stories being hummed and told, melodies that soothed and saved. It was an epic of peace. She smelled lavender and cinnamon and nutmeg.

"Snakes," he said again. Mercy's reverie dissolved.

Back in the truck, she tried to nail down the details. "But was that the real Scheherazade?" she kept asking.

She talked too fast, however, and Rasheed understood little enough English as it was. So Mercy began to hum what she could of Rimsky-Korsakov.

"Dad da DUM dad dadada dadada." She beat it out on the dashboard. Rasheed threw his head back in an explosion of laughter, exposing broken teeth, and drummed back.

The day was glorious, surreal, and ended with an invitation. Rasheed asked if it was okay for him to take her to see his wife. Mercy agreed.

Mercy smiled widely at the wife of Rasheed, whose name she did not catch, and the wife of Rasheed smiled back. Both women lowered their eyes as Rasheed tried to make introductions. Finally, he stopped talking. He took his wife by the arm and beckoned Mercy to follow him.

Tree branches canopied the porch. Rasheed reached up. His thin hand, corded with bone, disappeared into the foliage. His wife smiled shyly at Mercy, her full soft lips never parting. Rasheed brought his hands back to his chest near his heart. He held the largest avocado Mercy had ever seen.

It was the size and shape of a child's small toy football. Then he touched his wife's heart with the fruit and then his own and extended it to Mercy.

"For eat," he said.

Then they all bowed to one another some more before Rasheed took her back to the hotel.

Mercy was eating the avocado and watching a bush baby when she got the call.

"Miss, Mercy. Call for you. Telephone."

Only Linda, Dr. Wiggins' nurse, had the number. It had to be the test results. Mercy pushed away from the table. She walked reluctantly out of the sunshine into the shade of the lobby. The ceiling fan rattled above her as she approached the front desk.

"Hello?"

"Mercy."

"Mum?"

"Mercy, dear. There's been a fire."

Belle? Hurt? My house?

"Fire. Odell. Occasionally Yours is gutted, most of the upstairs, just...just charred. Two dead. There were some street kids partying up there. Two dead. One saved. Lulu's Rio."

"Rio?"

"He's alive, badly burned. He was the one who saw the smoke. Went in and saved that girl."

"Rio?"

"Lulu and Hap...they're going to need you. I knew you'd want to know. In case you wanted to come home."

If she could have, Mercy Beth Fanjoy would have sprouted wings.

*What a difference
a day makes,
a pay makes,
to play makes
to pray makes*

*What a difference
that you make
Today!*

—Foxy Moxy Roxy

Galpal Greeting Cards

Odell's downtown is in recovery. As are we. The work will never be completed. It's difficult to rejoice when those we love are in pain, but we will laugh again. A different kind of laughter from a place even deeper in the belly. There is nothing quite like the laughter of survivors. And we all are. The fire, which began in the old Manley building, reminded those who have forgotten and some who never realized that we really are a divinely imperfect dysfunctional bunch of oddballs in Odell. It has ignited and revitalized our entire community, not just the downtown core. Here's to us all in our glorious unfinishings! Here's to new connections. Electric Street will glow again.

—from the essay "Overwhelmed" in
*Mercy's Mid-Life Musings: A Kind
of Memoir*, published by White WaterLily Press.

The green room wasn't green at all. The walls were a harsh shade of grey—the dark of pencil lead, scouring pads, bullets. Mercy was in a television station somewhere in the outskirts of Toronto. It was almost a year since she'd been in Wiggins' office, thinking of death. But now, in less than an hour, she would make her debut on national television in front of a live studio audience. The show was called "The G Spot!" "G" was for the host, Georgette "Gee-Gee" Dobbins. It was a show meant to shock and tantalize, provoke thought and provide advice. "An intergenerational show for women of NOW," it boasted. Mercy was being interviewed as a result of her recently published book, *Mercy's Mid-Life Musings: A Kind of Memoir*.

Mercy gave a lot of credit to Ms. Hawkes, the editor who'd rejected her fictional biography idea. "Everyone Needs an Antagonist" was the first essay in the collection. "This Bus Runs on Natural Gas" won a national award from an environmental agency. One critic said, "Although Fanjoy has taken a swipe at everyone, and might have avoided using the term eco-Nazis had she an editor, or even better, avoided the incredibly corny 'Don't be sorry! Think Al Gore-y!' she makes a great case for injecting more humour into the global movement." That critic also cited her essay, "Healer,

Hooker, Homeless: Three Women of Old" as "charming and well worth the read and modest price of the book."

Today Mercy was beyond nervous. She'd done some interviews on local radio, but radio, in her mind, was fairly safe. "You can have bad hair and pimples and wear a garbage bag and no one knows," she wailed to Lulu. "Television, everyone can see you. Ask your sister for some tips, okay?"

"Ella told me to tell you not to fidget, keep your hair out of your eyes, and just suck it up. Besides, she said they'll have good makeup people." Mercy knew hair and close-ups were not really worth fretting about. Her wig was very natural looking, but she was almost as nauseous as after one of her chemotherapy treatments. And the producer had not given her a list of set questions. She felt utterly, completely out of control and at their mercy.

Mercy worried about how personal Gee-Gee would get in her line of questioning. If she was interested in talking about the essay "Matters of Taste: Who Decides?" there should be no problem. In that rumination, Mercy tackled both feminism and the M.O.M.S., detailing the fight to keep Foxy Roxy Moxy Galpal Greeting Cards in Odell. She also talked movies, books, hairstyles, and whether or not white shoes were ever a tasteful choice. But then there was "All ODD in ODD-ell," in which, with Belle's permission, Mercy came out of the closet as the mother of a lesbian. She'd interviewed two ministers who were forming the first interfaith gay and lesbian network in the Odell regional vicinity. While she was proud of the essay, Mercy was still not ready to go out on any controversial, overly personal limbs on television.

"Writing is one thing, talking another," she'd said to Lulu

that morning on the phone from her hotel room.

"Mercy, you will be fine. Rio will be watching." This made Mercy braver, somehow. She was also relieved she had Teeny Gaudet to depend on.

Teeny was with her now, in the grey green room, pacing back and forth.

Their reunion had occurred in the hospital cafeteria, when they'd both gone to be with Lulu during the weeks Rio hovered between life and death after the fire.

"Excuse me, could you pass me a Jell-O? Lime?"

Mercy resented the elbow at her side and the pushiness in the woman's voice. Without turning, she glanced at her watch and said, "One o'clock." She went back to her tray, pushing it along.

"Not time. Jell-O. Lime. Lime-en-essence! Mercy, it's me."

Mercy recognized her old friend's voice then. But even when she turned, she didn't recognize the woman in front of her as Teeny Gaudet. Instead, she saw a pear-breasted woman with lipstick on her teeth, smudged mascara, her hot pink polyester miniskirt clashing with her red sling-backs. Her hair was a bright forsythia blonde. She was not so teeny any more, either. Her publicity pictures had been kind.

"Teeny." Mercy stared, then reached out. They hugged as old friends do. When they sat down at a table, they stared at each other warily, each weighing the same eternal question: How does one begin again to trust? In this instance, history and their mutual love of Lulu, Hap, and Rio managed to transcend the past.

In the months that followed, Teeny became Mercy's confidante once more, her ideal reader and fiercest champion. Mercy, the compiler, combed the columns, essays, journals, and the Mercy files still in her head. Teeny, who had given up Burt the Burping Bear when she gave up alcohol and sex (sex addiction, anyway), decided to start White WaterLily Press and act as publicist for the book.

Teeny was contemplating a move back to Odell permanently. She was considering adopting a baby and maybe opening a consignment shop while continuing to work as publisher/editor/publicist when worthwhile projects appeared.

"Marketing! In this celebrity culture, unless you're a star with a book, you have to have a real hook. I had burps. What is your hook, Mercy? Why should I read this book?"

"Well, it's um…a thought-provoking reflection by…a small-town columnist and it serves the community?"

"No—you're hesitating."

"Sex, sexuality, suicide, religion, drugs, family feuds, the supernatural! Thoughts of the day."

"That's more like it. But it's still not a hook." So they'd gone and done it. They shamelessly promoted the book tabloid-style with an advance press release highlighting the essay "My Father Committed Suicide and Drowned My Dog, Sweet Jeezuz." She left herself out of it. Mercy also drew the line at using that for the title of the entire collection.

"Lord, Teeny, I have to at least pretend I have some integrity left," she'd protested.

"Unlike me, I suppose you are thinking."

"I didn't say that."

"But you think it. Look, Mercy, if we're going to be friends again, do you think you could try not to judge me by your standards?"

Mercy, knowing that was almost humanly impossible, nodded anyway. "I'll try my best. I'm not perfect either."

"No!" mocked Teeny.

Now, back in the green room, Teeny was doing her best to help Mercy overcome her nerves. "Be grateful for this opportunity. This is a good gig."

Mercy stifled a laugh. "Gig. Oh right, man!" In her mind a gig was something musicians did in smoky bars, before they found fame or fame found them. Mercy wanted to be back home in Odell just then. She wanted Rolaids or herbal tea. She had the hiccups.

"Makeup's on its way!" the associate producer, Tony, told them. "That'll relax you!" That's one charming smile, thought Mercy.

Just then, a chipper young woman with stilts for legs wearing a black leather miniskirt and a crisp white blouse, her breasts pointy as two Dixie cups, clunked into the room in platform shoes.

"Mercy Fanjoy? My name's Raine," she said, curtseying and spinning on her heels. "Raine with an 'e.' Come this way." Mercy rolled her eyes at Teeny.

"Go ahead, you'll be fine," Teeny said. "I'll wait for you here and talk to Tony until you get back."

★★★

Mercy still had the hiccups when she came back from makeup.

"Looks like you made out just fine," exclaimed Teeny. "You look stunning."

"You look like you're running a fever," Mercy replied. She

could hardly move her face the makeup was so heavy.

"I'm just getting nervous for you, I guess. Blood pressure. But you'll be amazing!"

"You handled questions like a goddamn professional," Teeny said later, over dinner.

"I had good coaches. That floor director was gorgeous, eh Teeny? Not like you not to notice!" Mercy clinked her wine glass against Teeny's club soda.

"I was focusing only on you. I loved the way you handled the question about calling it a 'kind of' memoir!"

"Is that in case Oprah calls you on her show?" Gee-Gee had asked, with a smirk. "I guess you need to be clear from the start."

"No," said Mercy. She'd tried to speak like Eunice Mc-Tavish, with quiet confidence. "First, it's a collage of mixed genres. Some reviews, some personal memoir-type essays, and my columns. I also fictionalized a few bits because if I told the real truth no one would ever believe me."

There were a few questions Mercy had stumbled over.

"Are you going to write another book? And how is your health?"

"Fine. The chemo seems to have worked. Another book? No. Maybe. I don't know, someday. For now, I'm going home and helping to run a new business. And I'm taking a Red Cross course in emergency response so I can be more useful. And maybe travel. I never did get to go on safari. But could you tell people they can order the book at www. mercysmusings.net? Some of the proceeds are going to the rebuilding of Odell."

"How wonderful," said Gee-Gee. "We'll put that up on our website." She smiled into the camera then turned to

Mercy suddenly.

"Now, before we go...This essay about your father—how unspeakable. How much do you think this incident affected your life? And how do you feel about it now? And do you ever wish you'd never read the note?"

Mercy began to hiccup. They cut to commercial.

Mercy's Minutes

Nov 2007, Issue 10

Hey all!

Thanks for your last round of emails, inspirational quotes, recipes, cartoons and white light beamings. And for purchasing Mercy's Mid-Life Musings. Catch the review in Mid magazine at www. midlifemadness.org. Sales are hot!

Even though Mercy's hair is starting to look fabulous, hats are still welcome as we are donating them to the hospital, for those we've met in the chemo waiting room. Speaking of which, check out "The Art of Waiting," unpublished verse by my mother that shows her wannabe Dorothy Parker satirical poetic side:

I waited in line ups at banks
I waited for phones to ring
I waited for love to arrive
I waited for everything

I waited for half of my days
I waited on tables a lot
Now I'm waiting for nothing
Forever!
No matter how long I've got.
(She says *the poem is still in revision and so is she!*)

New Soup Recipe:
One avocado.
One cup consommé.
Sherry to taste.
Simple! Perfect.

Progress Report on the Café:
ON schedule! We are ordering the fabric for the curtains and sofas next week.
Send in your ideas for names!

Update on Health:
It's been five months since the last chemo treatment and Mercy, Grambo (that's my fierce Grammy, Cassandra), Sage and Teeny—we're all going to Dr. Fergus in Halifax for the six-month check-up in a few weeks. So...KEEP up the positive vibes for my mama!

Remember to check out Aphrodite's if you are in Odell.
'til next page,
Belle FAN JOY!

QUOTE DU JOUR:

Kick the gluteus maximus ass of cancer!

It was a clear, crisp, Sunday morning in early December. Mercy jogged along the Odell Green, which had yet to see snow. She galloped off-trail, as close as she could get to the river, which, glittering in the snapping cold, was a sun-dazzled deep turquoise. After the hysterectomy and chemotherapy, she had lost and gained and lost weight. She'd also lost her hair. Now she had curls and just wanted to be strong. She loved to say she'd become a running joke. At times, in the middle of the night, she still wondered if she was running out of time.

Past the cathedral, over the underpass, she panted, then trotted along the two lengths of the train bridge. She looped behind the art gallery, the Odell Hotel, the post office, and the federal building. She crossed Regent Street and cut through Officer's Square, the parking lot of the craft school, the courthouse, and the library, past City Hall, saluting Oddie, the naked fountain cherub, until, playing her iPod tunes full blast, she coasted into Occasionally Yours. Or what used to be Occasionally Yours. A café and bar would take its place.

She met the contractor, put on some coffee, and stayed until the workers got settled. The store had been closed well over a year now; the café's opening was still months away.

Aphrodite's, the all-women's gym, had recently opened upstairs. Belle was co-owner and master yoga teacher. She had a space for her massage and raindrop therapy clients and a room for meditation. The entire building had been cleansed by a shaman, sweetgrassed and prayed over and "all negative energy released," according to Belle.

Mercy read the sign on the door:

Yoga to Quit!
You gotta quit!
And you will!

An introductory six-week
beginners' yoga session
to help the nicaffeine addict.

Yoga to Write! was the next course offering and Mercy had agreed to co-teach with Belle. Belle would do the yoga while she did the writing class. Mercy looked around, sniffing in appreciation. The muted pink, turquoise, red, and purple decor was stunning as well as soothing. The scent? Lavender, eucalyptus, rose geranium. Buddhas and dream catchers were everywhere.

"Mercy!" It was Hanna Davis-Perley on the treadmill, looking fit and glowing.

"Hi Hanna." Mercy waved but didn't stop. She liked Hanna. Noah had never looked happier. And how could Mercy not like someone who made someone she loved happy? But there were limits. "There's no law that says I have to chit-chat with her too often and hear about how she keeps getting kidney infections called honeymoonitis from too much 'O so incredible sex' from her man, right?" Mercy whined to BB.

"Boundaries are necessary for survival," BB agreed. "Especially when feeling oneness with another just isn't happening. Maybe next lifetime." Mercy loved BB for this. She was always reassured at the thought she had another chance at being a better human being.

Sit-ups were next on her agenda that fine Sunday morning. Mercy did fifty, her belly still a lumpy futon mattress. She then lifted eight-pound dumbbells in various configurations over her head, then did "kickbacks," hinging from her elbows, swinging fists forward, a tough move for triceps. Mercy worked for twenty-two minutes in the Sculpting Room. Next door, some newfangled kind of class called audioaerobics was in full swing: Women of all shapes and sizes were moving and vocalizing and kick-dancing to the song "Some Kind of Wonderful."

"YES WE ARE!" shouted the instructor over the music. "Wonderful! What are we? Wonderful!"

Mercy showered, dressed, and dried her hair.

As promised, she drove out to Louise and Hap's camp in Lower Ferryville to spend the afternoon. Her new car purred. She took the scenic route on the old Trans-Canada Highway, a ribbon of road paved overtop of the water like a causeway. There was less traffic on the old road, but she'd chosen it for another reason—she'd gotten into the habit of forcing herself to cross River St. John on the small barge. She was still deathly afraid of that body of water, but every time she managed the crossing, she noticed the tightness in her chest eased up just a little. The barge operator, Mark Foreman was his name, was a distant relative of Dodie Potts. Mercy felt safer knowing that. She liked his orange overalls and hip wader boots.

Today, there was a Christmas craft show in Lower Ferryville. She'd agreed to meet Lulu there. Mercy was early, so she took the opportunity to browse the stalls. In five minutes, she'd purchased stained glass angels for the tree, mustard pickles, elderberry jam, and microwaveable flannel bags for application to sore muscles. A log cabin quilt in shades of green caught her eye. She bought raffle tickets on the quilt, the proceeds of which were going to the regional schizophrenic society.

"You're Mercy Beth Fanjoy." The women tore her tickets and handed her back the stubs.

"Yes." Mercy glanced around, hoping no one had heard.

"I liked your book, well most of it, anyhow. I didn't read every part of it, you know. Loved the recipes. Should have put in more. Yep, liked it so much I gave it to my friend Barb. Woulda bought it for her but sheesh books are expensive, eh? Anyways, gave it to her 'cause she has a son she don't speak to 'cause you know…he's funny that way too. Like your daughter." She lowered her voice and whispered. "A homosexual. Fruitier than Florida oranges. 'Barb,' I asked her when I think she's read it, 'did you like the book?' She told me the book was real different, eh? Right filthy in parts, too. But not worse than some of them comedy shows on the CBC. That means she must have read some. So, you never know. You might have got her thinking. I mean, I wonder what Barb'd do if she had my son. See, I'm selling tickets because I'm a mother of a schizophrenic."

Mercy squirmed. "Well, thanks." She tried to slouch away. The woman, who wore earrings the size of hula hoops, was a redhead. A green bandana kept tight lambswool ringlets at bay. She looked like an Irish gypsy or a tarot card reader. And she kept blocking Mercy's way.

"Yep, I knew it was you. I recognize you from that cable show they replay a bazillion times. One time my son—"

Mercy did not want details she did not know what to do with. The woman pressed on, holding her by the forearm. "—Clorox bleach…burned his…" Mercy felt she was in handcuffs. Blood rushed to her head.

"Let go, please," she said. But the women didn't. She leaned even closer, breath emanating last night's pesto pasta.

"You should write about it, about the lack of health care and support for sufferers of mental illness in our region. People listen to celebrities."

Sweet Jeezuz.

"I'm not a celebrity!" Mercy yanked her arm away from the woman's grip. The woman backed away, looking confused. "Maybe you should write about it yourself," Mercy suggested more kindly, adjusting the many gifts in her arms and smiling brightly.

"I do already! But I'm not you. Who gives a shit what I think? I'm just a mother. Here's my blog, if you're interested. It's about learning to cope in the face of things."

"You have a blog? I mean, I will," said Mercy. "And I give a shit. I do! And mothers…mothers have a lot to say. Maybe everything." She was almost yelling.

Mercy wondered, not for the first time in her life, if maybe she suffered from multiple-syndrome syndrome. Fear of crowds? She remembered a time when Cogswell had admonished her, saying, "Mercy, this is no time for false insecurity. Get over yourself. You're a competent professional." But she was never sure what that really meant, and knew the god's awful truth: She was still too easily overwhelmed and constantly over-aroused.

In the face of things. She placed the phrase in her Mercy files; some habits were hard to break. She bought Sage and Belle each a rainbow-striped hemp snuggly—the baby was due in June. Mercy gulped; it was all she could do. Such joy could only be handled in gulps and gasps, washed down with gushes of hope. She was trying not to go crazy and buy everything she laid her eyes on. It was early still, but she was already knitting. She, who had only ever knit scarves, was trying to knit an entire layette.

She spotted a tray of homemade Nanaimo bars and bought that for Hubert, along with a lavender-scented eye pillow for her mother. "Belle is pregnant? How? No. Sweet Jeezuz, never mind I asked that. Well, after all, look at Mary Cheney! If a Republican lesbian daughter of the vice president of the United States could have a baby, maybe Belle of Odell, lesbian (or was it bisexual?) daughter of Mercy Beth Fanjoy, published writer, can too. I'm going to be a great-grandmother!" Cassandra had shrieked and hugged them both. Mercy inhaled her mother deeply, hugged her until she had to say, "Mercy, honey, could you let me go?"

No, thought Mercy, not really. How could anyone ever let go of a mother, the giver of one's life, the keeper of one's heart, the sharer of one's sorrow, the truest singer of one's greatest joy?

Mercy looked around the fairgrounds of Lower Ferryville. As she was prone to these days, she teared up in public from no other reason than an overwhelming surge of love and beauty.

"Mercy!" Thankfully, Lulu had arrived. Mercy composed herself. Was that wine on her friend's breath? Lulu looked like she had lost five pounds again this week. They didn't stay long at the fair. Lulu said she didn't like to leave Rio for long, but Mercy noticed Lulu didn't like being out anywhere for long herself. Everyone who knew Lulu agreed she was a boulder of strength and making out just fine, under the circumstances.

Rio was alive and home, finally, after almost a year in rehab. There were surgeries ahead, many of them. He spoke with difficulty, the skin of his neck grafted taut to his jaw. His arms and scalp were still layered in bandages. Mercy never knew where to look. Today, he seemed especially red.

"Belle sends you her love. She said I could tell you today that if it's a boy his name is Rio Nathaniel Fanjoy O'Donnell."

Rio's eyes danced at the news. Then he winced, as if even blinking was painful. The skin around his eyes was still raw, motley, ranging in colour from a waxy white to the pink of calamine lotion. The colours reminded Mercy of the illustrations of internal organs in her old nursing technician books. Lulu wheeled him back to his room. Mercy helped her arrange him into a series of slings in a hammock made to accommodate his wounds. Then she sat with him, reading from *A Prayer for Owen Meany* until he slept.

Hap was in the kitchen, smoking. He looked through Mercy when she entered and nodded.

Now Mercy and Lulu lazed out front in the swing on the porch.

"Have you heard from Valmont?" Lulu began.

"Not one word since I wrote the email that let him know how I feel. Scared him away, I guess. Who can blame him? I mean, he knows I'm clear and free and the prognosis is good, but I suppose he wonders how long it will last. He's already been widowed. So, no word in two months. I'd say that's a clear message. No big deal."

It was a big deal and they both knew it, but they had learned there were times when mutual falsehoods between friends were necessary. And kind.

"Any word on Nathan?" Mercy asked. Eunice McTavish's son was serving in Afghanistan.

"He emails once a week. Eunice is living in hell. Gerald is worse. You should go see her, Mercy."

"I'll call her tonight." The swing creaked as they swung back and forth. "I saw Doc Wiggins yesterday. He's doing a lot better. Fishing again. Only six weeks after his heart surgery."

"Is he really? Tough guy. Big, strong heart I guess. Mercy, I want your advice."

"Sure, but I was fired, remember? Besides, I ruminate. No advice."

"Ruminate then. Victoria Curtain called me. She wants

to come see us—to thank Rio. And she wants to bring Gloria."

"Gloria! What? She wants to thank him for saving her life, finally?"

"I told her that I would think it over. I mean, you know what it's like to be the mother of a troubled daughter."

"That was years ago. Belle eats just fine these days. I—"

"Sorry, I mean, Mercy, what would you do?"

"I don't know. Honestly, I don't, Lulu. I think it should be Rio's choice."

"I was afraid you'd say that. He's got at least one hundred surgeries in the next year. And he is still having those hallucinations."

"But it's Rio's choice. I'm not saying I don't feel for you, and you know I've never been overly fond of Victoria."

"I bumped into Vonda and she told me she was still worried about Vicky, and Gloria was on suicide watch. She's trying to get them to your mother's grief support group. Maybe Rio needs Gloria and could help her."

"You are so kind. What does Hap say?"

"Hap. Happy Kunkle? Have no idea. He hardly sleeps. He doesn't speak. He grunts. He's getting stoned, Mercy—smoking up. He's never been into pot. He goes into the woods for hours every day with that chainsaw. There he goes now." Hap was striding toward the trees, swinging the chainsaw, but stooped over as if he were bracing against a fierce wind, though the day was calm.

"I followed him once and watched. He goes at the trees like he's doing battle. He looks insane. We're...we're falling apart."

Then, time stopped. Mercy cradled her best friend,

Louise Lutes, in her arms, keeping her mouth shut and her heart wide open. Mercy wondered if sorrow like this ever ended, and feared for the first time that this family might not survive intact. How can you be happy when someone you love is in pain?

"What can I do for you in town this week?" Mercy asked as she got into the car. "Need anything? I'm making a trip to Goodfood's."

Lulu shook her head. "You've got enough to do with selling your house. Just keep visiting, Mercy, and maybe pray for us, okay?"

Mercy looked at the ignition as if it was the eighth wonder of the world. "Me, pray? I'm amazed you can still believe in a god." She started the car, still not looking up.

"How can I not?"

Mercy raised her head. Lulu looked down at her evenly.

"Look at Hap. That's the difference between us. He's got nothing to hang on to. Look, I'm having some rip-roaring screaming mad arguments with God right now, but it's not that I believe. It's...well...I *know.*"

"You know?"

"Yes, I know."

"You sound like my mother."

"I'll take that as a compliment."

Mercy drove back to Odell with Ray Charles and Gladys Knight belting out "Heaven Help Us All" on the radio. She'd never really heard the words before. She slammed her fist on the steering wheel. She raged. She ranted. Then, as if inhabiting the hearts of her two best friends, sorrow flooded over her and overwhelmed her, almost stopping her own heart.

A horn honked behind her. Mercy glanced in the rear-view mirror. There was no vehicle in sight. Her father's face flashed then disappeared. Then she saw herself. And she damn near drove into the river.

She swerved around the bend, blinded by light. The grass in the field ahead was lime green, phosphorescent, as if handfuls of Christmas icicles had been flung down, snagging between each blade and clover leaf.

Her wheels screeched and she was on the opposite shoulder of the road, careening towards the field. The back end of the car fish-tailed. She eased up on the gas and gained control again. The car slowed and slumped into a shallow ditch. Mercy pressed her head on the steering wheel. A flock of geese lifted from the field and filled the sky. The river flowed. She was shaking. She was alive.

"You don't just pray for yourself or anyone else like some kind of wish list to Santa Claus, Mercy. You carry their hearts inside yours for a while, maybe even give them yours. And you give what they need, not what you need to give— " The voice was clear. It was her own.

Prayer was the only thing Lulu wanted. Mercy cleared her throat. "Jesus-Conductor-Creator-Bhuddha-Mohammad-Mary-Faustina-Gladys and God only knows whoever else's holy spirit or lime-en-essence may be listening in, pray with me." She bowed her head.

"Hap," she whispered. "Lulu. Rio. *Sapiliqtailigit*. Never give up. Never."

The prayer did not lift her grief. The prayer did not magically heal her cracked heart. It scorched her soul. Light seeped in.

A few hours and a tow truck later, Mercy pulled up in front of the store. She was hungry and cranky and just wanted to get home. At least fifteen workers were still sawing and drilling. The painters had just finished the seventh coat of emerald green paint and had rolled up the tarp, but they were waiting, anxious to see if she liked the room. With a few mirrors and the right lights, the place would glow velvet.

"WOW!" she said to the painters.

"Different, ain't it?" one said.

"I like it," said another.

"I love it!" Mercy nodded. She wondered if the ghost of old Horace Manley would be impressed. She could hardly wait for Bee to see it. The front doorbell jingled. Had she left the door open?

"Bee? Is that you?"

"Merci!"

Grand opening Wednesday!

FREQUENTLY
ILLUMINATIONS
CAFÉ & BAR

Owners Mercy Beth Fanjoy, Teeny Gaudet and Bee Godwin invite you to LIGHTEN UP!

Enjoy wine, cheese and munchies and enjoy the art showcase. Works by Odell's craft school senior students as well as established local artists on display. Music by the Odell Blues Band. Poetry reading by Jan Muir, winner of the national Poetry Faceoff.

Raffle tickets sold, proceeds to the Burn Unit of the Odell Rehabilitation Centre and Tanzanian scholarships.

Check out our website and blog and WEEKLY podcast at
www.lasereye.com
Featuring recipes, art and poetry.

It was the night before Opening Day.

"I want us to be alone," he'd said to her. "It is important you be the first one to see my most beautiful job of lights I made before. Bring champagne and music," Valmont whispered in her ear. "I'll take care of the rest."

Valmont, flashlight in one hand, led Mercy into the room. He slipped in the CD she gave him, the one her mother told her to save for the right moment.

"Ready?" Valmont asked.

Mercy nodded. The music started. Murray McLaughlin began to croon "Love Just Can't Tell Time."

"Close your eyezz. Wait until I say 'now,'" Valmont called softly.

Mercy felt herself sway to the music. Was she vibrating? No—a head swaying was not a body vibrating, or so she reassured herself.

"I'm waiting," Mercy's nervous laugh was like a donkey braying.

She heard Val moving towards her. He wrapped his arms around her, turned her once. Mercy relaxed into the great stillness of his arms. Valmont's heart thumped in time with hers.

"Now," he said, and clicked a hand-held remote. The sound was like the courting song of crickets. Mercy opened her eyes, almost blinded by light.

There is this raw and naked now, Mercy told herself.

In this now, in this quivering dance of light and shadow, even in the dark, if you stay awake and have patience, eventually some things shimmer and clang. Then, if only briefly, you know you are, have been, or might be one true note being played. One of many; part of a necessary chorus. Until, in the beautiful blue-white sadness that is joy, everything disappears.

A CONVERSATION
WITH SHEREE FITCH

BY MARY JO ANDERSON

Is this a funny novel that is serious or a serious novel that is funny?

That is a really good question. If you can't figure that out, then I've done my job. I think tragicomedy might fit.

I felt it was time for me to sit down and tell an adult, contemporary tale, and I wanted it to be sad and funny. Writer Brian Doyle once gave me a phrase: "whistling in the graveyard." That is the chord I hoped to strike. But it can't be forced.

I think every writer tries to articulate the truth as they know it, and I do see life as mixed. I wanted to put a character in motion who wrestled with these emotions and ideas, and the "mixedness" of life at midlife.

There is a scene in which Mercy Beth Fanjoy has an epiphany: "That's when she learned a person could laugh and cry at the same time—a sun shower, one of life's secret survival strategies." Is the term "sun shower" one which you coined?

(Laughing) Yes, I remember the day that I wrote that. It refers to the kindness of the Hubbleys, Mercy's landlords, and the position Mercy was in. Mercy starts laughing and crying at the same time, and that line came out. I remember writing that and thinking, "How many times in my life have I felt that emotion?" There are those times when you don't know whether you're laughing or crying; you're doing both.

It's like a happy sad or a sad happy—who knows?

When I sit down to write a book I have different intentions at different times. But I always thought that if I ever wrote an adult novel I didn't want it to be a sober, serious, "megathing," or epic. (But maybe I'll try that before I die.) I wanted *Kiss the Joy As It Flies* to resonate with the life that I see. It's my job to bear witness and observe. I think I try to do that with most of my work.

How and when did this particular novel take shape?

In one sense, when I first started writing. The first creative writing class I took when I was twenty I wrote a short story from a boy's point of view. Then I wrote an adult short story that only got published a few years ago. In other words, I never started out saying that I wanted to be a children's writer. I just wanted to write. And what happened, of course, was that my children's writing got published, and that's where I decided to put my focus. I needed to know everything I could…about what made for excellence in children's literature. I went to school and concentrated on children's literature, and it was a wonderful journey. At the time, I remember thinking, "It doesn't mean I'll never try to speak in an adult's voice again, but it's going to have to wait awhile."

So you finally knew it was time to write a novel for adult readers?

Yes. I'd had a few short stories published—but again, I remained focused mostly on children's writing. Then, there was a news story, decades ago, that triggered a strong reaction. Haunted me, really. I found myself asking a whole bunch of "What if?" questions about the people in the story, and what would happen to them in the future, when they were adults.

So I began writing about a woman who was obsessed with getting a suicide note left by a parent. I had written it as a short story but it was just too big. I knew it wasn't a short story, but I was resisting the idea that it was a novel. I thought, "I'm not going to write a novel, this isn't the time, I have other things to do."

So I tucked everything away and kept tucking it away. It wouldn't go away. While I was finishing the final revisions for *The Gravesavers* [Fitch's first novel for young adults]—when the ink was still wet—Mercy Beth came rushing at me!

At the time I think my imagination needed to get away from commas, verbs, and the little nitpicky stuff of revisions. I just wanted to invent again. So Mercy Beth just came in and...took up occupancy in my room. That was when I realized that Mercy Beth was the same person in the short story from ten years before.

But I didn't want it to be "about" a suicide. I wanted it to be about life and Mercy told me she was a woman in the middle of a panic and had to take a fearless personal inventory of her life. It made sense to me. I knew I wanted a kind of everywoman anti-heroine. I've always been attracted to those sorts of protagonists.

It seems that it is very important when you tell certain key pieces of information and how you tell them. A key plot detail is not revealed until very near the end, for example. So how did you plot this novel?

How do you go about plotting any novel? I think I will, for the rest of my life, be asking that question.

As a poet, first of all, I just love the taste and the sound and the cling-clanging of words. It is very important to me that a page of prose reads as beautifully as it can. My love of the music of words is always there.

There are a million different ways to approach [the plot]... Isn't writing really a process of making decisions? Solving the problems of the plot sometimes makes you come up with a much better idea. It really does. When I started writing this book, I knew the plot but I didn't know the plot. I was originally going to give all kinds of hints to let the reader in on things. But then I thought, "No, that's part of Mercy's yearning."

I used to think that when writers said, "I create these characters and this world and then they take over," that it was just a little too airy-fairy. But there were things that appeared as I was writing, elements I couldn't have plotted, that I couldn't have planned. They were intrinsic and explained so much about Mercy Beth to me. But I didn't know that. I discovered it.

I already have forty pages of a book about Hap Kunkle [the husband of Lulu, Mercy Beth's best friend]. I want to return to creating the world of Odell over and over and over.

The book is very funny in a laugh-out-loud way that is rare. And your word play is inspired; you invent such wonderful words and phrases. I think of "permissionary," and "underdogmatist." Did you have fun writing this book?

Oh, I had a ball. But there were moments when I spilled some tears, too.

I had an experience that made everything "click." I went to a lecture in Washington, D.C., given by Jean Shinoda Bolen and Isabel Allende. Jean Shinoda Bolen looked into the audience and said something like, "You women, who are between fifty and sixty-five, this is your time. Whatever you do...you will know you are doing the right thing if—when you are doing it—you lose all track of time and what you are doing has a benefit for somebody else. And, it has to be joyful."

Then Bolen looked out into the audience and said, "For example, there may be some of you right here who want to write a book like Isabel [Allende], but it will be your own book. I say do it." And she turned her head and looked at me. Probably every woman there thought the same.

That was the night I came home and said, "I am going to do this book." It was a very literal "click." Bolen's words kept ringing in my ears: "It has to be joyful." And it's funny that joy ended up in the title, too.

Kiss the Joy As It Flies was fun to write. It was also challenging on many levels. But to be in the midst of inventing is always incredibly exciting to me.

You skewer or satirize a few different things don't you? Children's literature, academia, creative writing classes...

Well, since I am a children's writer I believe I can write about a children's writer. I think I got tired of reading about children's writers in novels written by people who aren't children's writers. In one way, I'm looking at Teeny Gaudet as the crassest, most commercial kind of children's writer, and yes, I had fun with it. But I also defended her if you look at Lulu's take on Teeny. Certainly, I wrote with a sense of laughing at, and with, us humans in various communities, and saw the absurdity in many places. I skewered the book world in general, really, and marketing and organized and unorganized religion, and so on and so forth. But it felt like making fun of myself, too.

There is a scene in the novel, set in the past, in which Teeny and Mercy are young girls. Teeny tells Mercy that she wants to be a writer and Mercy says that she'd like to write, too.

"No, but I'm serious," Teeny says. "I even enrolled in a course in writing for children. I'm going to start with something easy. Work my way up."

When I teach creative writing classes I often hear people say, "I've always wanted to write so I'm going to start with something easy—like children's literature." I usually say, "Well, you might have come to the wrong class."

What are the qualities of Mercy—or mercy, for that matter—which you explore in the novel?

Mercy's a "want-to-be" writer. She's never, in her mind, had success. I think she has had great success with her newspaper column, "Mercy's Musings," because she has brought together a whole community. But in her mind she hasn't. So, self-forgiveness, I suppose, might be one quality. Self-love. Maybe the healing Gladys wanted for all.

Mercy is very lonely. Going through a book called *Weird and Wonderful Words*, I found a German word, *Torschlusspanik*, which means "a sense of panic in middle-age brought on by feeling that life is passing you by." It literally means "shut door panic."

Mercy is a woman in the midst of a panic attack. Instead of going to people, she withdraws from people. When we meet Mercy, she is literally in a room with a shut door. This *Torschlusspanik* is Mercy Beth. In the end she discovers community in a new way, so belonging to part of a larger community is another aspect of Mercy…and mercy. With her daughter, among others, she is moving from judgment to acceptance and forgiveness over and over.

It seems this book could only have been written by a fifty-year-old woman author—by that I mean someone who has experienced life, as well as loss, and love.

I think so. That was one of the reasons I didn't write a novel earlier in my life. I thought, "I haven't lived enough, I haven't figured it out enough yet."

And I still haven't—I don't mean that I have. But I knew I was ready and I knew when I wasn't ready. I knew that I didn't have the vision, and I didn't have the perspective, as a younger person.

I truly think that all writing is a dance of the spirit. William Blake said, "Imagination is divine." I think that's true. So to write a book, there is some manifestation of spirit happening. That's just a given to me, that writing is a form of prayer—whether to celebrate or to rant. Years ago I realized that writing wasn't just about me, that there was something else, something big, that took part in it. What book doesn't have the writer's spirit in it?

When I sat down to write *Kiss the Joy As It Flies*, I knew that I wanted to write about a woman in the midst of a crisis about her mortality. And I wasn't going to pretend that the crisis wasn't a spiritual crisis as well as an emotional crisis. Mercy Beth can't pray. She has a mother who is a religious fanatic, her aunt is a devout Catholic, and so Mercy doesn't have any time for organized religion.

Some people do withdraw in times of crisis, and I wanted to write from the point of view of somebody who didn't believe. I wanted to explore what happens when Mercy withdraws. I didn't want there to be answers, I just wanted there to be questions. I will have done my job if two girlfriends read the book and at the end they ask each other questions. What do you think happens when we die? Do you believe in reincarnation? Is it better to know the truth or not know? Those were the questions swirling around in my head when I wrote the book.

At the same time, I do not think it's a book of ideas—it didn't start out that way. It started out with a really strong character and a voice. Then, as I shaped the story, all the larger, philosophical questions arose.

You created that wonderful word, "permissionary," which Mercy defines as "one who gives another permission to have faith in their unique authentic self." Who have been the permissionaries in your life?

My parents; Mrs. Goodwin, my grade two teacher; Fred Cogswell, man of letters; Mary Lou Stirling, professor of education and mentor to many women; Peter Gzowski; William

Blake; Hilary Thompson; Russ Hunt; and Donna Smythe, professor and writer. Her books, *Quilt* and *Subversive Elements*, are two stunning works from Atlantic Canada. I think they are creations of genius and very underappreciated.

I sound a little like Mercy Beth and her embarrassingly endless gratitude. I'm not Mercy, but like Mercy, I am a grateful sort.

Do you believe in angels?

I don't think they exist, but I see them everywhere. Especially in gardens. Maybe the best answer is to quote the title of a song by the great storyteller/poet/folk singer Chuck Brodksy: "We are each other's angels."

READING GROUP GUIDE

1) Do you think this is a serious book that is funny or a funny book that is serious? The term tragicomedy (first used by Roman playwright Plautus in 2 BC) refers to a "drama in which the action moves toward catastrophe like a tragedy but fortunate events intervene to bring about a happy ending."

Did you enjoy the fact that the novel had a happy ending? Do you think it is realistic?

2) Mercy Beth tells her creative writing class students to "find the recurring symbols in your own lives."

Do you think that life is like a book and that themes recur? What are the sources of these patterns or themes?

Cassandra, Mercy Beth's mother, says that Mercy was born "sunny side up."

How much does genetic disposition or inheritance influence the themes that replay though someone's life?

3) The novel opens with Mercy in her doctor's office being told she will need exploratory laparoscopic surgery. Mercy begins to take stock of her life. She even composes a list of "Things to Do I've Left Undone."

What would comprise your list? What if you could only list ONE thing to do, not ten? What would that one thing be?

Would you be able, like Mercy, to "not care what anyone thinks?" Would you not act differently at all?

Mercy wonders, "What will be my legacy?" What do you want your legacy to be?

4) Do you think Mercy has changed by the close of the story? Is she more her true self at the end of the novel? Is this because she learned the truth of the note?

Though illness or tragedy makes us face our mortality and compels us to change our ways, do you think most people permanently change their behaviour?

5) When Mercy initially faces her health crisis she wonders, "Why haven't I felt this alive always?"

Who is the person in the novel you think is the "most alive always" and why?

Who is the person who is able to see everything in the world as "so beautiful you cannot even imagine it"?

6) Stirling Cogswell is Mercy's mentor and dear friend. At his funeral she calls him a "true permissionary." Mercy's definition of a permissionary is "one who gives another permission to have faith in their unique selves and yet challenges them—always—to go the next step."

On the other hand, there are many characters in the novel who might be described as "missionaries." Discuss the characters whose intentions are to change people (and in particular, change Mercy) and *not* to permit.

Discuss the role of "permissionaries" in your own life. Do you see yourself as one?

7) Cassandra, Mercy, and at the close of the novel, Belle, are each mothers. They each keep secrets from one another. What do you think of them as mothers?

What do you think of Cassandra's attempts to keep the note and the truth from Mercy? How would Mercy's life have been different if she had always known the truth about the note? What do you think of Mercy keeping secret the identity of Belle's father?

8) Would you want to live in Odell? What does the community offer to its residents that appeals to you? What characteristics of the community do not appeal to you?

9) Have we all become what Mercy calls, "overly busy plate spinners"? Are you trying to simplify your life? Does technology help or hinder this?

10) Write your own obituary as it would read now. Write your obituary as it would read if you accomplished your dreams.

11) What do you think of the men in Mercy's life? Why do you think she truly loved Raymond Piper? Why do you think Valmont loves Mercy?